MATTHEW HATTERSLEY

A LINE IN THE SAND

MATTHEW HATTERSLEY

A LINE
IN THE
SAND

VIPER
books

For Alba and Suzanne

Vinci Books

vinci-books.com

Published by Vinci Books Ltd in 2025

1

Copyright © Matthew Hattersley 2025

A CIP catalogue record for this book is available from the British Library.
Paperback ISBN: 9781036709709

The EU GPSR authorised representative is Logos Europe, 9 rue Nicolas Poussion, 17000 La Rochelle, France
contact@logoseurope.eu

By Matthew Hattersley

The John Beckett Series

Darkness On The Edge Of Town
When The Kingdom Comes
A World of Sun and Violence
A Bullet For The Past
A Line in The Sand

Chapter One

Evan felt as if he'd been running for hours but was still nowhere at all. This was bad. He had to find safety. Sanctuary. He had to get away.

But even as this realisation hit, darker thoughts were already creeping in, tightening around his mind like a noose. Thoughts that told him he would never find safety in this world. Not now. Not after what he'd done.

Pushing these ideas aside, he gritted his teeth and pressed on. His side was burning with a stitch and his hair was wet with sweat, but stopping wasn't an option. Not now. Not with everything behind him. He had to keep moving.

His lungs burned with every breath, sharp and hot like someone had shoved a knife between his ribs. His legs were weak, threatening to buckle with every step, but he forced them forward, one after the other.

He ran as fast he could, running for his life, running until he couldn't run any more and had to stop, gasping for air. Leaning against a rock, he wiped his face with the back of his hand, smearing sweat and dirt into the streaks of blood already drying on his skin. It wasn't his blood, but he didn't have time to think about where it had come from. Not now.

It was early afternoon and the Vegas sun beat down hard, the higher than average October temperatures turning the desert into a furnace, the kind of heat that pressed down on you, made you feel small. He licked his cracked lips. What he wouldn't give for a cold beer right now. Hell, even a glass of water would do.

He'd lived in Las Vegas his whole life and the city had never been good to him. But it had been his world, and now he couldn't ever go back. He'd screwed that up, just like everything else he touched. His chest tightened at the thought but he pushed it aside. He couldn't afford to feel sorry for himself.

He glanced down at the sweat-darkened front of his shirt. His arms and shoulders ached, and his side still felt like someone had driven a spike into it, but rest was a luxury that he couldn't afford. They would be coming soon enough, and he had to get out of Dodge before they found him.

He set off again, pressing his hand against his ribs, breathing through his teeth as the pain flared. He'd only travelled a few metres when every muscle screamed for him to stop again. For good. To drop right there on the gravel and let it all catch up to him. But he didn't. He couldn't. His daddy had taught him to keep moving even when it hurts.

Especially when it hurts.

He stumbled, nearly going down, but caught himself just in time. Swiping at his face, he tried to steady his thoughts, though the heat made his head spin. The highway stretched endlessly ahead, a jagged strip of cracked blacktop slicing through the barren desert. He glanced over his shoulder, checking to see if anyone was following. That's when he spotted the gas station in the distance.

Shit.

What the hell had he done?

In the last ten minutes things had gone from bad to worse, from chaos to catastrophe. And no matter how fast he ran, some part of him knew he couldn't outrun it. He hadn't planned to stop there. He hadn't planned any of this. But his truck's gas needle had dipped into the red and there was nothing but open desert for miles. He'd pulled in because he had no choice, the old Buick coasting to a sputtering halt beside the first of the two pumps. At least he could fill up and get some water.

Or so he'd thought.

He'd stepped inside, hoping for a break, a chance to figure this out. Instead, he got some shitty kid behind the counter smirking at him like he'd seen it all before. He'd fumbled for his wallet, patting his jeans pockets as the sinking feeling took hold. He had the device. But no wallet. He could picture it on his dresser back home. He'd left in such a rush that he'd...

Fuck.

And of course, the kid didn't care.

"No money, no gas."

As he'd stepped away from the counter, he'd felt the hard steel of the revolver stuffed down the back of his jeans. His daddy's old Smith and Wesson. Could he? Should he?

The kid was behind reinforced glass, but maybe if he caused enough of a scene he'd turn on the pump. But before he even drew, the kid reached for the phone.

"You want me to call the cops?"

He'd turned and bolted outside, desperate. That's when the man came out of nowhere. Evan couldn't remember his face; he hadn't really looked. But he could still feel the grip on his arm. He'd tried to twist away but the man wouldn't let go, kept telling him to calm down.

Evan's hand had gone to his waistband before he'd realised what he was doing. He could still hear the shot that followed.

The memory of it made him stumble, but he caught himself and kept going, wiping a hand across his forehead to clear the sweat dripping into his eyes. He hadn't meant to shoot anyone, it just happened. One moment the man was pulling him back, and the next he was—

But he shouldn't have damn well tried to stop him! That was his fault, not Evan's. He'd panicked.

He hadn't even checked if the guy was dead. He couldn't. He'd taken one look at the body lying on the concrete, blood pooling beneath him, and his legs had taken over.

Run.

He could hear sirens now, faint but getting closer. The kid must have called them.

Cursing under his breath, Evan pushed himself to move faster. As he ran, he tapped his jacket pocket, checking for the device, needing the reassurance that it was still there.

It was. The thing that had set him on this hopeless path. Some kind of tablet but smaller, more like a phone, used in the warehouse for logging deliveries. And, as he'd discovered, so much more.

Why the hell had he taken it?

It had felt like the right thing to do at the time. Later it became insurance – a way out of the mess he'd made. Now it felt like a curse. He was running because of it. Hunted because of it.

A murderer because of it.

It was all Jen's fault. Or it was his feelings for her, at least. She made him want to be a better man, like old Jack Nicholson said in that movie. She made him want to do good. So he'd taken it, thinking it might stop the ones using it for bad things. Instead all he'd done was paint a target on his back.

And now he might never see Jen again.

His stomach twisted at the thought. She'd been the one bright spot in his life, the only person who had ever believed in him. She'd seen something in him that no one else had. Maybe something that wasn't even there. Shit, would they go after her too? He didn't think they would. Hoped they wouldn't. But hope didn't mean much these days.

He should have gone to the cops with the device the moment he realised he was being followed. That had been the plan, hadn't it? Do the right thing for once in his life. Walk into a police station, hand over the device, and tell them everything. A clean slate. Maybe even redemption.

But he hadn't done that.

He'd spotted the black SUV parked at the end of his street, seen the men watching him from the corner, and any plan he'd had evaporated in an instant. Panic took over, overriding reason, shoving aside whatever good intentions he'd started with.

Now he was running. From them, from the cops, from everything.

He swallowed hard, tasting dust and sweat on his tongue. He wasn't built for this. He wasn't clever enough, wasn't strong enough. He'd thought he could make Jen proud, thought he could make a difference. But he was just another idiot who'd gotten in over his head.

Paranoia kept him glancing over his shoulder, scanning the empty highway. It was still just him, the endless stretch of asphalt, and the heat waves rippling off the road. But they'd come. He knew they'd come.

Up ahead something broke through the shimmering haze. At first he thought it was a mirage, some cruel trick of the sun. But as he squinted, raising a hand to shield his eyes from the glare, a diner came into focus. One of those old-fashioned places that looked like it had been dropped on the side of the road fifty years ago and hadn't seen a lick of paint since.

He slowed his pace, weighing his options. Out here he was a sitting duck, a lone figure on an empty highway with nothing but endless desert on either side. The diner didn't seem much safer. It was too open. Too exposed. And if someone inside started asking questions, things could spiral fast. But it was something, and something was better than nothing.

He felt for the device. Still there. Felt for his revolver. Ditto. Neither felt like they'd save him, but the sirens were getting louder now. If the people he'd stolen from didn't catch him, the cops would. Staying put was asking for trouble, and he couldn't run for much longer. He needed cover.

Casting one last look down the highway, he took a deep breath and headed for the diner.

Chapter Two

Beckett clocked the guy the second he walked through the door. Other people in the diner saw him too, but most just looked up briefly before returning to their meals or conversations.

Beckett didn't.

There was nothing overtly wrong with the guy. He was in his early thirties, medium build, average looks, he carried no visible weapon. The kind of guy you'd pass on the street most days without a second glance. But Beckett didn't miss details. The man's clothes were streaked with dirt and sweat like he'd been on the move for hours. His hair clung to his forehead in damp curls.

But it was how the man moved that held Beckett's attention. His steps were jerky and hesitant, like he didn't know what he was doing here. Most guys walking into a diner have one thing on their mind – maybe two if the waitress is a looker – but this guy wasn't eyeing the menu or the female servers. He was looking for something. Or hiding from it.

His eyes darted around the room as he headed to the

counter, scanning every face without letting his gaze settle, like he was assessing threats and tracking exits. That was the giveaway.

A man who moved like that wasn't hungry or overheated.

He was scared.

Beckett didn't look away, but he didn't stare either. He just sipped his coffee and watched. From his seat in the far corner of the diner, he had the wall at his back and a clear view of the entire room. He'd chosen the spot instinctively, as he always did, even if it meant sitting apart from his fellow travellers. They'd been here twenty minutes, waiting out the heat and the delay caused by their broken-down coach.

The diner was small and run-down, barely holding itself together, the kind of place that survived on passing truckers and the occasional stranded tourist like himself. The walls were cluttered with old licence plates and tin signs advertising long-dead brands. A jukebox sat in the corner, but the lights were off and there was no music to drown out the clatter of plates and low murmur of conversation.

The waitress – a hard-faced woman in her fifties – worked the room with brisk indifference, her faded blue uniform straining at the seams as she dropped off plates and refilled mugs, not paying attention to anything she didn't have to. But Beckett was paying enough attention for everyone. He watched as the new guy leaned against the counter, rubbing at the side of his face, then patting at his pockets as if worried he'd lost something. He wasn't looking for a place to sit or for someone he knew. He didn't want to be here.

Beckett understood that feeling. He hadn't wanted to be here either. The difference was, he didn't have a choice.

Four hours earlier he'd been standing at the edge of the

Grand Canyon, staring out into the kind of vastness that made people insignificant. And it had felt like balance. A reminder of forces that had shaped the Earth over millennia, forces that didn't care about lines or boundaries or consequences.

Not that standing beside something of such epic grandeur hadn't given him cause to reflect on his own life. As usual when faced with such things, John Beckett's thoughts went to his past. To the things he'd done. The lines he'd crossed – and, more specifically, the ones he hadn't. He'd lived his life dancing on the edge of those lines, never fully crossing but never stepping back either. Looking down into the rocky abyss was a brutal reminder that nature was in effect its own line in the sand. The kind he respected but never fully obeyed. For a fleeting moment, though, he'd felt free. As free as a man like him could ever feel.

But the trip to the Grand Canyon was only meant to be brief, just a way to kill a few hours before his flight that evening. His passport and luggage were stashed at Harry Reid International Airport, and he was booked on a 7 p.m. flight to Germany, with a connection to Spain to finally see his niece, Amber, who he hadn't seen since both their lives had been thrown into chaos. She'd been staying with an old friend of his, a man Beckett trusted to keep her safe from the kind of danger that always seemed too close to his door. But with the CIA's Xander Templeton off his back – at least for now – it felt like the right time for a visit. Nearly two years had passed since he'd last seen her. She'd already turned nineteen a few months ago. A young woman. The thought of reconnecting with her stirred something in him that felt almost like hope. But there was also guilt there too, as well as a little unease.

He had hoped to work through his unrest during the

space, fresh air, and peace and quiet of the canyon trip, but his tight schedule had forced him to join a tour group instead. It wasn't ideal – too many people, too much chatter – but it had been the only option. And in the end it was worth it. The canyon hit him harder than he'd expected. The size. The emptiness. It was a worthy reminder that some things were bigger than him, a feeling that stayed with him even on the ride back to Vegas.

When the bus overheated outside Arrolime, he and the other passengers had filed out onto the highway under the blazing sun. Some grumbled quietly to themselves, others directed their frustration at the tour guide, but no one was happy. The diner had been their only option while they waited for a replacement bus.

So now here he was, sitting in a corner booth, irritated by the delay and watchful of the clock. He had six hours until his flight, ample time as long as nothing else went wrong. Which was why the man who had just walked in had his full attention. Beckett didn't like problems, and this guy looked a lot like one.

He kept his eyes on him, watching the way the man's hands twitched like he couldn't decide what to do with them, and the way his eyes darted to the window every few seconds. The atmosphere in the diner felt different now, charged, like the other customers were starting to pick up on something even if they weren't consciously aware of it yet. Beckett didn't move, his hand still resting lightly on the table. His instincts told him to stay ready.

"Hey, sugar, what can I get ya?"

Beckett glanced at the waitress who appeared at his table. He hadn't seen this one earlier, possibly she was on her break when he came in. She couldn't have been more than twenty-five, her blonde ponytail bouncing as she tilted her head, giving him a once-over.

"We got a fresh pot of coffee on, or the eggs are good," she added, with a flirtatious wink.

He returned a polite smile. "Eggs sound good. I'll take them scrambled, with toast if you have it. And a coffee."

"Good choice."

She lingered for a moment, her smile turning a shade more playful, but Beckett didn't bite. After a second she walked off, swaying her hips as she went, and he turned his attention back to the man at the counter.

The guy was now talking to the older waitress, who was wiping her hands on her apron and shaking her head. She looked worn out, like she'd been on her feet for decades. There was no warmth in her expression, no hint of a smile. What he was saying clearly didn't sit right with her. She shook her head again, more emphatic this time. Whatever he wanted, the answer was still no.

"I need you to fucking listen to me!" the man yelled, slamming his fist on the counter, hard enough to make a row of ketchup bottles jump.

Someone yelped. But the waitress held her ground, raising her hands in a plea for calm. "All right, sir. Take it easy. We don't need to make a scene."

But the man wasn't interested. He looked like a cornered animal. No plan, just panic. Beckett grabbed the edge of the table but he didn't move. Not yet.

"I need a car," the man was saying. "I need to get out of here."

"That's a big ask, sir." The waitress shook her head. "I can't help with that."

The guy was spiralling now, his entire body tense and jittery. He wasn't hearing her. He wasn't hearing anything.

His eyes darted to the door, then back to the counter, his jaw clenching and unclenching like he was chewing a scream.

Beckett rolled his shoulders back, steadying himself as he waited for the moment to break. He knew it was coming.

The guy cried out and reached around his back. Beckett tightened his grip on the table edge as a revolver was whipped out and pointed at the waitress.

The room froze.

For a split second everything was still. The waitress, already holding her hands up, looked more shocked than frightened as she stared at the gun. The man stood there, chest heaving, the revolver shaking in his grip.

Then all hell broke loose.

Someone screamed. A baby wailed. A chair screeched across the floor as it was shoved back hard. Diners scrambled under tables, overturning drinks and plates in their desperate bid for safety.

The man grew frantic, shouting at people to stay down as he swung the gun in a wide arc. His hand was trembling so badly that if he fired it could hit anything. Or anyone.

Beckett still hadn't moved and the guy hadn't noticed him yet. That was a good thing. But then Beckett heard it.

Sirens.

They were faint at first, but growing louder by the second. The man heard them too, his head snapping towards the window. Outside it was still just desert and empty road, but any minute now police cars would come screeching to a halt at the door, kicking up dust and commotion. Two, at least, judging by the sound.

The man gritted his teeth and turned back to the room, his eyes wide, panicked.

"Nobody move!" he shouted, waving the gun around as if he'd already lost whatever game he was playing.

Not good. Not good at all.

Beckett stayed where he was, his fingers resting on the handle of a fork for a moment before he dismissed the idea. Too risky. The man was scared and erratic, still pointing the gun at the terrified diners. It wouldn't take anything at all for him to pull the trigger, and then a fork wouldn't change a damn thing.

The sirens were almost on top of them now, closing in fast.

"Everyone shut the hell up," the man yelled, shouting for calm like that would do any good. "I need to think! Goddamnit!"

Beckett released a long, steady breath. The cops were almost here and the guy was running out of options. It wasn't time to move yet. But it would be.

Any second now.

Chapter Three

The gunman paced up and down the aisle between the
tables, the gun swinging wildly in his hand. "Nobody do
anything stupid or I'll kill you all!" he shouted, his voice
cracking with the strain.

Two English kids Beckett recognised from the canyon
tour party huddled under their table, clutching each other
tight. Near the door a young couple pressed themselves into
the corner of their booth, the woman cradling a baby like it
was her whole world. Other diners remained on the floor
where they'd scrambled when the gun came out, too afraid
to move, unsure if standing up or staying put would make
them a target.

"Evan, what the hell are you doing?" the guy hissed,
smacking himself on the side of the head. "Come on.
Think!"

He shuffled over to the window, but reeled back as if
he'd been slapped. A second later two patrol cars rolled to a
stop twenty-five metres from the diner, their red and blue
lights strobing across his twisted features.

"Shit!" He jabbed a finger at the waitress. "Close the blinds! Now!"

The older waitress froze, her eyes darting between the cop cars outside and the gun pointed at her. Beckett held his breath. She looked like she was weighing her chances, wondering if she could make it to the door.

Don't do it.

"Close the goddamn blinds!" the man screamed, thrusting the barrel inches from her face. She flinched as though he'd struck her.

"I'll do it," the young woman who'd served Beckett said, rounding the counter and hurrying to the first cord.

There were three large windows on this side of the diner, three blinds. It took her less than twenty seconds to pull them all down, the sunlight and flashing lights reduced to dim streaks filtering through the slats. She returned behind the counter to her older colleague's side.

Beckett leaned back. From his seat he could just make out the scene outside through a gap in the slats. The cops didn't look like they had the first clue what they were doing. No tactical gear, no snipers, no sign of a specialised unit. Just local cops. The closest unit when the call came in.

He turned his attention back to the man he now knew was called Evan. He was pacing back and forth along the length of the diner, dragging his hair into messy spikes as he raked his fingers through it.

"Shit, shit, shit," he muttered, spitting the words out like they left a bitter taste in his mouth. "Why'd you take that damn thing? Now look what you've done."

He brought his fist to his mouth, biting down for a second before his eyes darted to the people around him. Beckett raised himself slightly and Evan froze mid-step, his head snapping towards the corner booth. His eyes locked on Beckett.

"What the fuck are you doing just sitting there?" He stormed over and thrust the gun in Beckett's face. The barrel was shaking, but it was close enough to matter. "I'm not messing around here!"

Beckett met his gaze, calm and steady He kept his shoulders loose, his hands resting lightly on the table. "I'm just trying to stay alive. Same as everyone else here. Nobody wants this."

"English, huh?" Evan's grip on the gun tightened, the barrel now just millimetres from Beckett's nose. "Don't get smart with me, pal. You think I won't do it? Huh? You think I'm bluffing?"

Beckett held Evan's gaze as if the gun wasn't even there. "I think you're in over your head," he said. "I think you need help. A way out."

Evan frowned and sucked in a sharp breath like it pained him. His whole body bristled with barely contained fear.

"You've got to be clever about this," Beckett added. "You're in a tight spot. I get it. But pointing that gun at us isn't making it any better."

For a moment the tension in Evan's face lessened, as if the words had slipped through a crack in his panic. His eyes flicked toward the blinds, like he could somehow see through them to the patrol cars waiting outside.

"You've got people out there wanting an excuse to shoot you. You've got people in here terrified of what you might do." Beckett kept his tone steady, bordering on affable. Not a fake friend. Definitely not an enemy. "None of that gets any better if you pull that trigger."

Evan's grip on the gun faltered. He glared at Beckett, confused and uncertain.

"I can help you," Beckett told him, his voice quieter now, almost coaxing. "We can sort this out. But not if you lose control. Not if you hurt anyone. So put the gun down, and let's talk."

"What the hell is there to talk about?"

Beckett held his gaze. "What's your name?"

The man's lip curled, halfway between a sneer and a grimace. "Go to hell, English."

"Fair enough. But if we're doing this, we might as well do it properly. I need to know who I'm talking to. I think I heard you say Evan earlier. Is that right?"

The man didn't answer, but he looked to be calming down a little, looked like he was hearing him. But before Beckett could push further, a voice boomed from outside, distorted through a megaphone.

"This is the police. Put the gun down and come out with your hands up!"

Evan flinched, taking a step back. "No!" he cried out, shaking his head violently. "I'm not going back. I can't. They'll kill me!"

Beckett stole another glance through the blinds. His initial assessment seemed to be correct. The handful of local police were still chasing their tails out there.

"Shit. I'm screwed." Evan rubbed his face with his free hand, his cheeks puffing out as he exhaled. He was unravelling fast.

"Don't worry. This isn't over for you," Beckett told him. "My name's John. Am I okay calling you Evan?"

He glared at him. "Who the fuck are you? A cop?"

"No. I'm just a guy from England. Here on holiday seeing the sights. And I'd like to see more of them. If we're all going to walk out of here in one piece, we need a plan. So…?"

Evan blinked, caught off guard. "What do you mean?"

"Well… you're armed and you've got a room full of hostages," Beckett continued, still conscious of his tone. "That's not nothing. And now you've got the cops outside. What's our play? What do we tell them?"

Evan blinked at him as if the question had come out of nowhere. "Shut up," he said, but there was hesitation in his voice now.

"I'm not trying to be clever. All I'm saying is, if we want to get out of here, we've got to think this through. They're outside waiting for you to make a mistake. Don't give them what they want."

Evan didn't answer. Instead he started pacing again, his free hand tugging at his hair. "Shut up," he muttered under his breath. "Just shut up, shut up…"

Beckett glanced around the room at the diners huddled together, the waitresses behind the counter clutching each other's arms, undecided who was protecting whom. None of them were having the kind of day they'd expected when they got up this morning. "Look at these people. They're scared out of their minds. Everyone is. You don't want to hurt them. You don't want to hurt anyone, do you?"

Evan stopped pacing, his shoulders sagging slightly, his eyes dropping to the floor. "No. I don't want this," he said, lowering the revolver. "I never wanted this. I just…"

Beckett leaned forward. "Then let me help you."

"Help me?" He let out a bitter laugh. "How the hell are you going to help me?"

"By figuring out what happens next. By making sure nobody gets hurt, including you. But you've got to meet me halfway."

The man stared at him, his expression hard. For a long moment he said nothing. Then he sighed. "My name is Evan," he muttered. "Evan Gates."

"Great, now we're getting somewhere." Beckett smiled. "What are you doing here, Evan?"

"I don't fucking know!" He wiped at his eyes with his free hand, the gun now hanging limp in the other. "It's all a big, stupid mistake. I shouldn't have taken the damn thing. But... I can't go back. I can't..."

"Why not?" Beckett asked.

Gates gritted his teeth for a second. Then the words burst out of him, fast and desperate. "Because of the machine. Because I know what they're going to do. They'll have to kill me, they have no choice. I have to get away."

Beckett didn't react, didn't push. He let the tension settle before speaking. "What machine?"

Gates's head snapped towards the door as a sound from outside startled him. "Fucking cops."

Beckett slid closer to the edge of his booth, shifting his weight forward. Ready, if it came to it. As Gates moved toward the blinds, Beckett's stomach tightened.

"What the hell do I do?" Gates asked, pulling down one of the slats to peer outside. "What do I say?"

Beckett could now see the police crouched behind their cars, weapons drawn. And there was Evan Gates, framed perfectly in the open blind. Beckett wanted this over, but not with the man's brains splattered over the terrified families huddled in the diner. Besides, his instincts told him Gates wasn't the real bad guy here.

Beckett's focus shifted back to the cops. One of them was leaning forward, rifle raised, his finger tightening on the trigger.

"Evan, move!" Beckett yelled at him. "Now!"

The window shattered before the sound fully registered, the blinds snapping against the frame as shards of glass sprayed inward. Screams erupted, the diner descended into chaos, people hitting the floor, clutching one another, desperate to disappear.

Beckett looked over at Gates who had bolted to the back wall. The bullet had missed him by inches, slamming into the menu board above the counter – but it had only fuelled his desperation. His wide, terrified eyes darted around the room, the gun arcing wildly in front of him.

"Back off! Back the fuck off!"

Beckett could see raw fear in his eyes, a complete loss of control. He wasn't thinking anymore, just reacting. Pure survival mode.

And that was the last thing Beckett needed.

His grip tightened on the table, his mind racing. He had to stop this. Gates was on the brink, one misstep away from pulling the trigger on someone. But Beckett wasn't close enough. If he moved now, Gates might panic and start shooting. The line was razor thin.

Before Beckett could act, Evan lunged towards a teenage girl crouched on the floor, grabbing her by the wrist and hauling her up. She yelped, squirming as he wrapped an arm around her neck and dragged her to the window, moving the revolver to her temple. The boyfriend she'd been sitting with shuffled further under their table even as his gaze shot to Beckett's in desperation.

Do something, the glare said.

Beckett slowly shook his head at the boy, as through the shattered glass Evan screamed, "Get back! Get back or I'll fucking kill her!"

A baby started to cry, its mother frantically shushing it,

desperate not to draw attention. Everyone else remained frozen, too terrified to move.

Gates dragged the young girl behind the counter, the gun still pressed against her head. Her thin legs trembled in her denim shorts, a low whine escaped her lips. She looked ready to collapse. On the floor the boyfriend was quietly crying, his face red and hands balled into fists.

Beckett sucked in a deep breath. A panicked gunman facing off against trigger-happy local cops itching to make heroes of themselves. One wrong move now, and this whole situation could turn into a bloodbath.

Chapter Four

Beckett listened to the negotiator's voice crackling over the megaphone. Or rather, the voice of the local police chief or whoever had been hastily assigned to speak to the gunman. This was no trained negotiator. His voice was shaky and lacked authority.

"We know you're armed. We have footage of you shooting a man at the gas station a mile down the road."

Shit.

If Evan Gates had already killed someone, that changed everything. Not only did he know he was facing serious jail time and had less to lose, but he'd broken the seal – crossing the line from armed threat to active shooter. Not good.

"Let's end this peacefully. You don't have to do this." The voice halted briefly, as if the speaker was second-guessing his own script. "Put down your weapon and come out with your hands in the air."

Beckett's eyes stayed on Gates. It was painfully clear that the negotiator was out of his depth. Probably just some smalltown beat cop shoved into a situation far beyond his skillset. His voice had no command, no edge. And Gates had picked up on it.

He tightened his grip on the girl he'd taken hostage. "Peacefully?" he yelled back. "You think this is about peace? They want me dead. They want to ruin us all. You have no idea what's coming!"

Beckett's stomach tightened. The cracks in Gates's composure were widening with every passing moment. And now he was spouting paranoid gibberish to boot. Beckett reasoned he had only minutes before Gates lost it completely. Fear like that didn't sit idle; it built pressure. And when it was released, it was going to be bad for everyone.

"Come on, move!" Gates yanked the teenager roughly by the arm, dragging her back around the counter. She stumbled, struggling to keep up before he shoved her into a booth beside the young mother and her baby.

"Sit down!" he barked, the veins in his neck straining.

The girl collapsed into the seat, sobbing. The young mother turned to her instinctively, cradling the baby between them as if their thin bodies could somehow shield it from what was coming.

Outside, the negotiator's voice crackled again. "Please… let's talk about this. We can end this peacefully."

"Talk about what?" Gates yelled, though Beckett doubted the cops could conduct a reasonable talk-down this way. Why weren't they calling the diner's phone? Surely it had one. "You think this can be solved by talking? You think I'm playing games?" He waved the gun, making the young mother shriek and clutch her baby even tighter.

Beckett leaned forward. He didn't like where this was

going. Gates was like a wild animal, cornered and danger-ous. And cornered animals only reacted one way. Taking a steadying breath, he pressed his palms against the edge of the table and stood.

"Sit down!" Gates snarled, the revolver snapping towards Beckett. "I mean it, English!"

Beckett raised his hands, palms open. "Evan. Look at me. Just me. Forget them. Right now it's just you and me."

Gates shook his head. "You don't know what you're talking about. You have no idea."

"I know you don't want to hurt anyone," Beckett contin-ued. "You're a good guy in a bad situation. I can see that."

He kept his tone steady but his focus was razor-sharp, studying Gates and the room around him like a grand-master sizing up a chessboard, already three moves ahead.

"You're trying to survive, Evan. I get it. But pulling that trigger? It won't save you. It won't fix anything."

Gates's expression shifted, a flicker of confusion breaking through the fear. He blinked at Beckett, like the words had hit a part of him he rarely, if ever, confronted. Beckett took a step forward.

"I've been where you are," he lied. "Thinking the whole world is against you, like there's no way out. But you don't have to fight this alone." He offered a thin, reassuring smile. "Let me help you, Evan."

He took another step, the distance between them now just a few metres. His eyes stayed locked on Gates, though his peripheral vision kept track of everything – the hostages, the gun, the subtle shifts in Gates's body language.

"Look at them, Evan," Beckett said, nodding towards the people still cowering in their seats or pressed to the floor. "These good people aren't your enemies. They're just scared. Same as you. Same as me."

"Yeah? Well, you should be scared," Gates snapped. "We all should."

"Why is that? Tell me."

Gates sneered. "You wouldn't even believe me."

Beckett narrowed his eyes. Gates sounded paranoid as hell, but he believed what he was saying – at least, his own warped version of the truth. The bigger problem was, that he still looked like he was balancing on the edge, ready to break at any moment.

Beckett's attention went to the cops outside. It was a hot day, and with every minute that passed they would grow more fidgety, more eager to finish this, even if that was in the worst way possible.

Where the hell was the backup? The trained negotiators?

"You've got men out there with rifles and itchy trigger fingers," Beckett said. "They're just waiting for a reason to shoot you. Don't give them one."

He let the words hang for a moment before taking another step forward. The entire diner felt like it was holding its breath.

"You don't want any more blood on your hands, Evan. And you don't want to give them a reason to put a bullet in you. Not when you've got important information they need to know."

It seemed like his words were finally getting through. Gates lowered the gun slightly, the tension in his face easing just a fraction.

"We can fix this," Beckett added. "You and me. Just put the gun down." Gates's arm dipped, the revolver pointing at the floor now.

But then the voice came again from outside. "This is your last warning! Put the weapon down!"

The order cut through the fragile moment like a knife. Gates flinched, tightening his grip on the revolver, bringing his arm up once more. Beckett saw the change in him instantly – the panic flooding back, the fear taking over.

There was no time left.

Beckett closed the distance in two strides and grabbed Gates's wrist. The man tried to twist away, but Beckett grabbed his thumb, wrenching it back until it snapped, sending the revolver clattering to the floor. Gates screamed, but before he could react, Beckett kicked the man's legs from under him, dropping him to the floor where he pinned him with a knee on his chest.

It was over in less than five seconds.

"Suspect disarmed, scene secure," Beckett called out. "You're clear to enter."

The response was immediate. "Hold position! Do not engage!" a voice barked from outside. Then, "Move, move, move!"

Beckett got to his feet as the diner's door slammed open and three officers stormed in, two men and one woman, their weapons raised. Their aim snapped back and forth between him and Gates.

"Get on the ground!" one of the men yelled at him. "Hands where we can see them!"

Beckett held his hands high and open. "Easy," he said. "Everyone's fine."

"I said get down! On the ground!"

Beckett hesitated, but the Glock 22 aimed squarely at his chest made a solid case. He lowered himself to his knees, then face down onto the linoleum without a word.

A heavy knee pressed into his back, pinning him in place as his arms were yanked behind him.

Calm down, fellas.

26

He'd expected the local cops to be jittery, but this was excessive.

From his position on the floor, he caught a glimpse of two officers hauling Gates to his feet. "You don't get it!" he shouted as they dragged him towards the door. "It's already happening. We're all screwed. People will die. You're too late."

Even now, Gates wasn't letting up on his cryptic ramblings, and Beckett still couldn't be sure if they were the words of a paranoid man – or something worse. His thoughts were cut short as the cop holding him yanked him to his feet.

"Move," the officer snarled, shoving Beckett towards the door.

"Officer, he's not the guy," someone called out behind him. "He saved our lives."

"Thank you, sir," someone else added, possibly the waitress.

Beckett appreciated the comments, but he knew they wouldn't carry much weight until the cops cooled off. As they stepped out into the sunlight, he squinted against the glare, his attention fixed on Gates, who was struggling against the officers' grip as they shoved him into the back of a patrol car.

"You have to help me!" he screamed. "They're going to kill me. Then you'll all see." The car door slammed shut, muffling his voice but failing to silence it entirely.

He was insistent, and his words made Beckett uneasy. He hadn't changed his tune once throughout all this, and didn't seem like a man grasping at excuses.

Still, whatever Gates believed, it was no longer Beckett's concern. He had done his job, and he was ready to put this sorry episode behind him. All that remained was for him to make a statement, maybe fill out some paperwork, and then he'd be on his way to the airport. By tonight he'd be on a plane, heading to see his niece.

No more problems. No more stress.

At least, that's what he told himself.

Chapter Five

The Sierra Heights substation wasn't much to look at – a forgotten and overlooked offshoot of the Las Vegas Metropolitan Police Department, set up to handle the quieter, grittier corners of downtown. Just ten minutes from the Strip, it catered to the areas of the city that tourists ignored; the run-down blocks just past Fremont Street, the older residential neighbourhoods, the backstreets nobody wanted to walk after dark. The Downtown Area Command was stretched thin, overwhelmed by the chaos of Fremont's nightlife, the crowded business districts, and the endless churn of petty crime. Sierra Heights had been set up to take some of the weight off.

It wasn't a prestigious post. The building sat on a corner lot, surrounded by chain-link fencing and cracked asphalt. Inside, it was all peeling paint and scuffed tiles, staffed by a skeleton crew rotating through shifts. This was where the low-priority cases were handled. Noise complaints, issues with transients, the occasional bar fight.

Along with two interview rooms and an evidence locker,

the substation had three holding cells, but they weren't built for much more than holding drunks until they sobered up or detaining someone long enough for a transfer. Cramped and outdated, they were as unremarkable as the rest of the place.

Beckett glanced at the dashboard clock as the patrol car pulled into the substation lot. Almost two. Five hours until his flight. Like always, he was working a few steps ahead and had already done his calculations. If this didn't take too long he would still make it.

On the backseat he remained cuffed, while the same jaded, gruff cop from the diner sat up front at the wheel. He'd tried to explain himself during the ride – that he was just a bystander – but the cop didn't want to hear it. Once they were parked, he came around the car and hauled Beckett out.

"This way. And don't get cute."

He was marched inside, past the small reception area where a young officer glanced up, gave him a once-over, and returned to his paperwork. None of the cops working here looked like they were preparing to deal with the aftermath of a hostage situation.

"Wait here," the gruff one muttered, as they stopped outside a door marked 'Interview Room 1'. He unlocked the door and pushed it open, gesturing for Beckett to enter. "Someone'll be with you soon."

With the guy glaring at him, Beckett stepped inside and was met with a bare table, two standard folding metal chairs, and a bright fluorescent strip light hanging overhead. He sat in one of the chairs and turned to the cop. "Any chance of a glass of water?"

The man sneered. "Don't hold your breath." Then he closed the door, leaving Beckett alone.

It was a stuffy room with ineffective air conditioning, but at least he didn't have to wait long. Only five minutes later the door opened and a uniformed officer stepped inside. Beckett recognised her from the diner, part of the team that had stormed in once he'd secured Evan. She hadn't looked particularly confident at the time – more like she was doing her best to keep up with the chaos – but appeared calmer, more composed now, though still not completely at ease.

She looked to be in her early thirties. Pretty, with dark eyes that were even more striking given her blonde hair, tied back in a loose ponytail. The colour looked natural rather than dyed, almost white in places where it had been bleached by the desert sun. She had the kind of appearance that didn't need much effort to draw attention, though she seemed more focused on looking professional than polished.

She approached the table, pulled out the chair opposite him and sat, placing a clipboard and pen on the table. "Thanks for waiting," she said.

Beckett narrowed his eyes, trying to decide if she was making a joke. He leaned back in the chair. "Well, I didn't have much choice."

Her mouth twitched, almost a smile but not quite. "I'm Officer Maggie Lee." She clicked her pen and glanced briefly at the clipboard. "I've got a few questions for you."

Beckett leaned forward. "Listen, I know you're just doing your job, but I had nothing to do with the hostage situation. I was just in the diner waiting for a bus replacement. I don't have anything I can tell you that will throw any more light on the events."

Lee nodded but looked confused, like he'd thrown off her train of thought. It made him feel a little uncouth, but he just wanted to get this over with.

"I understand," she said. "But we do need a statement

from you. About what happened. You're not in any trouble."

"Good to know." He smiled.

"In fact, as I took names in the diner, a lot of the witnesses spoke very highly of you. You saved lives today."

"I just tried to calm things down, that's all."

This time she looked up and smiled properly. "What were you doing there, anyway? I take it you're quite far from home."

Beckett folded his arms. Now there was a statement and a half. "I was here seeing the sights," he said. "But I do have a flight out of here tonight that I need to be on. So, if we could make this quick, that would be wonderful."

"Of course, but... you know..." She gestured at the clipboard. "Protocol. We still need your version of events, and to make sure all the paperwork's clean." She leaned in and whispered, "For what it's worth, I think you handled things better than most of us would have."

Beckett raised an eyebrow. "Yes, I assumed the guy with the megaphone wasn't the department's top hostage negotiator. And don't get me started on whoever fired that shot. That could have escalated things in the worst possible way."

Lee gave him a tight, apologetic smile. "Yeah, I know. I'm... Well, I know."

Beckett sat up. He was warming to her. "I wouldn't put any of that in the report, though," he suggested, with a grin.

She snorted. "Good idea." Then she caught herself and cleared her throat. Back to serious mode. "Let's start with your name."

Ah.

A trickier question for a man like Beckett than she could ever know. The name on the passport stashed at the airport flashed in his mind. Joseph Sharp. But he didn't feel the need to use it here. He'd walked away from enough of his past to use his real name without it being too much of a risk. And for some reason he felt compelled to use it with her.

"Beckett," he told her. "John Beckett."

Lee jotted it down without looking up. "Beckett. All right." Her pen hovered for a moment before she continued, her tone shifting slightly. "You know, from what people told me, you showed some real negotiating skills in there today. Are you a cop or something?"

Beckett smiled. *Or something.* "No. Not a cop."

"Military?"

He rolled the question around in his head. And then his answer. "Sort of."

Lee stopped writing, giving him a quizzical look. "What does that mean?"

"It means I used to be. Sort of."

She narrowed her eyes. "You like being a bit of an enigma, do you, John Beckett?"

"It's not that. But I can't divulge much more."

"Oh?" Her brows arched slightly. Then her eyes widened. "Oh!"

Beckett shrugged. He didn't love dropping that kind of hint, but he was hoping it might speed things along, might get him out of here faster.

Instead, Lee seemed more intrigued. "So… what do you do now?"

"I'm just a civilian," he replied. "Trying to keep my head down and my hands clean."

"And how's that going?"

Beckett exhaled, the hint of a bitter laugh underneath. "Don't ask."

"Hm. You're not exactly a sharer, are you?"

"I'm here to give a statement, not my life story."

She stared at him for a second longer then picked up her pen. "All right, Mr Beckett. Let's continue. Walk me through what happened at the diner."

He glanced at the clock on the wall. He had time to humour her, so he started talking. Over the next five minutes he recounted events, keeping his answers short and to the point, laying out the facts without embellishment.

"What made you approach the gunman?" Lee asked, once he was finished.

"He was growing desperate. Someone had to calm him."

"Witnesses said you talked him down," she added. "What did you say?"

"I told him what he needed to hear."

"And what was that?"

He gave a small shrug. "That I wanted to help him. That there was another way out. By the way, the guy at the gas station – did he kill him?"

"You know about that?"

"Your negotiator," he said, recalling the look on Gates's face when that golden nugget went out over the bullhorn. "It was a bad idea, bringing it up."

She studied him for a moment, her lips in a slight pout. "You're very good at this."

"At what?"

She shrugged. "Responding to high-stress situations. You make it sound easy."

"It's not. But like I said, someone had to calm things. Where is he now?"

Lee's expression faltered, as though weighing up whether to share. "My colleagues have put Gates in one of the holding cells. Officers from the main precinct are on their way over."

"Is he still spouting off about a machine and people coming to kill him?" Beckett asked.

"I don't know. Did you think he was serious?"

"Not sure. But it might be worth finding out."

"It's not my jurisdiction."

Lee's gaze drifted back to her clipboard, and she looked almost sad. Beckett studied her, sensing something else beneath her professional exterior. A frustration, maybe. It was there in the way she carried herself, the stiffness in her shoulders, the edge to her tone when she asked a question. It pointed to someone who had spent years putting on a front, fighting to be taken seriously. That made sense. In a place like this, maybe as the only female cop, she'd have to work twice as hard for half the respect.

"It might be worth mentioning it to whoever's working the case," Beckett added. "He seemed genuinely spooked by something. When I looked into his eyes I got no hint of him being high or drunk. I just saw fear there. But it could be a ploy to deflect attention."

Lee was staring at him, like she was hanging on his every word. She caught herself and straightened. "What if it's not?"

"Then hopefully your colleagues at the precinct will figure it out," he replied. "But like you said – it's not your responsibility. Or mine."

Lee leaned back in her chair, studying him. "You don't get flustered, do you? Even when Jarvis was hauling you in here."

"Jarvis. That the friendly cop's name?"

She smiled, though there was no humour in it. "Yeah. He's... a lot. But what can you do?"

"Exactly. Pick your battles. You can't win them all."

The smile hovering at Lee's lips extended to her eyes as she tilted her head towards her shoulder. "You appear to be very good at staying calm under pressure. Handling people." She lowered her voice. "You made the chief look like an amateur today."

Beckett smiled. He liked how Lee thought. Most cops, especially at small substations like this, were too by-the-book, too rigid in their thinking to do good work. But Lee had real spirit and seemed to be just the right side of rebellious. It would fare her well if she ever got a chance to prove herself in a larger arena.

"All I did was try to calm things," he said again.

She pouted her bottom lip, nodding. "Okay, if you insist. Most people would've panicked. You didn't. That tells me you've done this before."

"As I already told you," Beckett said, "I have a military background. But that's all I can say."

"I could search your name."

"You could. But you'll find out less than I've told you."

"Wow." Her smile turned sly. "So you're secret service or something? What is it you have over there? MI6?"

Beckett shifted in his chair. "We don't need to discuss this. It's not relevant. And these days I'm a civilian."

Lee's expression shifted again as she sat upright. Less suspicion, more respect. "Right. Well, whoever you are, John Beckett, thank you. If it wasn't for you, we'd probably be dealing with a multiple homicide right now."

Before either of them could say more, they were interrupted by raised voices outside the room. More panic. Lee spun towards the door as someone banged on it, and a second later it flew open to reveal the young cop from the front desk.

"What is it, Stevens?" she asked.

"It's the gunman. Gates."

"What about him?"

The young cop paused, struggling to get his words out as he glanced from Lee to Beckett and back again. "He's… dead."

Chapter Six

Lee didn't stop to think. She leapt from her seat and was out of the interview room in a flash, the door slamming shut behind her. Stevens was already halfway down the corridor, glancing back and skipping sideways like he couldn't decide whether to run or wait.

"What the hell happened?" she asked, as she caught up to him.

Stevens, who usually thrived on the smalltown monotony of his role, now looked like a rabbit caught in the headlights. "I-I don't know," he stammered. "I was just walking past the cells, and then… then I saw… He's hung himself. Come see."

Hearing footsteps behind her as she hurried after him, Lee glanced back over her shoulder. Beckett had left the interview room and was following them.

Shit.

The chief wouldn't be happy about letting a witness leave the interview room, but there was no time to stop and deal with it.

"When did it happen?" she asked, as they moved down the hall. "How did it happen?"

"I don't know."

He reached the holding cell ahead of her. The door was open, but he stepped aside to let her go in first. A real gentleman.

Lee braced herself.

Whoa.

She'd seen dead bodies before – a couple of times at least – but never one so fresh. Gates hung from the bars of the cell window, the makeshift noose cutting deep into his neck. Thankfully, whoever had processed him had taken his belt and bootlaces, as per protocol, but he'd torn off his shirtsleeves, knotting them together to do the job. His face was swollen and purple, his eyes bulging grotesquely. Below him was a small pool of brown water where he'd voided his bladder and bowels.

"Jesus Christ," Lee muttered, the back of one hand to her nose and mouth while she checked Gates's neck for a pulse with the other.

Nothing. She stepped back, dropping her hand. The stench hit her, and she instinctively turned her head, her stomach lurching. Beckett stood in the doorway, poker-faced as he surveyed the scene. She half hoped he'd offer some kind of reassurance, be that steady presence she'd experienced in the interview room. But he just stood there, calmly looking around the room, like this was something he saw every day.

Stevens, on the other hand, was practically hyperventilating, pacing the small cell as if panic alone could erase the grisly sight before them. "Do we... Should we get him down?" he asked, his voice high-pitched and frantic.

Lee glanced back at Beckett, still hoping for... What?

Answers? A reaction? All she got was the same composed expression. She turned back to the body, pushing down the rising unease.

"What do we do?" Stevens asked again.

"First we calm down," she said, as much to herself as her colleague.

Beckett stepped past them, narrowing his eyes as he approached Gates's body. She wasn't sure what he was looking for. The guy was dead. That much was obvious.

"You shouldn't be in here," she muttered, unsure if he even heard. "Beckett, we need to get you back."

He turned to her, about to respond, but before he could, Jarvis stormed into the cell. "What the hell is going on?" he barked, his gaze snapping from Gates to Beckett. "Why is he in here?"

Beckett didn't flinch. "I followed the commotion to see if I could help."

"You… followed? Are you kidding me?" Jarvis turned on Lee. "This is on you. You're supposed to be keeping an eye on him."

"He's not a suspect," Lee shot back. "He's not the problem here."

"This man has no business being in a restricted area," Jarvis snapped, looming over her, his nostrils flaring as he jabbed a finger first at Beckett then back at her. "Do your damn job, Lee, or I'll do it for you."

Lee swallowed, feeling the heat rising in her cheeks. She knew Jarvis had a point – Beckett shouldn't have been in here – but she wasn't about to give the prick the satisfaction of admitting it.

"Relax," Beckett said behind them. "I've seen enough."

Lee turned to Beckett, grabbing his arm before Jarvis

could explode again. "Let's go," she said through gritted teeth.

She was pleased when he let her lead him out of the cell and into the corridor without further drama. Once they were clear, he stopped and turned to her.

"You look like you're about to fall over," he said.

"I'm fine," she insisted, her gaze steady, but the shaky breath she exhaled didn't exactly sell it. "We still need to finish your statement and get it signed off. So if you could…"

Beckett held his hands up. "Don't worry. I'm not going anywhere until you're done with me."

"I'd appreciate that."

"I also have something I need to talk to you about when you're ready," he added.

Lee leaned back slightly, trying to get a read on him. She'd wondered if he was being so cooperative because he thought she was out of her depth or something. Wasn't that just like a man. But maybe there was more to it than that.

"What is it?" she asked.Beckett glanced over her shoulder, his eyes tracking something behind her. She turned to see Chief Higson hurrying down the corridor.

"Lee! Get in here!" he ordered. "Now!"

"I'll head back to the interview room," Beckett told her. "But I do have a plane to catch, so let's not drag this out."

"I'll do my best," she replied, surprised by the flicker of gratitude she felt towards him.

The holding cell was buzzing with barely contained chaos as she stepped back inside, the stench of sweat and excrement an ineffective mask for the heavy sense of death in the air. Chief Higson paced in tight, agitated strides, his entire head flushed under his thinning hair. He looked like he was one wrong word away from either bursting a vein or throwing a punch.

"This is a total clusterfuck," he growled, glaring at no one in particular. "Vegas PD are on their way, and they're going to be all over this like flies on shit. Do you have any idea how bad this is? A dead suspect in our custody? Jesus Christ, we'll be the laughing stock of the entire department."

Stevens hovered near the corner of the cell, looking like he might pass out. He kept rubbing his palms on his pants, gaze flicking between Gates's lifeless body and the chief. "Sir, I-I don't even know—" he began. "I mean, one minute he was—"

"Shut it," Higson snapped. "Don't finish that sentence unless you've got something useful to say."

Lee stepped closer, forcing herself to focus. "We need to figure out how this happened, sir. Protocol was followed. So where's the gap?"

Jarvis, leaning against the wall with his arms crossed, let out a bitter laugh. "The gap?" he repeated, shaking his head. "The gap is we've got a dead guy on our watch and Downtown's gonna roast us alive. That's the gap."

Lee turned to him, her frustration boiling over. "It sounds like all you care about is how this looks."

Jarvis pushed off the wall and walked over to her. "And what are you planning to do about it, Lee? Crack the case wide open? The guy killed himself. End of story."

Lee clenched her fists. "I plan to do my job, Jarvis. Proper police work. Something you might want to try for once."

"Enough!" Higson barked, cutting them off. "We've got a dead suspect, a diner full of witnesses, and the main precinct about to breathe down our necks. Can we please save the pissing contest for later?"

He glared at the two of them until Jarvis turned away, muttering to himself. Lee kept her head up and her mouth shut.

Prick.

Higson stepped closer to inspect the body and Jarvis sidled over to her again. "This is on you, Lee," he snarled. "Your witness shouldn't have been anywhere near this."

"What?" She turned to him, not wanting to back down despite the tingle of nerves down her spine. "This isn't my fault. And it's not his, either."

"Isn't it?" Jarvis shot back, glancing at the chief, raising his voice. "You know, Lee here had that English guy wandering around like he owns the place. Who knows what he could've done?"

The accusation hit like a slap. She sucked in a breath, ready to fire back, but Higson stepped between them, his hands up like a traffic cop.

"Stop it," he told them. "This isn't the time to play detective, Lee. Let the main precinct handle this. I don't need you digging holes we can't climb out of."

"But, sir, I think if this happened on our watch, we should at least—"

"Officer, you're done here," Higson cut her off. "Go. Now. Take the English guy's statement, file your report, and move on. It's not our problem anymore."

Lee opened her mouth to argue, but closed it again when Higson's glare bore down on her. "You've made your point. Now back off. That's an order."

She let out a slow breath, swallowing the retort she had ready in the barrel. "Yes, sir," she said, before turning on her heels and leaving the room. Behind her she heard Jarvis muttering under his breath, but she didn't catch it.

Asshole.

Stepping into the corridor, she spotted Beckett leaning casually against the wall near the interview room, arms crossed, head tilted as he watched her approach. For reasons she didn't fully understand, she felt a wave of relief at the sight of him. He had a presence that was hard to ignore, and not just because of his steady demeanour. Looks-wise, he was more what you might call chiselled than textbook handsome, with defined cheekbones and a rough shadow of stubble along his strong jaw. His dark blond hair was unkempt but not too scruffy, and his blue eyes had an intensity that was almost unsettling. There was nothing showy about his appearance – just a rugged, lived-in look, like someone who'd spent more time outdoors than indoors. Right now he looked tired, but not in a frail way. More like a man who'd endured a lot and learned how to carry it.

"Thanks for sticking around," she said, her voice quieter than she intended.

"I had to stay." He leaned closer and lowered his voice. "There's something I need to tell you."

Her stomach flipped at the shift in his tone. "What is it?"

He glanced down the corridor before motioning for her to step back into the interview room. She hesitated, but followed him, the knot in her gut twisting.

Once inside, Beckett closed the door and led her over to the far corner of the room. "How well do you trust your colleagues, Officer Lee?" he asked.

She blinked. She wasn't sure what she'd been expecting him to say, but it wasn't that. "I trust them… enough," she said, searching his face for context. "Why?"

He held her gaze. "Do you know if any of them had a connection to Gates?"

"I don't think so. What's this about?"

"Gates didn't kill himself," Beckett said without a flinch. "Someone made it look that way. But he was murdered."

Chapter Seven

As was only fair when delivering information that was hard to hear, Beckett gave Lee a moment to process what he'd said. But after ten seconds she was still staring at him like he'd broken the news she only had weeks to live. Her wide brown eyes searched his face unblinking, as if trying to confirm she'd heard him correctly.

"You're saying he was... murdered?" she whispered. "But how?"

Beckett lowered his head to meet her face to face. "He couldn't have done it himself. I broke his thumb in the diner when I disarmed him. There's no way he tied that noose. Not a chance."

Lee blinked, then glanced at the door as if it might offer an explanation. "But..." She pressed her lips together, the words trailing off. Her gaze came back to him. "Who?"

Beckett exhaled. That was the question – and one he didn't have an answer to. He stepped back, putting some distance between them so they could think. Whoever killed Gates must have had good reason. He must've known something someone didn't want made public. Something damaging.

He rubbed at his stubble as he replayed the scenes in the diner. Gates had been jittery, agitated. At the time, Beckett figured the guy was just scrambling, desperate to justify himself in the middle of a hostage mess he couldn't handle. But now... maybe not. Gates was scared, kept saying they were coming for him. That they were going to kill him.

Turns out he was right.

Out of the corner of his eye he saw Lee pacing in front of the door, her face twisted in the way people get when they're trying to force themselves to think. She twirled a finger through her ponytail and then stopped.

"So you're saying someone here, someone in this station... did it?" she asked, doubtful.

Beckett met her eyes for a moment before nodding. He didn't like it either, but it was the only explanation that fit. After leaving the holding cell, he'd done a quick sweep of the station's security setup. All the internal doors leading to the holding cells were locked, and there were no other entrances or exits in that part of the building.

"I'm sorry," he said, watching her face fall as she struggled to find any other explanation. "But one of your colleagues killed him."

"That's insane." Her voice rose as she faced him fully. "There's only a handful of us here. Chief Higson, Stevens, Jarvis, and me. That's it."

"Exactly." He didn't say it like an accusation. Just a fact.

Lee chewed on her lip. "You don't mean the chief," she said warily. "Do you?"

"You know your colleagues better than I do."

"Yeah, and it wouldn't be him. He's pretty much a waste

of space these days, but he's not a killer. He's got grandkids. Just riding out his time up here, waiting for retirement."

"If you say so. So who does that leave? Stevens?"

Lee let out a sharp breath, part laugh, part disbelief. "I doubt it." She looked up at him, her expression tense. "Then you're saying it's Jarvis?"

"I'm saying he's the most likely choice. Is he always as highly strung as he was today?"

Lee considered it. "Maybe not quite as bad."

"Okay. And anything else different? Did you see him get a call or a text in the last couple of hours? Anything out of the ordinary?"

"Not that I noticed. But… why would he do something like this? What's he got to gain?"

Beckett watched her without comment. She shook her head, rubbed her fingers over her forehead. She looked frustrated, like she was trying to piece something together but couldn't make it click.

"I can't believe it," she said finally. "I always knew Jarvis was a prick. But I never would have thought him a— No. He's not a killer, he can't be. I mean… how? What for?"

"I'd say the better question to ask is *who* for?"

He let her sit with that a moment, wrestling with the idea. She was intelligent, and she had a good heart. Beckett had seen officers like her before – they had the potential to really move the needle when they were given the chance. And maybe this would be the case where Lee did that. But he wouldn't be sticking around to watch that happen.

He checked the clock over the door, the minutes ticking away. There were now only four hours until his flight. Time wasn't on his side.

"Why would Jarvis do it? It doesn't make sense." Lee

resumed her pacing, muttering under her breath. "Nothing about this makes sense."

Beckett tuned her out and walked over to the metal table in the centre of the room. Her notes and his half-finished statement were scattered across it. He picked up the pen and started writing, blocking out her mumbled monologue as she struggled to piece things together. He filled out the last few parts then signed his name. Setting the pen down, he turned back to her.

"There," he said. "Done."

Lee stared at him like he'd just kicked a puppy. She strode across the room to intercept him at the door. "I'm afraid you're not leaving," she said with authority, but then backed down at something she saw in his face. Perhaps that they both knew she had no grounds to keep him here.

She sighed, dropped her weight to one hip, and looked up at him with honest eyes edged with something like uncertainty. She lowered her voice. "If what you're saying is true, I don't know who I can trust."

"How do you know you can trust me?"

That made her pause. She looked like she might argue, but then shook her head. "I just do," she said, like that answered everything. "You're good at this. You see things others don't. Stay a little longer. Help me figure this out."

Beckett didn't move. He felt for Lee, he really did. There had been many times in his life when he'd been the lone voice in a sea of people who didn't give a damn. He understood how trapped she felt, how alone.

But…

He sighed, his thoughts drifting to Amber. She'd sounded so excited about seeing him again when he'd called a few days ago – or at least, as excited as any nineteen-year-old girl ever sounds. He'd promised her he'd be there this time. No excuses. No last-minute changes. He'd missed too much of her life already.

"I'm sorry, Officer Lee. But this isn't my fight."

"Well, great." She threw her hands in the air. "You just drop a big-ass grenade in front of me and walk away. No worries, soldier. I'll handle it *all* myself. Thanks for nothing."

Beckett didn't take the bait. "You'll be okay," he said, almost swayed by her sassy attitude and big brown eyes but not quite. "Find someone you trust in the unit that's taking over. Tell them what we talked about. Let them handle it."

She shook her head the way only a pissed-off woman can, glaring at him like she was daring him to blink first. "And how exactly am I supposed to do that without Jarvis or the chief finding out? If they think I'm going behind their backs, then…" She stopped, the fight draining out of her. "And if I'm wrong… they'll tear me apart. What little career I do have will be in the can."

She dropped her gaze, hands on her hips, her mouth twisted to one side like she was running some impossible calculation. "Are you really sure about this?" she asked when she looked at him again. "That Gates was murdered. By… one of us."

Beckett nodded. He explained to her how he'd checked the entrances and exits. "No one could've got to him without a keycard, and there's no way he did it to himself. Someone silenced him."

"But why?" she asked, half to herself. "What could he have known?"

"That's what you need to figure out," Beckett said. "In the diner he mentioned something about a machine. And people being in danger."

She eyed him. "That sounds big."

"It was big enough for someone to risk their job over. Big enough to kill for."

Lee groaned and rubbed at her face with both hands. "Jesus. I'm screwed."

"What do you mean?"

"I mean this whole place is a joke." She sighed, the mask really coming down now. "Everyone's more worried about covering their asses and having an easy life than doing real police work."

Beckett didn't respond. Her bitterness was clear, but he had nothing to add. Though he felt bad for her, he knew where his line was drawn.

"Tell someone from the main precinct what you suspect," he repeated. "Someone senior. Do it in an anonymous email if you'd prefer. But this is their jurisdiction now." He checked the clock. His window was closing fast but it wasn't gone yet. If he left now, he could make the flight. "I'm sorry, Lee. I really have to go."

She didn't say anything, but she didn't have to. He could see it all over her face – frustration, doubt, anger, most of it turned inward on herself if she was anything like the person he suspected her to be. She wanted to help, do more. But her hands would be tied. For a second he thought she might throw one last argument at him, but she didn't. She just stood there, watching as he turned and headed for the exit.

Chapter Eight

Heat rose off the road in shimmering waves, blurring the horizon as Beckett trudged along the roadside. The sun hammered down on him. Even in October, out here in the desert it was hot as hell. Sweat soaked his shirt and trickled down his back, but he hardly noticed. His thoughts kept circling back to Officer Maggie Lee.

He felt bad for leaving her in the lurch, but what else could he do? This was a police matter, not his. And yet the further he walked, the harder it was to ignore the voice in his head or the feeling in his gut. If Jarvis had killed Gates to shut him up, whatever this was had to be a lot bigger than one officer could handle alone. And deep down, Beckett knew Lee wouldn't just let it go.

Jarvis wasn't the one calling the shots; Beckett was sure of that. A lazy, middle-aged cop in a run-down substation didn't have the brains or pull for something this big. He was just a pawn, the kind of useful idiot powerful people kept on their payroll in every city to do their dirty work and keep things quiet. Jarvis wasn't the answer. He was just the starting point.

But it wasn't Beckett's problem.

It wasn't.

He'd seen it before, too many times to count. Corruption, incompetence, indifference. The pattern never changed. Whether in a war zone or a corporate boardroom, it was always the same – self-interest masquerading as necessity. Beckett hated it with a deep, burning fury. It was all ego and no decency. And good people like Lee always seemed to end up holding the shitty end of the stick.

Beckett didn't know much about the LVMPD, but he'd bet his last buck they wouldn't touch this case with a ten-foot pole. A suspect dying in custody was the kind of headache no one wanted. They'd bury it fast and move on, instructing those at the substation to keep a lid on it.

Reaching a dusty bench near a faded bus stop sign, Beckett sat, closing his eyes against the glare. He wanted to relax, but couldn't. The heat from the metal bench prickled through his clothes. The air was filled with the faint white-noise hum of insects, annoying once he'd noticed it.

Damn it.

It was bad timing, that's all it was. Maybe in different circumstances he'd have stuck around – helped Lee navigate the fallout, given her some counsel. But Amber was waiting. He should've been in an air-conditioned airport lounge by now, not baking under the Nevada sun.

He checked his watch. He'd only walked for thirty minutes but it felt longer. At least he still had time to spare.

The distant growl of an engine caught his attention and he opened his eyes. A silver car crested the horizon. He couldn't see the make – something old, boxy and loud – but somehow he already knew who it was.

Getting to his feet, he watched as the car slowed to a stop beside him. The window was already rolled down, framing Officer Lee's face.

"Don't tell me," Beckett said, "you're here to give me a lift to the airport."

It wasn't his best line, but Lee didn't even crack a smile. She looked worse than before. Tired, drawn, her dark eyes shadowed by worry. She was still wearing the uniform but without the radio and duty belt, and she'd rolled up the sleeves of her shirt.

"Please, Beckett," she said. "I need your help. I'm begging you."

He grimaced openly, glancing towards the city in the distance, and beyond that, the airport. He didn't think it needed saying again, so he didn't say it.

Lee sighed, his lack of subtlety not lost on her. "I know you've got a plane to catch, but there are planes out of here all the time. Can't you swap your ticket or something? Just for a day or so." She gave him a pleading sort of smile. "I need some guidance and I think an ex… you know… whatever you are, or were, you can help me." She shook her head as if angry at herself for flapping. "Please. I wouldn't beg like this if I wasn't desperate. And… I'm scared."

The admission wasn't hyperbole or a manipulation tactic. Beckett could see it had taken a lot for her to say it. "What's happened?" he asked.

"Downtown have just left," she replied, brushing stragglers of hair from her forehead that had come loose from her hair tie, and peering down the road like her colleagues might still be in listening distance. "They didn't stay long but they weren't happy. I tried to find someone, like you said, but they stonewalled me at every turn. They barely said a word to anyone. I heard them tell the chief they'd investigate, but they're already calling it a suicide, so why would they? And that's it. Gates's case is now officially out of our jurisdiction. Done. Just like that. Only it isn't, is it? Because I know I've got a corrupt cop in my unit and he murdered a prisoner for some reason. I can't leave that alone. I'm sorry, but I can't."

Beckett smiled at this. If it were him, he wouldn't be able to leave it alone either.

"What are you doing now?" he asked, glancing over the roof of the car. It was an old Chevy Sprint, beat up and compact.

"I asked the chief if I could talk to him in private, but he told me to go home, said I'd done enough for one day. I wanted to stick around, but I'd already clocked ten hours when I was only scheduled for eight. He said it wasn't worth the hassle to let me stay because of the unions. They've been poking their noses in recently about unnecessary overtime."

Beckett clicked his tongue. "You think that's all it is?"

"I don't know." She slapped her hands on the steering wheel. "I don't want to believe the chief's involved in anything other than being a lazy son of a bitch. But... shit, I don't know if they're trying to get rid of me or just keep me out of the way."

Beckett rested his forearm on the roof of the car and leaned forward. "What about Jarvis? How's he acting?"

Her eyes grew weary, unimpressed "I should've said something earlier," she muttered.

"There have been other things?"

"Not specifically. Just a feeling. I haven't trusted him for a while He's... slippery. Always has been. But the chief doesn't care. He's too old for this crap. Just wants to ride out his last years in peace." She looked up at him. "What should I do?"

"I'm not sure."

He straightened and stretched his arms. His head told him she should let it go. Keep her head down. Play it safe. But his gut, his instincts, and maybe even his heart said otherwise. She had a point. Maybe this did need investigating.

He glanced towards the city, finding it hard to ignore the crisscross of vapour trails in the sky.

Amber...

"Should I confront Jarvis?" Lee asked.

"No," he said, shaking his head as he refocused. "Not yet."

"Then what?" she asked. "Help me. I want to do the right thing, Beckett. But it feels like I'm walking into a minefield."

He sighed. She was a good cop in a bad spot, and it wasn't going to get any easier. Wanting to do the right thing was admirable, sure, but staying alive was more important.

He looked back the way he'd come and then towards the airport. Finally, his gaze returned to Lee, still looking up at him like he was the one with all the answers.

Could he walk away from this?

Could he leave her to face the shitstorm headed her way?

"Gates was talking in his cell," she said, dropping her elbow on the doorframe and lowering her voice "Stevens overheard him."

"Oh?" He leaned back, assessing if she was telling the truth or if this was just a ploy to make him stay. Either she was a good actress or he was a sucker for punishment. "What exactly did he say?"

"That's the only thing," she said, with a frown. "Stevens didn't catch much. Something about people in danger, something about a machine, same as what you heard. He said Gates sounded manic, kept talking about a catastrophe."

Beckett considered this information. He wasn't convinced Gates's warnings were the ramblings of a madman. "When are you back in?" he asked.

"Not until Saturday. It's my off days now. Why?"

Beckett checked his watch, though it was a pointless exercise now. His flight wasn't happening. He walked around to the passenger side, opened the door and got in. The car's interior smelled of hot plastic and something vaguely floral.

"Let's go," he said, clicking on his seatbelt.

Lee blinked, caught off guard. "Where to?"

"Your place. Somewhere we can talk safely." His knees were up to the dashboard. He felt around under the seat, yanking the lever to give him a little more leg room. "You can start by telling me everything you know about Jarvis. Then we need to figure out what Gates meant."

"What about your flight?"

He leaned back, his mind already working through the next steps. "It can wait," he said. "It'll have to."

Chapter Nine

Lee's apartment building was exactly what Beckett expected. A two-storey construction just off the Strip, close enough to hear the faint hum of distant traffic but far enough that the glittering lights felt like another world.

They entered through a glass door and into a long corridor. The walls were a faded beige colour, scuffed and marked like they'd seen one too many moving days. A small tiled entrance gave way to a lurid carpet that looked like it had been laid in the seventies and forgotten about. The air was close and smelled of nicotine and cleaning products.

They reached door number 17 and Lee stopped and pulled a set of keys from her pocket. "This is me," she said, unlocking the door. "I'm afraid it's not much."

She stepped inside, toeing off her work shoes just inside the threshold, and gestured him in. "Make yourself at home." She chuckled to herself awkwardly. "Coffee?"

"Good plan." Beckett closed the door behind him and glanced around as Lee went to the kitchen area on the far side of the open-plan layout, a breakfast bar dividing the space between kitchen and lounge. A worktop, stove and fridge were spread out along one wall, adjacent to a wide picture window, the only source of natural light. The small lounge was furnished with an old couch, a couple of chairs and tables, and a small flatscreen TV sitting on a wood veneer stand. Two doors led off the main room, presumably to a bathroom and bedroom.

The place was nicer than its exterior had suggested, and Beckett found himself glad of that fact. The furniture was mismatched but decent enough, and the overall feel matched what he knew of Lee so far – practical, no-nonsense, with a streak of something offbeat to keep you guessing.

On the wall beside the front door a row of posters caught Beckett's eye, a shrine to female action heroes. He recognised Ripley, Sarah Connor, The Bride from Kill Bill, but there were a few others he couldn't place. The display had the enthusiasm of a teenager's bedroom, but it told him Lee admired strength, especially in women. He respected that. There were no family photos, no knickknacks, no real clutter. It felt like a space someone lived in but had yet to make a home.

The rich smell of coffee filled the air and Beckett wandered over to the kitchen, watching as Lee reached up to grab two mugs from a cabinet. "How do you take it?" she asked, glancing back at him. "I'm going to guess black."

"God no," he said. "I am British, after all. If you don't have cream, milk will do."

She snorted, placing the mugs down on the worktop. "Milk. Right." She pulled a face. "It might have expired, to be honest."

"Then black is fine."

"Sorry." She rolled her eyes, and Beckett smiled. There was something oddly endearing about her.

"You live alone?" he asked, though he already knew the answer.

"Yep. Just me."

"Boyfriend?"

"Nope."

"Girlfriend?"

She frowned, then pulled a goofy smile. "No, I like men. Just the ones around here get antsy when they see the badge. I would say I'm destined to be a crazy cat lady, only I'm allergic."

Beckett didn't know what to say to that so he said nothing. Instead, he leaned against the breakfast bar, his eyes drifting around the room, imagining Lee sitting here alone at night after her shift was over. She seemed like a bit of a loner, but not lonely. There was a big difference. He knew that well.

She handed him a cup of black coffee and he took a sip. It wasn't as hot as he'd have liked and tasted a little bitter, but it would do. He watched her as she leaned back against the counter, brushing a strand of hair behind her ear. In this setting she looked younger, smaller somehow. Less like the eager local cop he'd first met and more like someone still figuring things out.

Still, she had a sharp wit and a quiet, unshakeable resolve he couldn't help but respect. She was a little kooky, maybe, but that only made her more intriguing.

Except he wasn't here to make friends.

They moved into the lounge. Beckett took a seat on the armchair facing the window and Lee placed her mug on the table without sitting.

"Can you give me two minutes?" she said. "I just want to get changed."

He sipped at his coffee. "Go for it."

She disappeared into the bedroom, leaving Beckett pondering in the quiet hum of the flat how the hell he'd explain his delay to Amber. When Lee returned a few minutes later, she'd swapped her uniform for black leggings and a grey t-shirt. Beckett's eyes flicked over her without thinking. She had a good figure, toned but not excessively. She noticed his glance and flexed goofily, showing off her biceps.

"Ready to take on the world," she said.

"You certainly look capable enough."

She dropped her arms. "I should probably work out more, but I guess I'm lucky. Naturally athletic, like my old man. He passed down some decent traits if little else." She perched on the arm of the couch.

"He was a fit guy?"

She snorted, looking over to the window. "Oh yeah. Strong. Up until the ninth beer and then his swing got a little sloppy." She peered at him, puffed out her cheeks. "Sorry, too much information. How you doing?"

He smiled. "Just enjoying my coffee."

She shook her head. "How do you stay so calm, Beckett?"

He set his mug down on the small table beside him. "Years of practice."

"You're not even a little freaked out about what Gates said back there?" she asked.

"We don't know what he's referring to yet."

She arched her eyebrows. "Yeah, but we know enough. A machine and a catastrophe. The whole 'end of the world' vibe. It sounds like some bad sci-fi movie, but if there's even

a chance people are in real danger we need to do something. Aren't you worried about what machine he's talking
about?"

"I don't let my mind go that far ahead. Not without
more to go on. Right now it's a puzzle. Could mean something big, could mean nothing. Either way, I don't waste
time chasing possibilities."

Lee raised an eyebrow, incredulous. "You can just… not
think about it? Seriously?"

"Seriously." Beckett leaned back in the chair. "It keeps
things simple."

"Simple?" she echoed, her voice rising. "There's a guy
dead in our holding cell, and you're calling this simple?"

"No. I'm saying there's no point worrying about things
until we have more facts. Right now we don't know what
Gates meant by 'machine'. We don't know what kind of
catastrophe he was talking about. Until we do, all we've got
is noise."

Lee let out a dry laugh. "You're something else, you
know that? What are you, a Zen monk disguised as a British
spy?"

"Can't I be both?"

"So you are a spy?" Her eyes lit up, and she leaned
forward as if the answer might spill right out of him.

Beckett looked her in the eye. "Listen, Officer Lee. I'm
here. I'm going to help you as much as I can. But don't ask
me questions like that, and don't expect answers if you do.
Understand?"

The excitement drained from her face, leaving only a
wry smile as she nodded and drew back. "Got it," she
muttered. She slid from the arm of the couch onto the
cushion and slapped her hands down on her thighs. "Geez,
I wish I knew what the hell I was doing. I wish I could stay

calm. Right now my head is spinning with a hundred different ideas. I feel dizzy. But I can't just shut it off like that. Because what if Gates was right? What if people really are in danger?"

"Then we figure out what the danger is, and we stop it. But only when we know what 'it' is. No point fighting shadows."

"And that works for you?"

"Yes. Focus on what you have to deal with and don't worry about the rest." He maintained eye contact as he spoke, making sure she heard him. "Too many people spend their lives fighting battles in their own heads. You can't win those kind of fights. If someone comes at me with a knife, I'll handle it. But until there's something I can act on, I try not to worry about it too much."

Lee looked him up and down. "Yeah, I don't doubt you could handle a fight if it came your way." Her tone was light, almost teasing, and for a second her candour threw him. But he brushed it off just as quick. She had a habit of saying exactly what she thought, with no filter and no pretence. He respected that.

"But here's the distinction," he added, steering the conversation back. "Worrying about the *possibility* of a guy coming at you with a knife is just as pointless a use of the imagination. The trick is to focus only on what you have control over."

Lee looked thoughtful, watching him over the rim of her mug like she was trying to figure him out. "Good way to be," she said. "If you can get in that headspace."

"I've had a lot of practice," he admitted. "Focusing on what's in my control is probably the only reason I've made it this far. I might've lost it otherwise. Or ended up…"

He trailed off, the unfinished sentence clear enough

without him saying it. The comment generated a long pause; Lee's turn to appear uncomfortable. She took another sip of her drink before setting the mug down on the coffee table. She looked serious suddenly, like she'd decided their getting-to-know-you session was over.

"I ran a quick check on Jarvis after you left," she said. "His record's clean, and I'm sure the chief would vouch for him. But I've heard things. He goes to this bar off the Strip. Jimmy's. It's a cop bar. Everyone with a badge ends up there sooner or later. I've heard a few rumours from some of the guys there about Jarvis sitting in on illegal poker tournaments and the like, and that he's up to his eyeballs in gambling debts. And now that I've been thinking about it, he has had some unexplained absences lately."

She leaned forward, tapping her knees rapidly with her palms as if playing an invisible drum kit. "Shit, this is starting to feel very fucking dubious all of a sudden."

Beckett considered her words. Gambling debts were a red flag, but not exactly a shock. Not in this town. But if Jarvis owed money to the wrong people, they'd have their hooks in him. Leverage.

"We're just a small substation," Lee continued. "Three officers and the chief. Why would anyone bother bribing one of us? We've got no power or pull. Most days we don't do much of anything. Why would Jarvis be tied up with anyone who'd want to kill witnesses?"

Beckett picked up his mug and took a sip, working through the possibilities. "Maybe whoever owns Jarvis is playing the long game. Strategically planting moles in small, low-profile departments like yours. Contingency operatives, hidden in plain sight. I've seen it before. They shuffle dirty cops into places like Sierra Heights under the cover of transfers or promotions, building a network that's wide but invisible. It's effective, especially in a place where corruption runs deep." He raised his mug in a dry, mock salute. "And let's face it – it doesn't get much more corrupt than good old Sin City."

Lee sighed. "Sounds plausible. So… what now?"

"We need to figure out what Gates was talking about." Beckett downed the remainder of the tepid coffee. "But first we need to learn more about him. Who he was, where he worked, who his friends were."

"I've got my laptop." Lee nodded towards where the machine was half buried under a stack of papers on the breakfast bar. "But I can't access work files from here. Our systems don't allow remote logins, for security reasons or whatever."

That was a shame. Beckett had been hoping they could make some progress from here. "Who's at the station now?" he asked.

Lee glanced at the clock on the wall. It was almost 6 p.m. "The same crew. Until the night shift takes over in two hours."

"And that is?" Beckett prompted.

Lee crossed her arms, a flicker of discomfort flashing across her face. "Jeff Montell. He's basically a glorified security guard. Most nights he kicks back in the break room with a family pack of chips on his lap, watching porn on his phone."

Beckett grinned. "Perfect. Think you can sneak me back in?"

"You're serious?"

"Deadly." He stood and stretched.

"Oh, well… yeah. Sure. I think I can."

"Great," he said, taking his phone from his trouser pocket. "How about another coffee while we wait? Oh, and I'll need your phone to make a few calls. Is that okay?"

"My phone?" Lee asked. "Why? What's up with yours?"

"It's died, and I need to cancel my flight then call my niece," he said, pushing down a twinge of guilt. "Let her know I'll be a few days late."

Chapter Ten

Dusk had well and truly fallen by the time Lee pulled her car into a spot near the substation's side entrance thirty minutes later. The building looked even more run-down and insignificant in the moonlight, a low, rectangular box of weathered brick and flaking render. Seeing the place through Beckett's eyes made her painfully aware of how amateurish the setup was. Security lights lit up the lot, but she knew the lone camera above the door was often never switched on.

She turned off the engine. "Here we are," she said, breaking the silence.

Beckett nodded but said nothing, just continued to peer through the windshield like he was seeing things important.

Her pulse thudded in her ears as she watched the station windows for any sign of movement. It wasn't her first time sneaking into the building after hours, but this time was different. She felt she was in a movie or something. She didn't know whether it was excitement or trepidation that had her grip the steering wheel tighter than she needed to.

Come on, Maggie, get it together.
You've wanted something like this.

She stole a glance at Beckett, who was still watching the station, his expression unreadable. She wondered if he ever felt nervous. He didn't seem like the type. Not a man who lets pressure get to him.

Weirdly, he seemed to have a calming effect on her too. His presence helped. She'd heard him on the phone earlier, talking to his niece, Amber. Lee couldn't make out the girl's exact words, but she'd sounded pissed as hell when Beckett told her he'd be a few days later than planned. Yet he'd been patient. Kind. Apologetic but firm. All good traits, she thought.

Not that she really *knew* him. It had only been a few hours. Hardly enough time to make your mind up about a person. Yet she found herself warming to him. Trusting him.

Even if he was incredibly enigmatic. And might actually be a goddamn spy.

She shifted in her seat just as he turned to look at her.

Shit.

She'd been staring.

He raised an eyebrow, his blue eyes catching the light. "You all right?"

"Yeah, I'm fine," she said, too quickly. Then, because it felt weird not to say more, she added, "It's just… breaking into the station. Not exactly a normal night for me."

Beckett smiled. "You're doing good. Don't think of it as breaking in. We're just information gathering."

She let out a short, breathy laugh, feeling some of the tension ease. "Right. Sure."

Beckett tilted his head slightly, studying her. "Are you getting cold feet?"

"No," she said. It wasn't a lie, but it wasn't entirely the truth.

"We're just ticking all the boxes. Nothing to worry about."

"But you shouldn't be here with me. If the chief finds out…"

"If he does, tell him I strong-armed you. Tell him whatever you need to about me. I'll be long gone and I don't mind playing the bad guy. It wouldn't be the first time."

Lee watched him, waiting to see if he'd elaborate, but of course he didn't. He never gave more than he had to. An enigma, through and through.

She rolled her shoulders back, forcing herself to focus. "Don't worry about me. I can handle myself."

"I know you can."

Annoyingly his words pleased her, even sent a ripple of nervous energy shooting through her that wasn't entirely unpleasant. Still, she wasn't sure who she was trying to convince more, him or herself.

Beckett leaned over to check the dashboard clock. It was 8:12 p.m. They'd been sat there five minutes already and there was no movement from inside the building. "Okay," he said. "Let's move."

They got out of the car, keeping to the shadows as they moved toward the station's side door. Lee's keycard made the entry easy, the soft beep of the scanner sounding louder than she'd like in the quiet.

Inside, the station felt different after hours, the fluorescent bulbs in the main hallway lighting up every crack in the plaster and every ball of dust in the corners. From somewhere deeper in the building she could hear the faint murmur of tinny voices. Recorded, not live. Montell was probably sitting with his phone out, watching YouTube or worse. Lee led the way, Beckett close behind her. They moved quickly past the break room where Montell was likely holed up, the faint glow of lights visible through the cracked door.

The data centre was at the far end of the next corridor, tucked into the back corner of the building. Though, calling it a data centre always felt like a stretch to Lee. It was little more than a cramped room with four ancient desktop computers shoved back to back on a cluster of rickety tables. There were two more computers, plus a printer and fax, in the dispatch centre, another misnomer, near the main desk. That was the extent of Sierra Heights Substation's IT department. The depressing thing was, usually it was more than enough equipment for their needs.

Lee beeped them through two more secure doors and they entered the data centre. She sat at the first workstation, jiggled the mouse to wake the screen, logged into the desktop without a problem and then into the police database. Beckett stood behind her, watching.

They'd already discussed the plan on the way over. She knew what she was looking for: Evan Gates's last known address. Normally, she was good with computers and felt reasonably confident she'd find it okay. But with Beckett standing so close, she found herself unable to type properly, and with each mis-stroke she got more worked up.

"Don't worry, it should be here," she whispered, as she opened the search portal. "Give me a second."

Beckett leaned closer, lowering his voice. "Montell going to be a problem?"

She shook her head. "Doubt it. Like I said, he's lazier than the rest of them. As long as we don't make much noise, he won't even notice we're here."

She typed in Gates's name and leaned back as the

system started its sluggish search. It was painfully slow, each second dragging as she felt herself watching the process through Beckett's eyes. She peered up at him. But his steady gaze, fixed on her, made her more uneasy.

"You okay?" she asked.

His eyes narrowed slightly. "I was just thinking – why are you doing this?"

"What do you mean?"

"It's risky for you. And you could've walked away hours ago."

She hesitated, debating how much to say. She knew if she started down this road she might never shut up. "Because someone has to," she whispered. "Because I'm sick of standing by while everything gets swept under the carpet. And the power dynamics here are a joke." She twisted in her chair to face him. "I don't know what it's like where you've worked, but here it's not easy being the only woman in the unit. I'm either invisible or under a spotlight. No in-between."

Beckett didn't say anything right away, and she was beginning to understand that was his way; letting silence do the heavy lifting. Finally, he said, "And yet you're still here."

"Yes. Because I have to prove I can be," she replied, noting the bitterness in her tone and sighing. "I grew up with two older brothers and a dad who barely noticed I existed. Spent my whole life trying to prove I was worth their time. Not sure I ever managed it. Or if such a feat was even possible."

Beckett nodded thoughtfully. "You're doing good, Lee."

She hadn't said any of that to get his approval, but all the same, turning back to the screen she felt a little steadier, a little more confident. Dang, he was good at this; she'd have to keep an eye on him. A second later they had a match.

"Where is it?" Beckett asked.

Lee squinted at the address. "An old complex off the Strip. Used to be a motel but was turned into apartments a few years back. Not the nicest of places."

Beckett looked at his watch. "We need to check it out. But first we should see what was logged in the evidence room when Gates was arrested." He straightened. "Might give us a clearer picture of what got him so spooked."

Lee nodded, her pulse quickening. "Makes sense but we have to be careful. Montell might be lazy, but he's still on shift. If he sees us in there, it'll raise a lot of awkward questions for me."

"We'll be careful."

He stepped aside, motioning for her to lead the way. They left the data centre and headed down the corridor towards the evidence room. It was on the opposite side of the building with another four locked doors to get through, but Lee was impressed with how quietly they moved. They reached the final stretch of the hallway. The evidence room was just around the next corner, but before they got there, footsteps sounded from up ahead.

Lee froze.

Shit.

"Keep going," Beckett whispered. "Find what you can. You can do this."

Without waiting for a response, he moved down to the fire door at the other end of the corridor.

"Wait. Where are you going?" she hissed after him.

"I can't be seen here," he told her, pressing down the bar and easing the door open. "Meet by the car."

The fresh night air spilled into the stale corridor as he

slipped out, pulling the door shut just as the footsteps rounded the corner.

Lee barely had time to collect herself before Jarvis appeared. "Officer Lee! What the hell are you doing here?"

She forced a casual shrug, thinking of the old duck analogy – calm on the surface, chaos underneath – as her heart played a dance beat against her ribs. "I couldn't rest. So I figured I'd double-check that all my recent reports were squared away," she said, as nonchalant as she could manage. "You know how it goes."

Jarvis sneered and stepped closer. His uniform shirt was rumpled, and he looked wired, like someone running on too much caffeine and not enough sleep. When he spoke, she got the faint whiff of liquor. "You're always so quick to file your reports, put the rest of us to shame. So what's really going on?"

"You know me," she said. "I like to keep abreast of things. You been in the evidence room?"

It was the only possible explanation for why he'd be down this side of the station. But instead of answering, Jarvis looked her up and down, leering in a way that made her skin crawl.

Why the hell did she have to say abreast *of things?*

"What's going on, Lee?" he growled.

She stiffened, instincts screaming at her to keep him away from the data centre. She was pretty sure she'd closed down the search portal, but the logs could still be traced. Blowing a piece of hair from her face, she forced a dry laugh. "Nothing's going on. You're the one who seems jumpy. What's got you so worked up?"

His lips curled into a lusty smirk. "Just making sure everything was handled properly today. For the precinct. Can't have us looking like amateurs, right? Speaking of which…" He took another step closer, lowering his voice. "You're lucky you're cute, Lee. Makes me less inclined to care about whatever it is you're doing here. But you be careful. People get hurt meddling in things that don't concern them."

She swallowed, fighting the urge to take a step back as he leaned into her space. He held her gaze for a long, uncomfortable moment before his grin widened, baring two rows of yellowing teeth.

He held up a piece of paper, a copy of what looked like Gates's transfer sheet. Downtown should have taken it with them, but they must have forgotten, considering he died before they arrived. "This is what I was looking for," he growled. "Okay?"

He put his face next to hers, his breath hot and sickly against her cheek. Then he laughed and walked away down the corridor.

Prick.

She looked at her hands. They were shaking slightly, so she made them into fists to steady herself. It was excitement, that's all it was. This was exactly the kind of situation she'd dreamed of dealing with when she first signed up for the force. Something big, something… dangerous.

Be careful what you wish for, Mags.

Once the coast was clear, she moved around the corner and let herself into the evidence room. The smell of dust and old paper hung heavy in the air as she scanned the shelves. It had been months since she'd been back here, but it didn't take long to find the logbook.

Gates's evidence was filed under his case number. She quickly located the clear plastic bag containing his personal effects and carried it to the table in the corner, spreading everything out under the harsh overhead light.

It wasn't much. A handful of loose change, the revolver, and an old cigarette card with a number for someone named Jen scrawled on the back in faded blue ink. Frustration built. She'd been hoping for more. Even the number was probably just some old date of Gates's. She was about to give up when it hit her.

Shit.

She picked up the evidence bag. In her haste to check what was inside, she'd brushed over one glaring detail. It hadn't been sealed properly. Was that just another oversight? Or had someone tampered with it?

Jarvis.

It was the only explanation. He'd been in here, no question. But whether he'd taken something, she had no idea – and no way to prove it even if he had. The thought left her cold.

Gritting her teeth, she shoved the items back into the bag and returned it to the shelf where she'd found it.

People get hurt meddling with things that don't concern them.

Jarvis's words echoed in her mind but she shoved them aside. She didn't know what Gates had been so afraid of, but there was no way she was backing down now. Whatever was happening, it wasn't over. Not even close. The case was growing more twisted and dangerous by the second, but one thing was certain – if Jarvis thought he could scare her into walking away, he didn't know her at all.

Chapter Eleven

Beckett waited by Lee's car, the metal still radiating the engine's warmth from earlier. It was a relatively humid night for the time of year. Even the faint breeze did little to cool it, only stirring the thick air around him. But Vegas never cooled off, not really. Too much asphalt, too much glass, too much heat trapped in all the wrong places. It was a city that held on to things, whether you wanted it to or not.

He shifted his weight, scanning the substation's dark, empty lot. It was quiet out here on the edge of the city, just the faint hum of air conditioning leaking out from the building's vents. A couple of cars passed in the distance, headlights slicing through the gloom before fading into the horizon. He remained still, waiting. It wasn't impatience, it was anticipation.

"Come on, Officer Lee," he muttered. "Get a wriggle on."

He was starting to worry something had gone wrong – probably with whoever had been coming from the evidence room. Jarvis, possibly. The thought gnawed at him, and he debated going back inside to check on her. He was just about to move when the side door creaked open and she stepped out.

She looked flustered, her eyes darting around the lot as she closed the door and headed his way, not running but close to it.

"Anything?" he asked, though the look on her face already told him the answer.

"Not really. Just the usual loose change and a chick's number. But…" She glanced over her shoulder then nodded towards the car. "Let's get in first."

She unlocked the car and slid into the driver's seat, eyes wide and alert. Beckett climbed in beside her as she started the engine.

"I think Jarvis was in there before me," she said. "I think he took something from Gates's personal effects."

Beckett pulled on his seatbelt. "We'll deal with him later."

"But what if it was something important? A vital piece of evidence?"

"Don't worry about that now," he told her. "Remember. You can only deal with what's in front of you."

Lee nodded, reluctantly. "What's in front of us is Gates's place."

"Exactly. And you got us the address," he replied. "Let's see if there's anything there that can help us figure this out."

Beckett watched her as she shoved the stick into drive and pulled out of the lot. Lee seemed to always drive like she had somewhere important to be, and he liked that. The neon lights of the city played across her face in shifting greens and blues, outlining the soft curve of her jaw and the determined way her lips pressed together with just the faintest hint of a pout. Occasionally she bit her bottom lip, a small, unconscious habit that seemed to surface whenever she was deep in thought. Beckett found himself lingering on her for a moment longer than he meant to before turning back to the road ahead.

"Do you think it's likely we'll find anything at Gates's place?" she asked.

"Could go either way," he replied. "Depends on what kind of headspace he was in when he left. He didn't have much on him, so he must have left in a hurry. There might be something to find. If not…" He let the sentence hang.

Lee nodded. "He was running, though. That much is obvious."

Beckett didn't answer immediately, sensing how keyed up she was. Full-on cop mode. She wanted all the answers and she wanted them now. He considered telling her to slow down, take it down a notch, but decided against it. He had to respect that her trade required a different mindset and attitude than his had. Frontline cops were all about the right-now and in-your-face, while his training had centred around staying out of sight and patience.

They turned onto a quieter road, the glow of the Strip fading into the distance behind them. The darkness made the space inside the car feel even smaller than it already was.

"This whole thing is just crazy," Lee said. "I keep thinking about the machine he mentioned. What do you think he was talking about?"

"Could be anything." He looked over at her. "But one step at a time, okay?"

Lee huffed, but it was good-humoured. "Right. Forgot who I was talking to."

He watched her for a beat, debating whether to share more. He'd been working through the same threads she was pulling at since they got in the car, but his thoughts weren't concrete yet, just loose connections. The machine, Jarvis, Gates's fear of whoever he thought was after him. It all added up to something, but the details were still too murky. If he said too much now, it'd only muddy the waters further.

They drove in silence for a few more minutes until Lee pointed ahead as Gates's apartment complex came into view. She pulled into an empty spot outside and killed the engine.

"Should I tool up?" she asked.

"Excuse me?"

"You know. Gun or Taser."

He smiled. "Neither. Let's keep this covert for now." He squinted up at the building, taking it in. "Ready?"

"Damn right."

They stepped out of the car and approached the dilapidated former motel. It was a U-shaped building with two storeys surrounding a central courtyard. The pool in the middle had long been abandoned; a few inches of green sludge remained at the bottom with several empty beer cans floating on the surface. A couple of old security lights screwed to the walls cast uneven shadows that made the place look even more miserable than it was.

They entered the complex through a creaky metal gate and made their way up to the second-floor landing. Lee reached Gates's door first, bristling with pent-up energy as she waited for Beckett to catch up. A tarnished brass number hung in the middle of the door. Number 7. Lucky for some. Not for Gates.

Lee knocked before he could stop her. They waited. She tried the handle. Locked.

"What now?" she whispered.

"Let me have a look." Beckett jiggled the handle, testing

its resistance. It was old, probably untouched since the place was built in the seventies. He crouched by the door, running a hand along the frame, checking for any give. There was some. Enough to work with.

Standing, he scanned the landing and spotted a crushed Coke can near the top of the stairs. He went over, flattened it further with his boot and picked it up. With a few quick tears, he peeled off a strip of aluminium and tested its edge with his thumb. Not ideal, but it would do.

Returning to where Lee was waiting, bouncing from foot to foot, he slid the strip between Gates's door and the frame, working it carefully along the edge until he found the latch. His first attempt didn't budge it. Adjusting his angle, he pressed firmly on the door with the flat of his hand, and the lock gave a soft click. He pushed the door open an inch and straightened.

"Old locks. They just need a little convincing."

They stepped into the apartment and the smell hit them immediately. It reeked of stale food, sweat, and something Beckett preferred not to think about. He closed the door behind them, letting the latch click into place, and stepped further into the room.

Not that there was far to go. The apartment was tiny. Just one room with a small bathroom tucked off to the side.

Lee went to switch on the light but he held a hand up.

"Let's not telegraph we're here," he said. She hesitated, then dropped her hand as he scanned the room. The glow of the landing lights filtering through the thin drapes was enough to make out the basics. A single bed and sagging couch both faced an old, boxy TV, while a kitchenette was buried under a mess of dishes and takeout containers. A small desk sat along one wall, and near the door a tall, narrow wardrobe was plastered with faded flyers and peeling stickers. Everything looked second-hand or salvaged. Nothing matched.

Lee turned to him, wrinkling her nose. "Always gets me how some people live."

"Think of everything as a clue," Beckett replied, his gaze falling on an old pizza box, its lid speckled with mould. "Almost everything. Let's split up. Check everywhere, see what shows up."

"Got it."

Beckett started in the kitchenette while Lee switched her phone torch on, avoiding pointing at the window as she ventured into the bathroom. A faint smile crossed his face as he heard a muffled noise of disgust. Turning back, he crouched by the sink and opened the cabinet. It wasn't much better on his end; he was immediately hit with the sour smell of mildew. He also found two empty spray bottles, a box of rat traps, and a single can of tomato soup that looked old enough to be a collectible. He pulled it out, turned it over, and tapped it once against the floor, half hoping it might be a dummy with something stashed inside. But no, just a can. He stood and moved to the cabinet above the stove.

Opening the door he was met with what appeared to be Gates's mug collection. Far too many for one man to own, all mismatched and worse for wear. One had a fading image of a bikini-clad woman holding a wrench, another bore the words *Don't Talk To Me Until This Is Empty*.

Lee emerged from the bathroom, her expression telling him all he needed to know about the state of it. She looked over and raised her eyebrows. "Anything?"

"Not so far."

He moved to the desk, where a stack of opened mail leaned against yet another stained mug. He thumbed through the pile, finding nothing but bills, junk mail, and a flyer advertising *All-Night Karaoke*. The closest thing to personal correspondence was a yellowed postcard with a generic beach scene on the front and no message on the back. He tossed the pile aside and headed for the bed in the corner before Lee got to it. It felt like the gentlemanly thing to do after she'd braved the bathroom.

The bed was as sad as the rest of the apartment, a single limp mattress covered by a thin, stained sheet, and a depressing yellow pillow that looked to be more sweat and skin cells than actual filling. Next to it was a small wooden, slightly tilted bedside cabinet, one of its legs replaced by a stack of beer mats.

The top drawer was stuffed with balled-up tissues, and Beckett slammed it shut immediately. The second drawer wasn't much better, crammed with what seemed like every takeout menu in Vegas and a stack of sticky notes. He sifted through them, finding half-finished grocery lists, random phone numbers with no names, and a poorly drawn doodle that could have been either a spaceship or a robot. In the last drawer he found a pair of mismatched socks, a bottle of cheap cologne, and an old pack of gum with one stick left inside. Not exactly gold.

"I can't find anything," Lee said, holding up a garish Hawaiian print shirt from the wardrobe. "Nothing of use, anyway."

"Me neither."

Beckett did a quick sweep of the bathroom in case she'd missed anything. It was the room where he would sometimes stash things if the need arose, so he knew it was worth another look. He closed the door and switched the light on. As Lee had intimated, the bathroom was worse than the main room. The stench of urine and bleach made his eyes and nose sting. Mould spread out from the corner of the ceiling, creeping along the grout lines and into the shower unit. The mirror above the sink was cracked in two places. He checked around the toilet cistern, then the medicine cabinet, finding a half-empty bottle of ibuprofen and an old toothbrush but nothing more. Shutting the cabinet, he stepped back and gave the room one final glance before turning off the light and heading out.

They regrouped in the kitchen area, Lee standing with her hands on her hips, her mouth twisted in frustration. Clearly she'd expected their big break to be waiting here, wrapped up in a neat bow.

"It's just crumbs and crap," she muttered.

"Well, why don't we run through what we know?" Beckett said, trying to keep her upbeat.

It did the trick. She nodded, exhaling like she was about to launch into a speech. "Okay. So we think Gates was running from something – or someone. And he was panicked enough to shoot that guy at the gas station and take hostages."

Beckett held a finger up. "Yes. But it wasn't just panic, it was desperation. My guess is he discovered something he wasn't supposed to. Something important enough to put a target on his back."

"Which is why whoever's behind this had Jarvis kill him," Lee added, with the energy of a star pupil eager to impress teacher. "To keep him quiet."

"That's the working theory," Beckett said. "But what did Gates know?"

Lee exhaled sharply. "This machine he kept going on about."

"Yes, but everything's a machine these days." He rubbed

at his chin. "Are you certain Jarvis took something from Gates's evidence folder?"

"Pretty certain. The plastic zipper wasn't sealed. Either it hadn't been closed properly in the first place or someone had been through it before me. Jarvis, most likely."

"So, let's say Gates had something these people wanted," Beckett said. "Or he took something they needed back. That would explain why he was running."

"And now Jarvis has it. Shit. This is huge. I can feel it. Why else would someone go to all this trouble?"

Beckett watched her as she talked, her words tumbling out in a rush. She was wound up, chasing the idea like a dog after a car. He appreciated her spark – it was what made her a good cop and a valuable ally. But it was also what could make her dangerous. She didn't know how to slow down, how to pace herself enough to see the risks. And like this, that spark could burn her out, or get her hurt.

And they still had no idea who they were dealing with.

"What could he have taken, do you think?" Lee asked, more to herself than Beckett. "Maybe it was the machine. Hey, maybe—"

"Lee," Beckett cut in.

She stopped mid-sentence, turning to him with wide eyes. "Yes?"

"Let's take a breath, okay?" he said, as gently as he could. "We've got nothing concrete yet."

"I know, I get it. It's just…" She leaned back against the counter, folding her arms tightly across her chest. "This is important - a chance to work on something that matters, and not just clean up everyone else's mess."

Beckett didn't respond, but he understood. She was trying to prove something. Maybe to herself. Maybe to someone long gone. But he could also see her enthusiasm starting to pull her off balance. And in Beckett's world, being off balance got people killed.

"Well, we're not getting anything else out of this place," he said. "Why don't we call it a night and—"

His eyes snapped to the window as a shadow passed across the drapes.

Someone was outside on the landing.

He froze. So did Lee. The angle of the light made it impossible to tell the person's size or gender. But they could both see the raised arm. And the unmistakable silhouette of a gun.

Chapter Twelve

Beckett grabbed Lee's arm, guiding her down behind the couch. "Stay down," he whispered. "I mean it."

His mind was already working through the possibilities. Maybe whoever was out there had been following them, or maybe Gates's place had already been under someone's watch. Either way, it didn't matter. What mattered was they had company, and that company was armed.

His instincts took over as he moved silently to the door, pressing himself against the wall beside the frame. The silhouette was gone now, which meant one of two things: they were standing just outside the door, or they'd moved on. He held his breath, listening for signs of movement. The landing was silent, and for a moment he thought they might have left, but then the handle rattled.

The door held firm. So did Beckett. But as his eyes locked with Lee's and he held up a hand to keep her still, he heard a soft click. Metal sliding into place.

Bugger.

He gestured for Lee to get down. Whoever this was, they had a key.

They were coming in.

Beckett pressed himself against the wall, holding his position as the door eased open. Light from the landing speared across the floor, and a second later the barrel of a pistol appeared, low and shaky. As a bony arm followed, Beckett stepped to the side of the doorway, grabbing the wrist behind the gun.

The intruder let out a startled gasp, instinctively jerking back, but Beckett held firm, twisting their arm upwards and forcing the pistol away from any potential target. The motion sent the intruder stumbling over the threshold, their balance off-kilter. Beckett pressed the advantage. Keeping a tight hold on their wrist, he yanked them forward and barged them onto the bed while wrenching the gun free from their grip.

"Geddahelloffame!"

Pistol now in hand, Beckett reached for the light switch, stepping back as the room was flooded with harsh yellow light.

"Who the hell are you?" the intruder growled, twisting to glare at him. "Fucking prick."

It was a woman, her thin face contorted with rage. She lunged for the door but Beckett grabbed her arm, forcing her back onto the bed.

"All right, let's calm it down," he said, levelling the pistol at her. "Who are you? What are you doing here?"

Lee got up from behind the couch and the woman's eyes darted between her, Beckett and the gun. For a moment he thought she might make another break for it, but then her shoulders sagged, and she raised her hands in a reluctant gesture of surrender.

"All right, man. Take it easy," she growled. "I was just checking on things, that's all."

Beckett kept the gun steady, his eyes narrowing as he studied her. She was white, possibly with a hint of Mexican, and could have been anything from early thirties to late fifties, it was hard to tell, she looked like life had chewed her up and spat her back out. Deep lines marked the corners of her mouth and eyes, and her unwashed hair hung in tangled clumps. She was also rake-thin but had clearly had a breast enlargement at some point. She wasn't wearing a bra, and her tight denim pedal pushers and leopard-print shirt looked well past their prime.

"Do you know the man who lives here?" Beckett asked her. "Evan Gates?"

Her bloodshot eyes met his, unfocused and glassy. She let out a coarse laugh, and the stench of alcohol on her breath was so strong Beckett could almost see the green haze wafting from her mouth.

"Yeah, I know the man who lives here. I know him *real* well." Her voice was rough and harsh, a lifetime of cigarettes packed into every syllable.

"What's your name?" Lee asked, stepping around the couch. She produced her badge from where it must have been clipped to her waistband under her t-shirt, holding it up as she moved closer. "Come on. Talk."

"Fuck off, cop," the woman sneered.

Lee gripped the badge tighter. "You want to do this downtown?"

The woman gave a dry, humourless laugh, her gaze flicking over the badge without a shred of concern. "Oh, yeah, that's *real* scary," she said. "Please, officer. Arrest me."

Beckett flicked the gun barrel. "Please, answer the question. Who are you?"

The woman stared at Beckett, her hands twitching at her sides like she was still struggling with which of the flight or fight responses to go with.

"We just want some answers," he told her. "You aren't in any trouble. No one is."

She glared at him, but then seemed to give up the ghost all at once, like she was suddenly too tired to care.

"My name's Jen," she muttered. "I live three doors down. Evan and I we… have a thing. Not your business what kind, but it's something. I walked past just now and I heard movement in here. I was just checking he wasn't being robbed." She flashed her eyes at Beckett. "Is he being robbed?"

"You think there's anything here worth robbing?" Lee cut in.

Beckett shot her a stern look before returning his focus to Jen. He was watching for the small tells in her posture, the flickers of emotion she couldn't hide. It all told him she was telling the truth. Now that her breathing had calmed and the wild edge in her eyes had dulled, he lowered the gun.

Lee stepped closer, her badge still in hand. She glanced at Beckett, eyebrows lifting slightly in a silent question, *Should I?* He gave her a quick nod and stepped aside. Even if Jen wasn't a fan of cops, this was better coming from Lee.

"Jen," she began, her tone softer now. "My name's Officer Maggie Lee. I'm afraid there's been a… What I mean is… I'm sorry to have to tell you that Evan Gates died earlier today."

Jen blinked. The words hit her hard. Beckett could almost see her sobering up. She stared at Lee for a moment before shaking her head. "What?"

Lee hesitated. "I'm so sorry. It happened at Sierra

Heights police substation. He'd been… Well, he was being held there, and…" She grimaced, glancing at Beckett for help.

"We're sorry you have to find out like this," Beckett added.

Jen's face crumpled as she looked between the two of them. "How?" she asked. "What happened?"

Lee opened her mouth to respond, but Beckett stepped in. "We're still figuring that out. But you might be able to help us. Did Evan say anything to you? Anything that might explain why he might try to leave town?"

Jen wiped her face with the back of her hand. "No. I'm not sure."

"And this is a hard question to ask," Beckett continued. "But is there any reason someone might have wanted him dead?"

Jen frowned. "He was killed?"

With Lee flashing her badge, Jen would assume Beckett was a cop too. No point complicating things by correcting her. "We believe so," he said. "It's an ongoing investigation."

Jen sniffed, her hands trembling as she pulled a crumpled pack of cigarettes and a bright pink lighter from her pocket. Beckett watched in silence as she wrestled a bent cigarette free from the foil, giving her the space she needed. It took a few shaky tries, but she managed to light it, the tension in her shoulders easing a fraction as she took a long drag.

"There is something," she said.

Lee raised her head. "Oh?"

Jen took another slow drag. "Evan started work as a security guard a few weeks back. Doing the night shift. I was pissed because… well, that's when we got together mostly."

Beckett met Lee's gaze. It wasn't much to go on, but it was something.

"Do you know where he was working?" Beckett asked.

Jen exhaled a large plume of smoke. "I'm not sure. But I do know he was worried. It was something to do with the company. Whatever they were up to."

"Did he see something? Or maybe heard it?" Lee asked.

Jen shrugged and stared at the floor. "He didn't like to talk about it. Just kept saying he didn't know what to do." Her voice cracked, and she took another drag. "I just know he was troubled. More than usual."

"And you don't know who he was working for? Not even a location?" Beckett asked.

Jen frowned, thinking. "Not exactly," she said. "It was for some big security company. They handle guards for all kinds of places – warehouses, nightclubs, casinos. You know the sort of thing."

Beckett nodded. It was often how it worked. Private outfits that acted as temping agencies for people who needed muscle. "You can't think of the name?"

She shivered slightly, wrapping her arms around herself. "Maybe Silver... something. Silver Shield?"

He looked at Lee. It sounded plausible. She stepped forward, her hand hovering awkwardly, like she wanted to pat Jen's shoulder but wasn't sure if she should.

"Thanks, Jen. Really. That's a big help."

Beckett placed Jen's gun on the arm of the couch and walked to the door.

"That's it?" she asked.

"For now," Lee said. "And if I were you, I'd keep my head down for a while."

Jen's glare snapped to Beckett, her face still pale. "Why? Am I in danger now?"

"No," he said, shooting Lee a hard look. He couldn't guarantee anything, but there was no use scaring the woman more than necessary. "But just in case, stay low for a week or so. And don't tell anyone we were here."

Jen sneered. "You think I'm going to tell anyone I helped the cops?" She let out a dry laugh, then gave a reluctant nod. "I appreciate you letting me know about Evan."

Beckett opened the door and went out first, checking the landing both ways before beckoning for Lee to join him. He shut the door behind her, leaving Jen still sitting on the bed, quietly sobbing. He felt bad for her, but there was nothing they could do now except stop the people who had ordered Gates's murder from doing anything worse. But first they had to find out who they were. As they headed back to the car his mind was working overtime, turning over everything they'd just learned.

They had a name now. Silver Shield Security. Their first real lead.

It wasn't much, but it was a start.

Chapter Thirteen

Back in the car, Lee sat staring ahead, making no move to start the engine. Her breathing still carried a trace of adrenaline, but Beckett was impressed with how she'd handled herself back there. A little clumsy at times, but without her more delicate touch, Jen might not have opened up.

"What now?" she whispered.

Beckett rubbed a hand over the stubble on his cheek. "We check out the security firm's head office."

She glanced at him, frowning. "Now? You think anyone's there this late?"

"I'd hope not," he replied. "That's the point. We can let ourselves in and find Gates's personnel file. That should tell us where he was working."

Lee stared at him like she wasn't sure she'd heard him correctly. "Another break-in? Do we have to?"

Beckett studied her. She was unsettled, caught between the rush of the chase and the weight of uncertainty. Out of her comfort zone, swinging between excitement and fear as her head tried to catch up with her heart.

He gave her a reassuring smile. "The less noise we make at present the better. If we can get the information without anyone knowing we're looking, it gives us the edge."

Lee nodded, but didn't start the engine. She was staring straight ahead again but he could feel it even stronger – hesitation, doubt, something brewing beneath the surface. The badge mattered to her. The rules mattered to her. And yet here she was, sitting in the dark next to a stranger with questionable methods.

"Something on your mind?" he asked.

"I just… This isn't my usual kind of job."

"I know that. But you wanted to do this. Didn't you?"

"Yes! But we don't even know where we're going."

"We can look it up on your phone."

She shifted in her seat, running out of excuses. "You really think we can break into two places twice in one night and it will all be fine?"

Beckett didn't answer. She already knew what he thought. He just sat there, letting her work through it. She stared at him a moment longer, then sighed and leaned back against the headrest.

"That a no?" he asked.

She shook her head. "It's not a no. It's just… Look, I don't want to get caught. I know your way is faster. And we need those records. But let's try my way first. We'll go in the morning. I'll flash the shield, get the details without breaking any laws."

Beckett cleared his throat. "You do know you're already breaking a few, though? This isn't your case and I've just impersonated a police officer on a late-night field trip to private property. If we're doing this by the book, you should be hauling me in right now." He was trying to lighten the mood, using humour to help her see the situation from another perspective. But from the look on her face, he'd have to try harder.

"Ah... shit," she muttered. "What the hell am I playing at?"

Beckett leaned in. "Lee, it's fine. You're doing good. You're on the right side of this."

She shot him a look, half defiant, half unsure. "Am I? Technically I'm still a cop, no matter where I am. There are rules and procedures I have to follow."

Beckett held her gaze, letting the silence settle.

"I want to wait," she said. "Please. We can go to Silver Shield first thing tomorrow."

"Fair enough." He leaned back, impressed by her resolve, concerned by the nerves she was trying her best to hide. "If that's what you want, we'll play it your way."

She exhaled, clearly relieved. Beckett turned his attention to the darkened streets outside. He understood her reticence. This way was cleaner, more above board. But he knew from experience that clean wasn't always clever, and they needed to be clever about this. Most security services, especially ones in Vegas, weren't the kind of places you barged into with a badge and questions. The last thing he needed was for whoever killed Gates to find out they were digging.

He glanced at his watch. Almost ten. His flight left three hours ago. The small amount of luggage he had, along with his passport, was in a safe deposit box at Harry Reid International. They weren't going anywhere and neither was he.

He rubbed a hand across his jaw, the fatigue catching up with him. He'd been running on instinct and momentum since the diner. Now the sharp edges were starting to dull. He closed his eyes for a second.

"You look like you need some rest." Lee's voice broke through the quiet.

He opened one eye. "Is that your professional opinion?"

"More like the obvious one." She shifted in her seat, and Beckett could tell she was watching him carefully, reading him the way a cop might read a suspect. "You've got nowhere to go, right?"

"I'll figure something out."

"You could stay at my place," she said, and then laughed nervously as if she'd heard how it sounded.

Beckett looked at her, keeping this professional at least. "That would help, but are you sure?"

She shrugged. "Where else are you going to go? Hotels are expensive, and I'm guessing you don't have one booked. Besides, I trust you."

"You hardly know me."

"I know. But you've risked your life for me already. You've listened to me, helped me, not spoken down to me or told me to wind my neck in and let it go. You've even missed your flight for me." She smiled. "It's more than my colleagues have done in the last five years. More than my family ever did."

Beckett smiled. "You're a good cop, Lee. You're a good person."

Her expression didn't change. "I'm not so sure about either of those. But thanks."

She started the engine, and Beckett let himself sink back into the seat as the car pulled out of the lot. The streets were quieter now, but Vegas never really slept. The neon glow from the Strip bled into the dark sky, lighting up the horizon like a forest fire.

Neither of them spoke on the drive back. Lee was focused on the road, and Beckett's thoughts were on Silver

Shield Security and whatever job they had Gates working. If they found that out, would it give them the lead they needed? He hoped so. He also hoped Lee was ready for whatever was waiting on the other side of their visit tomorrow.

He'd meant what he said earlier. She was a good cop, but his gut told him this was bigger and more dangerous than she realised. Gates might have been a bit lax in the cleanliness department, but there was nothing in his apartment to suggest he was anything other than a lonely bachelor trying to scrape a living in an expensive city, finding solace and perhaps a little pleasure in the arms of his neighbour whenever he got the chance. Yet earlier today he'd been scared enough to run, scared enough to grab a gun and take hostages. Whatever he'd stumbled onto, it wasn't small.

Fifteen minutes later they pulled into the lot beside Lee's apartment building. She shut off the engine, then turned to him. "We are doing the right thing here, aren't we?"

It was clear she'd been stewing on it the whole way back. Beckett turned to face her, forcing his expression into something close to reassuring.

"What do you think?"

She huffed. "I think something fishy is going on. I think a man has been unlawfully killed, and I think one of my fellow officers is involved." She looked away. "I also think I'm in way over my head and... Fuck it, I'm scared."

Beckett smiled. Admitting it was a good start. "That's normal."

She looked at him, taken aback. "Do you even get scared?" "Sometimes. But it's how we deal with it that matters. I'd say you're doing just fine. One step at a time, okay? Focus on what's in front of you. Stay out of your imagination."

She nodded, then sighed as if that was a big ask. "Yeah. I'll try."

They got out of the car and headed up to the apartment. Lee unlocked the door and stepped in first, flipping on the light. The place was just as Beckett remembered – small, sparse, a little quirky. But under the glow of the artificial lighting, and after the squalor of Gates's place, it felt a lot cosier.

"Here we are again. Home sweet home," she muttered, more to herself than him. Turning to Beckett she hesitated, almost awkward. "Sorry. It's not exactly Caesar's Palace."

Beckett grinned. "I wouldn't stay there anyway. Not my cup of tea."

"No. I imagine it's not." She smiled back, her gaze lingering on his lips a moment before she caught herself and spun away.

"Is something wrong?" he asked, having clocked her frown.

Lee scratched her neck, looking about her as if noticing the space for the first time. "No, it's just… uh… where are you going to—" She stopped herself, waving vaguely at the room.

"Don't worry," he said. "I've already made peace with a night on the couch."

She made a face. "It's pretty ancient. I mean you could always… But no, you're right. It's probably best that…" Her expression tightened as she realised what she was implying. "I'll get you a blanket. And a pillow. Hopefully it won't be too uncomfortable. But, hey – better than the floor, right? Consider yourself lucky." She laughed; a little too eagerly, Beckett thought.

He held up a hand. "Lee, it's fine. Thank you." He examined the couch in question. It was old and faded, and the cushions sagged in a way that promised a long night. "I've slept on much worse."

He sat, testing the cushion's firmness, or lack thereof. Lee hovered by the bedroom door, chewing her lip like she had something heavy on her mind.

"So you think we're doing the right thing then?" she asked. "That we'll get to the bottom of what happened?"

"That's two very different questions."

She smiled. "Okay. The second one."

Beckett held eye contact with her, his face serious now. "I think we will if you want to."

She thought about it, swallowed, then nodded. "I do want to. We have to, right?"

"I think we have a duty now," he said, choosing his words carefully. He wasn't just saying it for her sake, he believed it too. But he also didn't want to worry her more than she already was. "You're right, something big could be going down very soon and we need to find out what it is. If after that we hand the case over to the Metro PD or the Feds, so be it. But right now, no one else is looking in this direction. It's up to us to finish what we started."

She smiled but didn't look completely convinced. "I'll get you some bedding."

"Don't worry about it—" he started, but she was already disappearing into the bedroom.

While he waited, his attention drifted around the room, still not able to locate a single photo of Lee with any friends or family. He got up to tilt the blinds at the window. A cop's wage didn't pay for the best views in town. Just another apartment block across the street and the parking lot next door to it. Still, better than the rear alley and a row of dumpsters.

Lee returned clutching a pillow and a neatly folded blanket. "Here you go," she said, dropping them onto the couch.

"Thanks." He stood and pulled off his shirt.

As he tossed it onto the couch, he caught Lee staring.

"Sorry." She looked away quickly. "I'll leave you to it."

It was the scars. Always a bit of a shock to new people. "I guess I've been through a few wars," he said, but the comment landed flat. He exhaled. "Sorry, I was just getting comfortable. It feels like I've been wearing that t-shirt for days. I could probably do with some new clothes tomorrow."

"Or I could wash it?" she offered.

He grinned. He still had his wallet and about two hundred dollars in cash. "Don't put yourself out. I fancy getting a souvenir shirt anyway."

She raised an eyebrow. "Really?"

"When in Rome."

"Cool." She glanced at the floor, then at her bedroom door, then back at him. It was like watching someone trying to plan their next move in a game they hadn't played before.

"So… you good?" she asked.

"I'm good," he said, settling the pillow at one end of the couch.

"I'll just be back there." She jerked a thumb over her shoulder.

"Good plan."

"Okay. Goodnight."

"Goodnight."

She lingered half a second longer before turning abruptly and disappearing into the bedroom.

Beckett got himself comfortable. It was a warm night, but he kept his trousers on and left the blanket where it was folded on the arm of the chair. Kicking off his shoes, he lay back, the cushions sinking unevenly beneath his weight. He watched Lee's door for a moment, listening to the faint creak of her movements. He wondered if she'd be lying awake back there too, thinking about everything they'd discovered. Probably.

He let out a slow breath, calming his system. The pillow was lumpy against his head but he was tired enough that sleep wouldn't be far off. She'd switched out the light in the lounge, and the room was dark now except for a pale glow coming from under her bedroom door. He stared at the ceiling, his thoughts circling back to Gates and the panic in the man's voice as he spoke about *the machine*.

The machine and Silver Shield Security.

It wasn't much to go on, Beckett mused as he closed his eyes. But he was here now and he was prepared to see it through. It could be nothing, just the ramblings of a desperate man, but he didn't think so. His instincts were rarely wrong, and right now they told him one thing for sure. This was only getting started.

And it was going to get worse before it got better.

Chapter Fourteen

Las Vegas at night looked like it had been dipped in neon and polished to a high shine. From above, the Strip cut through the city like a switchblade, its billboards and hotel signs screaming promises of luxury and excess: oversized martinis, top-dollar steaks, platinum-card access to the best of everything. Casinos fired coloured spotlights into the sky, bouncing off the clouds like the Bat-Signal – though if Bruce Wayne were a real billionaire, he'd probably be drawn here by the spectacle of capitalism rather than some noble urge to fight crime.

Cabs and limos crawled bumper to bumper past fountains launching water jets into the air. Tourists snapped selfies in front of perfect replicas of the Eiffel Tower, Venetian canals, and an Egyptian pyramid. Music pulsed from every doorway, a driving bassline underscoring the city's obsession with wealth and vice.

Vegas was all show. Bright, loud, and proud. But two miles north, the glitz and noise faded and the lights dimmed. A sub-section of the Gateway District, Naked City sprawled out like a scar just beyond the glitter, a neighbourhood that didn't belong anywhere near Vegas's postcard-perfect images. Here the sidewalks were littered with drug baggies, broken glass and cigarette stubs. Storefronts sagged with peeling paint. Chain-link fences rattled in the breeze. Nothing moved quickly in Naked City unless you were chasing something − or being chased. It was the kind of place even cab drivers refused to go after dark. There were no tourists, no bright-eyed gamblers. Just people scraping by. It was a world of drugs, guns, and dead bodies. No glamour, no riches. No fun.

Down a side street that barely qualified as a road, an old building sat forgotten. It had once been a cheap motel, one of those places you paid for by the hour − all subdued lighting, plastic sheets and no questions asked. The sign out front had been smashed decades ago, and the boarded-up windows on the first two floors signalled there was nothing worth stealing inside. To any passerby, it was just another ruin in a part of town no one went. A place for rats and ghosts.

But Nina Sorrento − Red to those who knew her − liked it that way. It meant people stayed away. Even the rare cop who wandered this far into Naked City, driven by delusions of justice or foolishness, wouldn't give it a second glance. And that was the point. Because while the main building was a decaying husk, the lower levels were something else entirely.

Like a jewel-handled knife hidden under a filthy jacket, the basement was all Red's. Black walls soaked up the light, broken only by red neon strips that ran around the edge of the floor like arteries. A polished concrete floor gleamed faintly in the crimson glow, and at the centre of it all sat a long metal table. Against the back wall, two red leather couches faced each other beneath a huge industrial fan.

The place wasn't cosy. It wasn't meant to be.

Red liked it that way.

Tonight she sat at the head of the table, a phone pressed to her ear, her feline features set in a sneer of icy patience. She was tall and athletic, with broad shoulders and minimal body fat. Her hair was cut in a sharp, straight bob, jet black except for a streak of crimson down the left side, like someone had dipped their hand in blood and dragged it through. Thick black eyeliner ringed her dark eyes, and her lips, painted dark as night, were shaped into a defiant geisha pout.

She was a striking-looking woman, but Red's make-up wasn't about enhancing her beauty. It was war paint. Her clothes, too, were more armour than aesthetics. A sleek black tactical shirt was zipped up to her throat, paired with black cargo pants tucked into heavy boots. She had a good figure, but she never showed leg or even the hint of cleavage. Red wasn't that kind of woman. She didn't play anyone's game but her own.

Her free hand drummed lightly against the table, nails clicking against the surface as the man on the other end of the line rattled on.

Yes, yes, get to the point.

She caught sight of herself in a mirror on the opposite wall, her eyes flat and unblinking, the kind of stare that could, and did, make grown men sweat. Her patience was razor thin tonight, and every second on this call chipped away at it.

"Red, I need you to sort this."

She rolled her eyes at her reflection. He was worried

and he had every right to be. But he was wrong to doubt her ability to handle it.

"Just relax, will you?" she drawled into the receiver. "You don't have to keep telling me the same thing over and over. I'm aware of the situation."

"Are you? Because if this gets out—"

"I know. Don't worry."

She looked up as Morgan and Ross entered, motioning for them to sit while she finished the call.

Morgan was a mountain, six-four and built like a shipping container. A man who hit first and never needed to ask questions. Ross was a big guy too, but had a bit more about him up top. Not much more. But they were decent workers, and more importantly they were loyal. And loyalty mattered.

Ross caught her eye, giving her a half-shrug as if to ask, *What's the hold-up?*

She sneered and looked away.

"Listen to me," she said, pushing her chair back. "I'm going to sort it. Okay? I'm cleaning things up. Soon it'll be like nothing ever happened. Now leave me to what I do best."

She snapped the phone shut and tossed it onto the table before rolling out the tension in her neck, the stiffness a constant companion these days. It was always the same with these people – wanting everything done yesterday, dumping their mess in her lap and expecting her to fix it with a snap of her fingers.

But that's why they paid her what they did.

Vegas thrived on chaos, and Nina 'Red' Sorrento had built her reputation on being the one who could bring order to it. For the right price.

She'd once bought into a different kind of order. Duty,

service, loyalty to the flag. But two tours overseas had taught her the truth. Flags didn't mean much when you were left bleeding in the dirt while those giving the orders sat miles away, fat and clean. The second time it happened, her unit had been sent on a no-win op cooked up by politicians with no skin in the game. Three of her team didn't make it back. Red did, but not without a bitter lesson: patriotism, faith in the system, it was for suckers.

From there, it had been a lateral slide out of uniform and into something much darker. Contracting. Enforcing. Then Vegas, where people with power paid top dollar to make their problems disappear. Red didn't ask questions anymore. Her conscience had been burned off years ago, along with whatever respect she'd once had for authority. Now she was a fixer. Simple as that. Quick, clean, and with as little collateral as possible.

Morgan and Ross straightened as she crossed the room, sensing the show was about to start.

"Come with me."

She led them up a small flight of steps to a smaller room on the far side of the basement. Here, too, the walls and ceiling were painted black, and the only light came from a single red bulb hanging above a wooden chair bolted to the floor in the centre.

The woman in the chair whimpered as Red and her men entered. The duct tape binding her bony wrists to the chair arms had already begun to fray from her struggling.

"*Heese*," she mumbled over the ball gag in her mouth. "*Eye ownow owying.*"

The dull glow from the red bulb did little to dampen the deep lines on her face. She was junkie-thin and trembling like a shitting dog. She reeked of sweat and stale fear.

Pathetic.

Red hated junkies. She hated anyone with an addiction. They were weak, reckless, a waste of oxygen. She'd never touched anything herself – booze, drugs, none of it. She liked to stay sharp. Always.

"Did you hear what I told my boss just now?" she asked, leaning in. "I'm cleaning things up. Soon it'll be like none of this ever happened."

She yanked the ball gag free. The woman gasped, sucking in air like she'd been drowning. Red tossed the gag onto the floor.

"Soon it'll be like you never happened either," she said. "Unless you start talking. So come on – Jen – let's hear it."

The woman coughed, eyes wide with terror. "Please," she wheezed. "I told you everything. I don't know anything else."

Morgan and Ross had found this wreck of a woman in Evan Gates's apartment half an hour ago. She'd claimed she was his sometime girlfriend, and they'd brought her here for Red to deal with. Only she wasn't talking.

"All I want to know is who you were talking to before my men showed up," Red said. "They saw them leave. They know you spoke with them."

"I told you already."

"Tell me again."

Jen started to lose control, grunting like a pig as she struggled against the ties on her wrists. Red rolled her eyes. She needed this like a hole in the head.

"It was just... just a cop and a British guy," she stammered. "Like I told you."

"Names," Red snarled through gritted teeth.

"They didn't give me names. I don't know them, I swear. I don't give a shit. I'd tell you if I knew. I've told you everything."

Red leaned in until their faces were inches apart. "We'll see about that," she whispered, then drew back, snickering to herself.

Jen was trembling now, her breath coming in short bursts. Not breaking eye contact, Red reached into the thigh pocket of her cargo pants and pulled out the box.

It was just a dull pewter thing, scratched and dented. It could have held tobacco and cigarette papers. But inside was something far more valuable.

Red's tarot cards.

She flipped the lid, savouring the surprise on Jen's face as she slid the cards out into her palm. She'd had these specially made. The backs were a deep, blood-red lacquer, smooth and glossy like polished glass. She fanned them out with a practised flick.

"Wh-what's going on?" Jen stammered.

"She's showing you what's going to happen. Dumb bitch," Morgan snorted from the doorway, laughing with Ross.

Red shot them a glare and they fell silent.

They didn't get it, but they didn't need to. This wasn't for them. It wasn't for Jen either. Not really. Red already knew how this was going to end.

She held the cards out in front of her, making a show of shuffling them.

"I told you everything," Jen whined. "I swear."

"We'll see."

The woman was fully shaking now, her whole body vibrating like she was being electrocuted. She'd soon wish she was.

Red took her time. The cards were part of the game, part of the message. People feared the unknown, but Red had learned how to give it shape.

She slid a card from the middle of the deck and held it up to Jen with the flourish of a stage magician. She didn't look at it first – just watched Jen squirm. Then she turned it over, and a thin smile spread across her lips. She loved this part when it worked out right.

On the card was an image of a snake eating its tail.

The Ouroboros.

"Do you know what this one means?" Red asked.

Jen shook her head.

"It means cycles," she continued, rolling the words on her tongue. "Patterns. Lies being told again and again."

She let the words hang, then leaned in.

"Someone's spinning you a story, Jen. Or you're spinning me one."

"I'm not—" the woman's voice broke. "I swear I'm not lying!"

Red ignored her. She slid the card back into the deck and began shuffling again, taking her time, putting on a show. Because that's all this was – pure theatrics. She enjoyed reading the cards, but she was no mystic. Her real talent was making them mean whatever she needed them to. Then again, maybe that was all any tarot reader did.

Jen had been dead the moment Ross and Morgan dragged her through the basement door, the moment she'd looked into Red's face. But that didn't mean Red couldn't have a little fun.

"Oh!" she exclaimed, as she drew a new card and took first look. "The Tower."

Jen looked at her expectantly. "The Tower. Is that…?"

Red frowned, shaking her head. "God, no."

She turned the card over and the woman's already fragile demeanour crumbled. The sobs turned to frantic hiccups as she stared at the image of a derelict tower struck by lightning, flames dancing up its sides.

"What a damn shame." Red tapped the edge of the card against Jen's knee. "The Tower means destruction. Collapse. Your world comes crashing down, and there's no coming back. You see what I'm saying here?"

Jen's mouth opened, but nothing came out. She just shook her head, mascara tears streaking down her face.

Red placed the cards back in their box and slipped it into her pocket. Then she drew Suzette, her prized hunting knife, from her belt, tilting her so the blade gleamed red in the light. It was long and slightly curved, with serrated teeth running the length. Suzette had been by Red's side for years – quite literally. She was the best friend a girl could have.

"Please… Please, I told you everything—" The pathetic woman's eyes grew wider at the sight of the knife, her chest heaving as she fought to speak.

Red sneered. "Doesn't matter. You didn't tell me what I needed. And now the cards have spoken."

She didn't give her time to beg again. Stepping forward she slashed the blade across her throat, opening it up like it was a piece of fruit. Blood sprayed across the floor as the woman let out a grotesque, choking gurgle.

Red smiled. One of the tower card's traditional meanings was sudden unforeseen change. Well, you didn't get more sudden or unforeseen than that.

Jen slumped forward, the life draining from her, pooling beneath the chair like black oil. Red straightened, wiped Suzette's blade clean on her thigh, then slid her back into her sheath.

Ross and Morgan had been watching with the bored indifference of men who'd seen a lot worse. Red flicked a hand towards the body. "Clean this up," she ordered.

Morgan grunted as he fished a pair of latex gloves from his back pocket. Ross just shook his head and muttered something under his breath. But Red didn't care. Let them sulk. She had bigger things to deal with than her subordinates' job satisfaction.

There appeared to be more players on the board than anyone had anticipated. Which meant more for her to clean up. But it would also mean more money, so it didn't concern her too much. Loose ends were an issue and she was good at tying them off. She walked to the door, her mind already on the next task.

Whatever was coming – whoever else was involved – she'd handle it. She always did.

Chapter Fifteen

The pale light of dawn was seeping through the blinds in Lee's bedroom as she lay there, staring at the ceiling, trying to figure out how she'd ended up here. A dead man, a possible conspiracy, and a stranger asleep on her couch. A stranger who was… Well, she wasn't even sure what he was. And he wasn't really a stranger. Not anymore. But he was certainly intriguing, and the whole situation was strange.

Strange being a massive understatement.

But wasn't this exactly what she'd been craving? A real investigation, something to sink her teeth into?

She picked up her phone and scrolled through the local news, hoping for some kind of lead. Nothing. Just the usual noise. With a sigh, she got out of bed, wrapped her robe around her, and figured she'd sneak in a shower before Beckett woke up.

No such luck.

As she entered the front room he was standing by the stove, rooting through one of the cabinets. Thankfully, he'd put his shirt back on, but when he reached for a couple of mugs, the morning sun caught the thick muscles in his fore-arms, and for a second she felt a little lightheaded. Just hunger, she told herself.

Beckett looked over and smiled. "Good morning."

She didn't think she'd made any sound. "H-hey... Good morning. You're up early."

"Habit." He gestured towards a fresh pot of coffee. "I took the liberty. Hope you don't mind."

"All good."

Lee joined him in the kitchen, clumsily dancing around him as she half-heartedly checked the cabinets for anything resembling breakfast food. It had been a long time since there'd been a man in her place. And certainly never one who looked like Beckett.

"I'm afraid I've not got much in," she admitted, giving up on her hunt.

"It's fine. We'll grab something on the way." He smiled again, his blue eyes catching the sunlight streaming through the window, too bright and intense for this hour.

She set her phone down on the counter and poured herself a cup of coffee. They drank in silence for a few moments. It was sort of awkward but sort of not.

"Do we have a plan?" she asked.

Beckett pointed at her phone. "Mind if I use that?"

"Oh? You want to...?"

"I need to check something."

"Uh, sure," she said, snapping herself back to reality. She slid the phone his way, watching as he typed with his thumbs. "What are you doing?"

Beckett narrowed his eyes at the screen. "Searching the address. Here we are. Silver Shield Security. They appear to own a few locations around the city but the central hub is on Charleston."

"That's west," Lee said. "Not too far. I can drive us."

Beckett drained his mug. "Great."

"What, now?"

Beckett was already back on the couch, lacing up his boots. Lee finished her coffee. "I need to get washed and dressed."

"Okay. Be quick."

"Give me five minutes," she told him, hurrying back to her room.

Fifteen minutes later, Lee stood in front of the mirror in her bedroom, debating what she should wear. She wasn't used to this kind of case. At Sierra Heights, things were talked through for days before any real action was taken. But Beckett had an idea and acted on it immediately. She wasn't complaining. It was just a lot to get her head around.

But, jeans. That was simple enough. Not her tightest pair, though. This wasn't a date, for god's sake. She settled on a worn pair she didn't have to fight to button, then pulled a green sweater over her head. Her *lucky* sweater, though she had no real idea why she called it that. It had never brought her much luck.

She pulled her hair into a loose ponytail and applied some make-up.

No. Too much.

She wiped it off again with a pad and some strong remover, the chemical smell at least rousing her a little more.

She examined herself in the mirror. Maybe a little mascara wouldn't hurt? She reapplied it quickly, then grabbed her keys and badge.

Beckett was already waiting by the door as she walked through into the front room.

"Sorry," she mouthed, pulling a face as if it wasn't her fault.

But he didn't react, didn't seem pissed. Just smiled and opened the door. "Let's go."

"We'll have to make a detour," she said, eyeing him as she locked up. "You need new clothes, remember?"

He gave her a look but didn't argue. They got in her car and she drove them to the nearest department store. It wasn't a long stop; Beckett grabbed the first things he saw. A loose pair of black chinos, and a white t-shirt, aimed at tourists, with the words *High Roller* splashed across the front.

Lee grimaced when he picked it out.

"What's the problem?" he said, with a knowing grin. "I think it's very classy and subtle."

She laughed. "Yeah. Sure. Just like me."

They paid, and Beckett told her to go wait in the car while he got changed in the store. She hesitated for a second – uneasy about being on her own today – but told herself she was being ridiculous and did as he asked.

Outside, the sun had climbed higher and downtown Las Vegas was waking up. The hum of traffic was loud now, with cabs and delivery trucks weaving through the morning congestion. Tourists spilled onto the sidewalks, clutching oversized coffees and squinting against the glare.

Lee got in the car and pulled in a few deep breaths like every wellness influencer said you should. She was surprised to find it worked. A strange calm settled over her. She felt focused. Ready. Was that Beckett's influence? Maybe. She knew she'd been overwhelmed at first, running high on adrenaline and nerves, but now things felt real. And she was handling it. More than that – she was in it. Not just cleaning up someone else's mess, not playing the dutiful cop in the corner. She was proving herself. The thought sat heavy in her chest, but not unpleasant.

As often happened in quiet moments, her thoughts drifted to her career. Or what little there was of it. She could put in for a transfer to the main precinct, of course. Bigger cases, real detective work, something that mattered. It wasn't like she hadn't thought about it before. She had. Plenty of times. But every time she got close to making the move, something held her back.

Maybe it was fear – of failing, of proving everyone right. Even now, she could hear her old man's voice in her head, telling her girls didn't make good cops. That she'd be a lousy one.

She shook the thought away.

She had no idea what would happen if, or when, the chief found out what she was up to, but this was real police work, the kind she'd always wanted to do. She was damned if she'd walk away now. Plus, they were on the right track. She could feel it in her bones. Something was very wrong, and if Downtown weren't going to investigate, then she would.

She laughed under her breath, shaking her head at the very thought. It sounded reckless. Maybe even crazy. But it was true.

She jumped as the passenger door opened, and adjusted herself as Beckett slid in beside her.

"Hey, High Roller," she said, eyeing the t-shirt stretched across his chest. "Fits well."

He shot her a look as he buckled in. "Okay, fun's over," he said, though there was a hint of a grin. "Time to get to work."

Chapter Sixteen

The ride over to Silver Shield was quieter than their trip to the store, and more awkward too. Lee wasn't sure if it was the morning sun warming them through the windshield or Beckett's brooding presence, but something made the air feel tight.

"So," she said, trying to break it. "You're still not gonna tell me who you worked for? Or what you used to do?"

Beckett didn't look at her. "No."

"Not even a hint?"

"No. Sorry."

She sighed, a little too dramatically. "You're a tough nut to crack, Beckett."

"I've heard that before."

That was the end of that. She knew by now he wasn't the type to talk just to fill awkward silences. Still, it didn't feel as uncomfortable as it often did with people she'd only known a day or two. Lee liked to think she was a good judge of character, and despite his lack of conversation she only got good vibes from the Englishman. Well… she got more than that from him, but she was trying to ignore those feelings.

They drove on in silence for a while until Beckett leaned forward and peered through the windshield. "There it is."

Silver Shield Security's main office was the kind of place you could drive past a dozen times and never notice. A boxy old building on the edge of an industrial park wedged between a storage warehouse and a defunct car wash.

The parking lot was almost empty. Lee pulled into a space close to the door and killed the engine.

"This is the place?" she asked.

"Has to be."

On the far side of the building was a large loading bay, covered by a roll-down shutter. On this side, a single glass-panelled door led into what appeared to be a reception area. There were no windows anywhere in the building.

They got out of the car and headed for the entrance. Lee half expected the door to be locked, but Beckett pulled it open and stepped inside. She followed, staying close behind as she took in the reception area.

It was small and basic. Bare tile floors, a scuffed counter with the access flap propped upright, and a plastic plant in the corner that had seen better days. Behind the counter, a half-open door led to another room, possibly an office, with a second door on the far side that likely opened into the warehouse. There was no sign of a receptionist.

Lee followed Beckett to the counter where he leaned over and called out, "Hello? Anyone around?"

There was a pause. Then a man appeared at the door.

"Help you with something?" he asked, not even trying to hide his disdain at being disturbed.

Beckett straightened. "I hope so," he said, slipping into a perfect West Coast accent. "I'm Detective Beckett and this is Detective Lee. We're following up on an investigation and need to ask you a couple of things. Won't take long."

Lee's heart skipped a beat, but she kept her face neutral. *Detective Lee.* She liked the sound of it. It felt good. She even flashed the badge for good measure, too quick for him to see the details. That felt good too.

But the man's expression only darkened. "I never saw nothing."

"What's your name, sir?" she asked.

He held her gaze, unimpressed, then glanced at Beckett's *High Roller* shirt and let out a humourless chuckle. "Name's Ted Marshall."

Marshall didn't look like the kind of guy you'd want to cross. Late fifties, with a thick head of red hair, and what appeared to be a permanent scowl. His hands and neck were a gallery of faded amateur-looking tattoos. Snakes, gang signs, crosses. Lee figured a guy like him didn't get those in art class. He was an ex-con. Had to be. Probably spent a few years at High Desert or Ely.

"What's your role here at Silver Shield?" Beckett asked.

"Head operations manager. What do you want?"

"And what do you manage?" Lee asked.

He sneered at her like the question was the dumbest thing he'd ever heard. "We're Silver Shield *Security*. What do you think we do?"

"Humour us," Beckett said.

Marshall sighed. "We hire guys. Send them out where they're needed – casinos, warehouses, shipping yards. You name it. It's industrial contracts mostly."

"Do you remember an employee called Evan Gates?" Beckett asked. "He started working for you recently."

Marshall shifted his weight. "Doesn't ring a bell."

Lee didn't buy it. She could tell Beckett didn't either.

Marshall was putting on a good front, playing it cool, but the way his eyes kept skimming past them, never settling, gave him away. He wasn't just disdainful, he was nervous.

"We're a big outfit," he added, with a shrug. "Names blur together."

"Sure they do," Beckett replied, deadpan. He leaned closer to Lee but didn't take his eyes off Marshall. "What do you think, Detective? You think it's cops he doesn't like – or telling the truth?"

"Maybe both," she said, getting into the role.

Marshall bristled, his sneer returning. "You don't scare me. Coming in here like you own the place. I've done nothing wrong."

The guy glared back at them, playing hardball. But Lee wasn't walking out of here empty-handed.

"What's the matter, Marshall?" she said, taking a step closer to the counter. "We just need some information."

She glanced through the door into the office area, spotting a row of battered filing cabinets along one wall. "You've got personnel files? Records? Why don't you have a look to jog your memory? Or would you rather we come back with a warrant and a full team to tear the place apart?"

Marshall chuckled. "Good luck with that. I'm not giving you squat. Now get the hell out of here."

Lee ignored him, moving under the raised flap to the other side of the counter. "What else is back there?" she asked, as Marshall squared up to her.

"Get lost," he growled.

Lee sidestepped him, trying to see more. "We just want to have a look at Gates's file. Shouldn't take a minute.'"

Marshall moved fast for a man his size, getting in front of her so she couldn't pass. "I said *get lost.*"

Before Lee could react, he took hold of her shoulder and shoved, sending her stumbling into the wall. Pain jolted down her arm. As she steadied herself on her feet, Beckett moved past her, closing the distance in a flash, grabbing Marshall's wrist and wrenching it sideways. Marshall cried out, his balance shifting enough for Beckett to drive a leg through his stance, sweeping him off his feet. The big man crashed onto his back with a heavy thud, the air leaving his lungs in a choked gasp. Beckett kept hold of the wrist, twisting his arm while driving a knee into his chest, pinning Marshall in place.

"Are you done?" Beckett asked him.

Marshall grunted, teeth clenched against the pain. "Fuck you."

Lee leaned on the counter, catching her breath, more than a little impressed – and maybe a touch unsettled too. Beckett was the real deal. And not for the first time, she wondered why the hell someone like him was bothering to help someone like her.

Marshall writhed, sweat beading on his forehead. "Get... off... of me."

But Beckett tightened the grip. "I'm running low on patience, Mr Marshall. Do you remember Evan Gates yet?"

Marshall's face reddened. His jaw clenched, then he spat out, "All right! All right!"

Lee stepped forward. "Talk," she snapped.

He sucked in a breath, "Okay, yeah. Gates. I remember him. Worked a night shift. Warehouse job. Just off the Strip."

"Which warehouse?" Beckett asked.

"Warehouse 12, over on West Sunset," Marshall gasped. "It's owned by a company called Novara Logistics. Some

Silicon Valley shit. Computer parts, servers, that kind of crap. I don't know anything else."

Lee exchanged a glance with Beckett and nodded. *Novara Logistics*. She'd heard of them.

Beckett released Marshall's wrist and stood, letting the man scramble back against the wall, holding his arm like it might fall off. He was still angry, but the fight had drained out of him and the fear in his eyes said he knew better than to push his luck. Beckett took one last look around, then turned and walked out the door. Lee followed, letting it slam behind her as they stepped into the morning sunlight.

"You okay?" Beckett asked.

"Fine."

She followed him to the car, her mind spinning. *Warehouse 12. Novara Logistics*. If they were involved, this wasn't just some small-time operation. This was bigger and more volatile than she'd dared imagine. Novara was one of the biggest tech firms around, their tower near the Strip almost rivalling the Strat.

She glanced at Beckett as he climbed into the passenger seat. As usual, he looked to be miles ahead, piecing things together in that quiet way of his.

She started the engine. "We going there now?"

"No time like the present," he said. "If you're up to it."

"Yeah. Course."

She pulled out of the lot, eyes on the road, forcing herself to focus solely on what was in front of her, just like Beckett had suggested. He was right, of course, but it was hard to stop the dark thoughts creeping in at the edges of her mind. What had started as an exciting adventure was quickly turning into something serious. And a whole lot more dangerous.

Chapter Seventeen

Beckett knew Lee wanted to say something from the moment they set off. Five minutes passed before he shifted in his seat to look at her. She was staring straight ahead, her eyes wide and unblinking, lips moving silently like she was doing difficult sums in her head. He knew that expression. A thought trying to force its way out.

"What is it?" he asked.

She shot him a look. "What do you mean?"

"You've been chewing on something since we left Silver Shield. Talk to me."

She shifted uneasily in her seat. "It's just... don't you think that was a bit extreme back there?"

"We got what we wanted."

"Yeah, I know, and I sort of liked it. I think." She wrinkled up her nose. "But you could've broken his wrist. That wouldn't have looked good."

Beckett turned his head to the window, watching the blur of low-rent stores and strip malls fly past. "Who for? Those two made-up detectives?"

"I gave him my real name," she said. "We both did. What if this ruins things for me?"

Beckett got it now. She'd liked playing detective. More than liked; she wanted this so bad, it was everything to her.

"Don't worry," he said. "Marshall's not going to report anything."

Lee didn't answer. Just sighed.

Beckett studied her for a beat longer. Long enough to notice the freckles dusting her nose, the way the sunlight caught in her hair. She was over-eager, too quick to speak, and always pushing for more. Everything he wasn't. And yet, there was something about her energy he found… appealing. It unsettled him. He turned his attention back to the road because staring any longer wouldn't help.

"But you're probably right," he said. "I'll try and be less extreme. Sorry about that."

He felt her gaze on him for a moment before she mumbled, "It's fine." Out of the corner of his eye he noticed her shoulders relax a little.

Refocusing, he watched her phone screen mounted on the dash, tracking the route they'd pulled up before setting off. Warehouse 12, just off West Sunset Road. It looked to be a part of a bigger industrial site, sitting on its own lot. Too much space for a company that supposedly did 'nothing special'.

Lee steered them down a winding access road that didn't look like it saw much traffic. Beckett scanned the area. It was deserted. To their right, a high chain-link fence ran the length of the road, topped with loops of razor wire. At the end of the stretch stood a large building that looked like any other industrial warehouse. There were a few trucks in the lot, but no other sign of life.

"Place looks dead," Lee said, narrowing her eyes.

"Weird that, don't you think?"

Lee parked down the side of an old shipping container, putting the car out of sight of both the warehouse and the main road. Beckett noted it with quiet approval. She was thinking ahead.

"So what now? We just going to waltz in there?"

"Waltz, no," Beckett said, opening the door. "Investigate? Yes. Come on."

He led the way across the lot towards the far corner of the building where a fire door sat flush with the metal siding, no windows, no signs. He stepped up to it and tested the handle. Locked. He pushed his shoulder against it. Solid.

Damn it.

"I thought you said investigate?" Lee said. "This looks like another break-in."

He cleared his throat. "Semantics. I'd rather see if we can have a look around unfettered. Plus, I think we might be pushing our luck with the detective roles."

She looked a little put out, but this was no time for managing expectations or egos. He examined the frame. No sign of damage, no loose seams. He crouched, fingertips brushing the edge where the metal met the concrete. Still no cigar.

"What do we do?" Lee whispered.

He stood and gave the door a slight jiggle. Not loud, just enough to send a vibration through the frame.

There it was. A faint metallic rattle. He felt it, too. Like something wasn't sitting right.

Interesting.

He jiggled it again. This time it was more pronounced –

a fire bar out of tension on the other side. Sometimes, if the mechanism wasn't reset properly, the latch wouldn't fully engage. He adjusted his grip and shifted the pressure up and down, searching for the weak point. This time he felt it give. A metallic clink sounded through the door as the bar flexed enough for the latch to slip.

Bingo.

He froze, listening. No alarm. No voices, no footsteps. He eased the door open an inch and held it there. A beat. Still nothing. He pushed it open fully and stepped inside.

The warehouse looked even bigger from the inside. A cavernous space thick with the smell of oil, dust, and something faintly chemical. Tall shelving units ran down the length of the building, stacked high with boxes and crates wrapped in plastic. A herd of forklifts sat in one corner, motionless.

Something was wrong. It was too still. Too quiet. The fact there was no one around was useful, but a warehouse this size didn't just grind to a halt for no reason.

"We clear?" Lee whispered, shuffling in behind him. The space went darker as she closed the door. They moved forward, taking it steady, tracing the edge of the nearest shelving unit as their eyes adjusted to the gloom.

"You see anything?" she whispered.

"No. Not even security cameras."

"That's weird, right? A place this big?"

"Yeah," Beckett murmured. "It's weird."

They ventured deeper into the space to where the shelves opened out into what appeared to be a packing area. A noise echoed somewhere behind them, causing Lee to grab Beckett's arm.

"Shit."

Beckett remained still, ears straining for more sound, but nothing came. Just the structure settling. Expanding in the heat, maybe.

"We're okay," he whispered.

They kept moving. Ahead, a faint strip of light glowed beneath a closed door. Beckett stepped towards it, pressing his ear to the wood. Silence. He gripped the handle and eased it open. The room was large and windowless. Three heavy desks sat pushed against the walls, buried under stacks of boxes, files, and loose paperwork. Above one of the desks, an oversized whiteboard dominated the space, covered in transport schedules and maps pinned in place with small magnets.

Beckett made a beeline to the far desk and started flipping through the stacks of papers as Lee did the same on the middle desk. There were hundreds of invoices, manifests and delivery schedules. Everything looked routine, but the name Novara Logistics wasn't on any of it. That seemed odd.

He did a swift check of the other desks and the whiteboard, but couldn't find the name anywhere. No letterheads, no stamps, not even a stray memo. A warehouse owned by them, supposedly full of their cargo, yet not a single scrap of paper tying them to it.

"Looks like boring stuff," Lee said, squinting at a ledger. "Shipping statements, routes... but it's just codes instead of full details, so I'm not even sure what it means."

Beckett clicked his teeth as he took it all in. The problem was, they didn't even know what they were looking for.

"Keep searching," he told Lee. "But try not to make a mess."

She scoffed, meaning it was already a mess. And she was correct, but it was important to do this right. Beckett crouched by the first desk and pulled open the top drawer. Empty. He tried the next one. More invoices but nothing useful. Rising to his feet, his eyes drifted once again to the whiteboard. Most of it was clutter, but in the corner, half covered by an old maintenance checklist, a handwritten note caught his attention.

He pulled it free and read:

All outbound: use direct sign-off. Authorised personnel only. No exceptions.

The words were underlined twice, followed by a list of codes and what looked like coordinates. The edge of the paper was torn like it had been ripped from a larger sheet.

Lee wandered over and leaned in. "What's that?"

"Not sure. But it might be something."

Beckett scanned the board one last time, looking for anything they'd missed, before a loud clatter echoed through the warehouse. They both froze.

"That was definitely something," Lee whispered.

Beckett didn't answer. His instincts were shouting now. He crept to the door, easing it open just enough to scan the warehouse beyond. Nothing. He moved back into the room. "We should get out of here."

Lee nodded, setting down a stack of papers. "Yeah, I guess," she muttered, frustration in her voice. "There's nothing here."

Beckett was about to reply when he heard it. Footsteps. Coming from the main warehouse. Lee heard it too, her eyes wide as they locked with his. He focused in on the sound. Two sets of footsteps. Heavy. Wearing boots. They were moving closer to the office.

Then they stopped.

Beckett held a finger to his lips and gestured for Lee to move back against the wall. She did as instructed, pressing herself flat. He took a second to ground himself then eased closer to the door, every muscle coiled tight.

Whoever it was, they weren't leaving.

Chapter Eighteen

Instinct took over as Beckett stepped away from the door, moving into the middle of the room.

"Stay where you are," he told Lee, as the handle twisted.

He barely had time to turn back before the door slammed open, the impact against the wall echoing like a gunshot. Two men bundled through, one after the other, broad-shouldered and ugly. Lee let out a small yelp as Beckett stepped in front of her, feet planted, hands loose at his sides, tunnel vision locked onto the threat. The front guy was thick in the shoulders, bald, with a scar that ran down the side of his neck like a zipper. The second guy looked younger but no less mean-looking. He had dark, slicked-back hair and a squint like he'd smelled something rotten. His huge fists were thick with bulbous scars and thick calloused skin. Fighter's hands.

"The hell you doing here?" the older one growled. "This is private property."

Beckett tensed as Lee shifted behind him. "We're…

detectives," she said. "Metro PD." He didn't look around but he imagined she'd flashed the badge again.

"Oh yeah?" The younger man's lip curled and he shot a glance at his partner. There was no reticence or confusion in their expressions. Whether or not they believed Lee didn't matter. They didn't care.

The older one stepped forward. "We can't have you snooping around here."

"Yeah," his buddy chuckled. "Can't have it at all."

Beckett exhaled slowly, letting the tension fall from his limbs, his body loosening into something more fluid. Fight mode.

"Lee," he whispered, leaning back. "Get into the corner or under a desk. Stay back."

"What will you do?" she asked.

Beckett didn't answer. He didn't have time. The younger guy moved first, stepping forward with a grin that told Beckett everything he needed to know. He was over-confident. That was his first mistake.

Beckett ran at him, closing the gap before the guy knew what was going on. He feinted left and then pivoted hard, driving his fist into the man's stomach. He grunted, doubling over, and Beckett followed with an elbow to the side of his head. The man crumpled to his knees, clutching his skull.

Now the older man charged like a prized bull. Beckett turned just in time, sliding sideways as a heavy fist swung past his jaw, the air from it brushing his cheek.

This one was strong but slow. Beckett ducked under the next swing and drove a knee into the guy's gut, hard enough to knock the wind out of him. The man staggered, gasping, but he stayed upright. Beckett moved again, dummying left and slamming a palm strike into the man's jaw that cracked his teeth together. The guy's head snapped back, and Beckett grabbed his collar, driving him hard into the wall face first. The impact was heavy and brutal, but the man didn't go down. Instead he threw his weight backwards, catching Beckett off balance and knocking him into the centre of the room.

"Beckett!" Lee yelled, panic in her voice.

He turned to see the younger man back on his feet, face bloody. He lunged, tackling Beckett around the waist, driving him into one of the desks. Pain jolted up Beckett's spine, but he gritted his teeth, twisting hard to break free. A blow to the side of the man's neck loosened his grip for half a second. Just enough. Beckett pivoted away and drove his elbow into the guy's nose, feeling the cartilage snap.

The man howled, hands flying to his face as blood poured between his fingers. Beckett stepped in, grabbed a fistful of the man's shirt, and swung a brutal elbow to the side of his head, rattling his brain in his skull. The man's knees buckled and Beckett smashed his face into the corner of one of the desks. The crunch it made was sickening. The man slid to the ground, unconscious.

Beckett straightened, breathing hard, rubbing the sweat from his face. He had half a second to register movement before the older guy came at him like a freight train. The impact knocked him sideways into the wall. He pushed off, trying to find his feet, but the older man was relentless. Thick arms coiled around Beckett's neck from behind, locking him into a chokehold. The pressure was instant, crushing his windpipe, cutting off air.

He clawed at the guy's forearm, trying to find leverage, but he was like a granite statue, every muscle taut. Stars burst behind Beckett's eyes. His boots scrabbled against the floor, searching for footing. He twisted, trying to loosen the hold, but the man growled, tightening his grip.

"Get off him!"

Lee's voice echoed in his head, and then there was a crack of splintering wood. The older man jolted forward, a grunt ripping from his chest as his grip loosened. Beckett dropped low and stepped away, his vision clearing just in time to see Lee standing there, clutching the broken remnants of a chair.

The guy staggered, turning towards her, his face bright red. "You little fucking—"

Beckett didn't let him finish. Lunging forward, he grabbed the man's arm and yanked him off balance. The guy swung, but Beckett ducked, driving his elbow into the man's ribs. He grunted as the air left his lungs. Beckett spun behind him, locking one arm around his neck and wrenching upward. A classic blood choke. The second Beckett locked his fingers around his wrist it was all over for the guy. He thrashed around, straining to get some purchase, but Beckett held firm. After a few seconds the fight drained from the man's body and he sagged, out cold.

Beckett let him drop and stepped back, catching his breath as he took in the two men sprawled on the floor. Lee was still clutching the broken chair in her hands. Her eyes were wild like she was ready for more.

"Whoa," she gasped. "That was… awesome."

"Are you hurt?" Beckett asked.

She blinked, lowering the chair. "No… No, I'm good."

He crouched next to the younger man, rolling him slightly to check his pockets. There was nothing in his jeans or jacket. No phone, no wallet, not even a set of keys.

He moved over to the older man but it was the same story. He tugged back the sleeve of the man's jacket, checking for anything that might identify him, and found a tattoo on the inside of his forearm, just above the wrist. The ink was faded, but the mark was unmistakable. A skull circled by twelve stars.

Most wouldn't recognise the mark, but Beckett did. The insignia belonged to a group called *Black Talon*. The kind of outfit that didn't operate under anyone's flag, just whoever had the deepest pockets. Years ago, in Libya, Beckett had seen their work up close. They were skilled, ruthless, and deadly.

Beckett exhaled. Their presence confirmed what the little voice in his head had been telling him all along. If people like this were working for Novara Logistics, then the company was a hell of a lot more than it seemed.

He straightened, glancing at Lee who was lingering by the door, still worked up from the fight.

"Let's get out of here. Before someone else shows up."

They made their way back through the warehouse, breaking into a jog until they reached the car.

"Those were some mean security guards," Lee said as she opened her door. "A lot tougher than Evan Gates."

Beckett opened the passenger side. "Those guys weren't security. They were mercenaries."

"Mercenaries? What the hell does that mean?"

Beckett glanced back at the warehouse. "It means someone knows we're snooping around," he said. "And they're getting worried."

He climbed into the car.

"It means we're getting closer."

Chapter Nineteen

Jimmy's Bar sat on a side street near the far end of the Strip, a flat-roofed relic that had seen better days. The name was slapped onto the board above the door in faded yellow paint. No neon, no frills, just *Jimmy's*. The only window was a single pane of smoked glass at the front that kept the outside world from seeing in. You had to lift the door off its hinges slightly to open it. Regulars knew the trick. Those who didn't stayed away.

Inside, it was dark and smelled the way bars should smell, of stale beer and the cigarette smoke that had permeated the upholstery long before the smoking ban hit town. At the back of the long room, a single pool table stood on one side under a lopsided lamp. The counter took up most of the other wall, backed with shelves full of mismatched liquor bottles. The stools were cheap, their vinyl seats turning sticky when the heat ramped up. Not that it mattered. No women in skirts or tourists in shorts ever sat on them.

Jimmy's hadn't started out as a cop bar. It used to cater to the usual downtown crowd – gamblers, drifters, lowlifes – but by the late eighties, enough uniforms had started coming through the door to make the regulars uncomfortable. Over time they found somewhere else to drink, leaving Jimmy's to the precinct boys. Now it was strictly cops and ex-cops, a place to unwind – or at least pretend to.

The owner wasn't named Jimmy. No one knew why the bar was called that. No one cared enough to ask.

Officer Greg Jarvis sat hunched at the bar, eyes on the door as he nursed a beer that was mostly foam now. The two empty shot glasses told their own story, though they hadn't done much to steady his nerves. He ran a hand over his face, feeling the stubble against his fingers. It shouldn't be there – regulations and all – but he didn't care anymore.

He'd stopped caring about a lot of things. For instance, that he should be in work right now.

His uniform was still stuffed in his locker at the station, replaced by a wrinkled black polo stretched tight over a paunch he hadn't earned through good meals, just bad habits. His jeans and boots had seen better days, but his haircut was still military short, a hang-up from a time when things made sense.

He drained the last of his beer, eyes fixed on the mirror behind the bar. The way it tilted gave him a full view of the room, not that there was much to look at. A couple of off-duty cops playing pool in the middle of the day. Lou, the barman, collecting glasses. Normally, being here, surrounded by familiar faces and the low hum from the jukebox, grounded him.

Not today.

His gaze snapped to the door as someone walked in. A

big guy with ginger hair. Jarvis recognised him but didn't know his name. He was a cop. That was fine. Cops he could handle. Mostly.

He turned back to his empty glass, staring at the dregs. Too much on his mind. Not enough distance between him and his problems. They gnawed at him, whispered in his ear. The debts piling up. The promises he was breaking. He lifted the glass, hoping for a few rogue drops.

Nothing.

Even here, in a place that should have felt like home, he couldn't shake the feeling that the walls were closing in.

Though, he might have another option. If he could just figure out whether it was a way out. Or a trapdoor.

The thought made him signal Lou for another shot. He knocked it back in one, but it didn't help. The burn lingered in his throat as he stared into the empty glass, considering his next move.

He knew the smart thing to do was to get out of Dodge. Go dark for a while. But Vegas was his home and he didn't want to do that. And now that he had this… device, whatever it was, maybe it could save him. If the people who wanted it were desperate enough, maybe they'd pay. Enough to clear his debts.

It was risky as hell – pissing off Red and those she worked for could get him killed. But the way he saw it, he was screwed either way. His gambling debts had stacked up past the point of no return, and men like Al Starlight weren't just breathing down his neck, they were sharpening their knives. He was running out of time, out of options.

But this thing… if he played it right, it could be his way out. His debts cleared. His life back on track. Hell, maybe even a retirement fund if he leveraged it properly.

He just had to figure out how to use it.

Before one side or the other decided to bury him.

But the more he thought about it, the worse it got. His brain spun in tight circles, every plan unravelling before it was half formed. Could he really stand up to these people? Outplay them? Or would they gut him the second they figured out what he was up to?

He glanced around. He didn't feel safe anywhere, not even here. Paranoia. It was starting to eat him alive.

"Another round?" Lou asked, wandering over.

Jarvis stared at the collection of empty glasses in front of him. He'd love another round, but that was the dumb option and he had to be smart now.

"No, I'm good," he said, slipping off his stool and tossing a sloppy salute to the guys playing pool.

"See you later, Jarvis," Lou called after him as he headed for the door. He shoved it open and stepped out into the warm Vegas afternoon. The fresh air didn't revive him like he'd hoped, but maybe the walk back to his car would.

The streets were relatively quiet out this far. He shoved his hands in his pockets and set off, not drunk enough to sway, but drunk enough to feel untouchable. Problem solved. For now.

But as he walked, the sun's shadows seemed to follow him. Every sound prickled the hairs on the back of his neck. He looked back over his shoulder. No one there. Still, the itch wouldn't go away.

He passed an alley, unable to stop himself from peering down it.

Was that... movement? A figure? Maybe. Could've just been a cat. Could've been something else.

Shit.

He picked up the pace, fists clenched at his sides, his

breath hissing through clenched teeth. It was fine. Just paranoia.

Until he heard the footsteps.

He spun, locking onto the figure emerging from the alley. A man, taller than Jarvis, younger too. Late thirties maybe, wearing a faded hoodie, his hands stuffed in the front pocket. He stopped walking as Jarvis turned, a startled look on his face.

"What the fuck do you want?" Jarvis snarled.

The man took a step back. "I don't want nothing."

But fear-driven rage was already surging through Jarvis's veins, drowning out reason. Drowning out everything. If this son of a bitch was here to take him out, he wasn't going down without a fight.

He charged, pure instinct propelling him forward, slamming the guy against the wall of a boarded-up storefront. His head bounced off the brick with a sickening thud and before he could catch his breath, Jarvis yanked him forward and drove him back again, harder this time, then smashed a fist into his gut. Then another.

He kept going, driving his fists and elbows into the guy's head, feeling bone and cartilage give beneath the blows. It was a dog-eat-dog world, and he wasn't ready to be eaten yet.

The guy twisted, trying to break free, but Jarvis grabbed his collar and yanked him sideways. The sudden force sent him sprawling. Jarvis followed him to the ground, straddling his chest and raining down more punches. The guy was barely conscious but Jarvis didn't stop, snapping the man's head left and right with each blow, pounding him until his eyes were swollen shut and his nose was shattered.

Jarvis's knuckles burned. The skin was split and raw, and

his little finger was possibly broken, but he wasn't stopping until he was damn sure the punk wasn't getting up.

"Who sent you?" he barked, landing another punch.

There was no answer. Just shallow, broken breaths. Jarvis leaned back, fists still raised, chest heaving. The guy was limp. It was done.

He climbed off him and checked his pockets, pulling out an old leather wallet. His hands trembled as he flipped it open, his knuckles sticky with blood. Sunlight caught on the laminated edge of a driver's licence. He slid it out, wiping sweat from his brow as he read the details:

Anthony Morales.
D.O.B: 20/09/1994.

Jarvis ground his teeth. *Fuck.*

He flipped through the rest of the wallet, finding a work ID card a crumpled ten-dollar bill, a couple of credit cards, and a creased photo of a woman holding a baby. Just a regular guy.

Who he'd…

His chest tightened as the realisation hit. He dropped the wallet on the guy's chest. Anthony Morales. HVAC technician. Thirty-one years old. Not some hired muscle sent to take him out. Not anyone connected to the mess he was drowning in. Just some poor schmuck in the wrong place at the wrong time.

"Christ," Jarvis muttered, stumbling to his feet and wiping his hands on his pants. His breaths were coming too fast, his vision narrowing. He looked down at the swollen, bloody mess that was once the guy's face.

All right, get a grip.

He backed away, forcing down the panic rising in his

throat. Then he ran. His car was another block away, and his lungs burned as adrenaline surged through his system. He was almost there when something made him glance back.

An SUV.

Big. Black. Parked on the corner, same block as Jimmy's, with a clear view of the lot where he'd parked. There were no other cars around. It wasn't a waiting zone.

Shit.

He quickened his pace, darting down an alley, his shoulder scraping against rough brick as he turned too fast. Behind him, an engine roared to life. He kept going. The alley opened onto another street, this one even quieter. He ran across it, nearly losing his footing as he hit the kerb. Almost there. If he doubled back he could reach his car this way. But then the SUV appeared at the far end of the block, headlights on even in the daylight.

Jarvis ducked into a doorway, pressing himself against it as the vehicle rolled closer. The windows were blacked out so he couldn't see who was inside. But he knew. It was her.

As it neared he broke cover, sprinting past it and closing the last stretch to his car. The key was already in his hand, slick with sweat and blood. He fumbled with it, yanked the door open and threw himself inside, slamming it shut behind him. The SUV took a right, rolling up to the entrance of the parking lot. It idled there for a moment, just long enough to make his pulse hammer in his ears. Then it turned around and sped off.

Jarvis watched, frozen. Only when he was sure they were gone did he jam the key into the ignition. The last thing he needed was them tailing him back to his buddy's place where he'd been crashing. The engine started up but he didn't move. He just sat there, gripping the wheel so hard it split the cuts on his knuckles. Seconds ticked by. Then, slowly, he leaned his head back, tears streaking down his face.

He was losing the plot and needed to get his head straight. After that, he had to figure out his next move. Before someone made it for him.

Chapter Twenty

Nina 'Red' Sorrento was not happy.

She was currently pacing in front of an old metal work-bench inside Joe's Auto Repair, a run-down garage tucked away behind a row of pawnshops and adult video stores. It had once been a thriving mechanic's shop, back when this part of Vegas had something to offer. Now it was a shell – used by Red and her crew for meetings and, when necessary, extractions. The kind that required more mess and effort than she was willing to deal with at her place.

Inside, it still smelled like a garage – gasoline and burnt rubber – the kind of place where biker gear was practically the dress code. So, in that respect, Red fit right in. She was wearing a black leather jacket over leather pants that were so skintight she couldn't sit down. Not that she wanted to. Red wasn't built for stillness. She thrived on motion, on action. Always.

So she paced, and she thought, and she planned.

And she was not happy.

She shuffled her tarot cards absently as she walked.

Everything had been running smoothly, right on schedule. Until this mess at the warehouse.

She flipped over a card. The Ten of Swords. Not good. It was a card of ruin, of betrayal, coming when you were already on your knees. The end of the line. She tossed it onto the workbench, where it lay like a warning she didn't need. Good thing she didn't believe in this nonsense.

The rumble of an engine outside snapped her back to the moment. She kept pacing, not bothering to look up as car doors slammed, followed by a knock on the garage door.

"Enter."

The door creaked open, and Joey Boy stepped in, Dixon right behind him. Both looked worse for wear. Joey Boy's eye was swollen shut, and Dixon had a dirty bandage taped around his hand. Red cursed herself for not sending Morgan and Ross instead.

"Well?" she spat. "What happened?"

"We were staking out Marshall's place like you told us," Joey Boy replied. "They were there. A guy and a chick, just like you thought. We followed them to the warehouse."

Red crossed her arms. "Did they see you?"

"Not right away."

"What does that mean? I said to take care of them if the opportunity showed itself." She looked them up and down. "I take it that didn't go to plan?"

"We followed them into the warehouse," Joey Boy mumbled, avoiding her eyes. "But then—"

"You confronted them?" she cut in. "An English guy and a cop?" The junkie bitch had at least given her that much.

But the two men exchanged a look, frowning. "He wasn't English," Dixon said. "Or if he was, he didn't sound it."

Red rolled her eyes, trying not to lose it with these fools.

She'd been told the Black Talon were highly skilled opera-tives. Seemed she'd hired a couple of duds.

"But you handled it?" she asked.

The men exchanged another glance, and her stomach twisted.

"You *didn't* handle it?"

"I don't know what happened," Joey Boy said, defen-sive now. "The guy was… Shit, I don't know, he was fast. And he knew what he was doing. Said they were both detectives, but I've never seen anyone from LVMPD move like that."

"My guess is he's ex-military," Dixon added. "Special Forces, even."

Red snorted, fingers tightening around her arms. "Great. That's all I need."

She hated this. Losing control. Not knowing what was coming next. It bothered her, and it would bother her paymasters even more if they found out people were sniffing around this close to the event.

"We spoke to the guy Marshall at Silver Shield," Dixon added. "They gave him a hard time too."

"What did he say?" she asked.

"Just that they were asking about Gates. Where he'd been posted. He said that's all he gave them."

"Good news is they didn't find anything at the ware-house," Joey Boy added. "We got to them before they could. They took off."

Red stepped closer. "You're sure of that?"

"Pretty sure."

Red held his gaze before turning away, pacing again. None of this was calming her nerves.

"We done?" Dixon asked.

"No, you're not fucking done," she spat. "I need you to

track them down. Find out what they know and who they've told, and handle them properly this time."

"Handle them?"

Jesus Christ.

She thought these guys were supposed to be tough. She marched right up to them, close enough to smell the sweat. In her biker boots she had an inch on them both.

"Kill them," she enunciated, like she was speaking to a couple of morons.

Dixon and Joey Boy exchanged glances. "What if they really are cops?" Joey Boy ventured.

"What if they are?" She glared at the two of them. *Imbeciles.* "You make it look like a hit and run. A random attack. Whatever it takes. But don't come back until it's done."

"And if we don't?" Joey Boy snarled. "If we walk away?"

Red was on him in a heartbeat. "Try that. See what happens."

He sniffed and cleared his throat. "Fine. We'll get on it."

They both shuffled towards the door. The sound of it slamming behind them echoed through the garage, only adding to her irritation.

She turned back to the bench, fingers brushing the edges of the tarot deck. Taking a deep breath, she flipped over another card. The Six of Wands, but in the reverse position. She stared at it for a moment.

Victory, but at a cost.

"That's more like it," she muttered. "Whatever it takes."

Her phone buzzed in her pocket, interrupting her thoughts. She pulled it out. *Ross.* She swiped to answer. "What is it?"

"Just reporting in," came the gruff reply. "I've been tailing our pet cop like you asked me to."

"And?"

"He's definitely spooked about something. He just beat some random guy to a pulp outside Jimmy's. He panicked when he saw me, but he won't get far."

Red pressed her palm against the cold surface of the workbench. "Does he have the device?"

"I'd say so," Ross replied. "I think our theory was correct. He's holding on to it until he's sure he's in the clear. Makes sense."

Red closed her eyes. The cop was supposed to call the second he had the MDT, the mobile data terminal, in his possession. That it had been almost twenty-four hours and he hadn't touched base was another problem to add to an already growing list.

"Is he going to be an issue?" she asked.

"Maybe," Ross admitted.

Red exhaled through her nose. "Stay on him. Don't let him leave town. I'll deal with him when the time comes."

"Got it." The line went dead.

She dropped the phone on the table and stared at the Six of Wands.

Victory, but at what cost?

With everything spiralling out of control, its promise of triumph felt like a cruel joke.

A raw, restless tension crept up her spine but she refused to let it take hold. Fear had no place here. She'd faced worse, and she wasn't about to let this break her.

Whatever came next, she'd handle it. She had to.

Chapter Twenty-One

In her kitchen, Lee leaned against the edge of the counter, arms folded tightly across her chest to stop the tremor in her hands. The apartment was too quiet. She cast her attention around the room, searching for something – anything – to distract her from the chaos of this morning. Turning to the window, she drew in a few measured breaths. The adrenaline was still bubbling in her system, and she didn't want Beckett to see how rattled she was.

Though she had a feeling he already knew.

She rubbed at her temples, trying to shake the image of the two men, bloodied and broken, on the office floor. What weirded her out the most was that she'd kind of enjoyed the whole experience. At least, a part of her had. It had been scary as hell, but also exciting. Visceral. Real.

She moved over to lean on the breakfast bar. Beckett was sat on her couch, engrossed in whatever he was doing on her old laptop. He'd asked to use it the second they got back and hadn't spoken since. His focus was unnerving.

Intense in a way she'd never seen before, his chiselled features illuminated by the blue glow of the screen.

She tried not to stare, but couldn't help herself. The way he'd taken those guys apart back at the warehouse, it was something else. It was like he knew exactly what was going to happen before it did. Every move they made, he matched it. Perfectly. Like something out of a movie. Like Superman.

But she hadn't just stood there either, she reminded herself. She'd held her nerve. Done what needed doing. That had to count for something, right?

So if Beckett was Superman, maybe that made her Wonder Woman.

She caught herself smiling at the thought and glanced at the posters on her wall. Ripley and Sarah Connor stared back. Yeah. She'd been right there with him today, making it happen. Maybe not Wonder Woman, but useful all the same. It felt good.

But there was still her real job to think about. At present she worked five days on shift with two days off, then four days on and three days off. Today, Wednesday, was the first of her three days off, which meant she still had Thursday and Friday free. That worked out well. Gave her two more days to make some real headway in…whatever this was.

A case? Investigation?

A mission?

Yes. She liked mission. She'd go with mission. Though maybe she wouldn't call it that in front of Beckett. Not yet.

She glanced at the clock on the oven. Ten minutes left. The frozen pizza she'd thrown in when they got back from the warehouse was hardly gourmet, but it was all she had in the freezer. After the morning they'd had, speed mattered more than quality. She twisted the dial, bumping the temperature up a notch, then leaned her hip against the counter, arms crossed again as she waited.

The act of cooking – if you could call this cooking – for a man like John Beckett felt strange, almost absurd. A fleeting moment of domesticity in the middle of all this danger. For half a second she caught herself wondering what it would be like to cook for him regularly, but she shut that thought down as fast as it came. This was just business. Nothing more. And Beckett didn't seem fazed by it, so why should she be?

He was still the picture of focus, his broad shoulders hunched forward over the laptop. She knew he was digging into Novara Logistics, but whether he was getting anywhere was anyone's guess. His expression gave nothing away. She tilted her head, studying the strong line of his jaw, the slight furrow of his brow. Even sitting, there was an intensity about him, a raw energy that never faded. It was in the way he held himself, the alertness in his eyes, the way his fingers glided across the trackpad. On the surface he appeared as calm as a monk, but his mind had to be running a mile a minute, running calculations, solving problems, staying two steps ahead of the world around him.

She couldn't imagine living that way. Never fully at rest, always anticipating the next move, the next threat. It seemed both exhausting and undeniably admirable.

What was driving him? What was he getting out of all this? Why did he care so much?

She had no real answers, but one thing was certain, she'd never met anyone like him. She was still staring, smiling to herself, when he suddenly looked over.

Shoot. He must have sensed her watching.

Quickly looking away, she busied herself by rechecking

the temperature dial. But the heat rising to her cheeks wasn't just from the oven, and she knew it.

Once she'd composed herself and Beckett had returned to the laptop, she took a jug from under the sink and filled it with water. After placing it on a tray, she grabbed two glasses and was about to carry them all through to the lounge when her phone buzzed on the counter.

She glanced at the screen and her stomach clenched. "Ah... balls."

Beckett looked up. "What is it?"

"Chief Higson. What should I do?"

"Answer it. But don't give anything away. Not yet."

She picked up the phone and swiped. "Hey, Chief." She tried to sound normal. She wasn't sure she managed it.

"Officer Lee. Sorry to bother you on your day off."

"It's fine. What's going on?"

There was a pause. She could picture him scrunching up his face the way he always did when wading into a difficult conversation. "I'm just calling because... well, I don't suppose you've heard from Jarvis today?"

Her grip on the phone tightened, her mind scrambling for a response while her tongue tripped over itself. "N-No," she managed. "Why? What's up?"

"He was supposed to be on shift today, but he's not turned up," he replied, lowering his voice. "And I really need to speak to him about something."

Her knees went weak. She reached out, gripping the edge of the counter to steady herself. So this was it. All her suspicions confirmed. And her fears.

"Right, I see. That's... weird."

She glanced over at Beckett. He was watching her now, eyebrows raised. Like he already knew why Higson was calling.

"Anything I can help with, Chief?" she asked.

There was a hesitation, then, "No. Not for now." His tone had shifted, more guarded. And just like that, a new thought crept in.

Could he be part of this?

It was unlikely, for all the reasons she'd already given Beckett. But she couldn't be sure. And not knowing was driving her crazy.

"Well, if you hear anything from him... let me know," the chief said. "Enjoy your day off."

"Of course, sir," Lee replied. A lie. "I'll let you know."

"See you later." The line went dead before she could say anything else.

She lowered the phone, staring at the screen as it faded to black.

"Looking for Jarvis?" Beckett asked.

"Yeah," she muttered. "He was supposed to be on shift, but he's missing."

Beckett nodded. She wanted to ask what he thought but held back. She didn't trust herself right now to get through a sentence without her voice shaking.

She moved into the living room and slumped onto the far end of the couch, keeping space between her and Beckett. She didn't want to crowd him, didn't want to seem like she needed him to make sense of everything. Though maybe she did. She'd been angry and confused plenty of times on the job over the years, but this was different. This was bigger than her. Bigger than all of them.

Beckett didn't acknowledge her. He was still focused on whatever he was reading on the screen. As she watched, he leaned back and let out a low growl.

"What is it?" she asked, unsure if that sound meant something good or bad.

He remained staring at the screen, his lips pressed into a thin line. Lee shuffled closer, curiosity pushing her worries about Jarvis to the back of her mind. She leaned over to look, but the text was too small and the angle made it hard to read.

"Novara Logistics," he said, tilting the laptop towards her. "I've been looking into their public-facing operations. They're certainly on the rise. And they seem legit. At least on the surface."

"Yeah, that's what I thought," she said, trying to match his energy, not sure where he was going with this. "Though I've got to say, I'm not entirely sure what they do. Is it AI, and all that crap?"

"Not as far as I can tell," he said. "Mainly they're a tech services giant, providing high-capacity server space for the big players. Fortune 500 companies, banks, government agencies, private corporations. They also run an annual tech conference in Vegas, and market themselves as leaders in digital security. The website is full of corporate buzzwords. Data integrity, innovation, cybersecurity solutions."

"But there's nothing that helps us?" Lee asked.

Beckett rubbed his chin, eyes still on the screen. "I've seen setups like this before. With storage systems this large, Novara would have access to every digital aspect of these companies. Finances, intellectual property, the entire framework that keeps them running, and all their dirty secrets too. They'd have to be squeaky clean."

"So what are you saying? They're not involved?"

"They could be," he replied. "But they'd have to be incredibly clever about it."

Lee leaned in, their shoulders touching. "You don't sound convinced."

"I'm not. We've got nothing tying them to anything. Just hunches. In fact, all we have are hunches."

Lee chewed her lip. "So… what now?"

Beckett closed the laptop but still didn't look at her. She could see the wheels turning, the frustration building. She knew he wasn't the type to get flustered, but this was getting to him. Finally he glanced at the clock on the wall.

She followed his gaze. 3 p.m.

"Come on," he said, placing the laptop down and getting to his feet. "We should take a closer look."

"Novara?" she asked.

"Why not? Got anything better to do today?"

Lee opened her mouth to respond, but the only thing that came to mind was the pizza in the oven. She started to mention it, then stopped when she caught the look on his face. "One second."

She got up and headed for the kitchen. It was a nice idea while it lasted, but domesticity didn't seem to fit with Beckett anyway. She turned off the oven, leaving the pizza inside. Then she wiped her hands on a towel.

"Okay," she said, grabbing her keys from the counter. "Let's go."

Chapter Twenty-Two

Beckett could tell Lee was eager to get to Novara's head office by the way she wove through the late afternoon traffic on Las Vegas Boulevard like a rally driver. The Strip was alive with its usual commotion – tourists in shorts and sunglasses dragging wheeled suitcases, glittering billboards advertising magic shows and overpriced cocktails, and a kaleidoscope of casino signs all screaming for attention and patronage.

Beckett leaned back, his eyes fixed on the Strat Tower in the distance, its needle-like silhouette piercing the pale blue sky. Somewhere in its shadow was the Novara Logistics Tower – the company's corporate headquarters. They were close.

"How are we getting in there?" Lee asked, veering around a coach full of tourists.

"Let's stick with the detective line. It's worked so far."

Out of the corner of his eye, he saw Lee do an almost comic double-take. "Has it?"

"Well… not really. But what else have we got? We'll go

in under the guise of closing the case, asking a few routine questions about Gates's employment. From there, we'll get a better sense of our position. And theirs."

Lee shifted in her seat. "Works for me."

Ten minutes later she pulled into a deserted backstreet a block away from the Novara Tower. The low buildings and quiet streets gave the area a closed-off, forgotten feel. Beckett liked that.

Even from here, the Novara skyscraper dominated the skyline, the only thing close in height to the Strat Tower a few blocks away. As they stepped out of the car, Beckett squinted up at the glass façade, sunlight bouncing off it in bright flashes. The Novara logo – a stylised globe wrapped in arrows – was fixed to the building about twenty floors up.

He stayed alert as they crossed the Strip and approached. Cameras were positioned discreetly near the entrance and along the building's edges. Subtle, but impossible to miss if you were looking.

As they crossed the wide forecourt to the glass entrance, a doorman stepped forward, ready to let them in. Beckett glanced at Lee, and a silent nod passed between them. *Stay sharp, stay steady.* He hoped she'd manage it. The morning had rattled her more than she wanted to admit, but so far she'd held it together.

Beckett straightened his posture, holding his head high like he was meant to be there, as the doorman leaned over and opened the door for them.

"Thank you, sir," he said in his American cop voice, the same one that had appeared out of nowhere when he met Ted Marshall. He'd always been good at accents, at taking on different roles. Another skill that had kept him alive this long.

The overzealous air conditioning hit him the second he

stepped inside. The ceiling stretched high above, dotted with recessed lighting that didn't seem to do much since the sunlight streaming through the glass frontage handled the job. The other walls were bright white, interrupted only by oversized canvases. The kind of art that was designed to impress without saying much.

In front of them, the reception desk was a sleek expanse of white quartz that appeared to float in mid-air, suspended by some clever feat of engineering. Behind it stood a woman in a tailored black jumpsuit with gold accents at the cuffs and collar.

On the far side of the room, two large elevators stood side by side, and in the centre a wide stairwell led up to the next floor. Hanging above it, a giant screen played a loop of corporate clips, all glossy production and vague promises. Data centres glowing with endless rows of blinking servers. Cargo planes parked on sunlit tarmacs. Conference stages bathed in dramatic spotlights. The message was all about power, reach, and dominance, but the actual details of what Novara Logistics did was unclear.

Beckett watched, unimpressed. It was all style, no substance.

"Follow my lead," he whispered to Lee, striding towards the desk.

The receptionist didn't acknowledge them at first, her eyes still on her screen. Only when Beckett placed a hand on the edge of the desk and cleared his throat did she finally glance up, offering a polished smile that felt more like professional courtesy than a greeting.

"Good afternoon," Beckett said, adding some swagger to his American accent. "I'm Detective Beckett and this is Detective Lee. We're here to ask a few questions about one of your former employees."

The receptionist's smile didn't falter, but it didn't get warmer either. "Of course. Do you have an appointment?"

"No," Beckett replied. "This is a routine enquiry. Won't take long."

The receptionist hesitated, her eyes flicking briefly to her monitor. "May I ask who you're enquiring about?"

"Evan Gates," Lee said. "We need to confirm some employment details."

The receptionist's fingers hovered over the keyboard, but she didn't type. "I'm sorry," she said coldly, though still smiling. "I can't provide information without proper authorisation. Perhaps you could contact HR directly to set up an appointment?"

Beckett felt the tension creep into his shoulders. "Sure, we understand," he said, weaponising his own smile. "We're just tying up loose ends. But it is important. We want to close this case, and Gates's role here is still unclear." He leaned in slightly. "Maybe we could speak with someone higher up?"

The receptionist hesitated, her fingers twitching over the keyboard like she wasn't sure whether to type or call someone. She glanced over Beckett's shoulder, her focus shifting to something behind him.

"Hello, is there a problem?"

Beckett and Lee turned. A woman in a stiff grey suit was walking towards them. She was in her forties, with short brown hair and a distinct air of authority.

"I'm Susan Reynolds," she said, as she got up to them. "I'm the HR Manager here at Novara. Can I help you?"

Beckett smiled. "I'm Detective Beckett and this is my partner, Detective Lee."

Reynolds gave a curt nod, sizing them up.

"And, yes, you can help us," Lee added. "We need some

information on one of your employees. A man called Evan Gates."

Reynolds didn't blink. "Gates? I don't know anyone called Gates. What is this regarding?"

"Mr Gates is dead," Lee stated. "We're treating it as a homicide."

Beckett tensed. He wouldn't have put it that bluntly, but he kept his attention on Reynolds, watching for a reaction.

"Which department was he in?" she asked.

"He was a security guard," Beckett replied. "He was stationed at your warehouse on West Sunset."

Reynolds exhaled, a visible release of tension. "But he didn't die at the warehouse?"

"No."

"Then I'm afraid I can't help you," she said, more buoyant now, less guarded. "Novara Logistics doesn't employ security staff directly. We contract those services through agencies. We have a few."

"Gates was with Silver Shield," Lee said.

"There we go then. I'm afraid you've come to the wrong place. If Mr Gates worked at one of our warehouses, he would have been employed by them, not us. We don't manage or oversee their operations and I wouldn't have access to his file."

"I see." Beckett caught Lee's eye. He knew Reynolds was fobbing them off – she could probably pull a few strings and get the file. But he also got the feeling pressing harder wouldn't get them anywhere. Not yet. Push too hard, they might spook her enough to ring LVMPD for clarification. They didn't want that to happen.

Besides, he'd seen all he needed to.

It was what he'd expected. Big organisations like Novara Logistics operated with layers of insulation, never dealing with the grunt workers directly. That way nothing ever led back to them. Intermediaries handled the logistics, contractors did the dirty work, and subsidiaries took the fall. The trail always stopped before it reached the top, keeping the C-suite out of the line of fire.

"Thank you for your time, Ms Reynolds," he said, flashing a polite smile. "We won't bother you any longer."

He turned to Lee and tilted his head towards the door. She looked ready to argue but then thought better of it. Puffing out her cheeks in frustration, she followed him without comment.

As they walked, Beckett turned his attention back to the big screen. The rotating slideshow of corporate clips had shifted to a new slide: a bold graphic promoting a major tech expo happening this weekend at Novara Logistics' conference centre on the second floor. The next slide listed an impressive lineup of sponsors, including many of the major players in the industry.

The doorman pulled open the glass door, and they stepped back into the dry Vegas afternoon. Beckett was glad Lee waited until they were clear of the building before speaking.

"What the hell was that?" she snapped.

"What was what?"

"Why didn't we push for more information? We didn't get anything."

"That wasn't the point."

"Oh? Then what was?"

He stopped and faced her. "The point was to see what they knew. And my instincts tell me Reynolds already knew about Gates's death."

Lee frowned. "How do you figure that?"

"She didn't flinch when you brought it up," he said.

"There was no surprise, no follow-up questions. And the fact she didn't say anything, that's the tell. I'd say they're involved in this somehow. Even if it's just covering it up."

Lee huffed, arms dropping to her sides "So now what?"

"We dig deeper. And we pray for a lucky break. A lead."

"Easy as that?" She wrinkled her nose, doubtful.

"You never know."

It wasn't much of an answer and they both knew it. Beckett turned and set off walking. He knew Lee was annoyed at the lack of momentum, but patience was something she'd have to learn if she was going to step up to the next level. Besides, he didn't see this as a wasted trip at all.

He just wasn't ready to voice what he was thinking.

Not yet.

They walked the rest of the way to the car in silence. Beckett stayed a step ahead, his eyes scanning the streets and alleyways – partly out of habit, partly because he suspected they were now on the radar of people willing to do whatever it took to shut them down. He reached the car first, stopping by the passenger side and waiting for Lee to unlock it. But when he turned to check behind him, she was standing on the corner, phone pressed to her ear.

"What now?" he muttered, striding back to her.

She held up a hand as he approached, signalling for him to wait. She was nodding and grimacing, as she listened to whatever the person was saying on the other end.

"Yeah, okay," she told them. "And you're sure about that? Jarvis definitely left it out?"

She listened a moment longer, then caught Beckett's eye and grinned, excitement flashing across her face.

The Chief? Beckett mouthed silently.

She shook her head, turning away. "Okay, great. Thanks, Stevens. Like you say, I'm sure it's just an oversight." She ended the call and slid the phone into her pocket.

"Stevens?" Beckett asked. "The young cop who processed Gates?"

"I thought he might be able to help. You're not the only one who can have good ideas, you know."

Beckett assessed her. She was teasing, but he could tell she meant it. "I apologise if I made you think that," he said. "Please go on."

She stepped closer, glancing down the street before she spoke. "Stevens says the chief is in a spin because there's a discrepancy in Gates's paperwork. Jarvis only logged three items when they processed Gates. But Stevens swears there was a fourth item. Something that wasn't accounted for."

"What was it?"

"Some kind of electronic tablet," she said, her eyes flashing. "The size of a phone, but not a phone. That was how he described it. . Stevens watched him put it in the tray when they brought him in, but it's not in the report."

Beckett nodded. "That's something we can work with."

"Yeah." She grinned. "Now we're getting somewhere."

Chapter Twenty-Three

The dashboard clock read just after 4:15 p.m. as Beckett slid into the passenger seat beside Lee. She'd already started the engine, watching him as he buckled in.

"You want to check out Jarvis's place, don't you?" she said, more statement than a question.

Beckett smiled. Impressed. She was getting it.

Jarvis was lying low, possibly on the run, which meant he was scared. If he had taken the device, it confirmed it was central to whatever was going on. And if he was willing to risk his career and maybe even his life for it, then whatever was on there had to be important.

"Do you know his address?" he asked.

Lee shifted the car into drive. "Yeah, I know it."

They set off. Lee kept her eyes on the road, hands steady on the wheel. Beckett sat back, watching the world outside the window blur past. They were both turning things over, but now there was a sense of shared purpose in the air.

After a while the Strip faded behind them, the neon glow replaced by simple streetlights and suburban streets.

They drove on for another ten minutes before Lee turned into a neighbourhood just east of downtown.

"Paradise Palms," she said. "Not the nicest area."

Beckett scanned the houses as she slowed the car. They were mostly single-storey ranch-style homes with low-pitched roofs and small lots. A few were decent, but most showed their age. The wide streets were lined with tall palm trees, their fronds swaying lazily in the evening breeze.

Lee pulled to a stop outside a house halfway down the block. Beckett leaned forward, studying it. Another single-storey, with a wide alley between it and the house next door leading to what looked like a backyard. The windows were dark. No sign of life.

"This is it," she said.

They stepped out, and Beckett took the lead, heading for the backyard instead of the front door. If Jarvis wasn't home, he wanted to check the place out without drawing attention. If he was home, Beckett still preferred to confront him out of sight of the street.

The backyard was small, with a lawn that was more dirt and rubble than grass. A rusty barbecue grill leaned against a sagging fence which looked ready to collapse.

"I've only been here a few times," Lee whispered. "Just to pick Jarvis up. Never been inside, or back here."

"Someone has," Beckett replied, moving over to the back door. It was hanging open a few inches and the wood around the lock splintered.

"Shit. Should we go in?" Lee asked.

But Beckett was already moving. Silently, he eased the door open and stepped inside, Lee following a little too close behind.

The living room was a wreck. Drawers had been yanked from the sideboard and their contents dumped onto the carpet. The couch had been slashed open, the foam spilling out in ragged chunks, and a couple of throw cushions had met the same fate. A lamp lay shattered in one corner, and a coffee table had been flipped on its side.

Whoever had done this wasn't subtle. This wasn't intimidation, it was desperation. They'd been looking for something.

And now he knew what.

They moved methodically through the house, one room at a time. It was the same story everywhere – drawers ripped open, belongings tossed aside, every possible hiding place ransacked. The bedroom was a disaster. Clothes yanked from hangers, pockets turned inside out, the bedside drawers smashed on the floor. The bathroom had been torn apart just as viciously, the mirror cracked, cabinets emptied, even the shower rail bent out of shape.

They reconvened in the small kitchen, where every cupboard door was open, some barely hanging onto their hinges. A rubbish bag had been torn apart, its contents sifted through, leaving a foul smell in the air.

"Do you think they found what they were looking for?" Lee asked.

Beckett clicked his teeth. "The fact they ransacked every room suggests not."

"Okay." She crossed her arms, her face twisted in thought. "So Jarvis has it. This device."

"More than likely. Which means he's our best shot at getting answers."

Lee rubbed the back of her neck. "If he's still in town, I have an idea where he might be," she said. "Somewhere he feels safe. People there might have seen him, at least."

"Okay, let's move."

They headed back the way they came, but as Beckett

reached the door his instincts prickled. Through the glass, he saw them. The same two men from the warehouse, standing in the middle of the yard. They'd made no effort to hide. Just waiting.

He glanced at Lee and hesitated. But there was no point running. Like with most things in his life, the best way forward was through.

"Leave it to me," he said, pushing open the door and grinning at the men. "Good evening, gentlemen." He used his own voice this time, the American cop pretence feeling a little redundant.

The men sneered in unison. The older one stood nearest the alley, with the younger guy in the middle of the yard. They were bruised and bloody from the beating he'd given them, but looked eager for round two. Tough bastards, clearly. And now they carried weapons. Knives.

Beckett squared his shoulders. The look in their eyes, the way they'd positioned themselves, told him all he needed to know. Whoever was pulling the strings had given them new ones. This was no longer about intimidation or sending a warning.

It was going to get ugly.

"Beckett, be careful," Lee whispered from behind him.

"Stay back this time," he told her. "I mean it, Maggie."

Never taking his eyes off the men, he lowered his stance, feeling the weight settle in his thighs. If he let them come at him, he'd be dead before he had the chance to blink. No one won a street fight playing defence – especially not against two guys with blades.

He had to take the fight to them.

The older one was closest, just a step away. Beckett surged forward, closing the gap. The knife came up, aiming for his ribs, but he angled his body, knocking the attack away with his forearm. As the guy righted his swing, Beckett grabbed his wrist and twisted, forcing the blade down and away. Then he slammed his palm into the man's face, catching him square on the nose.

Cartilage crunched. Blood sprayed. The man staggered back, but Beckett kept hold of his wrist and drove a knee into his gut. He doubled over gasping for air, and Beckett yanked the knife free from his grip. Flipping it around, he buried it between the man's ribs, through muscle, sliding the blade straight into his heart. There was a sharp gasp. A jolt. Then the man dropped.

It had all happened in less than three seconds, but there was no time to think.

The younger guy roared and slashed at Beckett's throat. Beckett sidestepped, catching his arm mid-swing. The guy was strong – too strong to wrestle the blade away easily – but Beckett used his momentum against him, shoving him sideways into the rickety fence. The wooden slats shuddered under the impact, throwing him off balance for a split second. Beckett didn't waste it. He lunged, driving his shoulder into the man's chest and slamming him back. The fence groaned under their combined weight as Beckett grabbed his wrist, forced the blade wide, and then yanked the man's arm down hard over his knee.

The knife hit the dirt and the guy swung wildly, a desperate hook aimed at Beckett's jaw. He ducked, then drove a knee into the man's thigh. As the man staggered, off balance again, Beckett stepped back enough to bring his boot down on his knee.

The joint snapped with a sickening crack and the guy collapsed, screaming as he clutched at his ruined leg.

Beckett knelt, grabbing a fistful of the man's hair and wrenching his head back. "Who sent you?"

"Fuck you," the guy spat, his face twisted in pain. "You won't stop them. It's all in place. It's happening."

Beckett studied his face. He wasn't bluffing. But he wasn't going to talk either. Not now. Not ever. Reaching for the fallen knife, Beckett slid it into the man's neck. The blade met little resistance as it severed the jugular.

"Wrong answer."

There was a wet, sucking sound as he pulled the blade free. The man's eyes went wide, frozen in shock. He tried to struggle, but Beckett held him firm. Two seconds passed. It felt like a lifetime. The man jerked once. Twice. Then went still. Beckett lowered the man's head to the ground and stood, tossing the knife aside. He took a second to steady his breathing, staring down at the dead man.

Then he looked up.

Lee was standing in the doorway. Her face had drained of colour and her usually full lips were pressed into a thin, bloodless line. Beckett gave her a faint smile, one he hoped carried more meaning than words could. But he knew what she was thinking, knew exactly what this looked like. Except he'd had no choice. These men weren't going to stop. All bets were off now.

"We need to find Jarvis," he said.

Lee nodded slowly, her gaze flicking from the dead bodies back to him. "You probably need a new shirt first," she muttered, pointing a shaky finger at him.

Beckett glanced down at the *High Roller* shirt, now soaked with blood. "Good point. You go and wait in the car. I'll check inside for something of Jarvis's and meet you in two. He and I were about the same size, right?"

She nodded again, still looking like she wasn't entirely present.

"I'm sorry," he said. "But that had to happen."

"I know," she murmured. "It's fine. I'll be in the car."

She turned and walked back towards the front of the building, moving like she was still processing what she'd just seen. Beckett watched her go, then stepped over the bodies without a second glance, his thoughts already on what came next.

Chapter Twenty-Four

Lee's head was a mess of a hundred conflicting thoughts as she drove them away from Jarvis's house. She kept her eyes on the road and the car steady, but inside everything felt scrambled. Unsettled.

Beckett had killed two men in under a minute. She'd never seen anything like that before. It was so quick. So cold. No matter how hard she tried to push it aside, the image of the knife plunging into that man's neck wouldn't leave her.

She wasn't naïve. She'd seen plenty of fights. Seen men beaten so badly it was unclear whether they'd get up again. But this was nothing like that. This wasn't some scrappy street brawl. Beckett had killed those men like it was second nature.

And now here he was, sitting beside her, hands resting on his knees, looking out the window like nothing had happened.

At a red light she stole another glance at him. Not for the first time, she asked herself – who is this guy?

Beckett had swapped out his bloodied clothes for a pair of black jeans and a navy shirt he'd found in Jarvis's bedroom. The clothes fit him well, a little tight across his wide frame, but she wasn't complaining about that. And the darker colours seemed much more fitting for a...

The lights turned green and she set off again.

Much more fitting for a what?

A spy? A soldier?

A killer?

She pushed the thought away, not wanting to think too deeply about it. Most of the time, Beckett was charming and thoughtful. A gentleman, really. He wasn't overly emotional or expressive, but he was polite and she liked his dark wit which always seemed to catch her off guard. But then when things turned, when the violence started... she'd seen what else he could be. And that version of him scared her.

"Are you okay?" he asked, and she flinched.

"Yeah," she said, throwing him a smile. "I'm fine."

"Good. You did well back there."

And just like that, he was back to the thoughtful, calm, handsome man she'd first met.

She turned her attention to the road ahead, urging her thoughts to settle. He'd saved both their lives back there, she reminded herself. That was what mattered. He'd said it was the only way, and he was probably right.

She had to wonder if she was cut out for this life.

Most detective work wasn't this violent or bloody, but it still had its dangers. A few days ago, if someone had asked Maggie Lee about her career goals, she would've told them, without hesitation, that she wanted to see action, to be involved in proper police work for once. But now, in the thick of it, the reality felt... overwhelming.

She puffed out her cheeks and reminded herself why she wanted to be a cop in the first place. She thought of Ripley and Sarah Connor. She thought of her father, how he'd laughed for almost five minutes straight when she told him she was joining the force, how he'd told her she wouldn't last two minutes. Then she thought of how that was nothing new – he and her brothers had dismissed her for her entire life – and she pressed harder on the gas pedal.

Maybe she wasn't Ripley or Sarah Connor, but she sure as shit wasn't about to prove her family right, either.

"Where are we heading?" Beckett asked, pulling her from her thoughts.

"Jimmy's," she replied. "It's a cop bar just off the Strip. Jarvis is in there most nights and knows the owner well. I figure if he's still in town, it's one place he'll feel safe. Surrounded by the uniform."

"Good idea," Beckett said.

She kept her eyes forward. "If he's not there, someone might've seen him. Regulars at Jimmy's tend to keep tabs on their own. For better or worse."

"I like the way you think."

Two compliments in quick succession. She glanced over at him. He was watching her carefully, and when he smiled she found herself unable to hold back her own. She quickly snapped her eyes back to the road, just as Jimmy's came into view on the corner up ahead. She turned onto the street alongside it and parked next to a battered pickup.

Despite the sun dipping lower, the day's warmth still clung to the air as they crossed the street. Beckett, as always, was silent but alert, scanning his surroundings, taking in the beat-up old bar. She wondered what he made of it. Jimmy's wasn't her favourite place, by any means, but it felt like home turf.

She helped him with the door, and heads turned as soon as they stepped inside. Some looks were curious, others more guarded. The music didn't quite scratch to a halt, but the shift in atmosphere was close enough. Lee rolled her shoulders back. She recognised a few faces, but no one she knew by name.

"I don't see Jarvis," Beckett muttered, squinting into the gloom of the pool area at the far end. "You?"

Lee shook her head.

A couple of retired cops gave Beckett a sneering glance, then did the same to her before returning to their beers. They didn't like outsiders much in Jimmy's, and they weren't always welcoming to cops of her gender, either. Testosterone hung in the air like smoke, and it always made her feel like she had something to prove just by daring to walk in here.

Beckett, naturally, seemed unbothered by the attention. He moved through the room like he didn't care whether they wanted him there or not, and that alone made him seem like he belonged. It was the way he carried himself. Composed. Unshakeable. It gave him a quiet authority that was hard to ignore.

Lee couldn't help but feed off that confidence as they walked together over to the counter. Regardless of the macho energy coming off the regulars, this was still her territory. And after everything else that happened today, a bunch of cranky old men with their underwear wadded up their asses would be a breeze.

As they reached the counter, Betty emerged from out back, a towel slung over one shoulder. Lee liked Betty. She was usually the only other woman in here on the rare occasions Lee stopped in for an after-work drink. She was also tough as nails, one of the few bartenders who could handle Jimmy's and the crowd that came with it.

Tonight her hair was pulled back tight and she looked tired, but she perked up when she saw Lee.

"Hey, Maggie. What can I get ya?"

"Nothing right now," she replied. "I'm here looking for Greg Jarvis. I don't suppose you've seen him?"

Betty pursed her lips. "Sorry, doll. My shift only started at five. Haven't been here long enough to do a roll call." She smiled, then noticed Beckett and smiled a bit more pointedly. "You… uh… need him for anything important?"

"Could say that." Lee tapped her nails on the wooden bar top.

Damn it.

She'd been banking on this lead more than she realised. It was stupid, but she'd also wanted to impress Beckett. This could have been her shot. She turned to check on him. He was leaning his back against the bar, scoping out the room. For a second she worried he might do something that would get back to the chief. She hoped not.

"You could ask Lou," Betty added. "He's been here all day."

Lee turned as Lou came out of the storeroom, rolling a dented steel keg across the floor. He positioned it under the row of taps and wiped his hands on his jeans.

"Hey, Lou."

He frowned, thinking. "Lee, right? From Sierra Heights."

"That's it."

His eyebrows lifted like that meant something bad.

"She's looking for Greg Jarvis," Betty added.

"No shit." Lou shook his head with a humourless chuckle. "What the hell is going on with that guy?"

Lee stiffened. Her eyes flicked to Beckett, who had caught the comment and turned around. She hesitated, half expecting him to take over. Relieved when he didn't, she pressed on.

"Why do you say that?" she asked. "Have you seen him? Is he here?"

Lou frowned. "Yeah, I seen him. And I also got a call from your chief looking for him."

"Here?" Lee leaned in. "When was this?"

Lou glanced at the clock on the wall beside him. It showed almost five-thirty. He sighed. "He came in maybe half an hour, an hour ago. Second time today. I told him he was wanted back at the station, but he was already drunk as hell and didn't seem like he wanted to hear from your chief. I tried telling him that wasn't the right move, but he wasn't having it. Got nasty real quick. I've never seen him like that before. At least, not aimed at me."

"Shit. I'm sorry," Lee said.

"Not your fault. And I can handle myself." Lou held his hands up, directing the comment Beckett's way. "But the guy seemed really out of sorts. Twitchy. Angry. Like he couldn't sit still but didn't know where to go." He paused, still eyeing Beckett as if debating whether to say more. "Said he had something he needed to do and stormed out."

"Did he say where?"

Lou hesitated, then glanced around the room before lowering his voice. "If I was still a betting man, I'd put money on the Starlight Lounge. He's been spending a lot of time there. Sits in on a backroom poker game most nights. But be careful if you're going to go looking for him there. From what I've heard, it's run by some heavy people. Not sure if that's got anything to do with anything."

Lee glanced at Beckett who gave her a tight nod. "Starlight Lounge. Got it."

Lou raised a hand like he had more to add, but Beckett was already heading for the door.

"Thanks, Lou," she said, chasing after him. "You're a star."

Lou's voice followed them, something about keeping this quiet, but she wasn't listening. Her thoughts were already locked on Jarvis and the Starlight Lounge. If he was there, and he had the device with him, then they might finally get some answers.

She just hoped they weren't too late.

Chapter Twenty-Five

Beckett had a one-track mind as they left the bar. Normally he'd liked to take a beat, assess his next move from a place of calm contemplation, but they were too deep for that. Timing was everything. Momentum was crucial.

Lee matched his stride as they crossed the street. "The Starlight Lounge is down the far end," she said, veering into him slightly, guiding him the right way. "About a three-minute walk."

"You know it well?" he asked.

She shook her head. "Not firsthand, but I've heard about it. It's the kind of place you don't go unless you have a reason – and even then you think twice. Cheap booze, hookers at every table, full of crooks and wannabe gangsters."

"Sounds charming." Beckett could already picture it. Vegas had a lot of flash, but beneath the glitz there were plenty of much seedier places like the Starlight Lounge. The kind of casinos you never saw in those sweeping drone shots of the Strip.

As they approached, he saw he wasn't mistaken. The Starlight Lounge looked to be a converted cinema, wedged between a shuttered pawnshop and a strip club with a neon sign of a one-legged woman, her other high-kicking leg darkened by time and neglect. There were no windows in the Starlight Lounge, and the blacked-out doorway wasn't exactly inviting. Kerb appeal clearly wasn't a priority.

Lee stopped outside but Beckett kept going, pushing through the door without a second's pause. No time like the present.

Inside was no worse or better than the outside. There were no big-ticket shows or fancy gimmicks here, no scaled-down Eiffel Towers or roller coasters. Just the basics. Cards, dice, and desperation. The majority of the floor space was taken up by lines of ageing slot machines. Further along were the poker and blackjack tables, where clusters of drunks slouched over the baize, chasing luck that had left years ago.

Beckett cast his attention around the place, clocking exits, doorways, faces. A security guard stood halfway across the room near a change booth. A big guy, but slow-looking.

"See anything?" Lee asked, bustling in beside him.

"No. You?"

She narrowed her eyes, giving the room a quick once-over. "Not from here."

They moved further inside. Still no sign of Jarvis. Lou had seemed pretty adamant he was heading this way. But if Jarvis was neck-deep in Vegas debts, this seemed like the last place he'd want to hide out. What was his play? Was he here trying to use the device to settle his tab? Leverage it somehow? It was risky. But if it was the last act of a desperate man, it made sense.

He caught Lee glancing over at the bar, frustration edging into her expression.

"We'll find him," he told her. "I've never lost a…"

Lee shot him a look when he stopped. "What?"

Beckett squinted towards the back of the room. A female server was heading for a door halfway along the back wall behind the poker tables, balancing a tray of drinks in one hand. She stiffened slightly as she opened the door, like she was bracing for something, then disappeared into the corridor beyond.

"Follow me."

They moved quickly across the casino floor. Beckett yanked open the door, ushered Lee through, then glanced back to ensure no one was watching before slipping in behind her and pulling the door shut.

They found themselves in a long windowless corridor that stank of stale liquor and body odour. The muted din from the casino could still be heard, but layered over it was the murmur of voices and bursts of laughter coming from somewhere up ahead.

Beckett gave Lee a quick nod, and they moved on. At the far end of the corridor was another door. As they approached, it swung open to a burst of noise, and the server reappeared, her tray now empty and resting against her hip. Beckett kept walking, offering the woman a casual smile as they passed, which she returned half-heartedly, not the least bit bothered by their presence. They stopped outside the door.

"You think he's in there?" Lee whispered.

Beckett rolled his shoulders. "If he's not, someone in there should be able to point us in the right direction."

Before Lee could respond, he knocked once, pushed the door open and stepped inside.

Three men shot to their feet, chairs scraping against the floor, hands dropping instinctively to the guns on their hips.

"What's going on? This is a private game!"

"Calm it down, fellas." Beckett held his hands up, slipping into his American accent. "We don't want no trouble."

The room was small and square, thick with cigar smoke. A round poker table dominated the space, with stacks of coloured chips scattered across its surface. He scanned the room, sizing them all up, then locked eyes with the man who looked to be in charge.

"Heard you might be able to help us."

The man was tall and willowy, with a thick ginger moustache in the centre of a face that was all angles and hollows. A cream cowboy hat sat crooked on his head, and his cream Nudie suit jacket shimmered with silver embroidery under the lights, giving him the look of an ageing country singer clinging to a past that never quite was.

"Who the hell are you?" he barked, his fingers coiling around the handle of the revolver at his side.

Beckett kept his hands up and stepped forward. "I'm looking for Greg Jarvis. Heard he sat in on these games."

The man in the hat didn't flinch. "That piece of shit? What do you want with him?"

Beckett glanced around the room, flashing the other men a roguish grin. "The son of a bitch owes me money." He dropped his voice. "A lot of money. Been dodging me for weeks, and I'm done waiting."

The man studied him with pale, watery eyes. "Who's she?" he asked, nodding at Lee.

Beckett grinned. "My sister. Jarvis owes us both."

The man's smile turned lascivious, all gold caps and broken teeth. "Sister, huh?" He coughed, the sort of cough that sounded like a death knell. "Well, you want a piece of

Jarvis, you'd better get in line. That motherfucker owes me ten grand. And he's close to losing a finger or two over it. At the very least."

"You do know he's a cop?" Lee cut in.

Beckett tensed, but the man just barked out a laugh. "Yeah. And?" he growled. "He's a dirty cop. The kind no one's going to lose any sleep over. And I intend to get my pound of flesh, one way or the other."

Beckett held his nerve. "I hear you, friend. And I respect the pecking order. My sister and I just want to know where he is in the meantime. Don't want him skipping town on us now."

The man studied Beckett and Lee for a beat longer, then dropped back into his chair with a grunt, motioning for the others to do the same. "You just missed the pathetic prick," he snarled. "Came in here not five minutes ago, running his mouth. Said he had something valuable that could wipe the slate clean. Wanted my protection while he figured out how to squeeze the most out of it. Or some shit." He waved a hand like Jarvis was nothing. "I told him money talks in this town and that's all. Gave him twenty-four hours to pay up."

Beckett glanced at Lee, then back to the table. "Do you know where he went?"

The man folded his arms. "Nope. But if you see him, remind him Al Starlight's clock is ticking."

"Will do. Sorry to interrupt your game, gentlemen."

He took Lee's arm, steering her out of the room before she could say anything. Back in the corridor, they retraced their steps quickly, Beckett keeping his head down as they slipped through the door and back into the casino.

Out on the Strip they scanned the crowd for any sign of Lee's wayward colleague.

"See anything?" Beckett asked, relying on her more than his own memory of the cop's appearance.

Without answering, Lee jogged a few steps ahead, weaving through the foot traffic to the roadside. She was up on her tiptoes as Beckett got to her, straining to see over the heads of passersby.

"There. Got him!" She turned, pointing down the street.

Beckett followed her line of sight – and there he was. Officer Jarvis, the angry cop who'd manhandled him out of the diner. He was about fifty yards away, moving between two groups of tourists.

They crossed over and trailed him. As they got closer, it was clear Jarvis was drunk as hell, swaying and stumbling every few steps. He reached the doors of another casino, pausing just long enough to glance over his shoulder.

"Jarvis!" Lee shouted.

He turned, his face pale under the streetlights, eyes wide with fear – like all his ghosts had caught up with him at once.

Then he bolted.

Chapter Twenty-Six

Beckett and Lee pushed through the crowd, Beckett angling to cut Jarvis off as he veered away from the casino he'd been about to enter and darted down a side street.

"We can't let him get away again," Lee gasped, struggling to keep up.

Beckett didn't need convincing. He quickened his pace. Up ahead, Jarvis clipped a trash can, sending it skidding across his path, but he leapt over it, barely breaking his stride. Jarvis darted into the next alley and Beckett and Lee followed.

"Jarvis! Stop!" Lee shouted once more.

Her pleas were ignored. But as Jarvis neared the end of the alley, his foot caught on a loose trash bag and he stumbled, just for a second.

That was all Beckett needed. He surged forward, closing the gap in a heartbeat. As he reached him, the cop spun around, a knife flashing in his hand. Beckett reacted fast, swerving out of the blade's path and smashing his fist into

Jarvis's wrist. The knife clattered to the ground as Jarvis spun off balance and Beckett used his momentum to slam him against the wall.

"What the hell are you doing here!" Jarvis roared, throwing a wild punch. "Fucking limey prick."

Beckett ducked and pivoted, driving his shoulder into Jarvis's chest. He staggered, scrambling for the fallen knife, but Beckett scooped it up first and lunged, pinning Jarvis against the wall with his forearm across his chest. Before the drunken idiot could process what was happening, Beckett had the blade at his throat.

"Jesus! Wait!" Lee skidded to a stop beside them, panting. "He's a cop, remember?"

Beckett didn't flinch, keeping the blade tip poised at Jarvis's jugular. "Talk," he ordered.

Jarvis's eyes darted between them, wild and defiant. "Who is he, Lee, your new boyfriend? What the hell do you want?"

"Where's the device?" Beckett asked.

Jarvis's cockiness faltered, his face shifting from smug to scared. "I don't know what you—"

"Don't." Beckett pressed the blade harder, just enough to draw a bead of blood. "We're way past that. We know you took it. We just want to know what's on it."

"Who the fuck do you think you are?" Jarvis spat, his voice trembling despite the bravado and whatever he'd been drinking all day. "Why do you care?"

"Let's just say I'm a concerned third party." Beckett lowered his voice to a growl. "Now start talking, or I swear to god I'll slice your throat open."

"I swear," Jarvis stammered. "It's not what you think."

"Tell us what it is."

Jarvis struggled for a moment, muscles tense against Beckett's grip. Then, realising he wasn't going to win this, not in the state he was in, his body sagged. "All right, all right." He held his hands up. "But ease off a little, huh?"

Beckett didn't move.

"Beckett. Please." Lee placed her hand on his shoulder. "Let him talk."

For a second Beckett stayed put, his grip firm and the blade steady. Then without breaking eye contact he eased back a step, lowering the knife to give Jarvis room to breathe. Jarvis sucked in a sharp breath, brushing at his grimy clothes as if that might salvage his pride. It didn't.

He gave Beckett a once-over, scowling. "Seriously, what the fuck are you doing here?" His frown deepened. "And... is that my shirt?"

"Forget about it. What's going on, Jarvis?" Lee cut in. "We know what you've been up to. We know you killed the prisoner for someone. Who's calling the shots? Is it Novara?"

Jarvis flinched, caught off guard that she knew so much. "I can't say," he muttered. "If I do, they'll kill me. This is much bigger than I realised." He shook his head, despair creeping in. "I knew it was risky taking that damn thing, but I thought maybe I could get something out of it... You see, I'm in a lot of trouble and..." He trailed off, fear written all over his face.

Something told Beckett Al Starlight was going to be waiting a long time for his money.

"Where's the device now?" he asked.

"We know you took it from Gates's evidence bag," Lee added. "We know a lot of bad people want it. We can help you if you let us in."

"Appreciate it, *Officer Lee*," Jarvis drawled. "But no one can fucking help me."

"Who asked for the hit on Gates?" Beckett asked. "Was it Novara?"

Jarvis smirked. He looked as if he was going to swerve the question with a snide remark, but the fight seemed to leave him. He sighed again, his expression darkening. "Not directly," he said. "They're smarter than that. I get paid by a fixer crew headed by a woman called Nina Sorrento. They're all heavy cats. Ex-military types."

"Nina Sorrento," Lee repeated.

"Yeah. Though everyone calls her Red," Jarvis said, swaying a little then righting himself. "She's… a piece of work. Ordered me to kill Gates. Said there'd be a bonus in it for me. Though I've not seen a damn cent yet, and I need it like yesterday."

"So you thought you'd take what Red and Novara really want," Beckett said, reading the guilt in Jarvis's sheepish expression. "See how much they'd pay to get it back."

He shrugged. "It was the only option I had left. Debts with bad people, remember?"

"Where is it?" Beckett asked, already tired of this game.

"Go to hell. That's still my ticket out of here."

Jarvis tried to push past, but Beckett shoved him back, raising the knife to his throat.

"Don't!" Lee snapped, stepping beside Jarvis and glaring at Beckett. "He's still a cop. So am I."

Beckett paused, but then lowered the knife while keeping Jarvis pinned against the wall. "Search him," he said.

Lee hesitated for a second, then stepped in, patting Jarvis down.

"Get off me, Lee," Jarvis snarled, squirming. "I mean it."

Beckett held him steady as Lee reached into his jacket and pulled out a black device. About the size of a phone but bulkier, heavier.

"Give it back!" Jarvis growled, reaching for it.

Beckett held him back as Lee stepped away, turning it over. "What is this?" she asked. "Why do Novara want it so badly?"

Jarvis didn't answer. But there was fear in his drink-sodden eyes.

"This machine Gates was talking about," Beckett said, "is that Novara too?"

"I can't fucking say!" Jarvis yelled, sweat rolling down his face. "You don't understand – they'll kill me!"

Beckett's grip tightened around the knife handle. "Who? Red?"

Jarvis sneered. But then his eyes darted past Beckett and something shifted in his expression. Panic. Dread.

Beckett's instincts flared. "Down!"

He grabbed Lee and yanked her to the ground as a gunshot cracked through the alley. Lee screamed as Jarvis's head jerked back, blood and brain matter splattering up the wall. Beckett pulled her up and hustled her behind a metal dumpster as another shot pinged off the brick beside them.

Peering around the dumpster, Beckett spotted a black SUV idling at the mouth of the alley and silently cursed himself.

Bad form.

He hadn't heard it pull up. Hadn't noticed it. Now it was impossible to miss. The rear window was down, a gun barrel resting on the frame, but the angle and shadows inside made it hard to make out the shooter.

Ducking back behind cover, Beckett assessed the situation. Lee looked terrified, but they couldn't stay here. "Do you have the tablet?"

She patted her pocket.

"We need to move," he said, as a few more rounds punched into the metal dumpster just inches away. "On three. Ready?"

Lee nodded, her face tight with adrenaline. "One, two…"

"Three," they said in unison as Beckett hauled her up and they sprinted for the far end of the alley.

"Keep going, don't stop— Shit!"

He stumbled, gritting his teeth as something hot and sharp bit into his shoulder. It hurt like hell but he kept moving, grabbing Lee's hand as they burst out of the alley into a narrow street. Another bullet ricocheted off the wall behind them as they swerved into a tight passage between two buildings.

They ran to the end and kept running, zigzagging through alleyways and side streets until they spilled back onto Las Vegas Boulevard, near Caesar's Palace. Beckett drew to a stop, scanning the street for the SUV.

"Your arm," Lee said, on seeing the blood soaking through his shirt.

"It's fine." The dark fabric helped mask the wound from passersby, but it would need attention.

Lee was breathing hard, her hands shaking. "Who the hell was that?"

Beckett didn't answer. His focus was on their surroundings, scanning for signs of danger. Once he was confident they weren't being watched or followed, he reached into her pocket and pulled out the device. It was powered down but looked undamaged.

Lee stared at it, then up at him. "What the hell is on that thing?"

Beckett didn't know. But whatever it was, people were willing to kill for it. And whoever was in that SUV wasn't done.

Not by a long shot.

Chapter Twenty-Seven

It was a few minutes after eight when Lee pulled up outside her apartment building. The street was quiet, empty except for a stray dog nosing through a pile of garbage on the corner. The normalcy of it made the night feel even stranger. She killed the engine but didn't move. Beckett had been messing with the device on the drive back, trying to figure it out. Now his features were tight with focus as he stared, unblinking, out the windshield at something only he could see.

Lee unclicked her seatbelt and drew in a deep breath. Her thoughts were a mess. Jarvis was dead. Gates was dead. And the thing they'd died over was now in Beckett's pocket. She shut her eyes. She felt sick. Not so much from the blood, or from being shot at, or the smell of sweat and death clinging to her clothes. It was more the unknown. What came next? She couldn't decide if she was terrified or just plain exhausted. Maybe both.

She forced herself to move, opening the door and stepping out into the cool night air. Beckett followed, and as they walked towards the entrance, she glanced over at him. He didn't look scared – not even a little bit – and she was grateful for that. His presence steadied her. He was the kind of person you wanted around. In more ways than one.

Once inside her apartment with the door locked, Lee felt a little safer. But her nerves were still raw and her teeth and skin felt like they needed a good scrubbing. She kicked off her shoes and went straight to the sink, filling a glass with water. Her hand trembled as she drank, spilling some of it down her chin. After half a glass, she tipped the rest in the sink. Jarvis. Gates. The thought kept circling – was she next?

She set the glass down and turned around. Then drew in a sharp breath. "Oh… shit!"

Beckett had his shirt off. His shoulder was covered in blood. It was running down his arm in thin lines.

"You're hurt bad."

She hadn't forgotten, not entirely, but with everything that had happened, her focus had been elsewhere. Beckett hadn't even mentioned it in the car.

"I'm so sorry," she said, going to him. "Let me help you."

He grabbed his shoulder with one hand, squeezing the muscle as he inspected the wound like it was nothing. "It'll be fine," he said. "The bullet just grazed me. See?"

She leaned closer. It wasn't as bad as she'd feared, but it was still bad. A deep groove cut through the upper muscle, raw and angry, the skin around it swollen. "That is not fine."

"It will be."

She dragged her eyes away from the wound and looked into his. They were so blue, so penetrating, yet… kind, too. He smiled, and for a second she forgot how to breathe.

Not now, Maggie.

"I'll... get the first aid kit," she stammered, spinning so fast she made herself dizzy.

In the bathroom she flicked on the light and gripped the edge of the sink. Her reflection stared back, pale and rattled. She looked like hell. But her heart was pounding for a different reason now, and she didn't know what to do with that. She grabbed bandages, antiseptic wipes and gauze before hurrying back into the front room.

Beckett was perched on the edge of her couch, his wounded arm resting on his knee. He seemed unbothered, taking it all in his stride.

But of course he was. He was John Beckett. Some kind of Superman.

Lee set the supplies down and sat beside him, opening the antiseptic wipes. "This might sting."

She pressed the wipe against his raw flesh, but he barely flinched. The bleeding had stopped, at least. She dabbed away the dried blood from around the wound, then added a few drops of rubbing alcohol. Beckett sucked in a sharp breath, but that was it.

The silence felt charged as she worked. She kept her focus on the task, hands steady as she wrapped the bandage snugly around his arm. She told herself she was just being thorough, but the truth was she didn't mind the closeness, the heat of his body next to hers.

As she leaned in to secure the last strip of tape, Beckett turned his head, and for a heartbeat their lips were nearly touching. Lee froze, caught between impulse and uncertainty. But then Beckett cleared his throat and leaned back, breaking the moment.

"You're good at this," he said.

She chuckled. "I did want to be a doctor when I was little. I practised a lot on my dolls."

The words hung there, and she immediately wished she could pull them back.

Dolls? Really?

Here she was patching up some secret service operative – or whatever he was – and she was talking about goddamn dolls. She felt her cheeks flush with heat, but Beckett didn't seem to notice.

He flexed his arm, testing the bandage. "Perfect."

She stared at him. Yeah, she'd say so.

Sitting back, she relaxed her shoulders for what felt like the first time that day. Her gaze drifted to the device Beckett had placed on the coffee table.

"I managed to switch it on, but it's locked up tight," he said. "It has some kind of encryption I've never seen before."

"So we're no closer to knowing what's going on."

"Maybe," he said. "Maybe not."

"What do you mean?"

Beckett rubbed at his face. "Okay, this is only a theory. But did you see the big screen in the lobby when we were at Novara's head office?"

Lee thought for a second. "I think so. Why?"

"It was advertising some big event happening there this Saturday. Looked like some kind of tech expo."

"And you think it's connected?"

"I'm not sure. But it's worth considering. The only problem is, that gives us only three days to figure it all out."

Lee chewed her lip, letting the idea sink in. "But what's the link?"

"That's the tricky part," Beckett admitted. He leaned

forward, elbows on his knees, staring at the tablet again. "We've got this thing, but without a way in…"

"It's worthless," Lee finished for him, frustrated all over again. She crossed her arms, glaring at the device like it had personally offended her. "We were so close. And now we're stuck."

She got up and walked into the kitchen, grabbing two beers from the fridge and popping them open. Returning to the couch, she handed one to Beckett and sat, taking a long swig. She hoped it might dampen her frustration. It didn't.

"Christ, Beckett, what am I doing? Jarvis was my colleague, I should be calling this in."

He peered over his shoulder at her with one eyebrow raised. "Jarvis was his own worst enemy. And no, you shouldn't call it in. Not yet. Not until you can justify everything you've done over the last twenty-four hours."

That thought alone made her queasy. She pulled her legs up onto the couch and sighed. "I feel like I've messed up somewhere."

Beckett shook his head. "It's not your fault."

"Isn't it?"

"No. You're a good cop."

"But I'm not you. I'm holding you back." She took another gulp of beer, swallowing it hard enough to burn her throat.

"You've done good," he told her. "I've needed you every step, and you've been there. You should be proud of yourself, Lee. Really."

She nodded. She almost asked him to call her Maggie again, like he'd done earlier at Jarvis's house before he killed those men, but she stopped herself. Because was that all he thought of her as – his little sidekick? For some reason, she didn't like that. At all. She took a sip of beer and let it settle, but the feeling didn't go away.

"So what now?" she asked. "It feels like we're back at square one."

Beckett opened his mouth to respond, but paused, glancing around like something had clicked. "Not necessarily."

He spotted her laptop under the chair where he'd left it earlier, and leaned forward to grab it. "May I?"

"Go for your life."

She watched as he powered it on, the glow of the screen lighting up his face. He looked so focused, so intelligent as he began tapping away at the keys.

And he still hadn't put his shirt back on...

No. Stop that.

She sipped at the beer, meeting Sarah Connor's unflinching gaze on the poster across the room.

Get a fucking grip.

Lowering her feet to the floor, she sat upright, forcing herself to think professional thoughts, cop thoughts. Badass sidekick thoughts.

Beckett was squinting at the screen. "Of course," he muttered.

"What's going on?"

"Jean Dry Lake Beds," he said, spinning the laptop to show her the map on screen.

"O... kay..."

"It's about a forty-minute drive. Not too far, but I think we'll be better off waiting until tomorrow. So if you don't mind..."

Lee still wasn't grasping it. "Don't mind what?"

"Is it okay if I crash on your couch again? Then we can leave first thing in the morning."

"Oh." She let out a nervous laugh. "Yeah. Sure."

"Great. Daylight's better, and we could both use some rest."

Lee's stomach tightened. "Why? What's there?"

Beckett turned to her, and for the first time in hours, there was something close to a smile on his face. Not much, but enough to make her heart skip.

"Not what," he said. "Who."

Chapter Twenty-Eight

Daryl McKenzie stood over the open terrarium in the corrugated iron hut next to his trailer, holding a thawed rat by the tail. The thing dangled limp and pale, its eyes shut tight as if it already knew what was coming. Louisa, his favourite diamondback, lifted her head, tracking the slow sway of her breakfast.

The prey was close, but she waited. He waited too. Patience was a lesson he'd learned a long time ago, back when it wasn't a virtue but survival. He dangled the rat a little closer and Louisa struck.

"Good girl."

He watched her eating for a moment, then set the lid back on the tank. He liked snakes. You knew where you stood with them – right on the edge of getting bitten, but at least they were honest about it. People weren't like that. People smiled while they slid in the knife.

Once Ruby and Georgia Lee were also fed, he closed the door to the hut and made his way back to the long silver Airstream trailer next door that he called home. The air was already close as he stepped inside, but after the musty sawdust of the snake hut, the aroma in here was positively refreshing.

He took off his straw hat and crab-walked through the galley kitchen to the area at the back of the trailer that he called his control room. Three benches lined the rear and side walls, cluttered with gear. Against the remaining wall, a massive desk filled the space, stacked with computers and surveillance equipment. Above this, shelves were crammed with circuit boards, hard drives, and boxes of files and maps. Below, cables spilled from open drawers, snaking around a workbench crowded with soldering irons, cameras, and stained coffee cups. He didn't mind the clutter. It made sense to him.

He set the empty rat bag down and ran his fingers through his greying hair. He was wearing sandy-coloured camo shorts – the same pair he wore every day – and a faded Tom Waits t-shirt, loose enough to hide the bulk he'd lost. Seven years in the desert had left him grizzled and leathery, but he didn't mind. He'd left the clean-cut life behind with the CIA badge and the government pension. These days his security clearance was whatever he could hack into, and his retirement plan involved enough fire-power to outlast the apocalypse.

Outside, the sun was starting to rise over the horizon, lighting up the vast desert as far as the eye could see. He'd picked this spot because no one came here by accident. It was all dirt roads and empty space. A forgotten corner of Nevada, perfect for staying off the grid.

He was considering making a pot of coffee when a low, warbling chime cut through the stillness of the morning. The first of his alerts going off.

Moving instinctively, he tapped the keyboard on his

desk and the monitors flickered to life. On the main one, eight black-and-white feeds spread across the screen. He focused on the one in the top corner where the grainy footage showed a car kicking up dust on the track half a mile out. He leaned closer. A beat-up Chevy Sprint, by the looks of it.

"Interesting."

He wasn't expecting visitors, but he wasn't unprepared for them either. The car was travelling at speed and no one had a reason to be out here unless they were looking for him. He folded his arms, thinking through everything he'd been working on recently.

He was Daryl to his mom, and Mack to most who knew him, but online he had plenty of aliases, each one a nightmare for the likes of big tech and big pharma.

Still, he was always careful.

Wasn't he?

He scratched at his stubble as a second alarm chimed, this one higher pitched. Trouble coming.

Reaching down, he pried up a loose piece of lino under the desk. Beneath it was a metal box, built into the trailer's chassis with a biometric lock. It was where he kept his most *sensitive* items – drives and documents too risky to leave lying around. He opened the lid and pulled out a small hard-shell suitcase. Flipping it open, he swept in gear from the desk and shelves: flash drives, external hard drives, paper files filled with notes scrawled in shorthand no one else would understand. Then he snapped the case shut, dropped it back into the compartment, and sealed it with the metal lid and lino.

Moving through the trailer, he headed to where his bathroom used to be. He'd ripped out the fixtures his first week here – sink, toilet, even the plumbing. He didn't need it. Nature handled the basics, and for showers or anything more civilised, there was Jean or Primm down the highway.

He figured it was a fair trade. Comfort for security. Besides, nothing he'd ever owned came close to giving him the same satisfaction as his gun cabinet. Taking up the same footprint as the bathroom had, the walk-in cabinet was constructed of oak and steel, with reinforced hinges and a digital lock that lit up blue as he keyed in the code.

The heavy mechanical bolts thudded back, and the door swung open to reveal what he considered his real insurance policy. Rifles lined the back wall, gleaming under the LED strip he'd fitted along the top. Below, pistols sat in foam cutouts, arranged by size and calibre. Shelves above held rows of magazines, boxes of ammunition, suppressors, and spare parts.

The smell of oiled steel enveloped him as he stepped inside. It still calmed him, even after all this time. Guns didn't break your trust. Guns didn't lie. They worked or they didn't, and he kept his working.

He contemplated the AR-15. Custom build, match-grade trigger, holographic sight dialled to perfection. He'd put it together himself back when he still cared about specs and range. A sniper's weapon in a pinch, but too precise for what he needed now.

His attention shifted instead to the Remington Model 700. Precision craftsmanship, built for long-range accuracy and stopping power. He pulled it free, testing the weight. It felt as familiar as his own hands.

Perfect.

He slid a fresh .308 Winchester round into the chamber, locking it down as a new alert sounded, telling him the Chevy was getting closer. Without missing a beat, he pulled a tactical vest from the rack, slipped it over his head and fastened the straps tight.

Moving to the window, he eased the curtain aside. The morning was waking up around him, but his focus was locked on the car. The Chevy had stopped at the edge of his property. It was too far away to see who was inside, but that didn't bother him. The land all around was wide open.

Good for him. Bad for them.

He slipped an extra handful of shells into the loops on his vest, then closed the cabinet.

"All righty then," he muttered, resting his finger just off the trigger as he made his way to the door. "Let's see what ya got."

Chapter Twenty-Nine

Beckett stepped out of the car, stretching his arms as the desert sun hit him. Lee had given him a fresh shirt to wear that some undisclosed guy had left at her apartment. She'd been a little awkward handing it over, quick to point out the guy was a creep she hadn't seen since. But it fit well enough. A little tight, but it would do.

The desert stretched out around them, the horizon rippling faintly in the haze rising with the sun. Beckett squinted at the trailer two hundred metres away. It looked exactly as he remembered it. Like a long silver rocket, a relic from a lost decade. The large shack bolted onto its side now leaned slightly, patched with sheets of corrugated metal and plywood.

There were more radio antennas than last time, towering over the compound in every direction. But these days, Beckett figured, there was more to keep tabs on. Even from this distance he could hear the low hum of the generator beside the shack. He'd also clocked the covert security cameras mounted at intervals on the drive in. Mack's paranoia had been growing over the years, but clearly it had only got worse.

Then again, with the kind of information the two of them had been privy to, maybe it wasn't paranoia. Maybe it was just a sensible response to a world gone mad.

Lee slammed her door, drawing his attention. She moved around the car to stand with him, shielding her eyes as she looked around.

"You going to tell me what the hell we're doing here now?" she asked.

Beckett smiled. He'd been quiet the whole drive, sorting through what he knew to be true, what he suspected, and what he still needed to figure out. He'd also been thinking about the best way to approach this. He and Mack had been through a lot together, but showing up uninvited was a risk. Not to mention rather impolite.

"Don't worry," he said. "We're just calling in on an old friend."

"Friend?" She raised an eyebrow.

"Well, acquaintance," Beckett admitted.

"Is he a good guy?"

"He's not a bad guy."

"Wow," she muttered. "How reassuring."

She looked hot and bothered, wiping sweat from her forehead and squinting at the trailer like it might suddenly take off.

"We'll be safe here," Beckett added, patting the roof of the car before heading towards the compound. "Unless you're scared of snakes, that is."

"What? Snakes?"

Beckett didn't answer. He was already walking.

Lee hurried after him. "What are you talking about? Snakes? Seriously, what kind of place is this?"

Beckett was about to reply when he caught movement at the trailer door. Mack stepped out, shotgun in hand. A second later a shot cracked through the air, kicking up dirt just a few feet in front of them.

Lee screamed, shifting behind him. "Jesus!"

Beckett held his hands up, calm, steady.

Mack tilted his head. "Who are you?" he shouted. "What do you want?"

Even from a distance Beckett could see he'd changed. He was leaner and darker skinned, with long hair that was now completely grey. He looked worn around the edges. But Beckett could say the same about himself.

He raised his head. "Was wondering if we might get a cup of tea, old bean?"

Lee hissed behind him. "A cup of tea?"

Beckett ignored her, keeping his eyes on Mack. After a tense beat, Mack lowered the shotgun an inch. Beckett waited a second, then lowered his hands too.

Shaking his head, Mack stepped off the porch and started towards them, the shotgun still in his grip but held loosely now.

"Come on," Beckett said, nodding to Lee.

Mack grinned as he got closer, swinging the shotgun across his back. "Hell. Didn't recognise you with the hair and scruff. I almost gave you a third red eye. You should have messaged me first."

Beckett held his arms out. "Would you have replied?"

Mack screwed up his face. "Not straight away, that's for sure." He laughed, and they shook hands before Mack pulled Beckett into a rough hug, slapping at his back.

"You son of a bitch," Mack said, stepping back and giving him a once-over. "Man, I thought I'd never see you again. Last I heard, you were a ghost."

"I am." Beckett leaned back, smiling. "You look good."

Mack snorted. "Liar. I look like Robinson Crusoe, but I don't mind. We make our choices and we live them. He stepped back, his gaze shifting to Lee. "And who's this?"

"Officer Maggie Lee," she said, extending her hand. "LVMPD."

Mack shook her hand, throwing Beckett a smirk as he did. "Teaming up with a cop? Things must be bad. Or are you two…?"

"No!" Lee cut in quickly. "We're working together. On… something."

Mack raised an eyebrow but let it slide, flashing her a wink. "Good to meet you, Officer Lee." Then he turned back to Beckett. "And look at you, man. How long's it been?"

"Too long."

"Yeah." Mack nodded. "Way too long." He paused, the grin softening just a bit. "Good to see you… man."

Beckett twigged the reason for the man's hesitation. "It's fine," he told him, glancing at Lee. "You can call me by my real name. That's who I am now. Just plain old John Beckett."

Mack snorted. "Plain?" He grabbed Beckett by the scruff of the neck and gave him a rough squeeze. "Nothing plain about this son of a bitch," he told Lee, who managed a polite smile.

He released him and turned back towards the Airstream. "Come on inside. I'm not sure about tea, but I was about to put some coffee on."

He led the way, propping his rifle by the door before entering the trailer. Beckett and Lee followed.

"Love what you've done with the place," Beckett said,

looking around, ignoring the look of discomfort on Lee's face.

Mack smirked. "Yup. Few more machines, few more bed bugs. What can I say?"

The place felt smaller than Beckett remembered. He shuffled further inside to give Lee space. Instead she came closer, leaning in and whispering, "Did you say there were snakes?"

"Next door," Mack cut in. "You can see 'em later if you want. After coffee." They shuffled around awkwardly in the cramped space as Mack moved over to the old gas stove in the corner, setting a dented kettle on top. "Sit," he said, waving his hand over the small table and two chairs. "Make yourselves at home."

Beckett dropped onto the nearest chair. Lee sat opposite, and they watched in silence as Mack spooned coffee into a filter jug. He hadn't asked what they were doing here. But Beckett could see he was already assessing the situation, piecing things together. This wasn't a social visit, and they both knew it.

Chapter Thirty

Once the coffee was ready, Mack poured it into three mismatched mugs and handed one each to Beckett and Lee before leaning back against the counter.

"Sorry, no milk," he said. "Don't keep it around."

"Black's fine," Lee replied.

Beckett just nodded and took a careful sip. It was strong. Bitter. A bit too much bite. Kind of like the man who made it.

"So... how do you two know each other?" Lee asked, then immediately looked startled. "Sorry, maybe I shouldn't ask."

"It's okay," Beckett said. "It's a fair question."

"No, really, I get it..." She shifted in her seat, focusing on her drink. But Beckett could tell she was curious. Anyone would be. Better to give her something than let her imagination run wild.

"Let's just say our paths used to cross here and there," he said. "Mack did what I did, only for the US. Different branches, same kind of work. Intelligence, mostly."

Mack raised his mug. "For my sins."

"I see." Lee nodded slowly, like she wanted to ask more but wasn't sure how far to push. "Cool."

"I'm not sure about that," Beckett said. "But this man is one of the best people I ever worked with."

"Back at ya, buddy," Mack replied, his grin fading as his eyes met Lee's. "You know, Beckett here saved my life."

Lee cleared her throat, shifting slightly in her seat, perhaps caught off guard by the sudden weight in Mack's words. "Oh. Wow."

He nodded, looking off into the middle distance. "It was back in Eastern Ukraine, around 20… 15?" He glanced at Beckett, who nodded in confirmation. "I remember it was cold as hell. I was running surveillance. Supposed to be routine but, as it often does, it went sideways. Fast. My cover got blown and I ended up in the basement of a nightclub that doubled as a black site for one of the local militia outfits."

He shivered at the thought. "Nasty crowd. The kind that doesn't waste time once they've decided you're holding out on them." He rubbed at his wrist absently, like he could still feel the zip ties. "Six hours in, they'd stopped asking questions and started working through the body parts they thought I could live without."

He glanced at Beckett. "And then he showed up. Even though he'd completed his part of the mission and was supposed to be on a plane back to the US. He heard I was in trouble and he came anyway. Put three of them down before they even knew he was in the room."

Mack shook his head, a grin tugging at the corner of his mouth. "Dragged me out of there bleeding and half conscious and didn't stop until we were at the safe house."

"Incredible." Lee's eyes darted to Beckett, searching his

face for something – maybe confirmation, maybe more detail – but he didn't give her anything. He just took another sip of coffee.

"My point being…" Mack continued. "Whatever you're doing here. Whatever you need. You've got it. Just say the word. Because If I can help, I will."

Beckett smiled at Lee, letting Mack's offer hang in the air for a couple of beats. The tablet device was why they were here, of course, but his upbringing nudged him to at least fake a little politeness before diving straight in with requests.

He glanced at the thick blackout curtain covering the rear of the trailer. "Do you still have all your toys?" he asked.

Mack raised an eyebrow. "You think I'd let my skills go soft?"

He stepped forward and yanked the curtain aside. The setup beyond looked like the cockpit of a spaceship, albeit a very messy one. Multiple monitors, solid-state and portable hard drives, keyboards, cameras, and a sea of tangled cables all fitted with surge protectors. A series of cooling fans on the ceiling kept the temperature steady.

"Whoa." Lee stood, drawn towards the glow. "I thought you were off-grid," she said, taking it all in.

Mack gave a lopsided grin. "There's off-grid, and then there's off-grid." He shrugged. "What can I say, I like to keep an eye on things."

"What kind of things?" she asked, sitting back down.

"The government," he said. "Here and everywhere else. Big tech, big pharma. The Man!"

Beckett snorted, shaking his head. "And here I was worried you'd mellowed."

"Not a chance. These days? You can't afford to."

Lee craned her neck, still eyeing all the equipment. "Okay, I've got to ask. How the hell are you powering all this out here?"

Mack grinned. "There was an old dried-up riverbed running down the side of this plot when I got here. It runs all the way over to Jean and Primm. Both towns are close enough for supply runs, but more importantly"—he pointed for emphasis—"that old riverbed was a perfect trench for laying cables. I ran lines right down it – buried them, filled it over."

"You buried cables all the way to the town?"

"Correct. Using an excavator and a dump truck I... *borrowed* from a construction site up the highway. Took a week. Some sweat. Plenty of beer. Was worth it. Ran my lines under the dirt and tapped into the grid right outside Jean."

Lee folded her arms. "You mean you're stealing power."

"Only from the likes of Starbucks and Chevron," Mack replied. "Call it my way of redistributing the wealth."

"Jesus." Lee shook her head. "Robin Hood with an Ethernet cable."

Mack didn't seem bothered. "They overcharge for burnt coffee and gas anyway. I'm not losing sleep if I eat into their profits."

"You always were resourceful," Beckett said, placing his hands on his knees, steering the conversation back. He turned to Lee. "I'm just going to have a quiet chat with Mack. Will you be okay for a few minutes?"

She looked up at him as he stood. "Oh, yeah. Sure. You got the... thing?"

Beckett nodded, catching Mack's eye and tilting his head towards the back room. His old friend took the cue and led the way. Beckett followed, leaving the curtain slightly open so it wouldn't look like they were shutting Lee out completely. But he needed to talk straight with Mack. No filters.

"All right," Mack said once they were settled back there. "What's the story?"

Beckett filled him in. Gates. Jarvis. The tablet. Novara Logistics. The trail of bodies left in their wake. He kept it short, no sugarcoating, and Mack didn't interrupt. He just listened, nodding here and there like he was filing each detail away. When Beckett finished, his old friend let out a slow breath and pursed his lips, weighing it all.

"What do you think?" Beckett asked.

Mack scratched his jaw. "I think it sounds like a lot of mess and a hell of a lot of risk. And I think you could walk away. But..." He grinned. "You're not built that way."

Beckett didn't respond. He didn't need to.

Mack clapped his hands together. "All right. Let's see this elusive device."

Beckett slipped it from his pocket and handed it over. Mack turned it around in his hands, inspecting it like he was already mapping its insides. "Looks like a mobile data terminal, an MDT," he muttered, running a thumb along its edges. "They're like mini computers. If it was used in a factory setting, it probably tracked deliveries and inventory. See this?" He pointed to the back. "Scanner right here. Can be used to read barcodes and RFID tags."

"I've been trying to get into it," Beckett said. "But there's weird encryption I've not seen before."

"Let's have a look."

He powered the unit on, his fingers tapping at the screen as he tested a few commands. Beckett stepped back, letting him work, and glanced through the doorway into the main room.

Lee was sitting with her eyes closed, as if focusing on her breathing. Given everything that happened yesterday, the danger they were in, and what this all meant for her job, she was doing remarkably well. She was much tougher than she realised – he had seen it in the alley, in the bar, even back at Jarvis's place when everything went sideways. She didn't flinch easily, and when she did, she pushed past it.

He watched her longer than he should have. The slow rise and fall of her chest, the faint crease between her brows even as she rested. Her hair was tied up, but a few strands had slipped loose, brushing the curve of her jaw and tapping at the open collar of her shirt. The heat in the trailer had flushed her skin, making the freckles on her cheeks and chest stand out more than normal.

Somewhere in the middle of all that, he caught himself smiling.

"What's the deal with you two?" Mack's voice snapped him out of it.

"Nothing to tell," Beckett said, turning back to him. "We're helping each other figure this out."

Mack smirked. "She likes you."

"No."

"Yeah." Mack tapped the side of his head. "I see it. And I see you. We all have our blind spots, Beckett. Even you."

Beckett shrugged it off, moving over to where Mack was hunched over the MDT device. "Any joy?"

"Not yet. You were right. This thing's a pain in the ass." He leaned back. "It's not going to be a straightforward crack. Looks like whatever's on here is rigged to wipe itself clean if someone starts poking around without the right access codes."

Beckett had feared as much. "But can you crack it?"

Mack shot him a look like he was crazy. "Who the hell are you talking to? Of course I can crack it."

Chapter Thirty-One

Back in Vegas, Red had just finished in the shower after washing away the night's grime and stress. She reached for the Egyptian cotton towel hanging on the rack, dried herself off, and ruffled it through her damp hair before stepping onto the cool tiles. The bathroom mirror was fogged with steam, so she wandered, naked, into the main space. The floor-to-ceiling windows had no drapes, but she didn't care. She'd worn so much armour throughout her thirty-two years – both mental and physical – that it felt good to let her body breathe once in a while.

It felt good to be home, too. She'd moved here recently, in a hurry, and hadn't put her stamp on it yet, but she'd get there. It was a decent place, all polished concrete floors and exposed brickwork. The Arts District wouldn't have been her usual choice of location. It was the kind of neighbourhood that had traded dive bars for craft breweries and gang graffiti for corporate-sponsored murals. But being somewhere so gentrified served a purpose. It was clean, safe, anonymous.

Then again, she'd picked her last place for those same reasons – low traffic, no nosy neighbours, easy exits – but all it took was one bad drain and the wrong plumber asking too many questions. The pathetic do-gooder had called the cops, and rumours about forensic drainage tests had started floating around. Red didn't wait to find out if they were true. She was packed and gone in under a day, all her rental paperwork shredded, and then the property management office torched just in case.

Lesson learned: never use your own bathtub to dissolve a body.

In the middle of the room she stretched, catching sight of her reflection in the large mirror propped up behind the red leather couch. She looked good. Lean, toned, muscle where it counted. Outside, the day had kicked into gear in the city that never sleeps. The sun was already beating through the windows, promising another day with temperatures higher than average. More heat. More sweat. Things hadn't gone well recently and she wasn't happy about that. But today would be better. She'd make sure of it.

But first things first. Coffee. Then a meeting with her team – or what was left of them after those idiots got themselves killed. Red always hired the best, and for Joey Boy and Dixon to be taken out so easily might've given her pause if she let doubts fester. But that wasn't her style. Keep moving. Don't look back. Do the job. Do it well.

She crossed to the kitchen, flicked on the coffee machine, and had just grabbed the jug to fill it at the sink when her tablet chimed on the counter.

"Shit."

Normally, she wouldn't have answered. This was technically her downtime, and she guarded it like it was sacred. But she'd set a specific ringtone for *him*, and it was *him* calling now. His calls weren't optional – not when he paid her the kind of money that rewrote priorities.

Dispensing with underwear, she grabbed a pair of tight black jeans and a black mesh top from her laundry basket, sliding them on without a second thought. Grabbing the tablet, she headed for the desk in the corner, propping the device up on its stand and swiping the screen to connect the video call.

This better be good.

The display flickered, and then there he was – Lucian Holden, the man behind the curtain. Red leaned back, waiting while the feed corrected itself and his features sharpened. The billionaire CEO of Novara Logistics was probably a handsome man at some point in his life, but now he looked too fake to look anything but… odd. He was in his fifties, maybe older, though it was hard to tell with the skin on his cheeks and around his eyes stretched so tight. The work he'd had done was clearly expensive as well as extensive, but it left him looking artificial, like an android trying to pass for a human. But even with his rictus face, Red noticed his composure slip just slightly as his eyes widened.

Then she realised.

She was wearing a mesh top without a bra underneath, her breasts highlighted further by the blue glow from the screen. Holden had obviously been startled by the sight of her exposed breasts, but screw it. Whilst she didn't like showing off her body for the titillation of men, she enjoyed seeing them squirm.

"Did I catch you at a bad time?" he asked.

To his credit, he didn't seem fazed, but this only rein-forced her long-held belief that he wasn't driven by sex.

Money and power were what turned him on. Probably the only things that did.

She crossed her arms. Playtime over. "Never a bad time for you, sir. What do you need?"

He rolled his eyes dramatically. "What do you think? I want an update."

Red exhaled through her nose, keeping her irritation in check. She didn't like being handled in this way. She'd told him she'd get the job done and he should trust that. But Holden was paying her too much to say no.

"Our pet cop is dead," she said. "He won't be causing us any more problems. Or talking to anyone he shouldn't."

"You're certain?"

"I took him out myself last night."

Holden's eyes stayed locked on hers, giving her the kind of stare that made most people fidget. Red didn't. She'd dealt with men like him her whole life.

"And the data terminal?" he asked.

Red gritted her teeth. She hated admitting failure. Hated the taste. Holden picked up on her hesitation and gave a dramatic sigh.

"You don't have it?"

"Not yet. But I will. We ran into some... complications."

"Complications?" Holden repeated the word like it was something dirty. "I don't pay you for complications, Red. I pay you for results."

She gripped her thighs, digging her nails into the flesh as she fought the urge to snap back.

"And you'll get them," she said. "The job's not done yet."

Holden patted the air like he was trying to calm himself.

"Where is the data terminal?" he asked, speaking slowly like she was a fucking child.

Red dug her nails in deeper. "Jarvis's colleague has it," she muttered, swallowing the bitterness. "The female cop. We'd flagged her a while back, but nothing about her suggested she'd be a problem. She's a nobody. But now she's working with some English guy we can't get a read on. He came out of nowhere and has become a real spanner in the works."

"Who is he?"

"Like I say, we don't know. I'm working on it, but we think he's ex-military. He took out two of my men and was with Jarvis when I eliminated him. I tried to take him and the cop out at the same time, but they... got away."

Holden's eyes remained locked on hers as he shook his head slowly. For a second he reminded her of a teacher she'd had at the military academy. Another smug, passive-aggressive prick.

"I'll find them," she added. "Today. I've got my best people on it."

Holden steepled his fingers under his chin. He was good at this, waiting, letting the silence stretch just enough to make you feel you had to fill it. But she didn't. She held her ground, kept her mouth shut, and let him sit with it.

"Your best men?" he said at last, as if she'd said something cute. "The same kind of men who were just killed by this Englishman?"

"I am going to sort this," she told him. "You have my word."

Holden drummed his fingers on the desk. It was the first sign of agitation, but coming from him it might as well have been a scream.

"This is already spiralling out of control, Red. I don't like it. I pay you to clean up things. I was told you were the best."

"I *am* the best."

"Then prove it. Because if the event on Saturday doesn't go exactly as planned, it'll be disastrous. For everyone."

Red curled her lip before she could stop herself. She didn't like being pushed. She didn't like being questioned. And she sure as hell didn't like being threatened.

Holden pressed on, oblivious or just not caring. "We can't let any of this point back to us," he told her. "Not a single thread. Otherwise, all the work we've put in – all the planning, all the risk – will mean nothing." He leaned closer to the camera, his pale eyes drilling into hers. "And that would be catastrophic."

Red held his gaze. "I get it. And I'm handling it. Just make sure you're prepared for the carnage that follows. It's going to get messy."

Holden's lips twitched. Not quite a smile, but maybe he'd had too much work done to really show pleasure. "That's what I'm betting on," he said. "Quite literally."

Red smirked. "Don't worry, sir. I'll get the job done."

"You'd better."

He reached forward and the call cut out. Red sat for a moment, staring at the empty screen. The rebellious teenager inside her – the one who'd been expelled from two schools for fighting – urged her to flip it off. But what was the point? Holden wouldn't see it, and even if he did he wouldn't care.

She stood and rolled the tension from her shoulders. The call had left a sour taste, but that was nothing new. She crossed to the kitchen, grabbed the coffee tin, and started scooping.

It was time to go to work.

Chapter Thirty-Two

Outside Mack's trailer, the sweat dripped down Maggie Lee's face as she paced back and forth. She folded her arms. She unfolded them. She put her hands on her hips and then ran her fingers through her hair, scratching at her scalp as she puffed out a deep sigh.

She hated this. The waiting.

And the October heat didn't help. The sun was relentless overhead, shining down from a cloudless sky, making her more impatient, more restless. She was wired from too much adrenaline and too little sleep. At any one moment she felt scared, exhilarated, or tense as hell.

A lot of emotions to deal with.

Part of her wanted it to be over. All of it. No more dead cops, no more guns, no more people trying to kill them. But another part didn't want it to end at all.

A lot of *conflicting* emotions. She hated it. She loved it. Her head was a mess.

She glanced at Beckett, sitting on the steps of the trailer like he didn't have a care in the world, like this was just another day for him. It made her want to scream. Or maybe shuffle up next to him. She hadn't decided which.

"How long is this going to take?" she asked, stopping mid-step.

Beckett looked up, squinting in the sunlight. "As long as it needs to."

"That's not an answer."

"It's the only one I've got." He stretched his legs out in front of him. "Mack's the best there is. If anyone can crack this thing, it's him."

She blew out a breath and folded her arms again. "I just don't like doing nothing."

"Yes, I picked up on that." He smiled. "All in good time, Maggie. We're safe here."

Maggie.

It was only the second time he'd called her by her first name, and for a moment it sent a warm ripple through her. But it didn't last and was quickly replaced by a stronger sensation. The fear creeping back in. She wanted to believe she was safe. She really did. But the longer this dragged on, the more people tried to kill them, the harder it was to hold on to that.

Beckett must've seen it in her face because he shifted over, patting the step beside him. "Sit," he said. "Take a break. You're no good to anyone if you burn out before we've even started."

She hesitated, pretending to consider the offer for a moment, then sat. Inside the trailer, Mack was singing Springsteen's *Thunder Road* as he tapped away at his keyboard.

"Don't we need to get back to Vegas and do more digging?" she asked. "We know they're up to something big, and if you're right about it going down this weekend, we're running out of time." She gestured behind her to the trailer. "What if he can't crack that thing? Shouldn't we be doing something in the meantime?"

"Doing what, exactly?"

She blinked. "I don't know. Anything. We follow the leads we've got."

"What leads?" Beckett's voice was calm, like he was walking her back from a ledge. "That device is the best lead we've had. Mack will get it open. Then we'll see what's got everyone so desperate they're willing to kill for it."

Lee closed her eyes, trying and failing to enjoy the sun on her face. "I just hate waiting," she said.

"I know. But patience isn't the same as doing nothing. In the meantime, why don't you tell me everything you know about Novara?"

She ran a hand through her hair. She could see what he was doing, but what the hell, there was little else to do. "I probably know as much as you at this point," she admitted. "All I know is the CEO is a guy named Lucious – or maybe it's Lucian – Holden. He's the face and founder. A typical big tech guy, from what little I've seen of him. He moved his head office to Vegas about six years ago now. Bought up half that block off the Strip and built the Novara Logistics Tower."

Beckett didn't respond, so she kept going. Turns out she knew more than she thought.

"I think they started out in Silicon Valley, doing the kind of stuff no one really understands but making a ton of money doing it."

"And Holden?"

"A pretty odd guy. He's had too much work done, if you know what I mean. Looks like an AI image of himself." She hesitated. "Not my kind of guy."

She cringed internally as she said that. The way she'd looked at Beckett and practically fluttered her eyelashes didn't help. But he seemed oblivious as he looked away and frowned.

"What are you thinking?" she asked.

"Just trying to put it all together."

She got up and stretched, arms reaching high above her head, easing out the tension in her shoulders and chest. When she glanced back, she caught Beckett watching. Just for a second. Then he looked away like it hadn't happened.

But it had.

Lee tried not to read too much into it, but she felt that warm ripple again, stronger this time. She liked that he was looking. More than she should, considering the circumstances. She pushed the thought aside. Now wasn't the time.

"Beckett!" Mack's gruff voice cut through the moment.

Beckett jumped up and Lee hurried into the trailer after him, her heart racing as they shuffled through the living area and kitchen to the back, where Mack was sitting in front of a desk of monitors.

"What have we got?" Beckett asked him.

Mack tilted one of the screens to show him. "I got through the first layer of encryption and found a few things. Financial logs, delivery schedules, inventory reports. But no smoking gun or anything yet." He jabbed a finger at the device. "Problem is, this thing's built like an onion. Layers on layers. And the deeper you go, the uglier it gets."

"How ugly?" Beckett asked.

Mack tapped on the keyboard, and a new window popped up on the screen, showing what looked like a login page asking for a username and password. Beneath it, lines of code were scrolling fast, like the computer was running a process in the background, trying different combinations to break through. It looked complicated.

"The second layer's locked tight," he told them. "Plus, it's booby-trapped. I trip it, the whole thing wipes clean. Whatever's buried in there... they really don't want anyone seeing it."

"Can you unlock it?" Lee asked.

Mack blew out a long breath. "Right now I'm trying to bypass the security protocol, but it's like working with a grenade pin half pulled. Give me time, or we lose everything."

"How much time?" Beckett asked.

"Depends. Could be an hour. Could be a day. This thing's not standard. Someone built it custom and they knew what they were doing. But I have found something you need to see." He tapped a few keys and the screen shifted to a new window filled with rows of data.

Beckett leaned closer, resting a hand on Mack's shoulder. "What are we looking at?"

"These are some of the shipping manifests and inventory sheets I've pulled from the device's memory card. But look at this." Mack traced his finger down a section on the screen. "Single shipments with multiple dates and drop points. And notice how vague the descriptions are, even for inventory. And then there's this." He tapped the keyboard and another window flashed up showing a grainy scan of what looked like a hand-drawn instruction manual. Lee wasn't sure what she was looking at, but the shift in Beckett and Mack's expressions told her it was bad.

"Looks like some kind of explosive device," Mack said.

Beckett nodded. "Is it part of a shipment?"

"That'd be my guess."

"Where's it heading?"

Mack growled. "Haven't cracked that part yet. But they're moving stuff all over, splitting shipments to keep things scattered, harder to track. But look here." He picked up a notepad covered in scribbled notes. "Some shipments are tagged as 'Project C' with delivery addresses across the city – distribution hubs, warehouses. But there's more." He turned back to the screen. "There's an email saved on the memory card that mentions an event this weekend."

Lee and Beckett exchanged a glance.

"At the Novara Logistics Tower?" Lee asked.

"Doesn't say."

"Any links to Novara?" Beckett asked.

Mack shook his head. "If they're behind it, you can bet there's a long chain of cover between them and whatever this is." He waved his hand over the screen. "Looks to me like whatever's coming, they've been planning it a long time."

Lee looked at Beckett. "We head Downtown. Warn them about this. Get backup."

"Bad idea," Mack replied before Beckett could answer. "If there are powerful people behind this, and it's looking that way, you don't know who else they've bought. Could be the cops, Feds, anyone. If you mouth off to the wrong people, who knows what could happen."

"He's right," Beckett agreed. "We need to keep this between the three of us."

"So, what?" she asked, unable to hide the frustration in her voice. "We sit here and wait? That's your plan?"

"We don't even know what we're dealing with," Beckett replied steadily. "Not fully. We need to give Mack time to get past this kill switch and pull everything off the device."

He seemed so calm and measured, acting like the walls weren't starting to close in around them. It annoyed her, and it reassured her, and she still hated how both things could be true at once.

"And while we sit around, there's every chance they're moving that bomb into position," Lee snapped. "Tell me I'm wrong."

Beckett stayed silent. She glared at him, wishing he'd say something. Did he think she couldn't handle it, was that it? Was he regretting having her here?

She sucked in a deep breath, telling herself she was overthinking it.

She could do this.

She could. If she kept her head.

"I just want to stop this, whatever it is," she said, relieved when her voice came out stronger than she felt.

"I know you do," Beckett said, just as firm. "So while Mack works on extracting the rest of the data, we'll pay Holden a proper visit."

Mack snorted. "I knew you were going to say that." He grinned and shot Lee a wink. "You sure you know what you've got yourself into with this guy? He doesn't stop, you know. Ever."

Lee squared her shoulders. "That's good," she told him. "Because I don't either."

Chapter Thirty-Three

Beckett cracked the window, letting in a rush of air as the neon glow of Vegas shimmered on the horizon. The dashboard clock read 3:26 p.m., but Lee was driving like it was zero hour − hands clenched on the wheel, foot heavy on the gas.

Beckett didn't blame her. She was worried and frustrated. So was he. They just had different ways of showing it. They'd left Mack back at the trailer, still picking through the tablet's encryption like his life depended on it. And maybe it did. They'd given him Lee's number and Beckett trusted him to call when he found something.

"If this is tied to the event, does that mean the bomb is meant for Vegas?" Lee asked, voicing the question circling in his own mind. "It doesn't make sense. Novara owns half the damn city. Holden lives here. Why blow up your own backyard?"

Beckett stared straight ahead, his thoughts racing. "Could be leverage. A threat. A bargaining chip."

"For what? Holden's a billionaire."

Beckett gave a dry smile. "And how many billionaires do you know who are satisfied with what they've got? They're the most power-hungry people on the planet. That's usually how they become billionaires in the first place." He rubbed his face, thinking. "Besides, who says this is about money? Could be political."

"Yeah, I guess. But won't any power move expose them?"

"Not if they've planned it right. But until we know more, I don't think it helps to speculate. One step at a time."

"Sure. Whatever." She didn't look at him, just kept her eyes locked on the road, but he could hear the edge in her voice.

"Let's focus on what's in front of us," he continued. "On what is."

"Yeah, yeah, I know, not what *isn't*." She almost smiled. "But they wouldn't really blow up Vegas, would they?"

He glanced over. She was scared, holding it together by sheer force of will. He thought about softening the answer, but she deserved the truth. "I don't know. But that's what we're going to find out. I was thinking we'd visit Holden at home. Tonight, when he's vulnerable. That way I can be more forceful in my questioning."

Lee eased off the gas. "What does that mean, more forceful?"

"Whatever it takes to get the truth."

"Beckett... no. You can't."

"Sometimes it's the only way."

Their eyes met, and for a moment he saw the honest beat cop, still wrestling with the situation she'd been dragged into.

"Please. Not yet. Let's try this by the book first."

"The book went out the window a long time ago," he said.

"But I'm still police," she replied. "I can't just torture someone because we *think* he's planning something. That's not how the law works."

"We need answers, Maggie. And we need them soon."

"I know that, but let's try his office first and talk to him on the level. Please. He'll likely be there, with the event coming up."

"And if that doesn't work?"

She sighed. "Then we'll do it your way."

They drove on in silence, not exactly tense but far from easy. After twenty minutes, Lee pulled up on the same side street as she'd done twenty-four hours ago. The Novara Logistics Towers loomed above them, its glass and steel façade gleaming in the late afternoon sun.

Beckett was on high alert as they got out and made their way to the main entrance, scanning for threats, details, anything that might give them an edge. Through the glass, the lobby looked busy. Good. Crowds made it easier to blend in.

There was no doorman today, so they entered through a set of revolving doors and moved over to a seating area in the corner. Lee followed Beckett's lead as they sat, letting the noise and movement wash over them, observing in silence. Men and women in expensive suits came and went, delivery guys signed off packages, tourists snapped photos of the ultra-modern space like it was part of the Vegas experience.

After a few minutes, Lee leaned in and whispered. "What now?"

It was a good question. There was no chance they could

just walk up to the desk and ask to see Holden. They needed to be smart. Or devious.

Beckett narrowed his eyes, studying the lobby. The same stern woman from yesterday was at the front desk; she'd recognise them instantly if they tried the polite approach. Cameras were everywhere, but that was expected and not too much of an issue once you knew where the blind spots were. Two security guards hovered near the elevators, with another pair stationed by the stairwell. A promo video for the weekend's expo played on a loop across the giant screen.

"Anything?" Lee whispered.

"Working on it."

Across the far side of the lobby, a deliveryman was wheeling a cart piled high with parcels towards a service area, distracted by the clipboard in his hand.

Beckett nudged Lee. "Follow me."

They got to their feet and he made a beeline for the delivery cart. As they neared, he waited until the guy was looking at his notes, then angled his body to shield the action as he grabbed one of the larger parcels from the pile. Tucking it under his arm like it belonged there, he kept on walking.

"What the hell are you doing?" Lee hissed, catching up with him.

"Improvising," he replied, nodding towards the nearest elevator, where a group of people were stepping inside. "Come on."

They slipped in just as the doors were closing. The other occupants barely glanced up, too absorbed in their phones to care. Beckett pressed the button for the top floor and moved to the corner, keeping the parcel balanced under one arm as the doors slid shut. No one spoke as they began their ascent, but he and Lee exchanged a glance, the tension between them heavy but not unpleasant.

The Novaro Building was sleek and modern, designed with just two elevators instead of the standard setup of multiple banks serving different floors. As the car reached the fifth floor, it eased to a stop, and the doors slid open onto a long corridor flanked by glass-walled meeting rooms. Most of the passengers stepped out here, leaving only Beckett, Lee, and a well-dressed older woman. Beckett kept his eyes forward as the doors closed again.

Floor seven came next, at which the woman stepped out without a glance back. As the doors closed, Beckett gave the button for the top floor a few extra taps, as if that might hurry things along.

"Do you actually have a plan?" Lee asked, turning to face him as the car began to climb.

"Of course," Beckett replied, eyes on the rising floor numbers. "The plan is to speak to Holden. Try not to get thrown out of a window."

Lee snorted a short laugh, perhaps despite herself. "That's it?"

"Do you want the long version?"

"Let me guess. Something like, get in, get the information, get out."

He turned his head slightly, just enough to catch her expression. "*And* don't get thrown out of a window."

Lee shook her head at him but her smile lingered. Beckett smiled back. It was the kind of levity they both needed right now, a thin crack of light to cut through the tension.

"Seriously, though," she said. "What's the plan?"

Beckett shrugged. "That is the plan."

She rolled her eyes and silence settled between them

once more. He could feel her eyes on him, but when he glanced over again she quickly looked away, clearing her throat. He turned back to the numbers, straightening his posture as they neared the top floor.

Keep it together now.

After a few more minutes, the elevator finally stopped at floor sixty-four and the doors slid open with a soft hiss. Beckett stepped out first. The landing was quiet, with subdued lighting and dark, polished floors that felt more high-end apartment than corporate space. A set of double doors stood open opposite the elevator, revealing a wide staircase beyond, its edges lined with subtle LED strips.

"The penthouse must only be accessible by stairs," Beckett whispered, nodding upward. "That's where Holden will be."

They moved through the doors and started up the stairs. On either side, large screens displayed abstract digital art – waves of colour and light pulsing and shifting in slow, hypnotic patterns. At the top they stepped out onto a wide landing. Directly in front of them was a glass wall with a single glass door in its centre. Beyond it was a small reception area, all black marble and concealed lighting, complete with another stern-faced woman in a sharp suit.

She didn't look up as they approached. Beckett motioned for Lee to step back behind a section of wall that jutted out to conceal fire-safety equipment. While she stayed hidden, Beckett moved up to the glass door, adjusting his grip on the parcel before pressing the intercom button.

A faint buzz sounded from the other side, and the woman at the desk finally looked up, her perfectly sculpted eyebrows lifting slightly when she spotted Beckett standing there.

He grave her a crooked grin and lifted the package.

She frowned and shook her head. *No*, she mouthed. *Deliveries downstairs.*

Beckett held up the package again, jabbing a finger at the label and shaking his head. *No, this one's special.* He mouthed the words. *Top floor.* His expression one of dim-witted earnestness.

The receptionist pinched the bridge of her nose. "No. Downstairs," she called out, loud enough to be heard through the glass.

Beckett tilted his head, squinting at her like he couldn't understand. He shrugged, pointed at the parcel again, and mouthed, *Important*, then mimed placing it gently on her desk as if to say, *I'll just drop it off and leave.*

The woman's frustration was immediate, her polished veneer cracking as she leaned over and jabbed a button on her console. The door buzzed, and Beckett pushed it open with his shoulder, parcel still in hand.

"What the hell are you doing?" she snapped, rising from her seat as Beckett stepped inside.

Lee slipped through the door behind him, moving quickly to his side. The receptionist froze mid-stride, her annoyance sharpening into alertness.

"Get out of here. Now! I'll call security."

She turned, heading back behind her desk, but Lee stepped in front of her. "Officer Lee, LVMPD," she said, flashing her badge. "I need to speak with Mr Holden. It's a matter of urgency."

The woman glared at her, face twisting with indigna-tion. "Not a chance," she hissed. "He's incredibly busy. And you have no idea how much trouble you're asking for right now."

Beckett moved in beside Lee. "I'm afraid it's not a

request," he said. "We need to speak to him and we aren't leaving until we do."

"And I already told you, he's busy." The woman shifted around Lee to put the desk between them. But Lee was persistent.

"We can get a warrant if that's what you want. But I figure Mr Holden would prefer to keep this low-key. For now."

The woman opened her mouth, ready to argue again when a high-pitched voice cut through the room. "What is all this?"

They turned in unison, the receptionist's demeanour shifting instantly. Indignation replaced by panic-tinged professionalism.

"M-Mr Holden, sir," she stammered. "I'm so sorry. I was just asking them to leave."

Lucian Holden stood at the far side of the room, framed by the opening of a narrow corridor. He was wearing a midnight-blue suit and looked younger than Beckett expected. Or rather, not younger, just more airbrushed. His features were almost too symmetrical and his skin had the taut, waxy sheen of too many cosmetic procedures.

"What the hell is all the shouting about?" he asked, glancing at Lee before settling on Beckett.

"Sir," the receptionist started, her voice wobbling slightly. "They—"

"Burst in," Beckett interrupted, stepping closer to Holden. "Because we need to talk to you. Now."

A trace of recognition flashed in his pale blue eyes before his polished composure snapped into place. He didn't look surprised – not exactly. More like a man who'd known this moment was coming but wasn't happy it was here. His pink lips curled into a faint smile, the kind that offered no real warmth. "I see," he said.

The receptionist picked up the phone. "But, sir, I can—"

"No. It's fine," Holden told her. "I'll handle this."

Turning back to Beckett and Lee, he gave them a grin that could cut glass. "Please, follow me," he said. "We can talk in my office."

Chapter Thirty-Four

Holden led them through a set of brushed-steel doors, which opened silently as they approached, and into his office. The footprint was huge, occupying nearly half the top floor of the building. Beckett took it all in as they walked, instinctively mapping out exit routes like he did when entering any new room. On the far side, a staircase led up to a mezzanine level that overlooked the main space, with glass doors opening onto the roof.

The rest of the room screamed money and ego, hyper-modern with touches of eccentricity that felt like an extension of the man himself. The wall to their right was a seamless sheet of glass, offering a sweeping view of Las Vegas Boulevard below. From this height, the glitz and gaudiness of the Strip seemed like another world entirely. Along another wall, a row of minimalist display cases showcased what looked like art sculptures, though they might've just as easily been pieces of cutting-edge tech gadgets.

"Wow," Lee muttered, as the doors sucked shut behind them. "Impressive."

Beckett stayed quiet, more interested in what the space revealed about its owner. To him, it was the office of a man desperate to show he was ahead of the curve and more interesting than he was.

Lee walked over to the glass wall, looking out over the city. "Nice place," she said.

"Thank you," Holden shrilled, clasping his hands in front of him.

Beckett hung back. There were no visible cameras or mounted security systems, and that was telling. A space this high up, isolated from the rest of the building, meant no one could see or hear what happened.

"Is it just you up here?" Beckett asked.

Holden turned. "Most days, yes. I use it as a thinking space as much as an office. It's quiet. Private. The way I like it." He gestured vaguely towards the ceiling. "And I have a private helipad on the roof so I can fly in and out. Convenient for meetings, travel – whatever the day requires." He smiled. "But please, Officers. You must tell me what this is all about. Come."

He led them over to the seating area in front of the glass. A crescent-shaped leather couch curled around a black coffee table, its polished surface made from some kind of precious stone. Opposite the couch were two oversized chairs that looked like leather bean bags.

Holden eased into one of the chairs, crossing one leg over the other. "Please," he said, gesturing towards the couch.

Beckett sat at one end, leaving the middle for Lee. He kept his focus on Holden as they got settled.

"Now, what I can do for you good people?" Holden asked.

Beckett leaned forward. "I'm Detective Beckett. My

partner, Detective Lee, and I are investigating a few leads in a case and believe you might be able to help us."

Holden raised an eyebrow. "A Brit working for Vegas PD. That's not something you see every day."

Beckett didn't bite. He'd ditched the American accent because he was done playing games. "We have reason to believe there's a potential terrorist event planned for this weekend," he said, watching Holden for any subtle give-aways. "And this site could be a possible target."

Holden's expression shifted just enough to register shock, but it was too smooth, too controlled to be genuine. He leaned back, fingers steepled. "Terrorist event?" he repeated. "Are you sure?"

"I don't suppose you've seen or heard anything?" Beckett asked. "Or have any… insights you can share?"

Holden shook his head, the picture of polite incredulity. "Detective, I'm afraid you've been misinformed. What could I possibly know about something like that?"

"He didn't say you knew anything," Lee cut in, a little eagerly.

She shifted slightly closer to Beckett, but his focus never wavered from Holden. The man's performance was almost flawless, but Beckett had been around too many liars to be fooled. The gestures, the eye contact, the surprised expressions, it was all just a bit too deliberate.

"Well to be clear, this is the first I've heard of anything like this," Holden said, with a polite smile. "Please, enlighten me."

Beckett got in quick. "Does Project C mean anything to you?"

"No. Should it?" Holden replied, not missing a beat.

Beckett studied the enigmatic CEO. He'd seen better performances, but what struck him wasn't the quality of the act, it was the indifference. Holden wasn't even trying that hard. The way men are when they know they're untouchable.

Or think they are.

"We have a big event happening here this weekend," Holden explained. "A tech expo with key industry figures flying in from all over the world. I'll be delivering a keynote address to a room full of hundreds. So if this is a real threat, I'm rather surprised someone higher up than you hasn't informed me."

"We have reason to believe there's an explosive device currently on its way to Vegas," Lee said. "Do you think your event could attract such a target?"

Holden's expression shifted, the performative shock giving way to an air of professional concern. He uncrossed his legs and leant forward. "Of course, if there's a legitimate threat of a bomb or a terrorist plot, action must be taken. I assume the FBI is already involved?"

Not waiting for an answer, he continued. "I'll reach out to my contacts there immediately, see if they've picked up on anything in their channels. They might have intel you're not privy to."

He paused and Beckett saw his lips twitch. It was a blink-and-you-miss-it moment, but he was trained to pick up on these things. Holden thought he'd bested them.

"And of course I'll brief my security team," he added. "We take these things very seriously, Detective. A high-profile building like ours is always a target. But I must say, this is the first I've heard of such a threat." His eyes moved between Beckett and Lee. "Thank you for bringing this to my attention. But, honestly, I think you're mistaken. If there were a real threat of this magnitude, someone higher up would have flagged it. The FBI, Homeland Security –

someone would have informed me already. We're very well-connected, after all."

He smiled almost indulgently, reminding them exactly who held the power in the room. "Still, we'll remain vigilant. You have my word."

Beckett leaned back. Holden clearly relished playing the role of cooperative CEO, but it was obvious now that he was toying with them. His mention of contacts in the FBI and Homeland was pointed. He knew they had no real power or authority to stop him. He also knew they had no proof, nothing to tie him to anything.

But that was fine. Beckett had what he needed.

Lee cleared her throat as if readying herself for round two, but Beckett raised a hand to stop her. "Thank you, Mr Holden," he said, getting to his feet. "We appreciate your time. Please do remain vigilant."

"Of course." Holden stood also, casually brushing invisible lint from his impeccably tailored blazer. "Now, if there's nothing else, I'll have to ask you to leave. As you can imagine, my schedule is packed."

He crossed to his desk and pressed a button on the side. A second later, the steel doors slid open and two large men entered, their black suits doing little to conceal the muscle underneath.

"Gentlemen, please escort our guests back downstairs," Holden said, his voice maddeningly jovial as he gave Beckett and Lee a regal wave. "Thank you for stopping by."

Chapter Thirty-Five

Lucian Holden stood in the centre of his suite, clenching and unclenching his fists, the glass wall reflecting both the meticulously designed office and his carefully curated features. His reflection looked the same as it always did, handsome, neat, immaculate, but beneath the surface he was seething.

The cop and the Englishman. How the hell had they got up here? How had they heard about Project C? And why the hell were they still breathing air?

It was the audacity that got to him. Not only had they made it past his security, but they'd sat in his bespoke chairs, questioned him in his private sanctuary.

And they'd walked out alive. That was the part that burned the most.

He relaxed his hands, fighting to maintain the calm exterior that had carried him so far. His reflection continued to stare back at him, expressionless but somehow accusatory, and he felt the weight of his own expectations threatening to crush him.

Lucian Holden didn't let people like that win.

He won. Always.

He crossed the room and sat at his desk, tapping the hidden biometric scanner embedded in the wood. In response, a monitor rose smoothly from the desk's surface, sliding up through an almost invisible seam. Simultaneously, a concealed panel at the front of the desk shifted open, and a slim keyboard extended outward. The monitor flickered to life as his fingers hovered over the keys, ready to initiate a video call to Red.

She would explain herself. Now.

But before he could start the call, his phone buzzed in his jacket pocket. Maybe it was her. He pulled it out and glanced at the screen.

Damn it.

The anger drained in an instant, replaced by a cold twist in his gut like something had curdled inside him. Stress wasn't good for him; he knew that. Cortisol aged you. His hand trembled as he stared at the phone.

Not Red. Worse.

He closed his eyes, gulping in deep breaths. Belly breaths. Inhale, hold, count it out. At the same time he pressed two fingers beneath his ear, massaging in slow circles the way his longevity coach had shown him.

Activate the vagus nerve.

Lower the cortisol.

The phone continued to chime. Persistent. He exhaled slowly, releasing the breath in a long controlled stream, then tapped the screen to connect.

"Mr Holden. We thought you weren't going to answer." The voice on the other end was female with an Eastern European accent. Russian, perhaps. He'd not heard from this one before.

"I was away from my phone," he replied. "But I'm here now."

"Good. Because we need an update."

Holden cleared his throat, which had gone dry suddenly. "Everything is going to plan," he said, choosing his words carefully. "There have been a few complications, but nothing unmanageable."

"Complications?"

"Nothing I can't handle." There was no way he was going to mention his recent visitors or their mention of Project C. That was his problem to fix.

The line went silent. Never a good sign. Not with these people.

"You don't have to worry," he added, angry at himself for flinching first. "It will happen as we arranged."

"We hope so, Mr Holden."

He closed his eyes, imagining her on the other end of the line, in some secure bunker somewhere. Her voice was growing on him. Stern, efficient, kind of sexy if you liked that sort of thing.

Not that it mattered. He'd likely never speak to her again or know her name. The Consortium didn't deal in names or titles. They were an organisation that existed in the shadows, the faceless architects pulling strings in boardrooms and governments around the world. And Holden was fast becoming one of their greatest assets.

Or so he liked to think.

"Have the preparations for the contingency been completed?" he asked the woman.

"Of course," the voice spat. "All the false flags are in place. Transaction trails routed through compromised accounts, anonymised with chained crypto tumblers and funnelled through offshore shell corporations. The metadata's been scrubbed and spoofed to send the intelligence community where we want them to go. When it's traced, it'll be irrefutable."

Holden released the breath. "Who's taking the fall?"

"We've tied it to Al-Tariq Al-Jadid, a group already on Middle East watch lists for hostile cyber operations. When the financial trail is uncovered, it will corroborate intelligence chatter seeded months ago. Key pieces are already circulating on dark web forums. Analysts will be chasing leads within hours of the event."

Holden swivelled slightly in his chair, fingers tapping lightly on the desk. "And if someone decides to dig a little deeper?"

"They won't," came the abrupt response. "The narrative's been constructed to match existing expectations. No one digs past the surface when the surface looks credible. The financial forensics are airtight. Communications between members of the group have been fabricated, encrypted, and then conveniently decrypted. When the time comes, the FBI, CIA, and every alphabet agency in the country will be busy chasing ghosts in a foreign war zone. All roads lead to our scapegoat, nowhere else."

Holden allowed himself a tight smile. "And Novara?"

"To the world at large they'll seem like just another victim of the attack," the voice replied. "In the wrong place at the wrong time. Innocent, blameless, and devastated by the fallout."

"And the public?"

"They'll demand answers, as they always do. And they'll get them. Enough to satisfy the media and placate the masses." The woman paused, as if for effect. "Your job, Holden, is to ensure nothing disrupts the narrative before it's fully played out. Can you handle that?"

"Of course," he replied. "Novara Logistics will play its part beautifully."

"See that it does. Because if anything leads back to us, Novara's fall will look like a minor setback compared to what comes next. And if you want to remain in our orbit, Mr Holden – if you want to move into our ranks – you need to pull this off. There's no margin for error. Understood?"

"Loud and clear."

"Good."

The line went dead before he could say more. He placed his phone on the desk and shuddered. For all his power and wealth, the stakes had never been higher. The line between success and failure was razor thin.

He leaned back in his chair, his gaze drifting to the view through the floor-to-ceiling windows. The Vegas skyline gleamed in the late afternoon sun, a shimmering mirage of excess and ambition.

He had two days before it all went down. Forty-eight hours to pull everything together and eliminate every loose end.

And he'd start with that meddling cop and her pet Englishman.

Chapter Thirty-Six

The sun was slipping below the horizon as Beckett and Lee retreated to a small diner on the outskirts of the city to regroup. The diner was similar to the one where Gates had been arrested, where all this started, a relic from the days when a bit of neon and the offer of free refills was enough to pull in the customers. Its leather booths and tabletop jukebox pickers gave it a certain retro charm, but Beckett wasn't here for nostalgia.

He sipped the coffee he'd ordered, the low hum of conversation and the clatter of dishes grounding him as he thought.

Across the table, Lee sat with her arms folded, staring into her mug like it owed her answers. She was frustrated, that much was obvious. Definitely at Holden's evasiveness; maybe at Beckett too, for not pushing harder. He understood how she felt. Holden had got under his skin too. But they'd got all they could out of him today. Beckett was sure of that.

"We'll get there, Maggie," he said, tilting his head to catch her eye. "There's still time."

"We've got nothing," she muttered. "Holden acts like he's untouchable and we don't even know what Project C refers to." She shook her head and took a sip of coffee.

Beckett returned to his own cup. He could offer her more reassurance, but she wasn't going to hear it while she was feeling this way. She needed to let her system settle so she could think clearly again. In his experience, that always happened if you left the process alone. Besides, his silence didn't mean he wasn't processing what had been said – that's all he'd done since they left Novara Logistics Tower.

All they knew was an explosive device was being brought into the city. From what he'd gathered from Mack's findings so far, it was being transported as spare parts to avoid detection. But that meant the device still needed to be assembled somewhere. If they could figure out where, they'd have a shot at stopping it.

But with two days to the event and not much else to go on, it was a big ask.

"Should we head out and see Mack?" Lee asked. "See if he's found anything else?"

Beckett leaned back. "Let's give him a little longer. He's got your number. He said he'd call when he had something."

"But all this sitting around..." She lifted her shoulders. "It's making me feel out of sorts."

She sighed and let her shoulders drop. "I know I'm letting myself get too caught up in my imagination – or whatever it is you said not to do. I just want to stop these bastards."

"I know." He instinctively reached for her hand, but caught himself and pulled back, offering her a thin smile instead. "I got the sense earlier that Holden already knows who we are. We can't afford to keep popping up on his radar without a proper play. And we need more intel before we can act."

"You think that intel is on the device?"

Beckett nodded. "What we've seen so far is damning, but nothing that couldn't be spun if the right people got involved. The fact that Novara's gone to such lengths to get the device back tells me there's more on there. Hopefully enough to give us a clearer picture of their plan. I'm also hoping Mack can pinpoint where the bomb's being assembled and where they plan to deploy it."

Lee puffed out a sigh. "That's a lot to hope for."

"This isn't something we can rush. If we're reckless, we'll show our hand." He glanced out the window. "This might be Vegas, but I don't gamble if I can help it."

He shot her a proper smile but she looked away, still tangled in her frustrations. He kept staring and smiling and eventually she caved, a reluctant smile forming as she shook her head. That was a good sign. She was coming out of her spiral, back into the moment. That's where he needed her to stay.

"Not a betting man, then?" she asked.

He tilted his head, considering it. "Well, most of my life has been calculated risks and gambles. But *calculated* being the key word. We can't do this blind, Maggie."

She huffed, her eyes narrowing. He could tell she still wanted to push, to do something – anything – and right this second. But she also knew he was right.

"Fine."

Just as she seemed to relax, Beckett noticed a man near the counter. He was leaning against the steel top at the far end, pretending to talk on his phone, but he kept glancing over at their table, watching them. He was heavy-set, dressed in dark jeans and a blazer-cut leather jacket. There was something about his posture that screamed ex-military. Beckett couldn't pinpoint why exactly. He just knew.

Shit.

He extended his arm across the back of the booth, looking casually out the window as he spoke. "Don't look now, but we've been followed."

"For real?" Lee stiffened but didn't move.

"Almost certainly. A big guy at the counter. Just him as far as I can see." He turned back, pretending to read the specials board as he weighed their options. Whatever happened next, it had to stay on their terms, no giving this guy the upper hand.

Sitting up, he locked eyes with the man, holding the stare too long to be anything but deliberate. The guy lowered his phone and Beckett jutted his chin.

What do you want?

The man sneered, an unconvincing attempt at bravado. He'd been made and now he was scrambling to figure out his next move. Beckett didn't flinch, didn't blink, just kept his gaze steady as the man shuffled towards the exit.

"Can you pay for the coffees?" he asked Lee, getting to his feet.

"Yeah, sure." She hesitated. "What are you going to—"

"I'll be fine. Head to the car. Get in and lock the doors. If anyone shows up but me, drive around the block. I'll find you."

Without another word he moved to the door, stepping outside into the fading light. The man was already further down the street, walking briskly, not quite running. Most likely he'd been ordered to keep an eye on them until more muscle arrived. But judging by his size and build, he was far better suited for direct, brutal work than covert surveillance.

Beckett hung back but matched the guy's pace, not letting him out of sight. At the next crosswalk the man hesitated, glancing over his shoulder. Their eyes met, and Beckett gave him a subtle nod.

I'm coming for you, mate.

It was like the guy heard him. He bolted, sprinting across the street and veering down a narrow passage between two bars.

"Damn it."

Beckett raced after him, rounding the corner just in time to catch a glimpse of the man disappearing into an alley further along. He was a big man but out of shape, and Beckett closed the distance in seconds. Halfway down the alley a chain-link fence about hip height separated the rear entrances of two casinos, and as the man vaulted it, his foot caught and he stumbled.

Beckett cleared it a moment later, grabbing the guy's collar and slamming him against the wall before he could regain his footing.

"Get the fuck away from me!" The man twisted, desperation giving him a burst of strength as he swung wildly. Beckett saw it coming, leaning just out of range before driving his elbow hard into the man's solar plexus. He staggered, grunting for air, and Beckett grabbed him by the shoulders, kneeing him in the groin to make the point stick.

"Who sent you?" he growled, as the man's groans echoed down the alley. "Was it Holden?"

The man bared his teeth, still doubled in pain. "Go to hell."

Beckett clicked his tongue. His patience was wearing thin. He grabbed a handful of the guy's hair, then grabbed his wrist, twisting his arm up behind his back. "You've got two choices," he snarled into his ear. "Talk, or this gets a lot worse for you."

"Not a chance. They'll… kill me."

Beckett tightened his grip. "Who do you work for? Are you part of Red's crew?"

He slammed the man against the wall, forcing him to face him. Beckett could see in his eyes he was on the right track. The guy shook his head, his breath coming in laboured bursts. He looked done, and for a second Beckett thought he might actually talk. But then with a sudden burst of energy the guy lunged, slamming his shoulder into Beckett's chest, hard enough to send him staggering back. Beckett pushed off the wall to right himself, but the man was already sprinting down the alley like his life depended on it.

Beckett cursed and gave chase, but the guy had a head start and knew the terrain. At the end of the alley he grabbed a metal cart stacked with broken-down boxes and yanked it into Beckett's path. Beckett sidestepped, but the cart clipped his leg, throwing him off balance. By the time he steadied himself, the guy had bolted through the back door of a casino, letting it slam shut behind him.

Beckett pushed through moments later, stepping into a large loading area where men in white uniforms were hauling food crates from the back of a truck. None of them gave him a second glance, too busy with their work to notice him or the man slipping through a door into the belly of the casino.

He'd lost him. But the encounter told him they were under heavier surveillance than he'd expected.

Beckett retraced his steps, brushing himself down as he returned to the alley. If they weren't careful, it wouldn't just be one clumsy thug tailing them next time. It would be an ambush. And he had no interest in walking into that blind.

He jogged back to the car, slowing as he reached the driver's side. Lee was sitting behind the wheel, alert but tense, her jaw stiff with worry. He tapped on the window and gave a quick wave before hurrying around to the passenger side.

"What the hell happened?" she asked, scanning him for injuries as he climbed in beside her.

He tugged the seatbelt across his chest and clicked it in place while gesturing for her to start the car. "Change of plan."

Chapter Thirty-Seven

Mack drained the last of his Miller, wiping his mouth with the back of his hand. It was thirsty work but he was almost there, having been at it since Beckett left, working to extract the last of the data from the device. Just a few more files to download and he'd have the full picture. Or so he hoped. So far the puzzle still had as many gaps as answers.

Reaching down, he grabbed another beer out of the small fridge at his feet, cracking it open on the edge of the desk and taking a slow sip, eyes still fixed on the screens in front of him.

He hunched forward, his eyes darting between his notes and the dog-eared map of southern Nevada on the wall, trying to tie the threads together. The main monitor showed a cascade of windows – tables of data, image files, PDFs pulled from the mobile data terminal. In the top corner of the screen, progress bars crawled towards completion as the final data was extracted.

On another monitor, satellite images depicted industrial sites in and around Vegas, but so far none matched with the delivery coordinates he'd discovered. On the final monitor, he was piecing together his findings in a more organised data sheet – financial records, manifests, purchase orders – fragments of information pulled from the partially decrypted device. Every so often he scribbled on his notepad, writing his key findings, things he needed to raise with Beckett when he returned.

He straightened as a fresh batch of data downloaded, a scan of a handwritten memo. It was all shorthand and code, but he recognised one series of numbers as geospatial coordinates. He punched them into his system, then paused, his attention shifting from the screen to the map, then back again. He jotted the numbers on his notepad, circling them a few times.

The location, an old uranium and copper mining site within the Grand Canyon, had now surfaced twice in the decrypted files. The shipment manifests showed heavy volumes moving through it. But there were no storage facilities down there. Or so he thought.

Maybe that was the point.

Mack gulped down another mouthful of beer. Two files were still downloading, their progress bars creeping forward like they had all the time in the world. A watched pot never boiled. A watched progress bar never finished.

He drank. He waited. By the time the files finally completed, there was less than a quarter of the bottle left.

"Okay then, let's see what we've got."

He clicked on the first file, pulling a face as the data filled the screen.

"Well… shit."

Another schematic filled the main screen. It appeared to show the same explosive device as they'd already uncovered but this was more complex and detailed. Mack squinted, dragging the image around with his mouse. To the untrained eye it might look like a bomb – a big one at that – but Mack had seen something like this before. The intricate wiring and unusual components pointed to something else.

But why…?

He leaned in, studying the details. Supercapacitors. Cryogenic cooling systems. Magnetic coils wrapped in exotic alloys. A table at the bottom displayed energy output projections well beyond the range of conventional explosives. And the materials didn't match the usual profile – no C4, no TNT, no signs of shrapnel casings or containment fields for directional blasts.

He scratched at the stubble on his chin. He needed a shave. But not now. Definitely not now.

"If this isn't about blowing things up… then what?"

He clicked off the schematics and pulled up another document showing a logistics manifest. He scan-read a list of more shipment dates and materials all routed to the same mining hub carved into the side of the Canyon. He shook his head. It wasn't hard evidence, but the pieces were starting to fall into place.

And it wasn't a pretty picture.

He was halfway through jotting down a more detailed set of coordinates when the alert alarm went off. He didn't react at first. Beckett and his cute little protégé were bound to show up eventually.

"Told you to wait for the call, but sure, why not?" he muttered, underlining and circling the coordinates.

He stretched his shoulders and leaned back, reaching for the beer. He had it to his lips when the same alarm sounded again. Each alert had a different tone and this same one going off again meant there was more than one vehicle approaching.

He lowered the bottle. That wasn't right.

Pulling the keyboard towards him, he brought up the security system.

Shit.

The monitor showed an overhead view of the desert surrounding his trailer, captured by a remote camera positioned on a high rock formation to the east. Three black SUVs were coming in fast, their sleek chassis showing high contrast in the fading light. Tinted windows concealed whoever was inside, but Mack's gut didn't need a visual. Every instinct told him this was bad.

Muscle memory kicked in as more alarms chimed and he moved into what he called his *retention protocol*, a routine he'd drilled countless times for the day when the knock finally came. He'd always known it would. That was the price of knowing too much and staying off the grid. He transferred the remaining files onto an external hard drive, the same one holding the rest of the data, then yanked the connection. Next, he flicked a few switches on his custom-built control panel, cutting power to the computer and all six monitors.

Grabbing his stack of notes, he set the hard drive on top before dropping to one knee, fingers tracing the hidden seam in the lino. Peeling it back, he revealed the reinforced steel box embedded in the trailer floor and pressed his thumb against the biometric lock. The latch clicked open and he pulled out the hard-shell case, placing the notes and hard drive inside, before securing everything without a trace. For good measure, he grabbed the edge of the small refrigerator and dragged it over the hidden compartment.

Intel secure, he got to his feet and moved through to the front of the trailer. Through the side window he could see the headlights of the SUVs cutting through the low haze of desert dust on the far side of the basin.

He had minutes. Maybe less.

Still following protocol, he made for his makeshift armoury, keying in the code with steady fingers. The doors swung open and he stepped back, taking a moment to inspect his babies.

He reached immediately for the AR-15, pulling it free from its bracket. Light, versatile, dependable – it'd always been his go-to. The custom red-dot sight was already zeroed, the collapsible stock perfect for tight spaces or open ground. He checked the chamber, cycled the bolt, and slung it over his shoulder.

Next he grabbed the Mossberg 590. As always, the weight of the pump-action shotgun felt reassuringly heavy in his grip. Reliable and unpretentious, the old girl was a workhorse. He thumbed a few slugs into the tube and stuffed a handful more into his pocket. Satisfied, he adjusted the sling so she hung snugly across his back.

To round it out, he slung an ammo belt packed with extra magazines and shells over his shoulder, Rambo-style. Not that Mack appreciated Hollywood's take on war – or vigilantes. They never got it right. Always made it look too easy.

He spared a glance at the twin Glocks nestled in their foam cutouts. Tempting, but unnecessary. If it got to the point where he needed a sidearm tonight, things had already gone to hell.

Stepping back, he scanned the cabinet one last time to make sure he hadn't missed anything. Three SUVs. Full of god knows what. Hired guns, most likely. Mercs. Or amateurs with big egos and just enough training to be dangerous. Either way, he was ready for them. He'd been gearing up for this moment for seven years. Maybe longer. Maybe his whole life.

With a grin, he closed the cabinet and turned to the cracked mirror over the sink. His reflection stared back, wild-eyed and ready, an arsenal strapped across his body. His smile widened as adrenaline surged through his veins.

"Butch and Sundance time, baby. Let's dance."

Chapter Thirty-Eight

Red cricked her neck as the SUV rolled to a stop twenty metres away from the trailer, the silver panels shining in the setting sun. She leaned forward, peering at it through the tinted windshield. She saw no movement from inside. No signs of life. But this was the place. It had to be.

As the rest of her crew pulled up, she unclipped the handheld radio from her vest and keyed the mic. "Form a wedge," she ordered. "The front vehicle will hold position, the rear two flank the sides and lock it down. Don't leave the rat a hole to crawl out of."

There was no acknowledgement, just the sound of engines revving as the SUVs shifted into formation. She watched them spread out in a shallow arc, boxing in the trailer from three sides. A classic pincer formation.

"What now, boss?" a voice crackled over the radio.

"On my signal," she replied, tapping her fingernails against the grip of the assault rifle resting between her knees. An HK416, customised with a holographic sight and vertical foregrip. Perfect for jobs like this, where the message needed to be loud, violent, and final.

She kept her eyes on the trailer. Still no movement. But if her intel was correct, he was in there. The scout she'd had trailing the Englishman and his little sidekick all day had followed them straight to this place.

And if her subsequent intel was correct, the owner would know he had visitors.

Red knew exactly who they were dealing with out here in this desolate corner of nowhere. A former CIA operative gone native. Paranoid and armed to the teeth, according to his nearest neighbours over in Jean. An odd guy, they'd said. A recluse.

Not that she cared who he was or how crazy he played it. A guy with too many guns was still just one guy. She'd put down tougher targets before.

She keyed the mic again. "Okay, let's open this up. Remember, we've got a psycho in there. Maybe two if the Brit stayed behind. But we take them alive. For now." She glanced at the two men in the back, rifles ready. "You good?"

They nodded in unison, the driver too. She turned back to the trailer and hit the mic. "On my count. Three... two..."

They moved on one, Red shoving her door open and swinging the HK416 into position as she climbed out. Dropping to one knee, using the open door for cover, she opened fire, stitching a burst across the trailer's front and blowing out the nearside tyre. She kept firing. The trailer's sides looked to be reinforced, but from this range her rounds punched through the metal.

Her men in the other SUVs followed suit, muzzle flashes

lighting up the dusky sky as their assault rifles unleashed a deafening storm of gunfire, hammering the trailer with relentless force.

With no immediate response, the gunfire began to wane. Red looked around, assessing their next move when the trailer door flew open, slamming against the frame. A man burst out, already firing, screaming like a banshee as he cut down two of her men in rapid succession, then sprinted for cover around the far side of the trailer.

A madman, just like she'd been told, but one who knew exactly what he was doing.

Red dropped to a crouch, taking cover behind the SUV as a burst of rounds shredded through the opposite door, cutting down the driver. To her left, one of her men sprinted for cover behind a rock, but he didn't make it half-way. The madman snapped off a single, surgical shot through the man's neck, sending him spinning into the dirt as he choked on his own blood.

Four men down. Gone in seconds.

Red gritted her teeth, pressing her back against the SUV as bullets tore into the vehicle's side. Her rifle was ready, but she didn't move just yet. She'd underestimated the crazy bastard and it had cost her.

The gunfire paused for half a breath as he ducked back behind the trailer.

"Hold your positions!" she hissed into the radio. "We need him alive."

But she realised now, this wasn't a man fighting for his life. The crazy bastard was already dead and he knew it. People with that mindset were always the most dangerous.

She adjusted her grip on the HK416 and leaned out, trading fire as the gunfight raged on. A relentless cacophony of rounds, slamming into metal and dirt, screaming through the air. Red barked commands into the radio, keeping her remaining men coordinated, but the prick wasn't giving them an inch.

She fired off sporadic, unaimed bursts towards the trailer, more out of frustration than strategy. But he kept coming, a relentless onslaught of firepower that seemed to be never-ending. Another of her men went down, clutching his chest as he collapsed against the wing of his SUV.

Red ducked back behind the open door, adrenaline surging as she ejected her spent magazine and slapped in a fresh one. "Keep him pinned!" she yelled, popping back up to take another shot.

She tracked him through her sight, catching his shoulder as he turned. He staggered but didn't fall, spinning to fire another burst, which spiderwebbed her windshield. He was a tough old bastard. But she'd got him rattled.

She waited, tracking him through the chaos until the opening she needed appeared. As he stepped out from behind the trailer she shot him again in the same shoulder, a better shot this time. He jerked sideways, his rifle dropping slightly. She shifted her aim and shot a zipper line down his left leg, taking out his kneecap and splintering his shin. He yelled out and this time he went down. Hard.

"Move!" she barked. Two of her remaining men sprinted towards the guy, weapons raised.

The madman squirmed, fumbling for a pump-action shotgun strapped to his back. But her men got there first and a boot to the face shut that idea down fast. Another hard kick to the ribs knocked the fight out of him with a pained grunt.

Got you.

Red sprang to her feet before taking a moment to

compose herself. It was over. She'd won. She could relax now.

Resting her rifle over her shoulder, she strolled casually over to the man, now held at gunpoint as he lay in a widening pool of blood. She didn't smile. Didn't throw out any clever lines. There was no satisfaction in this. Not yet.

But it was coming.

Chapter Thirty-Nine

Mack knew he wasn't walking out of this one.

But that didn't mean he was going to make it easy for the two pricks dragging him into his trailer. They were big guys, but as they hauled him up he thrashed and fought, dead-weighting his body while spitting blood and bile, calling them and their mothers every name under the sun. When that didn't slow them down, he latched onto the metal doorframe with his one good hand but they just prised it away.

"You pathetic bastards. That all ya got?"

His jaw felt loose, like it'd been knocked out of alignment, and a heavy pain radiated out from the bullet wounds in his shoulder, spreading down his arm like wildfire. He couldn't move his hand on that side. The nerves were shot; severed, maybe. But his left leg was worse. His knee was shattered beyond repair, and every jagged movement sent fresh stabs of agony ripping up through his pelvis. And that was just the big stuff. A hundred smaller injuries fought for attention in the background, layers of pain piling on. The blood soaking into his cargo shorts felt warm and sticky, which told him it was still flowing. Not exactly comforting.

He knew no one was coming to save him. Beckett hadn't called so was probably still tied up in the city, chasing his own leads. There was no one else. No saviours. No last-minute cavalry. Just him, a wounded man dragged into his trailer by a pack of hyenas.

But he wasn't about to roll over. Never.

It was clear these goons were here for the data terminal, and his only consolation was knowing he'd extracted everything useful from the device and secured it well enough to keep the bastards from getting it.

He sucked in a breath, tasting blood and dust, as they dragged him through the front of the trailer, crunching on broken glass and debris from where they'd blown in the windows during the firefight.

"Careful," he growled. "Don't make a mess."

The one on his left grunted and yanked him harder, slamming his shattered leg against the edge of the table. Pain speared through him, but he bit down on it, letting it fuel his anger rather than his despondency.

With the cooling fans switched off, the back of the trailer was hot and airless. At some point he'd lost his sliders, and his bare feet left two trails of blood on the linoleum.

"Stop being so prissy!" Mack snarled at them. "Dragging me around like I'm some goddamn doll. You want to finish me, do it already. Show some fucking initiative."

They didn't respond. Professional, these guys. No banter, no wisecracks. Just meatheads with a job to do. That almost pissed him off more. They dumped him unceremoniously into his chair at the rear of the trailer, the jolt sending fresh waves of white-hot pain through his body. He ground his teeth and forced himself upright. His shoulder was useless, the arm hanging limp, and his leg felt like it didn't belong to him anymore.

The men took up position, one behind him, the other standing to the right of the curtain. The one by the curtain drew a Glock and aimed it straight at Mack's face.

"How rude," Mack muttered.

His breath was laboured now, and he was covered in cold sweat. He was bleeding out, he knew it. But he wasn't going to die cowering.

The sound of more boots against the steel steps of the entrance drew his attention. He looked up as the curtain was whipped aside to reveal a woman with jet-black hair streaked with a bold slash of red. She had an athletic build, wearing combat fatigues tucked into black boots and a leather jacket hanging open over a fitted tactical vest.

Mack watched her as she gave each man a nod. The one behind him leaned in, yanking his arms behind the chair. Pain ripped through him, but he kept his focus on the woman.

She had good bone structure, but any hint of beauty was overshadowed by the meanness in her eyes and the tight set of her jaw. Her lips were painted black and she was wearing too much eye make-up. Too much for a gunfight, at least. He almost cracked a joke about it but held back.

On a good day, in the right bar with the right amount of Jim Beam inside him, she might have sparked some attraction in him.

Not today.

He didn't need to ask who she was. She was clearly the ringleader of this little band of mercs. The one pulling the strings.

She sauntered over, leaning down until her face was

inches from his. "You fought well, old man," she purred huskily. "But not well enough."

Mack blinked through the sweat dripping down his temple. It was a hackneyed line and he'd expected more from her, given the spectacular entrance and everything.

"Go to hell," was all he managed back.

The woman's expression didn't change. Maintaining eye contact, she reached out and jabbed a finger into the gunshot wound on his shoulder.

"Motherfucker!" The pain was blinding. Like molten metal poured straight into his flesh. Mack arched against the chair, a strangled yell ripping from his throat as the goon behind him held him down. The woman in black didn't let up, her finger digging deeper, clawing at tendons and raw nerves.

After what felt like a lifetime, she pulled her finger free and wagged it in his face, now dripping with his blood.

"Where are they?" she snarled, her breath hot against his skin. "The girl cop and the Englishman."

Mack's chest heaved as he forced his head up. He opened his mouth, letting his expression sag into something that resembled sorrow, maybe even submission. He held it just long enough to see the delight on her face. Then he grinned.

"Still – go to hell."

He got a slap around the face for that. More insulting than painful. He righted himself immediately, staring up at her with numb defiance.

"I don't have the patience for this, old man. Tell me where they are."

Mack forced a chuckle. It hurt to even do that. "You're starting to sound desperate, darling. You know that?"

"Fine." She nodded at the goon behind him and two

massive hands clamped down on his shoulders, pinning him to the chair. "You're tough. I get it," she continued, leaning back. "Loyal, too. But everyone has a limit."

She smashed her fist into his nose. The impact exploded through his sinuses, fireworks behind his eyes, his vision blurring. He turned his head away, struggling to breathe. Blood filled his mouth, thick and metallic. He spat it onto the floor at her feet.

She hit him again, this time catching his right eye. "Where are they?" she barked.

Mack blinked the room back into focus, squinting through the swelling, then gave her a big shit-eating grin. "You know you hit like a little kid."

The goon behind him grabbed a fistful of his hair, jerking his head back. The woman stepped closer and glared at him, breathing heavily, her fists clenched at her sides. Then she straightened and glanced around the space, taking in the powered-down monitors, the disconnected hard drives, the stacks of handwritten notes. A lifetime of paranoia, condensed into one suffocating little space.

"What do they know?" she asked again, her voice lower now but with a sharper edge.

Mack chuckled again, though it came out as more of a wheeze. "I don't know who or what you're talking about, darling. I'm just a humble guy doing his best to keep his hands clean. Just me and my snakes out here."

The woman turned, snatching a knife from her man's belt. In two strides she was in front of him, pressing the blade against his throat.

"Where. Are. They?"

Mack didn't flinch. "You think you scare me?" he rasped. "Lady, I've faced down worse than you in my life. Next question."

Her patience snapped. She drove the knife into his side, just below his ribs, and twisted.

"Shit! Fuck!" He gritted his teeth, jerking against the hands keeping him pinned as she slid the blade free.

He coughed, a fresh spatter of crimson speckling the desk in front of him. But when he lifted his head he was still smiling.

"Next question," he snarled.

The woman stepped back, holding the knife loose in front of her, like she was debating whether to stab him again. His defiance seemed to both infuriate and amuse her all at once. Good. If this was his curtain call, he might as well have some fun with it.

"You're going to tell me," she said. "One way or another."

Mack shrugged. "Then you'd better get a move on."

He watched her through half-lidded eyes as she paced, thinking. She seemed ice-cold calm once more. That wasn't a good thing.

Stepping closer, she reached into the thigh pocket of her cargo pants and made a show of pulling out what appeared to be a deck of cards.

"You going to do some tricks for me?" he asked, swallowing back the pain. "Or are we playing strip poker?"

Her mouth twisted into a malicious smile as she slid the cards from their box and began shuffling. After watching her do a few cuts, he realised it wasn't a regular deck. The illustrations on the front weren't of kings or queens, but of suns, magicians, and hanged men.

Tarot cards.

He scoffed. *Of all the bullshit.*

"Really?" he croaked. "Didn't have you pegged for a fortune teller."

She cut the deck again and drew the top card. Her smile spread as she turned it towards him.

The card showed a crumbling spire struck by lightning, flames spilling from its windows, figures falling. He grimaced, mostly from the pain, but also from the absurdity of it all.

"The Tower, huh?" he muttered. "Is this about my dick?"

"You really want to die funny, don't you?" she snapped, shoving the card in his face. "The Tower means danger, crisis. Destruction. The moment everything you've built comes crashing down around you."

Mack pursed his lips, trying to make a mocking noise like he was scared, but it just came out like a wet rasp. He glanced at the guy holding the Glock.

"That sounds bad, right?"

The man ignored him.

"And towers that don't speak?" the woman went on. "Towers that are silent and unhelpful? They fall harder. More painfully."

With a sudden shriek she lunged, driving the knife into his chest. The blade punched through muscle and bone into his lung. The right one. He felt it go, felt the pressure release and then come back tenfold. He tried to scream but nothing came out.

The woman was frenzied now, yanking the knife free and stabbing him again, lower this time, angling up into his gut. Spleen, kidneys, it didn't matter. Mack didn't feel anything anymore. That was the only relief as she kept going, his body jerking with each brutal strike. His vision blurred, darkness creeping in from the edges, but he forced himself to focus.

"Don't worry," the woman snarled, her lips brushing his

ear as she twisted the knife deep into his chest. "I'll find them. And when I do, it'll be just as painful. No one messes with Red Sorrento."

Mack laughed weakly, but it was more air than noise. He wasn't even sure what he was laughing at. Maybe nothing. Maybe everything. He just wanted to piss her off one last time. Maybe she'd lose it and he'd get away with a bullet in the head. Nice and quick. *Quicker.*

He gasped as the world around him started to fade, the trailer and his attacker's face blurring into one hazy smear. His body felt heavy as lead, and the numbness wasn't just from blood loss anymore.

This was it.

As the darkness closed in he forced himself to lean forward, lips trembling as he formed his final words.

"We know it's not a bomb…" he whispered, blood bubbling at the corner of his mouth. "But if Beckett finds you…" He coughed; the taste of iron thick in his throat. "You'll wish it was. You and Holden."

His body sagged against the chair, the last of his will pouring out with the blood pooling at his feet. His vision tunnelled until nothing hurt and nothing mattered. The world was gone. He'd done his part.

He let out a deep sigh as the black enveloped him. Then there was quiet.

Then he was gone.

Chapter Forty

Dusk had turned fully to night as Beckett and Lee left the city and sped along the winding highway. They hadn't spoken much since leaving the outskirts of Vegas, but there wasn't much to say. Both were lost in their thoughts, eager to find out if Mack had uncovered any new intel.

Beckett glanced at the clock on the dashboard. A few minutes past 7 p.m. Mack had been working on the encryption for best part of the day. If there was more to uncover, he'd have it by now

They'd find out soon enough.

The desert stretched out around them, pitch-black, the stars scattered across the sky like bullet holes in a sheet of steel. Lee kept her foot down, hugging the curve of the low metal barrier as the road snaked around a jagged outcrop of rock. As they rounded the bend, Beckett leaned forward, squinting through the windshield as the first glimpse of Mack's trailer came into view below.

His stomach dropped.

Shit.

The trailer was on fire. Even from this distance he could see the orange glow spilling across the desert, casting jagged shadows over the sand. Black smoke seeped out of the windows into the night sky.

"No. That can't be…" Lee gasped, as if saying it out loud might change what she was seeing. She leaned forward, pressing the gas harder.

"Wait," Beckett said, scanning the scene below. Three black SUVs were speeding away from the burning trailer, heading straight for the highway.

"What?" Lee asked, her foot easing off the pedal. "What is it?"

He pointed. "We've got company. They're moving this way."

Lee hit the brakes and stared at the SUVs for a moment, before glancing in the rearview mirror and then to the steep drop just outside her window. They were high up, nothing but a thin three-foot steel barrier between them and oblivion.

"We need to turn around," Beckett told her. "Now."

Lee grimaced as she stared at the steep drop-off to their left. "Here? Are you serious?"

"I can do it if you'd rather."

She straightened. "No. I've got it."

Beckett leaned over and cut the headlights. Lee shot him a quick look but nodded, understanding. Gritting her teeth, she cranked the wheel to full lock, reversing until the back bumper kissed the rock face, then easing forward to the low barrier, gravel skittering off into the void below. Her breathing was shallow and she kept making a clicking sound with her teeth, but she didn't waver.

Beckett raised his head to get a better look as she

reversed then shifted the wheel and edged forward again. "You're good. Keep coming."

She'd almost turned it around when the front tyres skidded on loose gravel, and for a heartbeat the vehicle felt like it was teetering. Lee froze, her foot hovering over the brake.

"Don't stop," Beckett told her. "Momentum, or we'll slide."

Lee snorted, shoved it into reverse and cranked the wheel hard. A second later the tyres found solid ground and they inched forward, the car now facing the way they'd come.

Beckett glanced over his shoulder. "Nicely done."

"Yeah, well," she muttered, brushing hair from her face, "try not to make me do that again." She jammed it into first and they sped back down the road, the glow of the fire disappearing behind the hill.

Beckett twisted in his seat, checking the rearview mirror. No sign of the SUVs yet. "Keep going," he said. "I saw a dirt track about half a mile back. Should take us down to the flats."

"You're sure?"

"Sure enough."

The track appeared just as he'd said, a dusty strip carved into the hillside. Lee slowed, handling the turn like she'd done it a hundred times, swinging the car around the hairpin bend and onto the uneven trail. It was barely wide enough for the car, the edges crumbling into darkness on one side, but it was their only option.

"Can I at least have some light?" she asked, flipping the headlights back on as the car lurched and bucked over the rough terrain.

Beckett didn't argue. Down here they were mostly hidden from the road. Whoever was in those SUVs – Red and her crew, most likely – would have to be looking hard to spot them.

They hit the bottom of the hill, the ground levelling out into open plains. In the distance the trailer burned like a beacon, but the SUVs were nowhere in sight.

Lee kept her foot down as they raced across the dusty flats, the acrid stench of smoke growing more intense by the second. As she swung the car around to the front of the trailer, they saw the bodies and bullet casings, the blood and shattered glass. Beckett counted five dead in total, all in black jeans and tactical vests. Red's crew.

No sign of Mack.

Before the car had fully stopped, Beckett was out, leaving his door hanging open. "Wait here," he shouted over his shoulder. "I mean it."

"Please be careful!" Lee called after him, but it barely registered.

Moving purely on instinct he leapt up the steps and into the trailer, where the heat hit him like a sledgehammer. It was like stepping into a pizza oven, but he could tell the fire was fresh, the flames still searching for fuel.

He had a minute. Maybe less.

Ripping off his shirt, he grabbed Mack's half-full coffee jug and poured the lukewarm liquid over the fabric until it was soaked, then he wrapped the wet shirt around his mouth and nose.

Flames were licking up the thick curtain dividing Mack's living and working spaces. Beckett braced himself and yanked it back, ducking as a wave of smoke poured out, clawing at his eyes.

Back here the heat was ferocious. Flames chewed at the

walls and crept along the ceiling as he forced his way forward, boots crunching on shattered glass.

Mack was slumped in his chair, eyes closed. Beckett didn't need to check for a pulse to know he was dead. The multiple stab wounds told him that, as did the blood that had turned his shirt and cargo shorts dark red.

Damn it.

There was no time to mourn his old friend. That would come later if he made it out of here. The air was growing hotter, the flames larger. He gagged as he moved over to the desk, the chemical burn of melted plastic crawling down his throat. Another half minute and the whole place would go up.

Cupping his hand over his mouth and nose, he assessed Mack's setup. Everything looked powered down rather than fried from the fire, and there was no sign of the device. That gave him hope. The wily old dog would have seen the intruders coming and activated his protocols.

Good old Mack.

Beckett grabbed the back of the chair Mack was slumped in and dragged him aside, then knelt inspecting the space under the desk. The fridge was new. Practical, but also an extra layer of security for what he knew was hidden underneath. Pushing through the heat, he gripped the small appliance and heaved it aside. Leaning back in, his fingers skimmed over the worn lino until he found the hidden seam. He hooked it with a nail and peeled it back to reveal the metal strongbox embedded in the floor.

"Ah… bugger." The lock mechanism lit up as he pressed the corner. A biometric scanner. Fingerprint required. And not his.

He glanced up at Mack's body in the chair, his large frame limp and uncooperative.

Shit.

He knew what needed to happen. He hated it, but Mack wasn't exactly in any position to argue.

Pushing the thought aside, Beckett jumped up and hurried to the front of the trailer, rummaging through drawers until he found a large serrated knife. Not ideal, but it would do.

Back at Mack's side, he grabbed the man's limp right hand and set it on the desk.

"Sorry, mate," he muttered, bracing himself.

Shoving his humanity aside, focusing solely on survival, he sawed through the flesh and tendon at the base of Mack's palm. After a few strokes he hit the saddle joint, grabbed the thumb and popped it free. One final cut and he was holding Mack's severed thumb.

He pressed it to the scanner, unlocked the metal box, and lifted out the hard-shell case. Inside it was exactly what he'd hoped for – the mobile data terminal, the hard drive Mack had been downloading files onto, and a stack of notes on yellow legal paper. Beckett scooped up the whole lot and jumped to his feet.

The smoke was nearly floor-to-ceiling now. Beckett made a quick detour to Mack's gun cabinet, noting the door wasn't fully closed and prying it open with a few hard tugs. He grabbed two assault rifles, two Glocks, and a small utility satchel hanging on the back of the door. He stuffed everything inside the satchel, as well as the Glocks, ammo, and a pair of night vision binoculars. He had what he needed. Time to move.

The fire was consuming the trailer with ravenous intensity as he pushed through the thick smoke and burst out the door. The air outside was easier to breathe but still thick with hot ash. He kept the damp shirt pressed to his mouth as he sprinted for the car.

Lee was waiting by the driver's door, her expression tense. "Thank god!" she gasped, relief cutting through her voice as she climbed behind the wheel.

Beckett tossed the weapons and satchel into the back seat before climbing in beside her. "Mack's dead," he said.

She nodded like she knew. "Bastards." She glanced at his soot-streaked torso and the blood on his hands as she started the engine. "What now?"

"Your place," he said, tapping the dashboard. "Those SUVs looked like they had somewhere else to be, so we should be in the clear for a while. Let's see what Mack left us."

She didn't need telling twice. As they drove away, the trailer let out a sharp pop as a gas canister exploded, taking out the shack next door and sending flames surging higher into the night sky. Mack's snakes were all dead. So was he. That was how it was sometimes.

Beckett didn't look back.

Chapter Forty-One

Lee kept her eyes on the road as much as possible, but Beckett was shirtless and her gaze kept drifting to the jagged scar on the side of his chest. She hadn't noticed it before, she couldn't have been looking at it from the right angle. It was kind of bulbous and purplish, and could only have been caused by something like a knife, or shrapnel. It was just another reminder that John Beckett was far from the uncomplicated, reasonable man she wanted him to be.

She forced her attention back to the road, chewing on her lip. The smell of smoke still lingered in her throat. Should she say something? Try to get him to open up? Apologise? It would feel hollow, pointless even, but she also knew that Mack was dead because of her. Because of this fucking conspiracy she'd dragged Beckett into. All at once she felt stupid, guilty and – not for the first time – like a pathetic child playing at being a cop.

She stole another glance at Beckett.

Did he hate her now?

Maybe he should.

She pulled into the small lot outside her apartment and killed the engine. Now was the time to say something, to break the tension. But before she could, Beckett was already out of the car, the satchel from Mack's place slung over his shoulder. She watched him, frozen, as he dragged the rifles from the back seat, popped the trunk and placed them inside.

"Leave them there for tonight," was all he said. Then he slammed the lid and headed for the building.

She followed him, unlocked the front door, and led him up the stairs and down the corridor to her apartment. All without a word from either of them.

Inside, the familiar smell of her apartment did nothing to settle her nerves. If anything, it put her more on edge, making her wonder if she smelled the same, of coffee and lavender. There were worse things to smell of, she told herself. Though maybe all this was just her brain latching onto something trivial to distract from the guilt and anxiety swirling beneath it all.

She turned to Beckett, trying to force out the words that had been lodged in her throat since they left the trailer. "John, listen, I—"

"It's okay, Maggie."

He smiled, and there he was – the composed, considerate man she needed right now. The heaviness of everything he'd seen and done was still there, of course, pressing down on him like it was pressing on her. But her heart swelled a little at how he acknowledged her pain and guilt, trying to ease it in the only way he knew how.

"Mack knew what he was signing up for," he added. "He lived life on his own terms, and I'd like to think he died that way too."

Lee swallowed and nodded, but it didn't help. She still

felt crappy. And sad. Crappy and sad – it was familiar ground, at least.

"And now we've got these." Beckett pulled Mack's hard drive and notepad from the satchel. "He did his part. Now it's on us to finish the job."

She gestured to her laptop sitting on the chair cushion. "Can we use my old machine to see what's on there?"

"I'm hoping so," he said, placing the items on the coffee table. "But I'd kill for a shower first."

"Yeah, of course," she blurted, glancing at his bare torso. "Though I don't have any… spare shirts…" She trailed off, her cheeks warming. But Beckett didn't seem to notice.

"Don't worry about it," he said. "I'll pick something up in the morning. Too late now. We need rest."

She walked with him over to the bathroom door. Beside it, her bedroom door was slightly ajar and she was suddenly very aware that Beckett hadn't seen inside it yet. As she caught sight of the unmade bed, the pile of laundry on the chair, and the collection of dirty mugs on the nightstand, her self-consciousness only grew.

"I'll… um… get you a towel."

Her cheeks flushed warmer as she yanked the bathroom door open a little too fast. She pulled a towel from the cabinet and handed it to him.

"Thank you."

"I'll just be… through here."

He nodded, watching her with a half-smile as she backed out of the room and pulled the door closed behind her.

At the sound of running water she slipped into her bedroom, trying to focus on tidying. She grabbed the pile of laundry from the chair and stuffed it into the closet, then smoothed the sheets over the bed, doing her best to ignore the fact that a thin partition wall and a shower curtain were all that separated her from Beckett's naked body.

"Get a grip," she muttered, dropping into the chair at her vanity and tilting the mirror towards her. She wished she hadn't. Her reflection stared back, damp hair sticking to her forehead, eyes tired and rimmed with red. She pushed her hair back and straightened her posture, but it didn't help. So she just sat there, staring at her reflection without really seeing it. It had been one hell of a week.

She was still sitting there when Beckett emerged from the bathroom. She caught sight of him through the doorway and got up to join him in the front room. He'd pulled the jeans back on, but his hair was damp and the warmth of the shower still clung to his clean skin.

His shoulders rippled as he ran a hand through his wet hair, more scars revealing themselves as he lifted his arm.

"Thanks," he said as she moved past him. "I needed that."

"No worries." She tried not to look at him without it seeming weird. "The laptop is unlocked so why don't you see what we've got? I'm going to grab a shower too."

Beckett sat and picked up the laptop as she headed into the bathroom. In the doorway she paused, her hand resting on the frame as she glanced back. He was already in full-on Beckett mode. Eyes sharp and alert, jaw clenched, completely absorbed as he read through Mack's notes.

She wondered how he did it – kept going when everything felt impossible. If he wasn't here, she'd have fallen apart long before now.

But he was here.

And she was grateful for that.

Shaking off the thought, she closed the bathroom door

and stripped, bundling her clothes into a pile in the corner. Avoiding her reflection in the mirror, she turned on the shower and stepped in. The water was scalding as it hit her skin but she didn't care. In a way she liked it. She scrubbed away at herself, wishing she could scrape off the stress and guilt along with the dirt and sand. When she was done, she leaned her head under the jets and squeezed her eyes shut, trying to block out everything but the sensation of water on her skin.

After a few minutes, she switched off the shower and dried herself, wrapping her largest towel around her. Clutching the bundle of dirty clothes, she shuffled through into her bedroom, doing her best to ignore Beckett still sitting on the couch. In her room she pulled on a clean pair of joggers and a loose t-shirt, rubbing her damp hair with a fresh towel as she headed back to the front room.

Beckett's attention was flicking between the laptop and the yellow notepad. "Not a bomb," he muttered. "What the hell does that mean?"

Lee stood by the wall, watching him. Her focus shifted quickly from his muscular torso to his face. He still looked unshakeable, but there was a tension in his expression now that made her uneasy. She crossed the room and sat beside him.

He didn't look up, too engrossed in trying to decipher Mack's messy scrawl. "This all has to mean something," he said, half to himself. He flipped another page, scanning it before tossing it aside. "Damn it, Mack. Couldn't you have been more organised?"

Lee pressed her lips together. Mack probably had a plan to explain everything to them himself. Only, he never got the chance. She reached for one of the discarded pages, squinting at the mess of scribbles. The handwriting was almost illegible, but on the reverse side, written in the corner, was a clear list of numbers.

"Have you seen these?" she asked, holding the page out to Beckett.

He leaned in, frowning as he scanned the numbers. "Interesting."

He opened a new tab on the laptop and typed the first sequence into a map search. Within seconds, an aerial view of the west rim of the Grand Canyon appeared, with a red pin marking a spot just north of Peach Springs.

Lee stared at it. "What is that?"

Beckett zoomed in. "An old mine by the looks of it. Could be where they're taking the components once they've been delivered to the various hubs. Got to keep them somewhere and this makes sense. Out of town, off the radar."

"You mean that's where they're assembling the bomb?"

"If it is a bomb."

She twisted to face him. "What do you mean?"

He shook his head, his frown deepening as he stared at Mack's notes. "I'm not sure yet."

Lee let the words hang. She wanted to press him but there was something else she needed to say, and if she didn't do it now she'd lose her nerve.

"I was thinking," she started, glancing at Sarah Connor for a little borrowed confidence, "maybe we should tell Chief Higson what we know." She waited for Beckett to respond; when he didn't, she kept going. "He might be able to help, and a bit of backup wouldn't hurt."

"There is no backup," Beckett muttered, still preoccupied with the notes. "Not for this. We already know Holden's got people in his pocket – cops, FBI agents, probably politicians. We can't trust anyone." He rubbed a hand across his mouth, staring at something in Mack's notes like he'd seen a ghost. "And it gets worse."

Lee groaned. "Jesus. I don't want to know." She slumped back against the couch, staring up at the ceiling.

Beckett turned to look at her. "You can walk away," he said quietly. "No one would blame you."

She met his gaze. He meant it. He was giving her an out.

For half a second she considered it. But one look at the wall where her lineup of badass women stared back sharpened her resolve.

No. She'd been in this from the start. She wanted this.

"I'm seeing this through," she told him.

He smiled. It was clear he could see she meant it. But sitting here in her apartment, the adrenaline of the day fading into a dull ache, everything felt too close.

"I just wish we knew what we were dealing with," she said.

"We will," he replied. "It's all in here. We just have to piece it together."

"And what if we're too late? What if we fail? What if I mess everything up for you?"

Beckett held her gaze. "Give yourself more credit, Maggie. You've been great up to now."

She shrugged, staring at her hands clasped in her lap. "You have. I'm just along for the ride. Slowing you down if anything."

When she looked up again, Beckett was still watching her. "I couldn't do this without you. You're a lot more able than you think."

"I don't feel it," she whispered.

"Well, let me tell you a secret," he said, a wry grin

spreading across his lips. "You don't have to feel it. You just have to keep going."

Lee smiled, her heart beating faster now. She didn't know what to say, so she didn't say anything. The silence stretched. Not awkward, just charged.

Beckett reached for her hand and it sent a jolt through her like a live wire. Her instinct was to pull back, but she didn't. "You should get some sleep," he said.

"We both should," she replied, though neither of them moved.

Then Beckett leaned forward, and without thinking she mirrored him. The space between them shrank until it was almost non-existent.

"Maggie..." he started, but whatever he was about to say was lost as her lips met his.

The kiss wasn't rushed or frantic. It was soft. Certain. And for one brief, perfect moment, the chaos of the world faded away.

They pulled back at the same time, both catching their breath. "I'm sorry," Beckett whispered.

"Don't be." She held his gaze.

"That was..."

"Yeah," she agreed, her heart thudding. Then, scrambling for something to say, she added, "But I think I should get some sleep. I need some rest before tomorrow. Big day, I imagine." She stared at him without blinking, wondering what the hell she was saying – because every part of her wanted to do the exact opposite.

Beckett smiled like he understood. "Probably for the best." He turned back to the notes. "I'll keep going for a bit longer, but I'll turn in soon myself."

She stood, and was wondering if she could come back from this when he glanced up.

"Okay if I take the couch again?"

"Oh." She nodded, wanting to say so much more than, "Yeah. Sure."

"Thanks."

Her mind was racing, but Beckett's attention had already shifted back to the laptop and Mack's notes. She needed to get her head back in the game, too.

Leaning down to grab her damp towel, she caught a glimpse of the map of the Grand Canyon still open on the screen – a blunt reminder of what lay ahead. Straightening, her gaze shifted to the notes in Beckett's hands, landing on a single word scrawled in big capital letters and underlined twice:

CONSORTIUM.

"What does that mean?" she asked.

Beckett puffed out his cheeks, his expression darkening. "Trust me, Maggie," he said, "you really don't want to know."

Chapter Forty-Two

Beckett wasn't sure what to make of the kiss with Lee last night. It had come out of nowhere – unexpected, but not unwelcome. Far from it actually. But neither of them mentioned it as they prepped for the day ahead, both acting as if nothing had happened. Which was for the best. The air between them was charged, but there were bigger things to focus on.

Much bigger.

Beckett hadn't slept much. Too much on his mind, too tuned in to every sound outside, ready for the wrong kind of visitor. So far, hiding out at Lee's apartment had kept them off Red's radar, but they were pushing their luck.

Physically, though, he was fine. He'd run jobs like this more times than he could count, relying on nothing but adrenaline, his wits and caffeine to keep him going.

They spent the morning poring over maps, Mack's notes spread across Lee's coffee table like pieces of a jigsaw puzzle. Somewhere in the planning, Beckett gave her a crash course on handling an assault rifle. They were holed up in her apartment, so she didn't actually fire it, but she seemed to grasp the theory well enough, her nervous energy only slightly masking her determination to get it right. She claimed she'd be fine if it came down to it, but Beckett hoped it wouldn't get that far. His plan was to keep things as covert as possible.

It was the afternoon by the time they were in her car, heading towards the mining site Mack had flagged on the edge of the Grand Canyon. The two assault rifles were in the footwell between his legs, along with the satchel containing boxes of ammunition and a hastily packed med kit. Beckett held Lee's phone rested on his thigh, the map software showing the route. The red pin marking their destination was close now, less than a mile away. As the highway narrowed up ahead he pinched at the screen, zooming in on the area.

"Slow down," he said. "We're getting close."

Lee eased off the gas, and as they rounded a bend the terrain suddenly shifted, the smooth asphalt giving way to sand and rocks.

"There." He pointed towards a rock formation about a hundred metres from the roadside. "Pull up behind it. We'll go the rest on foot, but it should keep the car out of sight."

"Got it."

Lee steered off the road and slowed to a stop behind the largest section of rock.

"You okay?" he asked.

She nodded, but she didn't look okay.

He offered her what he hoped was a reassuring smile. "One step at a time. We can do this."

The dry desert air wrapped around him as he climbed out and unloaded the equipment. Despite the car's air con, sweat was already forming on his back. He adjusted his new brown shirt, the one Lee had picked up for him that morning along with a pair of beige pants. She came around the car, brushing a strand of hair from her damp forehead. She was wearing similar colours as him, a cream short-sleeved shirt, chocolate-coloured leggings, and tan hiking boots. Their makeshift nod to desert camo. Not perfect, but a hell of a lot better than the *High Roller* shirt.

Their eyes met, and she gave him a nervous smile.

"Let's go," he said, pulling the binoculars from the satchel before slinging it and the rifles over his shoulder.

He led the way along the ridge, keeping close to a row of rocks that stretched down towards the site. The terrain was uneven, the sun beating overhead making every step feel ten times more difficult. Lee did her best to match his pace, stifling yelps as she skidded on loose stones. As they neared the site, Beckett stopped and motioned for her to hunker down in a shallow alcove worn into the rock.

"Wait here," he whispered, handing her one of the assault rifles. "If you see anyone with a gun, shoot them. Don't even think about it."

She took the weapon and nodded. "Where are you going?"

"For a better look."

He leaned his rifle and the satchel against the rock, slung the binoculars around his neck, and climbed onto a flat section overlooking the point the map had led them to. As he moved to the edge, he realised the binoculars were almost unnecessary. They were closer than he'd expected, the mine entrance less than seventy metres away.

Outside it, three shipping containers were arranged in a staggered formation, like a wonky 'Z', their metal walls painted a dull brown that blended with the surroundings. Two prefab huts stood further along, and the ground around them was a churned-up mix of dirt and sand, criss-crossed with cables running towards a generator on the far side.

"What's going on?" Lee whispered.

Beckett lifted the binoculars, zeroing in on the details. "A lot of activity," he murmured, watching as men moved crates back and forth. "Seems we picked the right day. Or the wrong one."

He moved his focus around in a slow arc, scanning more of the area. A truck was parked near the largest container, its rear door rolled up. There were more men here – he counted twelve in total – all armed, all dressed in dark cloth-ing. Two were unloading wooden crates, hauling them towards the container, while others stood guard or super-vised. Every so often one of the men reappeared from inside, tossing an empty crate onto a growing pile near the truck.

He also clocked three open-topped jeeps parked up on this side of the site, not far from the containers. Beyond them, a helicopter sat on a cleared patch of ground. As he watched, another figure emerged from the main container. A woman. She seemed to be in charge, barking orders at the men carrying the crates.

She was dressed all in black, her hair the same colour except for a single streak of crimson slashing through it like a warning flare.

Red.

Had to be.

Beckett slid back down the rock and removed the binoc-ulars as Lee looked up, tense with anticipation.

"Red, the one that Jarvis mentioned," he said. "She's here, running the show."

"It's definitely her? Holden's fixer?"

"I'd say so." A thought came to him; that this Red person was probably the one who'd killed Mack. A quiet rage twisted in his gut, but he pushed it down, locking it away for later. "She's got a crew with her. They're moving crates into one of the containers. If I had to guess, they're assembling the bomb here."

Although, according to Mack it wasn't a bomb. He'd written as much: *Not a bomb.* But whatever it was, it was going to be some kind of problem. And judging by the pace of the operation, they were close to finishing it.

"What now?" Lee asked.

"We need to get closer," he said. "I need to see exactly what they're moving and how far along they are."

Lee nodded. "Let's do it."

Beckett slung his assault rifle over his shoulder and adjusted the strap. He checked his ammo, making sure everything was secure and within reach, then gave Lee a quick once-over. "Keep the safety on until you need it," he whispered. "And remember – short bursts. Don't waste ammo."

She nodded again, gripping the rifle tight.

Together they moved out, staying low and close to the rocks. The ground sloped gently downward, the loose dirt shifting under their feet as Beckett led the way, every nerve in his body alert for movement. They paused behind a cluster of boulders. Beckett signalled for Lee to stay put while he peered around the edge. All clear. He waved her forward.

The shipping containers and prefab huts were now less than a hundred yards away, the faces of the men clearer. Beckett led them parallel to the main container, staying hidden behind it until they reached one of the huts. They crouched behind it, catching their breath, the corrugated metal warm against their backs.

The structure shielded them from view, but the sounds of boots crunching on gravel and voices barking orders were too close for comfort. Beckett leaned out, mapping out a route to the next hut. If he could make it there, unseen, he'd have a clear view inside the shipping containers.

Risky, but doable. He turned back to Lee, signalling with a few hand gestures that he was moving closer and that she should stay put. She understood, her hand tightening around her rifle. He could see the fear in her eyes, but she was fighting it with all she had and he appreciated that. They exchanged nods and Beckett edged forward, ready to move. But then – movement to his left. A lone sentry stepped out from a cluster of rocks. Beckett froze.

Too late. He'd seen them.

Shit.

The man cried out. "Red! Intruders! East perimeter!"

His hand shot to the pistol at his side. Beckett took him out with a headshot before he had the chance to draw.

But the damage was done. As the man's body hit the ground, all hell broke loose.

"Move!" Beckett growled, grabbing Lee's hand and yanking her towards the row of jeeps. They sprinted, heads down, as bullets whizzed past, shouts and gunfire blending into a chaotic roar.

The jeeps were unguarded, and as they reached the first one Beckett spotted the keys dangling in the ignition. A bit of luck for once, though it tracked with standard protocol – military vehicles were often left with the keys in for rapid deployment. Like now. He threw himself into the driver's seat, cranking the engine as Lee scrambled in beside him.

"Go, go, go!" she yelled.

Beckett didn't need telling twice. He slammed the accelerator to the floor, the jeep surging forward in a spray of gravel and dust. Gunfire erupted behind them, bullets thudding into the dirt and pinging off the rear panels as he pushed the vehicle harder.

"They're on us!" Lee shouted, twisting in her seat to fire a burst at the men scrambling into the other jeeps.

"Hold them off as best you can," Beckett yelled, swerving onto a narrow trail that snaked into a small canyon running almost parallel to its much grander sibling. The terrain was brutal, dotted with jagged rocks and a steep drop-off on one side.

"Hold on," he snapped, yanking the wheel to dodge a boulder. The tyres screeched, the jeep skidding as they careened around a sharp bend, cliffs rising on both sides. Lee braced against the door, gritting her teeth as she steadied her rifle.

Beckett glanced in the rearview mirror as the remaining jeeps roared into the canyon, hot on their tail. The lead vehicle was closing fast, its driver weaving effortlessly through the rocky terrain while the gunman in the passenger seat opened fire.

"Keep them busy!" Beckett barked.

"I'm trying!" Lee shouted back, firing off another burst over the roll bar.

The canyon twisted sharply again, forcing Beckett to brake hard before accelerating into a straight stretch. The lead jeep stayed with them, eating up the distance with every second. As they hit a flat, open patch, Beckett yanked the wheel hard to the right, sending the jeep into a controlled skid, kicking up a thick cloud of dust and gravel. It bought them a few precious seconds as their pursuers slowed to hold steady.

"They're falling back!" Lee yelled. But any relief was short-lived as a jeep burst through the dust cloud, the gunman already firing. A round punched through the passenger door, missing Lee by inches. She flinched, then snapped into action, raising her rifle and squeezing off a heavy burst. Their pursuer's windshield spiderwebbed with cracks and the jeep veered away before slamming into a jagged outcrop.

"Good shooting," Beckett yelled, struggling to keep the jeep steady.

"Think it was a fluke," Lee replied, breathless but grinning.

"Well, keep doing it."

Up ahead the trail forked. One path leading to open ground, the other snaking steeply upwards to higher ground. Beckett made a split-second call and steered left, the engine growling in protest as they began to climb the sheer terrain.

Behind them the last jeep stayed in pursuit, its gunner leaning out and firing wildly. Lee returned fire, squeezing the trigger like she had an endless supply of ammo, spraying rounds with reckless abandon. She actually seemed to be enjoying herself now, her fear morphing into something else – adrenaline, maybe even exhilaration.

Beckett glanced at her, half impressed, half concerned. Confidence was good. Overconfidence could get them both killed.

"Got the bastards!"

Beckett glanced back just in time to see the pursuing jeep's front tyre blow out. He flicked his gaze between the road ahead and the chaos behind as the vehicle swerved hard, slammed into the canyon wall, and tipped over the edge. It tumbled down, smashing into jagged rocks ten feet below. The old vehicle crumpled on impact, folding the men into the twisted frame. If they weren't dead, they'd wish they were.

"That's all of them," Lee yelled, her voice shaky.

"But it's not," Beckett replied. "Red and the others are still back there. With whatever's in that shipping container."

Lee's face fell, the adrenaline rush fading fast. But there was no time for pep talks. They had to keep moving.

At the top of the incline Beckett swung the jeep around in a sharp turn, gravel spraying in all directions. As he straightened it out, he glanced over at Lee. Her face was streaked with sweat and grime, and her fingers trembled as she ejected the spent mag like he'd shown her. She was rattled, but there was a steely determination beneath it all. A resolve he'd seen before in people who'd faced the worst and kept going.

He felt it too, a tightening in his chest as he drove them back towards the site. This wasn't about surveillance anymore. It wasn't about gathering intel. It was about brute force. About stopping these people before they could make it to Vegas.

Lee reloaded her rifle, handling it even better than she had that morning. Sweat dripped into her eyes, but she wiped it away with the back of her hand and caught Beckett's gaze. She gave him a firm nod before snapping the mag into place.

That was all he needed to see. She was doing good, holding her own.

And they could do this.

But the fight was far from over.

Chapter Forty-Three

Beckett floored the accelerator, the jeep bouncing over the uneven ground as they sped back towards the shipping containers. He gripped the wheel tight, keeping the vehicle steady while his mind raced through worst-case scenarios. When they'd scouted the site earlier, Red and her crew had looked ready to move. Now he feared they already had.

Lee sat rigid in the passenger seat, her rifle resting across the door panel, eyes flicking between the road ahead and the side mirror.

"Get ready," Beckett told her. "This could get ugly."

But as the site came into view his heart sank, his suspicions realised. The site was empty. No movement. No guards. No sound beyond the rumble of the jeep's engine. He steered in a wide arc around the front of the first container, keeping his distance. Experience told him that just because you couldn't see the enemy didn't mean it was time to relax and let your guard down.

But the site was deserted.

"Damn it," Lee snarled. "We're too late."

Beckett edged the jeep forward, just enough to check the crux of the Z-formation. But as they passed the next container, two vans roared into view, engines screaming. They sped past the jeep and skidded to a halt, blocking the only open path back.

Shit. Ambush.

Beckett slammed on the brakes as gunmen spilled out from between the containers thirty metres ahead. Bullets thudded into the jeep, ripping through the metal and shredding the ground around them.

They ducked low behind the windshield and Beckett grabbed his rifle and the satchel.

"They've got us pinned!" Lee shouted, raising her rifle and firing a burst towards the attackers. Her aim was still steady, but she wasn't used to this level of pressure.

"Out! Now!" Beckett barked.

He released the door, firing over the hood to push the gunmen back. "Let's go." He slid out, using the door as a shield while laying down cover fire. As Lee scrambled after him, he stayed close, his body pressed against hers as they darted towards the narrow gap between the containers, bullets whizzing past.

Once there, Beckett peered around the edge, tracking the gunmen's movements. They were closing in fast, fanning out to cut off all escape routes. He fired a few controlled bursts, dropping one man before ducking back as rounds pinged off the container's edge. Metal sparks seared his forearm, but he didn't feel it.

As he squeezed off more retaliatory fire, he spotted Red emerging from behind the far container, rifle drawn, flanked by her remaining men. He leant back under cover, assessing the situation. The staggered layout of the shipping containers formed walls on both sides, with only narrow gaps between them. There was no way to manoeuvre the jeep through now, and advancing on foot wasn't an option.

Lee knelt beside him, leaning out to fire, her shots forcing two attackers to dive behind a stack of crates. One managed to fire back, the bullet slamming into the container inches from her head.

"We need to move," Beckett yelled. Turning, he spotted a cluster of rocks twenty metres away. From there they'd have a clearer view of the main site. And rock was better than metal when it came to stopping bullets. "Follow me," he told her. "Backwards in a straight line, shooting as we go."

She gave him a sharp look. "You lead the way."

He stepped out, laying down a barrage of suppressive fire as he moved, careful not to lose his footing on the loose gravel. Lee matched his pace, firing in bursts. Bullets zoomed past them, a few dangerously close, but they kept moving until they reached the rocks.

Hunkering down, they took a moment to catch their breath and reload. Beckett slammed a fresh mag into his rifle.

"This is bad," Lee gasped, wiping sweat from her forehead. "I can't believe we're still alive."

"Don't talk that way," Beckett said. "Get out of your head. Stay in the moment. You can do this. You're doing great."

She gave a quick, shaky nod, tightening her grip on the rifle. Beckett leaned around the side of the rock, firing off another burst while he assessed the scene. Red and her crew were still holding their ground, repositioning themselves facing the rocks. Lee rejoined the fight, squeezing off more rounds as bullets ripped through the air. Beckett dropped another target, opening up the man's chest and sending him jerking back against one of the containers.

A sudden flurry of gunfire forced Beckett to take cover. Bullets hammered the rock where his head had been seconds earlier, sending shards of stone flying. Lee hunched beside him and they exchanged a glance. She looked scared. He didn't blame her. Right now this could go either way. They needed a new move.

As the return fire died down, a husky voice cut through the chaos.

"Hey Englishman," Red called out. "You know you've lost this, right? You and that cop are already dead. Just like your pathetic friend. He died pissing his pants."

Beckett gritted his teeth but didn't respond.

"You really think you're going to stop this?" Red continued, her voice edging closer. "Everything is already in motion. You've got nothing. No plan. No hope. You've lost. Give up."

Beckett closed his eyes for half a second, shutting her out. She was trying to get in his head. She wanted him emotional, reckless, easier to kill. But at times like this Beckett didn't do emotion. He did instinct. He did tactics.

He did what he did best.

Motioning for Lee to stay low, he shuffled around to her side for a better angle. He spotted a man trying to flank them and took him down with a clean zipper up his neck and head.

"Can you shut her up?" Lee yelled, as Red kept taunting them.

"I'm working on it." He leaned out, taking aim, but Red had already ducked behind the nearest container.

Crouching low, rifle pressed to his shoulder, he tracked her through the narrow gap. She was speaking quickly, motioning to the rocks behind him and Lee. Two of her men broke off, using the uneven terrain as cover. They were trying to box them in. If they made it behind the ridge, he and Lee would be pinned from both sides with nowhere to go.

This was getting worse by the second.

He turned to Lee, who was pressed against the rock, rifle at the ready. She met his gaze with a wicked grin. "I've got a plan," she said.

Before he could stop her, she darted from cover, keeping low as she sprinted behind a line of boulders a few feet away. Beckett held his breath as she ran. Smart move – she was using the terrain to outflank the two men.

Smart, but risky.

He stayed locked on her position until she disappeared unseen behind the rocks. A second later the first of the two men circling them emerged from around the furthest container. As he stalked past, Lee popped up behind him. Two quick shots dropped him before he could turn.

The second man saw it happen and aimed at Lee, but Beckett leaned out and took him down clean and fast. That left Red and six more. But they couldn't stay pinned here. He glanced over. Lee had taken up a defensive position further along the boulders. She caught his eye, and he gestured for her to cover him. He had a plan of his own.

Running in a straight line away from his cover, he veered around the base of the Z formed by the shipping containers, angling to approach the remaining gunmen in a wide arc. It was a reckless move, leaving him exposed for several crucial steps. But as long as Lee kept them occupied, it might work.

At the far end of the first container he spotted two of Red's men using the adjacent one for cover, positioned at opposite corners. They were fixated on Lee, gunfire masking the sound of his approach.

In one swift motion he slipped an arm around the first man's throat and clamped a hand over his mouth. The man thrashed, boots scraping against the dirt, but his panic was drowned beneath the roar of gunfire. Beckett tightened his grip, twisting the man's head one way and his body the other. The sickening pop-crack of bone severing spinal cord vibrated through his arms, and the man went limp. Beckett eased him down, slipping a knife from the sheath on his belt before moving on.

The second man was firing wildly at the rocks where Lee was positioned. Beckett slung his rifle over his shoulder, raised the knife, and slipped out of cover. He closed the distance fast, driving the blade up through the man's ribs.

The guy let out a sharp gasp, cut short as the blade pierced his lungs. Beckett held the knife steady for a second, then yanked it free and slit his throat in one clean motion. With his hand clamped over the man's mouth for good measure, he lowered him to the dirt. He was dead before he hit the ground.

Two more down.

Red was running out of men, but Beckett knew better than to get comfortable. He retraced his steps along the container wall, paused at the corner to ensure he was clear, then stepped out.

Lee was still behind the rocks, firing controlled bursts as he'd hoped, keeping Red's remaining men pinned. Staying low, he raced around the first line of boulders and skidded in beside her, a barrage of bullets pounding into the dirt behind him. Too close.

"We've got them scared," she shouted over the gunfire.

Beckett nodded, but his focus snapped to movement at

the far end of the site. Two of Red's men had emerged from the main container, carrying a large, tarp-wrapped object towards the lead truck.

Bugger.

He adjusted his rifle, tracking their movements as they hefted the bundle up the truck's ramp and disappeared inside. That was it. The bomb.

"Damn it.

Pushing down his frustration he exhaled, steadied himself, and shifted his aim. The truck was Red's only way out of here, and he wasn't about to let that happen.

He sighted in on the front tyres and fired twice, each shot hitting its mark. The heavy vehicle sagged onto its rims, tilting under its own weight. At the far end of the site, Red spun sharply at the sound, glaring in Beckett's direction through the gap in the containers. Moments later the two men reappeared from the back of the truck, glancing around in confusion.

Beckett twisted away as a hail of bullets peppered the rock inches from his head. When he risked a glance, Red was gesturing wildly at the helicopter, shouting for her men to load the device there instead. The two men disappeared inside the truck, while Red and the remaining gunmen provided covering fire, keeping Beckett and Lee behind the rocks.

"We've got to stop them!" she yelled. But as she leaned out, her shoulder snapped back in a burst of red.

"Maggie!" Beckett was at her side in seconds, dragging her out of the line of fire. He propped her up against the rock to inspect the damage. The bullet had punched clean through, leaving a bloody exit wound in the back of her shoulder. Painful, but not fatal.

She winced but her eyes were fierce. "I'm fine," she gasped. "Stop them. Get the bomb."

Beckett hesitated, but the determination in her face made the decision for him. Snatching up his rifle, he broke cover and sprinted towards the helicopter as its rotors picked up speed, churning the air into a storm of noise and dust.

Firing as he ran, Beckett forced the last two operatives back towards the chopper. They scrambled to climb aboard. He dropped to one knee beside a container, bracing his rifle as they hauled themselves into the open side door. Their weight threw off the balance, the helicopter rocking unevenly as it fought to lift off.

He took aim, firing at the fuselage, but he was too far away to make the bullets count.

No matter. The men were still struggling to pull themselves inside, stalling its ascent. Beckett was about to advance when Red appeared in the chopper's doorway, her black hair whipping around her face. Without hesitation, she drew her pistol and shot both men in the head, their bodies tumbling backwards into the dirt.

Beckett rushed forward, but the unburdened chopper lurched higher, forcing him back.

As it rose, Red leaned out, locking eyes with him. A smirk tugged at her lips. "See you in Vegas, English."

The chopper banked hard and disappeared over the ridge. Beckett tracked it for a few seconds before lowering his weapon. No point in wasting ammo on frustration; that was rookie behaviour. But that didn't stop him from feeling every bit of it.

He turned and sprinted back to where Lee was slumped against the boulder, her hand pressed to her shoulder. Blood seeped through her fingers, but her expression was more anger than pain.

"I'm fine," she snapped before he could ask. "Damn it, we almost had them."

He crouched beside her, staring at the horizon where the helicopter had disappeared.

"Novara's big event is tomorrow," she muttered, letting her head rest back against the rock. "They're going to be in Vegas. With the bomb."

"I know," Beckett said, meeting her gaze. "So we'll just have to stop them there instead."

Chapter Forty-Four

Night had fallen as Beckett walked back across the motel parking lot, alert to any sign of trouble. It was a typical Vegas dive – run-down and ancient – with a flickering neon sign above the office, and three flights of rooms built around the central lot. The kind of place you only stayed if you had nowhere else to go, which made it grimly fitting for their situation.

Staying at Lee's apartment wasn't an option anymore. If Red's crew had tracked them to Mack's trailer, her place wouldn't be safe either. After a quick stop to grab a change of clothes, the hard drive, Mack's notes and her laptop, they'd found this place. For the past hour, Beckett had been holed up in a diner across the street, sipping bad coffee and keeping watch on their room. No one had followed. They were safe. For now.

He climbed the rickety stairwell to the second floor and made his way down the landing to their room. Outside he knocked twice, then a third time. "It's me."

A few seconds later, Lee eased the door open. Her hair

was wet and she was wrapped in a towel. She moved aside and Beckett entered, shutting the door behind him and locking it before checking the curtains at the window.

When he turned, Lee was sitting on the furthest of the two single beds, watching him with a strange expression on her face. Not totally despondent, but not far off.

"How are you feeling?" he asked, nodding to the clean white dressing on her shoulder.

"Okay," she said. "It was hard to wash my hair without getting it wet, but I sort of managed."

Beckett smiled, moving closer. He'd patched her up after they got here, using the supplies they'd brought from her medicine cabinet. It wasn't the best patch-up job he'd ever done, but it was enough.

"Can I check it?" he asked.

"Sure." She leaned forward, the movement making her towel slip lower. Beckett kept his focus on the wound, forcing his mind to stay where it belonged, and using his fingertips to peel back the dressing. The skin was still swollen and raw, but the stitches were holding and the iodine had done its job. No sign of infection.

"It's healing," he said, replacing the dressing. "You might have a scar though, I'm afraid."

"It'll match yours."

Beckett met her eyes, unsure if she was joking. From the look on her face, she wasn't sure either. He straightened, running a hand through his hair as Lee adjusted the towel around her. The moment felt brittle. Not so much uncomfortable, but heavy with everything left unsaid. He stared at the bandage, thoughts colliding. Their kiss. Mack. The fact that he'd let Red get away. Lee had held her own and he was impressed by both her resolve and her skillset. But he should have done more. He should have kept her safe. That was his job.

She must have sensed the tension in him because she made a point of holding his gaze. "I'm a big girl, you know, John," she said. "I was the one who dragged you into this mess, remember?"

Beckett nodded, offering her the start of a smile as he turned and sat on the edge of the other bed, facing away. He appreciated the sentiment, but she couldn't disguise the anger in her voice. Whether it was directed at him or herself it didn't matter. Mack was dead. Lee had been shot.

This was on him.

He leaned forward, elbows on his knees, staring into the carpet. Somewhere in the worn pile he saw Mack's body. He saw Red, smirking as the helicopter flew away. His anger was like a physical sensation, like a boot on his chest. People had been dying around him his whole career. He knew it was part of the job and always told himself it wasn't his fault. But it never stuck.

"Why won't you talk to me?"

Lee's voice snapped him from his thoughts. He looked up to see her standing now, her arms folded across her chest.

She glared at him. "You've shut down. *Again*. Do I not matter to you?"

"Of course," he whispered.

"Then let me in! Geez. We need each other. Now more than ever." She tilted her head, her expression softening. "I'm scared, okay? Terrified. I regret ever thinking this was some kind of adventure. I regret dragging you into it. I regret all of it."

Beckett looked away, unsure what to say. "It's not you," he muttered. "You did great. Don't be hard on yourself."

He reached for the low unit beneath the wall-mounted TV, pulling the laptop, notes, and hard drive onto his lap. It was late, and they were both exhausted, but there was no time to rest. He had to understand what Novara was up to.

Lee huffed pointedly as he opened the laptop, but he ignored it. Plugging in the hard drive, he spread Mack's notes across the bed beside him, his focus bouncing between the files on the screen and the scrawled handwriting.

Every few seconds he paused, leaned back slightly, and rubbed his thumb across his jaw, as if this motion might shake loose the answers.

Not a bomb.

Yet it looked like a bomb. Red's men had treated it like a bomb.

So what the hell was it?

The question gnawed at him as he examined the schematics for the tenth time, trying to marry what was on screen with the fragments of information in the notes. Mack could no doubt have explained it all in a few minutes, but without him to decipher the scrawl, Beckett was working blind.

One note stood out. *Tower roof.*

If this referred to the bomb site, surely it couldn't mean the Novara Logistics Tower. Holden wouldn't blow himself up.

So which tower? The Strat?

He felt like he was on the edge of something, but he needed more. Something concrete. He exhaled, trying to focus. This is what Beckett hated more than anything, being in the dark, feeling helpless.

The bed dipped as Lee sat beside him, close enough he could feel the warmth of her freshly showered skin. She smelled good, of soap and cherries. He braced for the inevitable questions, but she just leaned in, watching the screen over his shoulder.

"You should take a break," she said finally. "You're going to burn yourself out."

"I have to get to the bottom of it," he muttered. "There's not much time left."

"I know. And you will. But right now you need to rest. Just for an hour or two." She placed her hand on his arm. "You know, sometimes when I'm stuck on something, it's only when I step away that the answer comes to me."

Beckett forced a smile. "I get that, I do. But there's something here. Something Mack wanted us to see. I just need—" He stopped, shaking his head, frustrated with himself.

Lee reached over and shut the laptop. "Please, John. We've been through enough for one day."

He stared at the closed laptop, his hands still resting on either side of it. He wanted to carry on, but the exhaustion pulling at him made it hard to argue. They sat in silence for a while, side by side on the bed, the only sound the *vub-vub-vub* of the bathroom fan. It sounded as if it was on its way out.

"Do you ever let anyone get close?" Lee asked.

He shrugged. "It's hard for me to."

"Isn't that a lonely existence?"

Another shrug. "It's what I signed up for."

Lee edged closer, the curve of her breast brushing against his arm through the towel. He tensed but didn't move.

"You told me you weren't... in that line of work anymore," she said.

He turned to look at her, their faces only inches apart.

"I'm not," he replied. "But that doesn't mean it's over.

Not really." He paused, wondering how much he could and should say. "I don't let people get close because they don't survive. Not in my world."

Lee frowned, then smiled, then looked away. "I get that," she said, fidgeting with her hands. "I wonder sometimes if I'm cut out for this world too. I know it's nothing like what you're up against, but I hate it at Sierra Heights. I hate what low-level police work has done to the chief, even Jarvis. Everyone starts out as a cop wanting to do good, to make a difference. I really believe that. I have to. But somewhere along the line I guess they stop believing it's possible. The bad guys always win so why not join them? I don't want to end up like that."

Beckett smiled, tempted to tell her it wasn't always like that, but he stayed silent. What did he know about how the world worked, anyway? He'd spent most of his adult life in the shadows, far removed from normal people and their lives.

But one thing was undeniable – Maggie Lee was nothing like the smalltown beat cop he'd met just days earlier. They stared at each other, the silence no longer heavy but electric, alive with possibility. Beckett reached out, his fingers tentatively brushing against her cheek. She didn't pull away, and despite everything, in that instant nothing else mattered. A rush of dizziness hit him, a reckless abandon he hadn't allowed himself in years. But for once he didn't care. For once he wasn't the lone wolf running from ghosts.

He leaned in, so did she, the space between them dissolving until their lips met. Their kiss this time was not gentle, but enthusiastic and intense, a surge of fiery passion in the eye of the storm. When they came up for air Lee's hands moved to his shirt, her fingers trembling but determined as she worked the buttons loose.

His heart pounded as he got to his feet. Lee rose with him, helping him shrug off his shirt before stepping back and letting her towel drop to the floor. For a moment she looked uncertain, almost hesitant, but Beckett met her gaze and held it, taking in her strength, her beauty. Her nervousness melted away as she stepped forward, wrapping her arms around his neck. Their lips met again, a spark catching fire.

Then Beckett lifted her into his arms, and carried her to the bed.

Chapter Forty-Five

The covers were warm and smelled like him. Like last night. A good smell. A happy smell. Lee drifted awake slowly, caught between sleep and awareness. Her body felt light but sated, and more relaxed than it had in a long time. Yet beneath the surface something else stirred. A strange tangle of emotions teasing at her consciousness. Satisfaction, grogginess, contentment... and then, creeping in at the edges, a whisper of unease.

She turned lazily, her hand brushing the cool sheet beside her. And a sharp pain jolted through her shoulder.

Shit.

Her eyes snapped open, fully awake in an instant as the last few days came rushing back. She pushed herself up, eyes darting around the room. The other bed had been slept in, but it was empty.

"John?"

Where the hell was he?

Panic flared for half a second before Beckett emerged from the bathroom, a towel slung low around his hips, droplets of water clinging to his chest and shoulders. The tension in her chest eased as more memories formed. Pleasant ones this time. Very pleasant indeed.

He smiled. "Good morning."

She swallowed back her grogginess. "Hey. Morning."

She stretched and the sheets fell away, revealing her naked breasts. Instinctively she grabbed for the covers and then felt silly. Beckett laughed, but it was all warmth and she chuckled along with him, a shared acknowledgement that last night had been good. Very good. A stolen moment, anchoring them in passion and humanity amidst the terror and chaos. It was what they'd both needed, and maybe it was more than that, but she didn't think either of them would be ready to unpack it just yet.

"Did you sleep well?" he asked.

She smiled, still a little dreamy. "Very well. You?"

"I did. Once I moved beds."

She laughed. "Are you implying I hog the covers?"

"I'm not implying anything. But you should get up. We've got work to do."

Lee groaned, fumbling for her watch. She found it on the floor beside the bed. "Eight a.m.?" She dropped back onto the pillow with a sigh. "Shit. I'm meant to be back on shift in an hour."

"Call in sick," he said from across the room, and she frowned.

"God, I haven't called in sick since... ever. The chief will hit the roof, what with Jarvis and everything."

"He'll get over it. You have more important things to do today."

She glanced over at him. He was pulling on his pants, seeming not to care they were covered in dirt.. That was John Beckett for you – practical to the core, unconcerned with things like appearances. Yet as he slipped on his shirt and buttoned it, something about him seemed different. He still looked like a man carrying the weight of the world on his shoulders, but now he seemed ready to fight it rather than let it crush him. She studied him, lips twitching into a small smile.

Was that her doing?

"You're very chirpy this morning," she teased.

He smiled. "I've got something to show you."

"Oh yeah? Something else?" She raised a flirtatious eyebrow. But his grin faded, replaced by his usual stoic calm as he reached for the laptop.

"This," he said, sitting beside her and opening the lid. The screen was already cluttered with open browser tabs and files from Mack's hard drive. "I woke just after dawn with an idea I wanted to look into. So I got up and asked reception for the wi-fi code."

Lee snorted, sitting up to get a better look. "This place has wi-fi?"

"It's spotty. But enough for what I needed."

He pulled up a few articles and what looked like a stockbroker's site. Lee watched him as he worked, the fire she'd first noticed in him now burning white-hot again. It had faded over the last few days, but now it was back, intense and unwavering. And she had to admit it was exciting to witness.

Especially after what they'd done…

No, Maggie. Not now.

She tucked her hair behind her ears and forced herself to focus as Beckett tapped on the screen. "You see, we had it all wrong," he told her. "This isn't about blowing anything up."

Lee considered it, trying to match his enthusiasm.

"What is it about?"

Beckett brought up a new page, which looked to be a financial report, and scrolled halfway down.

"Novara aren't planning to destroy Vegas," he said. "They're going to shut it down. Erase it. The digital part, at least."

Lee frowned. "What do you mean?"

Beckett turned the laptop around so she could see. A bold headline dominated the screen:

Novara Logistics Builds Vegas Data Center in Multi-Billion-Dollar Deal

Lee pulled the laptop closer, skimming the article at speed, searching for the pot of gold Beckett had found. The covers slipped down around her again but she was too engrossed in what she was reading to care.

She could feel Beckett watching her, waiting for her to catch up. "Look here," he said, tapping on a subheading halfway down.

Sensitive Trading Platforms Hosted in Vanguard Server Farms

"These server farms are the backbone of trading platforms used by banks and hedge funds," he said. "Novara controls them now."

Lee nodded, trying to process it all. It was still early and there was a lot to take in. "So, what?" she said. "They're holding on to them for leverage?"

"Not quite." He took the laptop back and pulled up another browser tab showing what looked like a finance blog. "This is where it gets interesting. A few weeks ago there was a 'minor' power surge at one of these facilities. It barely made the news. But look here." He pointed to a comment under the main thread.

Lee read it. Then re-read it. The author seemed to be speculating on the ripple effect the outage had caused on trading platforms.

"Market volatility," Beckett said, as if it explained everything. "Panic trading. Billions in losses. If you ask me, that wasn't a coincidence. It was a test run."

Lee frowned. He'd pretty much lost her now. "A test run for what?"

"Mack was right," he said. "That thing – the machine, as Gates was calling it – it's not a bomb. It's an EMP device."

Lee blinked. "EMP?"

"Electromagnetic pulse," he explained. "A powerful enough device can emit a burst of energy that fries anything electrical within a few kilometres. Phones, computers, vehicles. If it's got a circuit, it's dead. Think of it as a blackout, but permanent."

"Jesus," Lee muttered, leaning back against the headboard. "And that thing is big enough?"

"Easily."

Lee sat up straighter, the pieces starting to align in her mind. "You think Holden wants to take out his own server farms? But why?"

"Money," Beckett said. "Power. The usual stuff. These server farms are housed in a huge state-of-the-art facility just a block from their head office, right off the Strip. According to Mack's notes, they're planning to detonate the EMP on the roof of the Novara Logistics Tower. If they pull it off, they'll wipe out their entire financial infrastructure in one hit."

He shook his head with a bitter chuckle. "The irony is,

they're the ones storing their own financial data for their lenders. It's a blatant conflict of interest, but a company as big and powerful as Novara has no doubt found a way to make it legal, or at least bury it deep enough that no one's looking. But this isn't just about wiping their debts. Look at this."

He swiped at the trackpad, pulling up a complex-looking graph.

"This is market activity from yesterday. Someone moved billions into short positions, dumping futures, betting against major indices. That's not normal trading behaviour. That's someone who knows the market is about to take a hit and is positioning themselves to profit when it does."

Lee's eyes widened. "They're betting on the collapse they're engineering."

"I'm almost certain of it," he replied. "An EMP that size will wipe out everything – financial records, trade history, debts, holdings – all gone in an instant. Chaos in the markets. And while everyone else scrambles, Novara and their associates – an organisation called The Consortium – will rake in close to a trillion dollars. And they'll use it to tighten their grip on everything that matters."

Lee's face hardened. "But how do they avoid getting caught? Something like this will leave big footprints. The FBI, Homeland Security – they'll dig into this and Holden will be exposed."

"They have to have accounted for that." Beckett tapped Mack's notes, then gestured to the laptop. "They've built in layers of misdirection. Novara isn't pulling this off them-selves. Everything's been outsourced to shell companies, and independent contractors and subcontractors. No single group knows what they're really part of. One company manufactures components; another transports them; then

Holden's hired goons manage the installation. No one who could roll on him has the full picture. Plausible deniability at every level."

"Conniving bastard."

"You said it." He paused, clicking over to a map of Vegas and its surrounding areas. "And I guarantee they've lined up a perfect scapegoat. A device like this is cutting edge, sure, but it's not unique. Rogue states, black-market arms dealers, extremist groups – any one of them could build something similar. My guess? Holden and his associates have already planted the evidence, fed just enough misinformation to ensure that when the dust settles the blame falls exactly where they want it."

Lee thought of the imposing man they'd met in the penthouse office of the Novara Logistics Tower, and could easily believe every word Beckett said was true. "So, you're saying they'll make it look like… what? A terrorist attack?"

"Most likely. The first thing investigators will look at is motive. Who benefits? On paper, Novara looks like the victim here. It's their server farms, their reputation on the line. And if the trail conveniently leads to a radical group or a foreign power, investigators get an easy target, one that fits the narrative. Something clean. Something the authorities will accept without question."

"And Holden?" Lee asked.

"He starts fresh with billions in his pocket. Him and The Consortium."

"I've never heard of these people," Lee said. "Who the hell are they?"

Beckett sighed heavily through his nose. "A very powerful organisation. But secretive. They had their grubby fingerprints on most of the cases I worked in the last six years of my career but I never got a real handle on them. I got close once, but the layers of protection around Novara are nothing compared to the maze of shell companies, rogue actors, and buried money shielding The Consortium. No one at MI6 or the CIA has any real clue who's pulling the strings. And after this, they'll be even more untouchable."

Her shoulders sagged. Sitting here naked and still sleepy, the weight of it all felt unbearable. "And they'll just get away with it."

"If we don't stop them." He closed the laptop and bowed his head.

"Well at least…" she said, cringing even as she spoke, "it won't be as bad as an actual bomb going off."

Beckett shot her a look. "It could be. An EMP that size won't just take out the data centres. The blast radius will knock out power grids and anything running on electricity. That means electric cars, rail systems, hospital equipment, even air traffic control."

She stared at the closed laptop, struggling to find her words. "The whole city could come crashing down. Literally."

Beckett nodded. "While Novara and The Consortium are chasing their billions, thousands could die in the fallout. Maybe more. Planes would lose navigation and maybe even fall out of the sky. Trains would derail. Traffic lights stop working. All with the emergency services offline. This might not be a bomb in the traditional sense, but the devastation would be just as bad. Maybe even worse."

This time words failed her completely. She opened her mouth but nothing came out. The quiet hum of the bathroom fan seemed deafening suddenly.

"The event is this afternoon," Beckett continued. "There'll be people from all over the world attending the expo. It's the perfect cover. That's when it's going to happen. We have to stop them."

"Just me and you?"

He nodded. "We can't trust anyone. Not now. The Consortium has people everywhere – law enforcement, government, even the intelligence agencies. If we tip anyone off, they'll know."

"But how do we stop something this big? It feels impossible."

Beckett got to his feet. "We don't have a choice. If they pull this off, it won't end here. They'll do it again. Bigger. Worse. They'll hold entire countries hostage. The world." His jaw tightened. "And on top of that, they've killed innocent people. They killed my friend. And they've pissed me off."

She stared at him, searching for a crack in his composure, some indication he wasn't as sure as he seemed. But there was nothing. Just deep, unshakeable resolve.

She lifted her chin. "Okay then. Let's do it."

Chapter Forty-Six

Lucian Holden stood at the window of his office, gazing down at the city he was about to ruin. Las Vegas stretched out beneath him, pulsing with its usual frenetic energy, the mid-afternoon sun shimmering off mirrored skyscrapers in every direction. From his vantage point up here in Novara Logistics Tower, it all looked so small. So manageable. Just like the people in it, oblivious to the chaos he was about to unleash.

He smiled at the thought, catching sight of his reflection in the darkened glass. He was looking sharp as hell and the Des Merrion supreme bespoke suit he'd commissioned for the occasion was perfect. Made from handwoven Italian silk, in midnight blue with custom gold stitching, it was power and elegance personified. His pocket square alone cost more than most people earned in a month. And that pleased him.

Turning from the window, Holden crossed the room to the handleless, brushed-steel door on the far wall. He pressed his palm to the biometric panel beside it and waited. A faint beep confirmed his identity and the door slid open to reveal a room bathed in cool blue light.

Inside, ten massive screens lined the walls, each displaying live feeds from various points around the building. Holden moved into the centre of the display, that familiar sense of control settling over him. This was his command centre, where he kept a close eye on those who worked for him.

Five of the screens were focused on the event space, where technicians were finalising setups, adjusting lighting, and testing the sound system. The stage in the main room was a picture of modern design, with a subtle charcoal backdrop and stark spotlights, the perfect setting for the day's star attraction – Holden himself. He was breaking convention today, delivering his keynote at the start of the day rather than the end. But there was a good reason for that, and it wasn't just because he thought of himself as a shrewd disrupter and iconoclast.

In the exhibition hall, staff bustled between booths, setting up tables and chairs, oblivious to what was coming. Downstairs in the lobby, the buzz of anticipation from the VIP guests was palpable even through the muted speakers.

"Idiots," he muttered.

They thought they were here for innovation, for progress. What they didn't know was they were just part of the plan, pawns on a board they didn't even know existed.

Another screen displayed the rooftop, where his private helicopter sat waiting, primed for immediate departure. The pilot was already in the cockpit, looking weary as he flipped through a manual. Holden couldn't have cared less if the guy was bored out of his mind. He was being paid to wait, and as long as he was ready to go when the time came, that was all that mattered.

A Line in the Sand

His smile widened. Yes. Everything was in place. All he had to do now was play his part and watch the world fall into chaos.

Leaving the control room he strode back into the main suite, stopping at the mirrored wall by the door. He adjusted his gold cufflinks – custom pieces in the shape of early microchips – and then examined the skin on his neck, satisfied that his daily hour of facial yoga was paying off.

This was how power looked.

Refined. Immaculate. Unstoppable.

He straightened his tie, his thoughts drifting to what lay ahead. He was an old hand at these things now, so his keynote speech gave him no concern. He'd speak for thirty-five minutes, just enough time to dazzle the audience and reinforce his status as the mastermind behind Novara's meteoric rise. Then he'd leave. Quietly. Efficiently. Thirty minutes after that, the device would activate and Vegas would collapse into darkness – both literally and figuratively.

The thought sent another smile spreading across his tight features, which was no mean feat considering all the collagen injections, dermal fillers, buccal fat removal, microneedling, and chemical peels he'd subjected himself to recently. Not to mention the monthly vampire facials, cryotherapy sessions, and bioelectric skin-tightening treatments he swore by.

But he was particularly pleased that the plasma-rich protein injections into his scalp were starting to show results. He was looking younger by the day. Soon his own mother wouldn't recognise him.

If he ever could be bothered to visit her.

His grin widened, the same rush he'd felt when he made

his first million flooding through him. The hunger for more. For his new life to begin.

"Soon," he told his reflection.

Because this wasn't just a masterstroke of engineering or finance. This was art. The EMP would cripple the city, its pulse erasing financial records, obliterating digital footprints, and plunging millions into chaos. Planes grounded. Traffic systems frozen. Communications severed. A modern city gutted in an instant.

And while governments scrambled and markets imploded, Holden and The Consortium would sit back and reap the rewards. The insider trades were already in motion, with billions riding on the collapse. Others would bear the losses. The profits would be his.

But for Holden it wasn't about the money. Hell, his personal fortune sat at three hundred and six billion last time he checked, he didn't need more. This was about his legacy. About reach. And most of all, it was about proving himself to the people who mattered.

The Consortium had promised that once this was done he would finally take his place at their table, a seat he had coveted ever since he first got wind of the elusive, all-powerful network.

Joining The Consortium wasn't just a business move; it was an ascension. They were the architects of the world's future, and he was on the cusp of becoming one of them.

Today was the day he proved himself. Not just to them. To himself.

The idea of failure didn't even cross his mind. He was untouchable. Every detail accounted for. Every risk mitigated.

He adjusted his watch, the polished face catching the light.

Two hours. Plenty of time.

He walked to his desk and eased into the grand leather chair, grounding himself for a moment before reaching for the custom-built laptop sitting on top. This was a machine not intended for casual use. He'd had it made last month, its casing constructed from matte carbon fibre for maximum durability and heat resistance. Inside, it housed a solid-state drive with hardware-level encryption, impervious to brute-force attacks or unauthorised access. There was no standard operating system, no frills, no webcam, no microphone – nothing that could leave him vulnerable. Just a stripped-down interface optimised for security.

He leaned over the backlit keyboard and logged in. The laptop was connected to a private satellite uplink, bypassing all public networks entirely. Once inside, he launched a specialised browser loaded with advanced encryption protocols – the kind that fragmented data into meaningless shards if anyone tried to intercept it. Moments later the screen flashed to life, displaying The Consortium's plain-text forum. Its minimalist design mimicked a simple Terminal window, an ideal façade for covert communication. Holden navigated to a hidden subdirectory and typed in the randomised access code he'd committed to memory.

The screen went dark for a moment, then a single message flashed up in green, old-school computer text.

C5: Status update?

Holden smirked as he typed his reply.

NLH: All good. Device armed. Countdown initiated. Two hours until activation.

A brief pause followed. He imagined whoever was on the other end taking a moment to appreciate how smoothly things were moving. Another message arrived.

C5: All contingencies in place. Proceed without deviation. No room for error.

Holden's smirk deepened. *Contingencies.* The Consortium's operatives were meticulous, their plans layered with misdirection and fail-safes. Even if someone managed to piece together the operation, they'd be chasing phantoms. It was all set. It was happening.

Another message flashed onscreen.

C5: The dominoes fall. Will you be clear of the board?

Holden shook his head. They appeared to be checking up on him, but fair enough. He hadn't fully proven himself yet. But today he would.

He typed back.

NLH: All on schedule. Thirty minutes post-event I'll be airborne. Vegas will be a memory.

Another pause, and then the screen refreshed.

C5: Remember. One brick sets the wall. This is just the foundation. The structure is coming.

He stared at the words, a slow thrill coursing through him. He was part of something far bigger than himself, something that dwarfed even his own ambitions. The Consortium had plans far beyond the Strip. Vegas was just the beginning. A test. A proof of concept. And he was the architect of its success.

He typed one final message.

NLH: In two hours, the lights go out.

No further message came. But that was The Consortium's way. Efficient. To the point. He stared at the screen for a moment longer, then shut the laptop, leaving the embedded protocols to scrub away every trace of their exchange.

Getting to his feet, he smoothed his jacket and checked his watch. The countdown ticked steadily in the back of his mind. Two hours. Soon it would be time to take the stage and deliver his speech.

After that he would cement his place in history.

He walked to the window, taking one last look at the city below. The clueless masses had no idea they were about to witness the birth of a new world order. *His* world order. The culmination of everything he'd worked for.

As he left his suite and stepped into the elevator, he allowed himself one last indulgent smile. The pieces were in place. The game was his to win. And there wasn't a damn thing anyone could do to stop him.

Showtime.

Chapter Forty-Seven

The area in front of the Novara Logistics Tower was a hive of activity, its expansive marble forecourt swarming with attendees eager to enter the imposing building. At the entrance, guests collected lanyards and expo packs from neatly arranged tables, while those already registered exchanged pleasantries and snapped selfies in front of a towering digital banner that read *Novaratech 25* in massive letters.

It was just past 3 p.m. and the expo was in full swing, but lobby security was tight. Only a handful of people were allowed through at a time, their bags checked before they were ushered between large white metal detectors.

Beckett and Lee stood on one side of the forecourt, watching the waves of tech bros, startup hopefuls, and industry titans milling around, waiting their turn.

"This is it," Beckett said, meeting Lee's gaze. Her cheeks were flushed and she seemed anxious. "You okay?"

"Yep. No turning back now."

She looked the part, like she belonged in this tech-savvy

crowd. Smartly dressed in a white button-down shirt tucked into dark green trousers, a pair of beige pumps completing the look. Her blonde hair was pulled back into a high pony-tail and her make-up minimal.

Beckett had also made the effort, having picked up a suit an hour ago in a department store further down the Strip. It was the first time he'd worn one since his last undercover mission. Back then, though, it had been a bespoke three-piece, the kind of attire befitting for the right-hand man of the boss of an organised crime gang. Today's suit wasn't that. It was a loose, off-the-rack number, worn over a pale blue polo shirt. But it fit the look favoured by the tech bros and industry types milling around them. And that was all that mattered.

He raised his head, spotting what he needed, and leaned closer to Lee. "I think we're in. Ready?"

"Always," she said, glancing around, though the slight tremor in her voice gave her away. "I know what to do."

He tilted his head towards the far side of the forecourt, directing her attention to a woman in her late thirties dressed in a lightweight blazer and slacks. She held a tablet in one hand, her other gripping the strap of a heavy canvas bag slung over her shoulder. She looked to be a journalist possibly, here to cover the event. Three lanyards hung loosely over the open top of the bag, swaying as she shifted.

Perfect.

Lee gave him a quick nod before setting off. Beckett watched, careful not to stare too obviously as she moved across the forecourt, weaving between clusters of attendees. When she neared the woman she slowed, brushing a hand against her side as if adjusting her clothes. Then as she moved past, her hand darted out, hooking the lanyards away in one smooth motion. No hesitation. She kept moving, continuing in a wide arc and only glancing back once she was well away from her mark. The woman hadn't noticed, still engrossed in whatever she was reading on her tablet.

Beckett met Lee near the entrance, and she slipped him one of the lanyards. "Good work."

She smirked, raising an eyebrow. "Well, I wasn't always a cop."

The line inched forward as they joined the stream of attendees being funnelled through the towering glass doors. A blast of cool air from the industrial-grade AC hit them as they stepped inside. A welcome change from the heat. Not that it mattered. Things were only going to get hotter from here.

Beckett glanced at the name on the lanyard. *Bradley Simons, Tech Now Press Team.* Good enough. He tilted it towards Lee, signalling for her to check hers.

She looked down and grinned, angling it so he could see. *Isabella Simons.*

"Hey hubby," she whispered.

Beckett allowed himself a smile before getting back to business as they neared the front of the line. They hadn't talked too much about sleeping together last night and he was glad of that. It had been good – great, even – just what he needed. But he wasn't one for dissecting his feelings. Everything else? Sure. How people moved, their micro-expressions, the fastest way out of any room he was in. But emotions? No. That wasn't his skillset.

At the checkpoint a stocky guard gestured sharply for him to step forward. He checked Beckett's pass, then gestured for him to raise his arms. Beckett complied, receiving the briefest of pat-downs before being waved through the metal detector. Lee followed, going through the same process with a female guard. No issues. She joined him in the main lobby.

The energy in the grand lobby was different from the last time they were here. Excitement filled the air as attendees clustered in groups, chattering about the event. *Novaratech 25* banners hung from the walls, and the massive display screen cycled through images of the speakers and event highlights.

Shit.

Beckett clocked Holden's name on the list. Filing it away for later, he scanned the room, quick and discreet. Two sets of armed guards were stationed on either side of the space. They looked heavy, not the kind of show security a company would typically hire for an event like this. Most likely Red's crew.

He touched Lee's arm to make sure she'd seen them, then gestured for her to follow. They moved into the crowd, heading towards the wide staircase between the elevators, where signs directed attendees to the upper floors.

"Keep moving, don't look at them," he whispered, as they approached more security guards at the base of the staircase.

She swallowed, keeping her face neutral, but he knew her well enough now to catch the flicker of unease as they began to climb. Without thinking, he reached for her hand and gave it a quick squeeze. It was unlike him, but just enough to steady her.

On the next landing more armed guards stood watch on either side. Beckett glanced around, then up. Above them, on a mezzanine level that wrapped around the atrium at the top of the staircase, a man in a suit with swept-back hair walked the perimeter keeping an eye on the crowds.

"This the floor?" Lee asked, lifting herself onto her toes to look around.

"Yes. This way."

He guided her over to one side, away from the main throng, and stopped near a pillar to take it all in. The rear of the landing opened into the exhibition hall, packed with people. Rows of booths stretched in neat lines, showcasing a mix of tech companies and cutting-edge innovations. Attendees wandered between them, some carrying branded tote bags, others snapping photos. Overhead, more banners proclaimed *Novaratech 25: Innovating Tomorrow.*

This was clearly the heart of the expo, and a sign nearby directed guests to the keynote venue on the floor above.

But Beckett and Lee needed to get to the roof, another sixty-three floors up.

And fast. Mack's notes had indicated the EMP was set to detonate thirty minutes after Holden's keynote ended. Beckett had just seen the schedule. Holden's speech wasn't closing the event – it was opening it.

He did a full turn, matching their surroundings to the details he'd memorised. Mack had done them the favour of downloading a schematic of the building. Beckett had no idea where he'd got it, or if it was even up to date, but it was their only lead.

If the schematic was correct, there was a comms room down a corridor to their right, with a service elevator nearby that ran up to the fiftieth floor. From there, a stairwell led to the sixty-fifth and the roof.

They were on target. But the place was more heavily guarded than Beckett had anticipated. Knowing there'd be heavy security on the door, they hadn't brought guns, but he was used to improvising. Adjusting in real time. That was the job. Out in the field, a rigid plan could get you killed. The first obstacle could throw everything off, and then what? No, he worked best like this. Adapting, watching, reacting. It was how he'd stayed alive this long.

With a subtle jerk of his head, he signalled to Lee, guiding her away from the crush of attendees jostling for space at the booths and tables. The excitement of the crowd gave them enough cover to slip into the service corridor that ran along the side of the building.

"Anyone see us?" Lee whispered, as they moved quickly down the narrow walkway.

"We'll know soon enough."

The corridor was dimly lit, the noise of the exhibition muffled behind them. They hurried through a series of winding hallways until they reached the comms room. Beckett stopped, inspecting the door. It was made of brushed steel and secured with a push-button lock.

"Shit," Lee muttered.

But Beckett had already anticipated this.

"Plan B," he replied, stepping past her and heading to the end of the corridor where he found what he was hoping for – a small utility room, unlocked. The stench of industrial cleaner hit him in the face as he opened the door, but he pushed through, examining the shelves and floor space. Mops, buckets, an old floor polishing machine. And in one corner, wedged between a stack of rags, a small metal toolbox.

Result.

He crouched, flipped it open and sorted through the contents, finding a decent-sized screwdriver and a wrench. Grabbing both, he jogged back to where Lee was waiting by the comms room door.

"We'll do this old-school."

Positioning himself in front of the door, he pocketed the wrench and worked the screwdriver into the narrow gap between the latch and the strike plate. With a little force he was able to push the spring-loaded latch inward, retracting it from the doorframe.

They were in.

He straightened and pushed the door open. "After you."

"Impressive," Lee whispered, stepping inside.

He followed her in and shut the door behind them. The setup in the comms room was standard. A bank of monitors, each labelled with corresponding camera zones, and a control terminal with a compact keyboard and trackpad.

Lee moved closer, eyes flicking between the screens. "Okay, so... what do we do?"

Beckett leaned in. The system looked relatively straightforward – each feed tied to a specific area, toggle controls to turn cameras on or off – but one wrong move, one alarm triggered, and Red's entire team would be on them.

"We need to redirect the feeds on the cameras covering our path," he whispered. "Which is mainly these feeds here, leading to the top floors." He used the trackpad to select the first feed.

"You sure this won't set off any alerts?"

"Shouldn't do, as long as we don't change anything outside the pre-ordained areas." He gestured to the monitor on the far left. "That one's showing the roof access hallway. We need to swap it with this stairwell camera here."

"Okay..." She pulled in a deep breath he didn't hear her release as he made the change. The image on the monitor flickered, then shifted to an empty stairwell.

"One down."

Now Lee blew out the breath. "Good work."

Beckett moved from screen to screen, swapping out each

key feed until they had a clear path to the penthouse level and then up to the roof, ensuring no one monitoring the security footage would see them.

Once the cameras were switched and no alarms had gone off, they waited, watching the feeds for this floor. When they were satisfied no one was coming, they slipped out of the comms room. Beckett took Lee's hand and they retraced their steps until they reached another passage. According to the schematics in his head, this would take them to the east side of the tower. At the far end was a pair of steel doors. The service elevator.

He pressed the call button, and somewhere above them the faint hum of machinery responded. As they waited, Lee bounced from foot to foot, her eyes darting to the corridor behind then back to the elevator doors. She was holding it together, but only just. A few seconds later the elevator pinged and the door slid open.

They stepped inside, and Beckett pressed the button for floor fifty, the highest this car would take them. As the doors closed, Lee shuffled against the wall, gripping the handrail. She didn't look at him but he could see the tension in her face.

"How are you doing?" he asked.

She shrugged. "You tell me. I've never done anything like this before."

"Then you're doing great. Just try to stay out of your head, remember. Deal with what's in front of you. One step at a time."

"Yep. Sure. Thanks."

They rode up in silence, past the twenties and thirties. A few glances, a couple of reassuring smiles. A quiet acknowledgement they were in this together. As they reached the top floor the doors slid open with a shrill ping, revealing a sterile, dim hallway.

Beckett stepped out first and looked around. Clear. The air was cooler here, the distant hum of ventilation systems the only sound. Lee followed, keeping close to his side as they moved. They were halfway down the corridor when a sharp voice rang out.

"Hey! What are you doing here?"

Beckett froze as a large man strode towards them, holding an Uzi at waist height. He was dressed all in black and was built like a middleweight boxer, all muscle and speed. His scowl deepened as he closed the distance, shaking his head.

"You can't be up here," he snarled.

Beckett shifted in front of Lee, angling his body to shield her while keeping his face lowered. He slouched slightly, hands loose at his sides, adopting a nervous, uncertain posture. "Oh, uh, sorry," he said, pitching his voice higher. "We were looking for the keynote venue. Someone said there was a shortcut—"

"This floor is off-limits," the guard snapped, jerking the Uzi towards the elevator. "Back inside. Now."

"Right, of course." Beckett shuffled a step towards the doors, hands still raised. "No problem. Totally my fault."

As the guard got closer he stopped, recognition dawning in his eyes as he looked them up and down. "Shit—!"

Beckett didn't let him complete that thought. He lunged forward, grabbing the Uzi's barrel and wrenching it aside. In the same motion, he smashed his elbow into the guard's jaw. The man staggered, knees buckling, and before he could recover, Beckett slipped the wrench from his pocket and brought it down hard against the guy's temple.

Lee appeared beside him as he eased the body to the floor. "Wow."

Beckett grabbed the guy's arms. "Help me," he said, dragging the body away from the elevator.

Lee got the legs and they carried him to an unlocked utility room a few metres down the corridor. Inside were shelves stacked with cleaning supplies and paper towels. Beckett found a coil of nylon cord hanging from a hook, and measuring out a length, he cut it against the sharp edge of a shelf bracket. Working quickly, he tied the man's wrists behind his back with a constrictor knot, then secured his ankles with another length of cord, anchoring it to the rack with a firm hitch knot to restrict movement. Next he grabbed a cleaning cloth from one of the shelves and tore it into strips, stuffing most of it into the guard's mouth before knotting a longer piece around his head to keep it in place.

"That should do it."

Lee nodded, her expression caught somewhere between relief and fear, like she was midway through a rollercoaster ride she'd never signed up for.

"Let's go," he said.

They stepped back into the corridor, shutting the door behind them. The corridor was silent, no one around, a stark contrast to the bustling expo many floors below. They couldn't hear it from here, but the event was now in full swing, and the clock was ticking.

If the EMP was due to detonate soon after Holden had finished his keynote, that meant it could happen anytime in the next hour, depending on how long he planned speaking for.

Beckett glanced at Lee, her demeanour now one of grim focus. "We have to get to the roof," he said. "Now."

Chapter Forty-Eight

The mezzanine level overlooking the first-floor landing offered Red the perfect vantage point of the bustling attendees as they milled about like cattle, each trying to look important and investible.

Red had seen it all before. Startup founders pitching bad ideas. Tech journalists pretending to be busy. Self-important investors nodding along, trying to appear like they understood what was being presented to them, when all they were really doing was waiting for those magic words, *Artificial Intelligence,* to spark their interest.

Idiots. All of them.

She touched her earpiece, activating the mic clipped to the collar of her leather jacket. "Five – any updates?"

A gruff voice crackled back. "All clear, Red."

Her men on channels six and seven, when asked, all responded in kind. "All clear."

Everything was running smoothly. Just as it should. This was why Holden had brought her and her team in. Why she was here now, micromanaging every detail, even if operating so openly made her uneasy.

She had to get this right. Holden was paying her an obscene amount to oversee this circus, but more than that, this job could elevate her standing in the underworld. Prove to the right people that she was someone who got things done. Someone to fear and respect.

Continuing her circuit of the mezzanine, she sneered inwardly at the eager smiles, forced laughter, and empty handshakes playing out below. The tech world's finest. All the ambition of a shark. None of the teeth.

She resumed checking in with her team.

"Eight, any updates?"

The comms crackled. No reply.

"Eight? Any updates?"

Then, finally, a voice. "Maybe there is. I ain't sure."

It was Morgan, his dumb monotone voice already grating on her nerves.

"What do you mean?"

"I think I just saw them. The Englishman and the cop."

She stopped dead, speaking through gritted teeth. "When?"

"A few minutes ago," he said. "Heading for the back elevator. The one you told us is for employees only. It *sort of* looked like them. But I wasn't sure."

Red gripped the steel railing, trying not to let her rage consume her. She closed her eyes, inhaling slowly, forcing herself to think. Morgan was a blunt instrument, not a thinker, but he'd been briefed with photos like everyone else on the team. And more than that, he'd seen them up close. He knew their faces.

"Why didn't you stop them?"

"I wasn't sure how," he admitted. "You said to bring them in alive, and I wanted backup."

Her knuckles burned as she clenched the railing tighter. "Then why didn't you call it in?" she hissed.

"I followed them up here to the fiftieth floor, figured Sixteen and me could box them in. But I just got up here and…" A pause. "No sign of them. Of any of them."

Red ground her teeth, the sound audible in her earpiece. She'd deal with Morgan later. "Return to your post," she snapped. "I'll handle it."

Muttering dark curses under her breath, she stormed down onto the landing, shoving past anyone in her way as she made a beeline for the door at the far side.

"Sixteen – any updates?" she snarled, pressing a finger to her earpiece.

No answer.

The crowd thickened near the entrance to the exhibition hall, but she moved through them like a battering ram, unwilling to slow for even a second.

Reaching the unassuming steel door, she keyed in the access code and pushed through, descending the industrial stone staircase to the basement where she'd set up her control hub. At the next set of reinforced doors she pressed her hand to the biometric scanner and the doors slid open. The hum of cooling fans filled the air. To her right, racks of servers lined the walls. In the centre of the room a wide desk housed four large monitors, their screens split into grids, displaying feeds from cameras throughout the building.

Red dropped into the chair and grabbed the keyboard, cycling methodically through each zone – the main exhibition hall, the lobby, floor fifty, the landing leading up to

Holden's penthouse. Everything looked normal. No sign of the Englishman or the cop.

"Sixteen," she tried again into her lapel mic, "any updates?"

Silence.

She frowned, adjusting the frequency. "Sixteen, do you copy?"

Nothing.

Her jaw tightened. "Damn it."

She pulled up additional feeds of the fiftieth floor and above, zeroing in on floor sixty-four, the camera trained on the staircase leading to Holden's penthouse.

Still nothing.

But they had to be somewhere.

She tapped her nails on the desk as the implication hit her. If they found the EMP before it went off—

No!

Wasn't going to happen. She wouldn't let it.

She returned to the feeds, winding each one back a few minutes, desperate to catch sight of them.

Come on. Show me something.

Maybe Sixteen was handling it. Maybe that was why he wasn't answering. Too busy gutting the wretched pair.

She hoped so, but her patience and nerves were wearing thin as she cycled through more footage. The service cameras were her last shot, but most feeds showed nothing but static hallways and empty staircases. Then, on the last feed, she caught something – a flash of movement on the service stairwell leading to the top floor.

"No…"

She leaned closer to the monitor, narrowing her eyes as she rolled the footage back and forth with the tracking wheel. The grainy image had caught two pairs of feet climbing quickly out of frame. The angle was terrible, the resolution worse, but she didn't need a clearer picture.

It was them. She knew it.

Her hand went to her comms unit, ready to alert the guards on the upper levels. But she paused. The thought of dealing with them herself was far too appealing.

Straightening, she reached down to her belt and drew Suzette from her rubber sheath. Now this was an ally Red could rely on. Suzette had been with her for years. First used to take down coyotes. Then the Taliban. Now anyone who displeased her. Maybe Morgan would feel Suzette's bite in time. But for now she had a date upstairs.

A slow smile spread across Red's face.

This wasn't about the job anymore. It wasn't about the money, or even impressing Holden and his associates.

Now it was personal.

That bitch cop and her meddling lapdog had been a thorn in her side all week, and now they were going to pay.

Still smiling, she slid Suzette back into her sheath, adjusted her comms, and strode towards the door.

Time to end this.

Chapter Forty-Nine

They'd nearly reached the top.

Beckett and Lee pushed hard up the final few flights of the service stairwell, gripping the handrail to propel themselves around each tight landing. There were only fourteen flights up to floor sixty-four – the level just below Holden's penthouse – but it felt like a hell of a lot more.

At last they reached the top, both pausing for a second to steady their breathing. Beckett moved to the door leading into the corridor and eased it open a crack, angling himself to get a clear view.

Shit.

A guard stood just a few feet away, his back to the door. Beckett froze, craning his neck. Further down, another guard stood against the wall, facing the staircase that led up to the penthouse. He shot Lee a warning look and held up a hand. One misstep, one creak of the door, and everything would come crashing down.

Keeping low, he gestured for her to hold the door open

while he slipped onto the landing. He kept his balance centred, his breathing still. As he got closer he slipped the wrench from his pocket, gripping it tightly in his hand. The metal handle pressed against his grip, reinforcing his fist the way a set of brass knuckles would. Normally when a punch is thrown, the fingers are driven back into the palm, absorbing some of the impact like a shock absorber. But with his grip around the wrench handle, his fist would hold firm, transferring more of the force directly to the target. At least, that was the plan.

When he was close enough he stood upright, readying himself. He'd done this before but it had to be done right. If it wasn't, neither of them were going any further. Twisting the way his boxing coach had shown him, putting his shoulder and upper body into the swing, he smashed his fists into the occipital region at the base of the man's skull. The blow was brutal and heavy and the guard dropped instantly, his knees buckling as he collapsed in a heap. Beckett caught him under the arms before he hit the floor, and dragged the limp body backwards into the stairwell.

"There's another one guarding the stairs up to the penthouse," he whispered to Lee, as he propped the unconscious guard against the wall. "But he's too far away for a sneak attack."

He straightened, rolling his shoulders back. "We have to assume they've seen photos of us. But they're looking for a man and a woman. One of us alone might be able to distract him long enough that—"

"You want me to try?" Lee asked.

He held her gaze. "I don't want to ask you if you have doubts."

"Of course I have doubts," she said, undoing her ponytail. "But I reckon I can pull it off."

She ran her fingers through her hair, shaking it into a side parting that swept across her brow. She looked good. Different enough that it might work.

"Okay, you're Isabella Simons, remember," Beckett said. "Hoping for an exclusive interview with Holden."

Lee wrinkled her nose. "He's not going to let me up there."

"He doesn't have to. You just need to distract him so I can take him out."

Lee looked nervous for a second but shook it off. She stared at him, something unspoken passing between them, a silent acknowledgement of the stakes. Beneath that, understanding. Trust. And something even deeper.

"Okay," she said. "Let's do it."

Beckett eased the door open and they slipped out. Moving unseen, he ducked into an alcove while Lee carried on, swaying her hips as she approached the guard.

As she neared, the guard turned, his hand instinctively moving to the weapon at his hip. "Who the hell are you?" he barked. "What are you doing up here?"

"Hey there," Lee chimed, adopting a sing-song Valley Girl accent. "The name's Izzy, how are you? So, I'm here covering the expo for *Tech Now* and..." She waved her lanyard and giggled, all wide eyes and fake flirtation. "...I was wondering if I might get a few words with our illustrious founder."

Beckett slipped out from cover, pressing himself against the wall. He was close enough now to be in the guard's peripheral vision, but right now the man's focus was on Lee. His expression hovered between amused and suspicious. Like he wasn't sure if she was insane or an opportunity waiting to happen.

"Please?" she added, stepping a little closer. "I won't tell anyone you let me."

"Absolutely-fucking-not," he snarled. "I don't know how you got up here, but you need to turn around and—"

Beckett closed the distance and struck before he could finish, driving the heel of his fist into the guard's windpipe. His eyes bulged and he staggered towards Lee, clawing at his neck, gasping for air.

Lee shoved him back and Beckett moved in, locking his arm around the guard's throat while his free hand gripped the back of the man's head, shoving it forward to tighten the hold. The guard thrashed in a futile attempt to break free, but the choke was applied perfectly, compressing the carotid arteries on both sides of his neck and cutting off blood flow to his brain.

A hold like this usually took six to twelve seconds to knock someone out. This time it took five.

"You really are good at this," Lee whispered, as Beckett eased the guard's limp body to the ground.

No time for pats on the back. Kneeling beside the unconscious guard, he stripped the man of his belt and rolled him over to secure his wrists with it. The hold wouldn't last long if the guy woke up, but judging by the way his head lolled to the side, Beckett doubted that would happen anytime soon. More collateral damage. But it came with the territory.

"He's got to be the last one," Beckett said, rolling the man onto his back. From here they had a clear path through the penthouse to the roof. According to Mack's notes and the schematics, that's where the EMP device would be. "You ready?"

Behind him Lee made a strange whimpering sound. "John…"

"Lee, what's—" He turned, the words dying in his throat.

Red was standing behind Lee, a large serrated hunting knife pressed to her throat.

Beckett started to get up.

"No! You stay down, English," Red snarled. "Or we'll see just how deep Suzette here can cut."

Lee stood frozen, barely daring to breathe as the blade bit at the thin skin on her neck. It felt impossibly sharp. So sharp she wondered if she would even feel it cutting her. She didn't know if that was a good or bad thing.

Was it cutting her now?

Was that sweat trickling down her neck, or blood?

Every muscle in her body tensed as a familiar feeling of panic blossomed through her system. It threatened to overwhelm her. Her legs felt like they were made of jello. She wanted to barf.

"John," she whispered, her voice trembling, barely audible. "Help me."

Beckett lifted his head, his gaze locking onto hers, pulling her back from the brink. *Stay with me*, his expression said. "Maggie, it's going to be okay."

His voice steadied her. Just enough to keep her upright. She let out a shuddering breath, forcing herself to focus on him, to fight against the panic wrapping itself around her heart.

Red chuckled, husky and humourless. "It's going to be okay, is it?" she mocked. "I wouldn't bet on that."

She dragged Lee backwards, the knife pressing harder against her throat. The panic surged again, stronger now, threatening to pull her under. A warm sensation on her neck told her the knife had definitely broken skin. Not deep. Not fatal. Yet. But enough to send her system into freefall, nerves firing in every direction. Her hands twitched uselessly at her sides as Beckett glanced at the guard's pistol. For a second she thought he might go for it.

But Red had seen it too.

"Try it," she hissed. "I'll open her neck up like the Grand Canyon before you have it out of the holster. You don't want that, do you?"

The blade pressed harder and Lee winced. Every instinct screamed at her to move, fight, do something. But her body wasn't getting the message. Red's nails dug into her arm, holding her in place as firmly as the knife at her throat.

"Don't hurt her," Beckett said. "It's me you want."

His eyes stayed on Red but he didn't move. Was he waiting for the right moment? Calculating his options? Lee hoped to god he saw an opening, but as far as she could tell, there wasn't one.

"John, she's going to kill us anyway!" she wheezed. "Please, just try it!"

Beckett met her gaze, his eyes widening slightly as if trying to tell her something.

But what?

He could probably get out of this situation in an instant. But she wasn't him. She wasn't Sarah Connor or Ripley. She was just... her. Margaret Rebecca Lee. A lousy beat cop with delusions of grandeur. And she was going to die here.

She sniffed. But if this was it, she was determined to do something. Anything. An idea formed.

"Please... don't..." she whined, shuffling forward, forcing Red to move with her. "I just—"

Desperation fuelled her as she threw her head back,

aiming to bust Red's nose. She put everything into it. But Red was faster. She shifted, anticipating the move, and Lee's head struck her shoulder instead, the impact jarring and ineffective.

"Stupid bitch," Red snarled, shoving the blade harder against Lee's throat, fingernails piercing her flesh.

Except Lee could sense it now. Red didn't have a real plan. She was stalling, assessing, weighing the odds. If she killed Lee now, Beckett would go for the gun without hesitation and she had no way of stopping him.

But Lee didn't want it to come to that.

Her throat tightened as the seconds dragged out. She watched Beckett, his eyes darting between Red and the knife, working the angles. Time was slipping away and Red was growing restless. It was a standoff − one that wouldn't hold much longer.

She had to act.

Now.

Red yanked her back a few more steps, dragging her towards the staircase leading to the penthouse.

No. Shit.

There were most likely guns up there and possibly more armed men. If Red made it to the penthouse, it was over. She could kill Lee, then wait for Beckett and take him out too.

A fresh wave of panic surged through her system. She could feel her pulse beating against the blade's edge but she clenched her teeth, forcing the fear down.

She couldn't let it take her. She needed to think.

Her mind flashed to another time, years ago, memories she'd buried deep. Her brothers, Robbie and Michael. Grabbing her by the throat. Twisting her arms behind her back. Laughing as they tormented her, testing her strength just because they could.

But she'd figured it out. There was a way out then, and maybe it could work now.

Her breathing slowed as she centred herself, trying not to focus on her rising terror. Could she do it? Her mind screamed at her to act, but her body was still holding her in place.

Come on, Maggie.

No time for hesitation. This was it. No other choice.

She closed her eyes briefly, a silent prayer to anyone who might be listening. Then all at once she went limp, her entire body sagging against Red like a puppet whose strings had been cut. The sudden dead weight threw Red off balance, just for a second.

But a second was enough.

Red stumbled and Beckett was on her in a flash, knocking the knife from her hand and slamming her into the wall with a thud as Lee staggered away.

He turned to check on her but she shooed him off, gesturing at Red who was already rallying. With a banshee shriek she lunged at Beckett, raking her nails across his cheek. He jerked back, sidestepping another wild swing and driving a boot into her midsection. The kick forced her back, but the woman was tough. She stumbled, grimacing, then charged again, dummying left and then slamming her knee into Beckett's groin.

Beckett recoiled with a sharp intake of breath, his hands instinctively moving to shield himself.

"John! No!" Lee's heart lurched as Red yanked a small finger blade from her waistband, readying to strike while Beckett was still incapacitated.

Instinct took over.

She spotted the hunting knife on the floor and dove for it, stumbling but using the momentum to propel herself forward. Pushing upright she charged at Red, raw adrenaline fuelling every step.

With a screech to rival Red's own, she barrelled into the taller woman, driving her full force into a nearby pillar. The impact jolted through her arms and shoulders but it didn't stop her. With a grunt she drove the blade upwards, plunging it deep into Red's chest.

For a second they just stared at each other, their faces centimetres apart.

"Fuck you," Lee snarled, finding her voice again, gruff with righteous fury.

Red's mouth moved, but no words came. Just a wet, gurgling sound as blood bubbled up from her throat.

Lee released the knife, her hand trembling as she stepped back. Red let out a deep groan, swaying unsteadily for a moment before pitching forward onto the floor.

She felt her own legs give way, and she toppled sideways into Beckett as he rushed to catch her.

"Hey, you're all right," he whispered, holding her tight. "You saved my life."

"Shut up," she muttered, her voice wavering between laughter and hysteria. But she turned into him, pressing her face into his chest, t the rise and fall of his breathing steady even now and grounding her. She felt numb. As if the weight of what she'd done hadn't fully hit her yet. Or maybe it had, and her mind just didn't know how to process it. She didn't cry. She wasn't even sure what she felt.

Beckett stepped back, his hands moving to her shoulders, his blue eyes searching hers. "Can you go on?"

"Yeah. I'm fine," she said, sniffing sharply.

"Are you sure?"

She nodded. "I'm sure."

Her gaze drifted to the doors leading to the stairwell up to Holden's office. She took a breath, steadying herself, feeling the last of her hesitation slip away.

She turned back to Beckett. "Let's go stop this thing."

Chapter Fifty

Beckett knelt beside the fallen guard and prised the gun from his holster. A Glock 19. Standard and reliable. He ejected the magazine, checked the rounds, and slid it back into place. He stood and moved over to Lee. She looked wired, the shock of what she'd done there in her eyes. But she was alert. Ready enough. She'd have to be.

He gave her a curt nod. Time to go.

They moved in silence up the stairs leading to Holden's penthouse suite. Beckett went first, the Glock leading the way. The air in the stairwell was cooler than the rest of the building, and it was so quiet up here. Almost too quiet. Beckett couldn't tell if that was because of some over-engineered climate control system or the weight of the confrontation ahead. Either way, there was no turning back.

Lee came up beside him, both of them staring through the reception area, its glass entrance open and desk empty, to the brushed-metal doors they'd entered with Holden the last time.

"We've got this," she whispered.

She was still charged, telling herself as much as him, but he didn't share her confidence. Something was off. They passed through reception, and when they were only about a metre away the metal doors slid open, revealing the dimly lit penthouse.

Beckett shot a glance at Lee. He didn't like this. Not one bit. Leading with the Glock, he moved into the Holden's imposing office suite.

"Ah, there you are."

Beckett's attention snapped to the seating area in front of the window where he and Lee had sat two days ago, and where Lucian Holden now lounged, holding a large handgun levelled right at them. Beckett raised the Glock in response, but Holden tutted, shaking his head.

"I wouldn't risk it," he said, nodding at the two armed guards positioned on either side of the room, rifles raised and ready.

Beckett's grip tightened on the Glock as he took it all in, running real-time assessments. If he dropped and shot the guy closest to him, he might have a slim chance of—

"For Christ's sake, drop the gun," Holden snarled, as if this should have already happened. "Now."

Beckett exhaled slowly through his nose. There was no play here. Not yet. "Okay. Doing it."

He raised one hand and carefully lowered the Glock to the floor with his other. As he straightened, Lee grabbed his arm, her fingers tight around his bicep. Beckett didn't look at her. His eyes stayed on Holden, waiting for what came next as the smug CEO rose and strode towards them.

"What a shame," Holden sneered. "You were so close." The gun in his hand stayed level on Beckett as his plastic features twisted into a cruel smile. "I have to say, I almost feel sorry for the two of you. Almost."

He reached into his jacket pocket with his free hand, pulling out a sleek black tablet. He turned it towards them. The display showed security footage from the floors below. He glanced at the screen, then back at Beckett.

"If I hadn't cut my keynote short, I'd still be down there with my people. You might have had a shot." He paused, his smile widening. "But you know what they say – leave them wanting more." His gaze flicked to Lee for a moment as if gauging her reaction, before turning back to Beckett. "And, honestly, I wanted to get up here fast. Had to make sure everything was set for my dramatic exit."

His gun didn't waver, but Beckett noted the shift in his posture. Relaxed now, as if enjoying himself.

"I'm not going to pretend I'm not pissed that you killed one of my best fixers," Holden said, swiping at the screen to pull up footage of the hallway below. Red, lying in a pool of blood.

"Ms Sorrento has been a useful tool for me over the years. But she isn't irreplaceable. There are plenty of other disillusioned souls who understand the value of working for real power. And soon I won't even need people like Red." He jutted his head forward, grinning at Lee. "You see, soon I'll be playing in a league you can't even begin to comprehend." He paused, smoothing a hand over his jacket. "But then, you won't be around to see it."

"So that's it," Beckett said. "All this just to get in The Consortium's inner circle."

Holden froze, his composure slipping for the first time. "What did you just say?"

Beckett leaned in slightly, keeping his hands loose at his sides. "I know all about the people you're working for," he said. "My friend Mack – the guy you had killed – had recognised one of their payment aliases on a document he pulled from your data terminal. He's been monitoring them for years. They're not as invisible as they think."

Holden's eyes widened, the conceit slipping a touch. "You got that off the device?"

"Yeah," Lee spat, finding her voice now. "The same one you've been killing people over."

Holden sneered. "Yes, a very unsatisfying turn of events." He waved the gun lazily like a lecture pointer. "All because of that blasted warehouse drone. If he hadn't stolen it, everything would have run so much smoother." His expression darkened as he turned back to Beckett. "I wouldn't have to kill the two of you, for instance."

"Fuck you," Lee snapped, moving closer to Beckett. "You can't do this."

"Can't I?" He raised the small tablet he was holding, swiping at the screen with the pinkie of his gun hand before tilting it towards them. The screen showed a countdown timer in bold red digits. Fifty-eight minutes and counting. He pulled a face of mock fear. "Oops."

"It's on the roof?" Beckett asked.

Holden hesitated for a second. "It is." He paced in front of them, still waving the gun at them. "The culmination of years of planning, the best minds tech money can buy, and yes, a little extra help from some very *influential* partners." His grin widened as he turned to face them. "You can't stop it, of course. But by all means try. It'll be amusing."

He continued parading up and down, waxing lyrical about how ingenious he was, how they were powerless to stop him. But Beckett's attention was on the guards. He noted their stance and demeanour, the way they watched Holden, waiting for orders. They were professionals, alert and ready, but there was something else, too. A hint of impatience, the kind that came from standing too long and listening to a boss who liked the sound of his own voice.

"I've been asking around about this interfering Englishman," Holden continued, pocketing the tablet and wagging a finger at Beckett like he was scolding a wayward child. "You're a tricky one to get an angle on, but I've been doing my research. One of my contacts believes you're not a detective at all, but John Beckett, ex-MI6."

Lee stiffened. Just enough for Holden to notice. He paused mid-stride, his grin spreading as he turned to her. "Struck a nerve, did I? Interesting."

He shifted his focus back to Beckett, pointing the gun at his chest. "Word is, before that you were Black Ops. But no one's really sure what you are these days. A ghost, maybe?" His smile sharpened. "One thing they all agreed on, though – you're a dangerous son of a bitch. No wonder you've been causing me so much trouble. I should've dealt with you earlier."

"Yes." Beckett lifted his chin. "You should have."

Holden let out a high-pitched chuckle. "Don't worry. All in good time. And before you start thinking your presence here might derail things for me – I haven't shared that little titbit with anyone at the… organisation you referred to. Don't want them to think I can't handle things. Or worse, get spooked by a potential gremlin in the works." He smirked. "No, I'll deal with you myself. Much cleaner that way."

He stopped pacing and leaned in slightly. "But before we do anything rash, let me offer you a way out." He smiled. "You're wasted in whatever shadowy little corner you've been hiding in. Join me. Work for me. We could do great things together."

"Go to hell." Beckett's response was immediate.

Holden's smile didn't falter, but his eyes hardened. He stepped back, spreading his arms. "You know what your problem is? Misguided idealism. You're still clinging to some outdated code. Like you're fighting the good fight."

Beckett held his gaze. "You want me to help you destroy Vegas? You're insane."

"Vegas? You think this is about Vegas?" He shook his head. "This is about resetting the board. Tearing up the rulebook and writing a new one."

He stopped, levelling the gun at Beckett. "You know what? I take it all back. You're out of your depth here. I see it now. You still think power is about governments, agencies, men with guns. It's not. It's about leverage. Controlling markets, economies, entire infrastructures. And after today, when the lights go out and the world scrambles to understand what happened, I'll be the one holding the switch."

He turned the gun towards Lee, then back to Beckett, making sure they both understood. "You know what the best part is? The CIA, whoever, they'll have no choice but to pin the attack on Al-Tariq Al-Jadid, the terrorist group my colleagues have been feeding intel about for over a year. An operation this size needs a villain, and we've made sure they have one."

Beckett listened without comment, his focus elsewhere, again on the two guards. Their weapons were still raised, but their attention had drifted since Holden launched into his ego-fuelled monologue.

"If you know my partners, Mr Beckett," he went on, "then you must also know that they don't just write the script. They direct the entire show."

"You won't get away with it," Lee spat.

"You still don't get it, do you?" Holden tilted his head, regarding them with amused disdain, like a cat toying with trapped mice. "We already have got away with it. This doesn't stop with me. Or them. Cut off one head and two more take its place. We are legion. We can't be beaten."

"What happens to Novara?" Beckett asked.

Holden inhaled deeply, as if relishing his own brilliance. "A regrettable casualty. One of many companies lost in the chaos. And yes, that does pain me a little." He sighed. "But progress demands destruction. So often in this world we must tear something down to build something better. Novara was my chrysalis. And now I'm ready to emerge stronger, untouchable."

By now his pacing had become almost theatrical, like he'd stepped straight out of a bad movie, fully aware of the villain trope and relishing every second. A phoney persona to match his phoney face. Maybe he thought it added to his mystique. Maybe he just liked the sound of his own voice.

Beckett shifted his weight onto the balls of his feet, keeping the movement subtle. The guards' stances had loosened, their attention drifting further as their boss carried on grandstanding. No doubt they'd heard too many similar speeches from him and were tuning out.

Good.

He could use that.

Beckett readied himself, slowing his breath and steadying his pulse. He only had one shot at this.

He had to make it count.

Chapter Fifty-One

Holden turned towards the window, gesturing at the neon cityscape below. "Look at it," he said. "The Strip. The skyline. A glittering monument to excess. And soon? Nothing but darkness. Ashes." He chuckled, almost as if he couldn't help himself.

Beckett remained still, waiting, reading the moment. One false move on Holden's part and he could do it. But it had to be perfect. Split-second timing.

The guards held their positions, weapons trained on Beckett and Lee, but their discipline was eroding with every passing second. Holden, meanwhile, was still pacing, waving his gun through the air. He was also still ranting, basking in his own genius, but Beckett wasn't listening anymore. His focus was locked on the next few seconds.

He checked the guards again. One was shifting his weight from foot to foot. Too eager. He'd be first. The other stood statue-still but with tension in his shoulders. Not conducive for a precise reaction. He'd be second.

Decision made, Beckett leaned forward, staying loose but primed. Holden turned, pacing towards him now, the gun swinging carelessly, too caught up in histrionics to pay full attention.

This was it.

The opening he needed.

Beckett lunged, grabbing Holden's gun arm and shoulder. Shifting his weight, he yanked Holden off balance and spun him around, using the momentum to wrench the pistol free and force him into position as a human shield. Before the first guard could react, Beckett shot him between the eyes and was already turning to the second before the body hit the ground. The other guard flinched, jerking into action, but with Holden in the way he hesitated – just for a second – and in that time Beckett put a bullet in his skull, sending him spinning sideways into the glass wall.

"Get off me. Fuck!"

Holden struggled against Beckett's grip. He was stronger than he looked, all sinew and hard muscle, but Beckett was stronger. He shoved Holden away and pointed the gun at his head. "Stop," he snarled. "Now."

Holden did as he was told, his shoulders raised and rigid. He glared at his fallen guards, then back to Beckett, his lips curling into a cruel sneer.

"How do we stop the EMP?" Beckett asked, adjusting his grip on the pistol for Holden's benefit. But if he noticed, it didn't shift the sneer from his face.

"You need a deactivation code," he said. "And I'm the only one who knows it. If you kill me it'll go off. Nothing you can do to stop it."

"So what's the code?" Lee demanded, stepping forward.

The sneer became a smirk, then a sly grin. His confidence creeping back. "I can't tell you that, I'm afraid," he replied. "I'll be as good as dead, so you might as well shoot me here and now. But then…" He sucked air through his teeth. "You'll have failed. Best just accept it. You've lost."

Beckett kept the gun raised as he studied Holden. He wasn't bluffing. He had them over a barrel. But there had to be a plan B. There always was; even if he had to conjure it up from the depths of himself. He glanced up at the mezzanine level leading to the roof. At the same time, Lee stepped forward.

Too close.

Holden grabbed her and pulled her towards him. She cried out, and before anyone could move, he had a small revolver pressed against her temple.

"Little tip I learnt from my new friends," Holden snarled. "Always carry a backup."

"Let her go," Beckett growled.

"Put the gun down."

Beckett adjusted his aim, tracking the narrow slice of Holden's head visible behind Lee's. The guy was smart, keeping most of his body shielded, but Beckett had enough of a target – and he was almost certain he could get a kill shot before Holden pulled the trigger on Lee. But *almost* wouldn't cut it. And besides, it wasn't just Maggie's life at stake. If Holden went down, they had no way of stopping the EMP.

Lee sucked in a sharp breath as Holden drove the barrel harder against her skull. "John, just shoot him. We'll figure it out. We'll sort it. Just… take the shot."

Beckett kept the gun steady and his breathing controlled, but he couldn't risk it. He wouldn't.

"Hold on, Maggie," he said. "You're going to be okay. Keep your eyes on me."

Holden sniffed. "How pathetic you both are. No idea. No vision. You've lost, Beckett. Now back off, or she dies."

Beckett still didn't move. Just shifted his focus to Holden. "You know, time's running out," he said. "The longer you stay here, the closer you get to being caught up in the chaos. Or caught by the Feds. You don't want that."

Holden let out a high-pitched growl. That was a good sign. He was rattled. But Lee was growing more anxious as he backed away, dragging her with him.

"John... help..."

"Stay calm, Maggie. I need you to stay calm."

Her breaths were coming faster now, panic blooming. "He's going to kill me," she said, voice breaking. "You need to do something."

She wasn't wrong. Holden's composure was unravelling fast. He tightened his grip on Lee's, forcing her to stumble as he dragged her back another step.

"Drop the gun, Beckett! You're not the hero here. I am. I'm the fucking hero. This is what the world needs. A reset. A clean slate!"

Beckett kept his aim steady as he ran through the options, weighing each one against the reality unfolding in front of him. Holden was drunk on power, riding the high of his delusions. The way his movements were becoming more erratic and unpredictable confirmed what Beckett already suspected. Lucian Holden was a man teetering on the edge. A live grenade, seconds from detonation. This whole arrangement having taken a greater toll than the smooth persona had projected.

"All right, take it easy," Beckett told him. "I'll do as you say." He began to lower the pistol, his eyes never leaving Holden's.

Holden let out another shrill chuckle but his grip on Lee

stayed firm, and for a moment Beckett worried he wouldn't take the bait. But then, with a cry, he shoved Lee away, forcing Beckett to shift his focus as he moved to catch her. As he did, a gunshot cracked through the air and he felt the sonic pulse of the bullet as it tore past his ear, close enough to make his skin prickle.

"Move!" he barked, shoving Lee behind the leather couch as another shot whizzed past. The bullet slammed into the window behind them, exploding the reinforced glass into a mess of splintered veins.

"Idiots!" Holden roared, his voice raw and unhinged. "You can't stop me. Nothing will!"

Beckett crouched low, one hand anchoring Lee against him, the other on the trigger of the Glock, ready to return fire. Before he had a chance, another shot thudded into the top of the couch, forcing him back.

"Stay down," he told Lee, lifting his head just enough to get a clear angle. He fired three quick shots in response, but with no time to aim they were a gamble. As the bullets zipped past, Holden was already on the move, sprinting across the vast office and bolting for the spiral staircase leading to the landing above.

Shit.

Holden's words from their last encounter flashing through his mind as the man raced up the mezzanine stairs.

Private helicopter on the roof.

Beckett vaulted over the back of the couch and tore across the room as Holden disappeared through the glass doors. Reaching the staircase he grabbed the handrail, skidding to a stop before launching himself upward, taking the steps two at a time. At the top he glanced around to see Lee right behind him. They ran across the landing and he yanked open the glass door, leading with the gun as he stepped out into the warmth of the late afternoon.

The rooftop stretched before them, a broad, flat expanse of tar and reinforced metal dotted with ventilation units and satellite dishes. It was roughly the size of an Olympic swimming pool, and Holden was already halfway across it, sprinting towards the helicopter idling on the far side, its rotor blades spinning faster, gaining speed.

Beckett pressed on, firing twice as he ran. Shooting on the move was never going to deliver the perfect shot, but he was hoping to slow the man down at least. The first round went wide, but the second found its mark, slamming into Holden's shoulder with a burst of red. He stumbled but managed to stay on his feet. Spinning around, he returned fire – once, twice – then nothing.

He glared at the revolver in disbelief.

Out of ammo.

Exactly what Beckett had been counting on.

Gritting his teeth, he raced forward, closing the gap with every stride as Holden flung the useless revolver aside and bolted for the helicopter. The rotors were already a blur, their pounding rhythm hammering the air as the downdraft slammed into the CEO, knocking him off balance. But sheer desperation kept him moving, driving each step.

Beckett pushed harder, closing the distance by several more metres before dropping to one knee. He raised the Glock, lining up a non-lethal shot. He was highly skilled at extracting information from people, and this poison-filled tech bro wasn't going to be the exception. If he could take Holden down, there was still a chance of getting the deactivation code before the EMP went off.

On the far side of the helicopter he spotted what had to be the device – housed in a large metal suitcase with thick, coiled wires running between a central core and an LED timer. At the heart of the setup a cylindrical emitter pulsed with blue light. From this distance he couldn't make out the numbers on the timer, but he didn't need to. Time was running out.

He steadied his aim and exhaled, his finger tightening on the trigger. But before he could fire, the helicopter pilot leaned out of the cockpit, gun in hand, and shot first. The round screamed past Beckett, missing him by inches, before ricocheting off something metallic behind him.

Cursing under his breath, Beckett bolted for cover behind an air vent as the pilot shot again. The round zipped overhead, and Beckett leaned out, aimed and fired, taking out the pilot with a precise head shot. The man's head snapped back before he slumped forward against the controls, and for a tense moment the chopper pitched sideways before the autopilot kicked in, levelling it out just above the helipad.

Holden let out a desperate cry and ran once again towards the helicopter.

"Wait!" Beckett yelled, running for him.

But Holden kept going, stumbling and nearly falling as he jumped for the edge of the door, his body swinging dangerously as he fought to haul himself inside.

Beckett stopped a few feet short, raising the Glock.

"What are you waiting for?" Lee yelled, coming up beside him. "Shoot that motherfucker! He can't get away!"

But Beckett held his fire, still running split-second assessments, as Holden clambered higher, trying to reach the cabin. The lurching helicopter had thrown the pilot halfway out, and Holden seized the opportunity, reaching for the pistol still clutched in the dead man's hand. Wrenching it free, he turned and aimed.

That was Beckett's cue.

He fired a single shot, the round punching through Holden's skull above his right eye, killing him instantly. As his body slumped out of the cabin, the sudden imbalance jolted the helicopter, causing it to tilt towards them. The rotors let out a strained whine and it seemed ready to spiral out of control. Then with a shudder, the autopilot engaged and once more it levelled out.

Lee grabbed Beckett's shoulder. "The EMP!" she shouted, breaking into a sprint towards it.

"Maggie, wait."

He ran after her, coming to a stop beside the device. They stared down at it. The air around it crackled with static, prickling at his nerve endings and making his insides feel weird. Even above the roar of the chopper blades, the pulsing hum was loud. The central core seemed to be powering up.

He knelt, leaning in for a closer look, but the EMP was unlike anything he'd seen before. No clear panel, no obvious disarm point. He had no idea where to even begin.

"What do we do?" Lee yelled over the noise. "We've got forty-five minutes before it goes off. Can we call it in?"

Beckett ran the numbers in his head. Even if they got through to someone immediately – someone who believed them and scrambled the right team – it was a toss-up whether they'd get here in time. And after what Holden had said about fail-safes, Beckett had no choice but to take the bastard at his word.

"There's no time," he told Lee. "And we don't even know if it can be disarmed. We need to deal with it ourselves. Some other way."

She nodded. "Any ideas?"

He got to his feet, casting his eyes over the horizon. He looked at the helicopter, then he looked at Lee. A plan formed. A long shot.

One hell of a long shot.

But it was all he had.

Chapter Fifty-Two

Beckett crouched beside the EMP device, running his fingers over the thick coils and reinforced metal core. He gripped the sides of the suitcase, testing its weight. Heavy, but not impossible to move. What unsettled him more was the energy radiating from it, the low hum pulsing louder as the digital timer counted down.

He inspected the soldered joints and the casing, searching for any way to interrupt the mechanism or access the internals. Nothing. It was sealed tight. He wiped the back of his hand across his forehead, sweat dripping down his face. Holden hadn't been bluffing. There was no disabling it without the code.

Standing, he turned to Lee, who hovered nearby, her eyes darting between him and the flashing timer. "Help me carry it to the helicopter," he said.

Lee's eyes widened. "What?"

"I'm going to fly it out of here. Get it away from anything it can take down."

"You can fly that thing?" she asked.

"Well enough."

Lee hesitated, clearly wanting to argue but coming up short. She looked from the device to Beckett, then sighed.

"Jesus. Okay. Fine."

Beckett ran back to the chopper, climbed aboard and shoved the dead pilot out of the cockpit. Familiarising himself with the controls, he lowered it back onto the helipad, keeping the rotors going. They didn't have time for a restart.

Once it was stable he jumped back out, and together with Lee they hauled the large metal case onto the floor of the cabin.

"What are you planning to do?" Lee yelled over the thrum of the blades.

He paused, glancing towards the horizon. "I need to weaken the blast. Maybe even cancel it out completely. All I can think of is to drop it in the Colorado River, just past the Hoover Dam."

"That's still a way off," she said. "How long do you think it'll take to get there?"

"Thirty, maybe forty minutes," he called back, moving towards the cabin.

Lee frowned and leaned in to check the timer. Beckett saw her face drop as she registered the time left. Forty minutes. She looked up at him.

"If this goes wrong, if you don't make it in time, you'll be caught in the blast."

"Better me than the people in this city."

"Is it?"

Her eyes were wide and awash with colour and desperation. The thud of the chopper's rotors echoed in his chest. She was terrified and uncertain, and he understood. He felt it too. It was hard, but he had to do it. It's what he'd been trained for. What his father would have done.

It was what John Beckett did.

"I have to go," he yelled over the din. "Now."

"Wait." Lee's hands balled into fists at her sides. "I'm coming with you."

"Not a chance. It's too risky."

"Yes!" she shot back, stepping closer. "I didn't come this far to bow out now. I'm not letting you do this alone."

Beckett frowned, ready to argue, but Lee didn't give him the chance. She turned, grabbed the edge of the cabin, and hauled herself up.

"Come on," she said, looking down at him from the cabin door. "Every second counts."

Beckett ran around the other side and climbed into the pilot's seat beside her, the metal floor cab vibrating beneath him. Grabbing the cyclic and collective, he took a moment to cast his attention across the vast array of gauges, dials and controls, relying on instinct and muscle memory as he flicked a few switches and brought the engine fully to life.

"Put this on," he yelled, reaching back and grabbing two headsets from the cabin. He handed one to Lee, then plugged his into the comm panel, adjusting the frequency dials to sync their channels.

"Have you got me?" he asked, tapping the ear cup of his headset.

She threw him a smile. "I've got you."

But the smile faded as she glanced back at the EMP device, its blue light casting an icy glow across the back of the cabin.

"Thirty-six minutes!" she said, her voice crackling in his ears.

"Okay. Let's do this."

Lee grabbed his sleeve as he pulled the chopper into the air, the lift-off a little too aggressive. The rotors strained against the turbulence, and for a moment the whole aircraft felt unsteady. But as Beckett adjusted, guiding it away from the tower and into open sky, they started to level out.

It was early evening now, and below them Las Vegas stretched out like a grid of glittering lights, oblivious to the catastrophe ticking down above it. Beckett gritted his teeth as he fought the controls, feeling the drag caused by the weight of the EMP. The altimeter was dead, either fried by the EMP's interference or caught in the first wave of its growing pulse, forcing him to rely on instinct over instrumentation. Beside him Lee was gripping the cabin's edge for dear life, but doing her best to stay focused. He appreciated that.

They continued on in silence for a while, aware of every second of every minute. The hum from the EMP, the rhythmic thump of the rotors, the static crackling in the headset, it was starting to feel suffocating. Finally Lee twisted around, unable to hold back any longer, and checked the countdown timer.

"Twenty-five minutes!"

Beckett kept his attention fixed on the controls, forcing himself to stay in the moment. This would go right down to the wire. There was a real chance they wouldn't make it out. But running the odds wouldn't change them. Either they'd make it or they wouldn't. Anything beyond that was a distraction he couldn't afford.

The power in the device was building, each pulse of static sending shudders through the metal frame, vibrating under his hands. The strong winds at this height weren't helping, buffeting the chopper from all sides as he adjusted the collective, fighting to keep on a steady south-eastern trajectory. Above them the clouds flickered with bursts of blue light from the EMP, each flash making the cockpit feel more unstable.

Then out of nowhere the interference worsened. Sporadic bursts of static crackled through their headsets, cutting in and out. Sparks spat from the base of the instrument panel, drawing a sharp yelp from Lee. He didn't blame her. It was getting dicey as hell. But he gritted his teeth, tightened his grip, and kept his eyes locked on the horizon.

Lee glanced at the timer again. When she turned back, her expression told him everything he needed to know. He squinted through the cockpit canopy, scanning the terrain for signs of water. He flicked on the searchlight, but the beam revealed nothing but an endless stretch of rocks and sand.

Another surge rattled the helicopter, the controls momentarily resisting his inputs. Beckett wrestled with the cyclic, forcing the craft back on course. The weight of the EMP was making them sluggish, and the constant energy pulses weren't helping. Sparks crackled along the edges of the cabin, skittering across the panels.

"Come on," he muttered to the chopper. "You can do this."

They were jolted sideways as another pulse from the now almost fully operational device rocked them. Beckett gritted his teeth and tightened his grip on the controls.

"How long?" he asked.

Lee stared at him, her face pale in the pulsing blue glow. "Fifteen minutes," she said, then shook her head. "Less now."

Beckett nodded. In many ways they had accomplished what they'd set out to do. There was nothing out here but rock. If the EMP detonated now, no civilians would be at risk. No grids would fail. No planes would drop from the sky.

But a helicopter would.

If the device went off while they were still on board, the blast would rip through the cabin, fry every system in an instant, and send them plummeting to their deaths.

He forced his focus back to the horizon and pushed the thought down. He'd been in worse scrapes, he told himself. Though right now none came to mind.

The helicopter bucked again, the cyclic jerking in his hands as the energy pulses grew stronger. The hum from the EMP was near deafening now, vibrating through the entire cabin. Lee gripped her seat with both hands, knuckles white as she braced against the jolts.

"Hold steady," Beckett growled, though he wasn't sure if it was meant for her or himself. He wiped sweat from his eyes with his shoulder. It had been a while since he'd flown a chopper, and between the weight of the EMP and the interference from its surges, every adjustment was a fight.

Time stretched and warped as they pressed on. Minutes ticked by. Beckett kept his eyes fixed on the terrain below, willing the bay to appear. Lee had now turned around in her seat, fixated on the timer. She'd been like that a while, shoulders tense, not speaking. Beckett wanted to tell her it wasn't helping – that watching the countdown wouldn't change the outcome – but he stayed quiet. She was scared, and what right did he have to dismiss her fear?

His own was creeping in too.

It was an almost alien sensation, made worse by the fact he usually found a way to channel that energy elsewhere. But now it lurked at the edges of his psyche, gnawing at his focus, feeding him doubt. He tightened his resolve and shoved the feeling aside as best he could.

Still, he couldn't help himself from glancing back, catching sight of the glowing numbers as they ticked down.

Five minutes.

4:59… 4:58…

Shit.

Lee turned to him, and his stomach twisted at the sight of her tear-streaked face. Her lips trembled as she forced herself to speak. "I… think this is it, John. We aren't going to make it, are we?"

Beckett opened his mouth, then shut it again. He sighed. He had no words.

"I just want to say thank you," she added. "For helping me, for believing in me. For… everything."

Beckett's throat tightened, but he kept his focus on the horizon.

"It's been amazing being with you these last few days," she went on. "I want you to know I've really grown to… care about you. A lot. I just wanted you to know that—"

"Save it, Maggie," Beckett cut in. "We're not going to die. Not today."

"How do you know?" she cried.

Beckett didn't reply. He didn't want to lie to her, but he had to think that way. It was the only mindset that would keep him going. He refocused as the helicopter shuddered again, the console flaring with another burst of interference. Gritting his teeth, he scanned the darkness ahead.

Then – finally – the searchlight caught something below. A faint glimmer, rippling and shifting in the darkness.

"There," he said. "Look. Water."

Lee leaned forward, practically leaping out of her seat as she saw it too. "Yes," she screamed.

But they weren't there yet. As the dark expanse of the Colorado River and Las Vegas Bay came into view, the EMP's energy pulses became relentless, growing more intense and frequent with every passing second. The control panel flickered as gauges spun out of sync, and a sea of warning lights bathed the cockpit in an ominous red glow.

Beckett flicked switches and adjusted levels as best he could but it was touch and go. His grip on the cyclic was so tight it felt like an extension of his own body.

"Are we going to make it?" Lee asked, her gaze darting between the EMP's timer and the water below.

"We have to."

They were almost over the bay now, breakers in the inky water reflecting streaks of evening moonlight. Beckett adjusted the collective, lowering the helicopter as they closed in. Every movement was a battle, the hum so loud it felt like the air itself was vibrating.

"How long?" Beckett yelled.

Lee leaned back to check. "Two minutes."

Shit.

It was too close. Static screeched through his headset as he glanced at the altimeter. The controls groaned in his hands, resisting every adjustment.

He made his decision.

Yanking back on the collective, he cut their forward momentum, sending the helicopter into a steep dive. Lee shouted something, her voice lost in the chaos as the g-force slammed into them and Beckett fought to keep the descent controlled, adjusting the cyclic to correct their angle.

As the water rushed up to meet them, Beckett held his nerve, waiting until the last possible second. At around fifty metres he wrenched the chopper level, muscles straining as he fought to stabilise the hover. The airframe jolted violently, the EMP's energy pulses rattling through the structure, but he held it steady.

"This is it," he yelled. "Get that thing out of here."

Lee unbuckled her harness and pushed herself up, steadying herself with a hand on the roof as she moved into the rear where the EMP was throbbing and spluttering. Beckett watched as she dragged the heavy metal casing towards the doorway.

The timer showed thirty seconds.

"You can do this."

Beckett turned back, his hands and forearms burning from the effort as he fought to keep the helicopter stable. The timer in his head ticked on.

Twenty-five...

Twenty-four...

Lee slid the door open and the chopper lurched as the sudden shift in airflow made it even harder to control. Beckett adjusted his grip on the controls, willing her onwards. She could do this. She had to.

The wind howled through the cabin, bustling at her as she fought for balance. She gritted her teeth, braced herself against the frame, and with a desperate grunt shoved the device with everything she had.

A deep metallic scrape tore through the cabin.

Fourteen...

Thirteen...

She'd moved it far enough to get behind it. Dropping onto the floor, she planted her feet against the casing and pushed. Hard. The device slid, teetered for a second on the edge, then tipped over and tumbled into the night.

Ten...

Nine...

They leaned over as best they could, watching as the

metal box hit the water, sending a towering spray into the air. It bobbed for a few moments before slipping below the surface, the blue light fading as it sank.

Three…

Two…

Then, the detonation.

A massive ripple of electrical energy burst beneath the surface, the shockwave radiating out in perfect circles. The helicopter rocked violently, the force slamming into the frame like a battering ram. The electronics flickered again, before the cockpit was plunged into darkness.

No.

Beckett's stomach clenched as the rotors stuttered and the chopper dipped. Gritting his teeth he yanked at the controls, relying on instinct as he fought to level them out. The systems sputtered once, twice, then blinked back to life.

The rotors caught.

They were still airborne.

"It worked!" Lee screamed, breathless and ecstatic.

She slid the door shut and slumped back into her seat, chest heaving. "You did it!" she said, reaching over to grab his face and kiss him. The sudden movement threw him off balance, the chopper jolting slightly, but he quickly corrected.

As she pulled away, he turned to her and smiled.

"No, Maggie," he said. "*We* did it."

Chapter Fifty-Three

An hour later, Lee sat across from Beckett in a small diner just off the highway. It was one of those places that hadn't changed much since the eighties, not unlike the diner where she'd first set eyes on John Beckett. She couldn't decide if that was fitting, ironic, or just asking for trouble – but she was too tired to think about it deeply.

She leaned back, half smiling to herself. It was strange. That first meeting with him felt like a lifetime ago, though it had only been days. She glanced out the window. The sun had long since set, and the Vegas skyline shimmered on the horizon, blissfully unaware of the disaster it had narrowly avoided.

Beckett had landed the battered helicopter a mile out in the desert, well away from prying eyes. The walk back had been a mix of elation and exhaustion, their adrenaline finally wearing off, replaced by the sheer weight of everything that had happened.

Now, they sat in a booth near the window, trying to act normal as they waited for coffee and pie. Lee shivered, the diner's climate control doing nothing for her fatigue and hunger. A part of her wished Beckett would shuffle in beside her and warm her up. But she knew he wouldn't think to do that, and she wasn't going to ask.

"It's crazy, isn't it?" she said, finally breaking the quiet. "To think what we just went through?"

Beckett looked up from where he'd been staring at the scratched surface of the table. He gave her a faint smile and a nod, but that was all. Still a man of few words, even now. But she didn't need him to say anything. His presence was enough.

The server arrived, setting down two steaming cups of coffee and slices of cherry pie on mismatched plates. Beckett thanked her, and Lee took a welcome sip of coffee as the woman shuffled away. It was strong and bitter, but right now it tasted like nectar.

The pie was even better. She forked up a large mouthful and chewed. Across from her, Beckett was still staring at nothing.

"What is it?" she asked.

He glanced up. "Just thinking about what Holden said."

"Oh?"

He leaned back and gazed out the window as if the far-off neon of Vegas might offer him the words he needed.

"The attack. The Consortium's plan. I don't think it was just about wiping out financial data or manipulating the markets. It wasn't about profit. Not really."

Lee frowned. "Then what was it about?"

"Same thing as always. Control. By pinning the attack on a rogue state, they'd create chaos, destabilise regions, justify wars. The Consortium thrives in that kind of environment. If they can control the narrative, they control everything."

Lee puffed out a sigh. It was a lot to take in, but she had no reason to doubt him. "Do you think Holden was in on it all?"

Beckett's expression darkened. "Holden thought he was important. That he mattered to them. But really he was a tool, the same as the EMP, same as the scapegoat plan. The Consortium are growing more powerful all the time. They don't care about people like Holden. The truth is, they don't even care that we stopped them. They'll have ten other operations running right now. They're untouchable." He picked up his mug and took a sip, pulling a face like it was too hot or too bitter. Or maybe he was just angry.

Silence settled over them once more as they ate. The pie was damn good and Lee finished hers in minutes. Sitting back, she wiped her mouth with a napkin and stared out the window, trying to look past the ghost of herself reflected in the glass. She looked tired. Messy.

But she was alive, and after the last few days that was saying something.

"Are you okay?"

She turned to find Beckett watching her.

"I don't know," she admitted. "Holden's dead. Jarvis is dead. Gates too. And no one's ever going to believe what happened tonight. If I tried to explain it, they'd think I was crazy or some wacko conspiracy theorist."

"Like Mack?"

"No," she said softly. "Not like Mack. He was a good man."

Beckett smiled. "Yes. He was." He glanced down, smiling into his coffee before rolling his shoulders back. "But as for explaining this to people – don't."

"What, none of it?"

"No. Don't explain it. Don't write it up. Let it go." He

wrapped his hand around his mug. "Like you say, no one will believe you anyway. And if you try, you'll just make yourself a target."

She sat up straighter. "But I'm a cop. I can't just turn my back on this."

"Yes. And you're a damn good cop, Maggie. You saved lives tonight, and no one's ever going to know it. But if you try to handle this the way you're used to – with rules, with bureaucracy – it could get you killed. You've seen how these people work. They have eyes and ears everywhere. You know it's true. You're smarter than that."

She stared at him, her defences dropping as his words sank in. "So, what? Walk away? Just… quit?"

"No, don't quit. But bide your time. Pick your battles. Figure out who you can trust."

She thought for a moment. "Do you think I should put in for a transfer? To the main precinct?"

"Do you?"

She nodded, slowly. "Yeah, I do. I really do. It's something I've been thinking about for a long time, but something has always pulled me back. Fear, I guess. Impostor syndrome. But after this week… after everything… I think maybe I'm ready."

Beckett grinned. "You're definitely ready."

"What about you?" she asked, fighting the warm glow his words gave her. "What's next?"

He glanced towards the window. "Visit my niece," he replied. "I made her a promise. And it's been too long."

Lee smiled, watching him as he finished his coffee, trying to memorise the lines of his face when he wasn't looking. He seemed calmer now, leaning back in the booth, but there was still something guarded in the way he held himself.

She wondered, not for the first time, what it would be like if things were different. If they weren't two people caught in a storm they barely understood. If he could stay. If she could go with him. The thought made her chest ache, but she swallowed it down the way Beckett always seemed to.

He caught her looking and held her gaze as something deep and unspoken passed between them. Her throat tightened, but she refused to let it show.

Instead, she offered a faint smile and set her mug down. "I meant what I said on the chopper," she said, her voice steady despite everything swirling inside her. "I want to thank you. For everything. For sticking around. For trusting me. You're a good man, Beckett."

"Beckett?" he said, raising an eyebrow.

She shrugged, leaning back in her seat. "Figured that's what you prefer."

"It's what I'm used to." His smile was a knowing one, almost wistful – like he understood exactly what she was doing.

Calling him by his last name made it easier somehow. It kept things at a distance. Kept her from saying what she really wanted to.

Because what would be the point?

This was always the way it was going to end.

Once they'd finished their coffees, Lee told him she'd see him outside and went to settle the check. Buying the guy pie and coffee felt like the least she could do. As she waited for the server to process her card, she watched him through the glass, standing there like a lone wolf in the wilderness, his face stern but his eyes full of compassion and intelligence. He looked as if he had the weight of the world to carry and the shoulders to match, and she knew she could never compete with that.

When she stepped outside, he turned and smiled, his entire face lighting up. For a moment she considered saying what was on her mind, what she'd wanted to say in the chopper. It was right there, on the tip of her tongue. But for whatever reason, the words wouldn't come.

Instead, she nodded in the direction of Vegas, and they started walking. It would take at least an hour to reach her apartment, but it was a nice night, and neither of them seemed in a hurry.

They'd been walking a while when she caught Beckett looking at her with a strange expression on his face.

"What is it?" she asked.

He shrugged, his usual stoicism softening just enough to make her heart tighten. "I need to thank you as well," he said.

"For what?"

"For helping me figure out this mess."

"Oh." She turned away. "It's fine."

"And for reminding me there's still a heart beating behind all the scars and calluses. That I'm still alive. In every way that counts."

She turned back to him, unable to suppress a sly smile. "It was good, wasn't it?"

"It was great. You're great."

She felt her cheeks warm. She wished more than anything that he could stay, even for a few more days. But it was unfair to ask. She knew him well enough to know he wasn't the kind of man who stayed anywhere for long.

"You're a good cop, Maggie," he said. "And a wonderful person. Whatever you do next, you'll be excellent at it."

She nodded, happier to be back on steadier ground

conversation-wise. They walked for a while longer, letting the night air settle around them.

The city lights were in sight when Lee finally spoke again, hoping to put to bed the last of the doubts nagging at her.

"Do you think we stopped them?" she asked. "Or just delayed the inevitable?"

Beckett shrugged. "Probably both. But it's enough for now."

The walk back to her building felt shorter than it should have. When they reached the front door, Lee turned to face him, her hand resting lightly on the frame. "Do you want to… come in?"

He sighed. His eyes said yes – they said more than yes – but she already knew what his answer was.

"It's fine," she told him. "I understand."

"It really is for the best. I think."

"Sure."

"Will you be okay?"

She nodded. "Will you?"

He hesitated, like he was actually considering the question. Or like it was the first time anyone had asked him in a long time.

"Yes," he said, after he'd thought about it long enough. "I will."

"I guess this is goodbye then." She kept the smile on her face. Kept it there with all her might, for fear of what might happen if she let it drop. But she didn't move, still leaning against the doorframe. If he wobbled even for a second, she'd drag him inside.

But then he cleared his throat, and she knew it wasn't going to happen.

"I'm sorry, Maggie," he said, leaning in. "My world is a

complicated one. But I have your address, and I'll try to keep in touch. Maybe even visit, if you'd like that. But I can't make any promises. The truth is, I don't know where I'll be in a few months. I don't even know where I'll be next week."

"It's fine. I won't hold you to anything." She paused, then chuckled. "Hell, you know what they say, *Beckett* – whatever happens in Vegas…"

He laughed, and so did she. For a moment it felt lighter. Easier. Even if the ache still lingered.

Beckett took a step back. "I'll see you around."

"Yeah."

Their eyes met, a lingering glance that said everything they couldn't. Then Beckett turned and walked away. Lee stayed where she was, watching him go, wondering if he'd look back.

He didn't.

She smiled to herself, watched a moment longer, then stepped inside and closed the door.

Chapter Fifty-Four

Beckett sat in the stiff, plastic chair of the departure lounge, a single carry-on bag resting by his feet, his passport balanced loosely in his hand. Around him, Harry Reid International Airport was a collage of motion and noise – an overhead speaker droning on about delayed flights, a crying child two rows away, the chime of slot machines carrying over from the concourse, an unmistakable reminder of where he was.

Beyond the glass walls, planes taxied on the runway in the late afternoon sun. It was now Monday, two days since he and Lee had stopped the city from grinding to a halt.

It already felt like an age ago.

He shifted in the chair, its hard edges refusing to let him settle. Or maybe it was nothing to do with the chair. He watched as an American Airlines flight took off for some unknown destination, a failed attempt to distract himself from the thoughts circling in his head.

His flight would be boarding soon. First to Germany and then on to Spain. It had been almost two years since he'd seen Amber, and the time in between had been filled with too many excuses. He wondered if he'd even recognise her. If she'd recognise him. She was a young woman now, and he had a nagging suspicion that the distance between them could be measured in more than miles. He was already bracing himself for plenty of eye rolls, but it would be good to see her.

He exhaled and closed his eyes, his thoughts drifting – like they had done more than once in the last forty-eight hours – to Maggie Lee.

He thought about the way her eyes lit up when she argued her point, refusing to back down until she'd got through to him. Or the way she carried herself in those quiet moments, when the adrenaline had faded but she tried her best to stay grounded. He sighed. It had been a long time since he'd felt this way about anyone.

If she'd asked him to stay, would he have?

He didn't know the answer to that, and he'd long since trained himself not to worry about such questions. That kind of thinking had no place in his life. A life built on momentum, not attachments. On action, not regret. Letting people get too close was the quickest way to lose focus. And losing focus was a dangerous mistake in his world.

But there was something about Lee. She was different in a way he couldn't ignore. For the first time in years he'd let someone in.

The problem was, that scared him more than any gun to his head ever had.

A muted television above the airport bar caught his eye, the rolling news channel flashing bold headlines across the screen. One in particular stood out.

Tech mogul Lucian Holden found dead in his apartment of a suspected heart attack

Beckett snorted and shook his head.

A heart attack.

He knew better than anyone that the gap between what the mainstream news reported and the truth was often a mile wide, but whoever had orchestrated this spin had acted fast. It was almost impressive. But it was also the kind of influence that made him uneasy, no matter how long he'd lived in its shadow.

It was a reminder of just how dangerous The Consortium really were. Their reach was expanding. Their grip tightening. If they could bury something like this in only two days, what else were they capable of?

Still – Beckett exhaled and pulled his focus back – it wasn't his problem.

Not today, at least.

A voice over the Tannoy snapped him back to the moment. His plane was boarding.

He stood, grabbed his bag, and slung it over his shoulder. For a moment the thought surfaced again, the same one that had been at the back of his mind ever since he'd left Lee's apartment. Since he'd left Lee. But once again he shook it off; headed for the gate, shoulders back, eyes forward. The madness of the last few days was behind him, and he wasn't looking back.

This was his way. It always had been. It was who he was. A lone wolf knows better than to stop moving.

Because moving on wasn't just a choice.

It was survival.

More by Matthew Hattersley

vinci-books.com/final-kill

Betrayed by her agency. Hunted by her past. A lethal assassin on the run.

Turn the page for a free preview…

Final Kill: Prologue

Darkness.

Confusion.

Then a familiar taste in the back of her throat. Iron. Blood.

Damn.

She fought herself awake, realising immediately she was on her knees with her hands tied behind her back. It wasn't the best situation to find oneself in on waking.

Peering through the shadowy veil covering her face, all she could make out were vague shapes and distorted silhouettes. She did, however, notice her left eye was swollen shut. Which was when she remembered the rifle butt.

Oh shitting hell…

The general.

"Hey, Ratty," she called out, fully conscious now and straining at the thick hessian sack covering her face. "Are you there?"

"Right beside you, kiddo. You hurt?"

"Not too bad," she told him. "Where are we?"

"Underground. Some kind of cell."

She struggled at her constraints. "I guess I went off script again."

"You sure did. I mean, you might have pulled it off. If you had eleven arms."

Images of the attack flashed across her mind. There'd been seven of them – mercenaries. She'd killed four of them before the others had overpowered her. Not bad going considering she'd been armed with only a pocketknife.

She flinched, remembering something else. "I want to speak to Ramos," she called out into the room.

"Save it, bitch," a man's voice came back. "The general is on his way."

The general – General Luis Carvalho Ramos, to give him his full title – was a local politician and part-time gunrunner, whose approach had become too erratic and violent even for the corrupt officials here in Fortaleza. Considering the city was widely known as the murder capital of Brazil, that was saying something.

She shifted her awareness back to the room, slowly lifting her hands to her belt. The air was cool but stagnant, and she had a sense they were underground. With great care and the slightest of movements, she slid the push dagger from out of the concealed sheath in her belt. Whoever had tied her up had missed it. But everyone did.

Concentrating on moving only her wrists, she sawed at the thick rope. Like always, her senses were heightened, but her hearing was even more so - over compensating for her lack of sight. She heard grunts from outside the room. Heavy booted footsteps, coming her way.

A moment later the door crashed open and a voice boomed, "So, these are the pigs sent to kill me?"

The same voice as before answered him. "Yes sir. I've

had run-ins with this organisation in the past whilst working detail for Al Shaitan in Sudan. They're assassins but call themselves Elite Eradication Specialists."

"Well, not elite enough, huh?"

"No, sir."

"Let me see them."

She flinched as the heavy sack was ripped from her head. She blinked her eyes into focus as Ramos loomed down at her. He was an old man, much older than his picture in her file, and with a disgusting, thin moustache that twitched as he spoke.

"Seems you aren't as good as they say, bitch." He grabbed her by the throat, forcing her to peer at him. "You might have killed four of my men, but the buck stops here. Who sent you?"

She smiled, exposing a set of blood-stained teeth. "I'm going to kill you," she whispered.

Ramos laughed and leaned closer, his foul breath in her face. "No. I don't think that's going to happen." Straightening, he moved over to the back wall to join the remaining mercenaries. There was four of them now, including the general. All armed.

She sucked in loo long deep breaths, all the while sawing at the bindings around her wrist. She was almost through the first rope. Thirty seconds more and she'd be free. If she lived that long.

Ramos walked over and removed the bag from her partner. "What the fuck are you supposed to be?" he asked, curling his lip at the large, muscular man with camouflage-green hair and silver rings running down the curve of each ear.

"Go to hell," Davros Ratpack snarled back. Although not so easy with a bust lip. "Just get this over with."

"Oh no, amigo, I like to savour these moments," Ramos sneered. He pointed a stubby finger her way. "She screwed you both, this one, huh? Crazy bitch. You know, I've half a mind to let one of you go – so you can tell the world that the great General Ramos cannot be killed." He sighed, theatrically. "But I don't think I will."

She watched the soldiers as they bristled with readiness. No doubt they were all highly trained, with years of combat experience under their belts, but they were also overweight and pushing fifty. Two of them carried Walther MP submachine guns, and the other a Kalashnikov assault rifle - an AK-something-or-other, it was hard to tell with the light in her face. Ramos himself carried a Colt pistol, or perhaps an IBEL, the Brazilian-made equivalent. Either way it added up to a lot of firepower.

She kept going with the push dagger, fine-tuning her play as she gauged the situation. From this angle the soldier with the assault rifle would have to step back to take a shot. He'd be third. Ramos – who had now holstered his pistol and was lighting a fat cigar – fourth. She glanced at the soldiers holding the subs – one aimed at her, one at Davros – they'd be first and second. She bowed her head as one of the ropes fell away.

One to go.

Ramos blew a large plume of cigar smoke into the room and smirked. "So, tell me, who wants to die first? You? Or you?" He waved the cigar between her and Davros, bathing jubilantly in their apparent fear.

"Why not both at once?" she replied, readying herself, almost through the last rope.

"Not a bad idea."

He blew another large cloud into the room and turned

to his men, about to give the order. But before any words could leave his mouth, she was on her feet.

Springing forward, she moved between the muzzles of the two Walthers, slashing with the push dagger across the throats of both soldiers. Blood spurted from the open wounds as she spun and flung the dagger at the soldier with the rifle, embedding the sharpened steel between his eyes. As he groaned and fell to the floor, she grabbed one of the Walthers, turning it on the solider carrying it before finishing off his friend. As the two men buckled against each other she aimed at Ramos – now frantically trying to release his gun from its holster. He jerked erratically in a macabre dance for a few seconds, before she released the trigger and the great General Luis Carvalho Ramos dropped to the floor with a thud.

She pulled in a deep breath as she surveyed the scene. Not bad going. All of them dead in under three seconds.

She walked over to her partner, a smirk forming. "What? You didn't doubt me, did you?"

"Oh no. Not for a second," he said. "You crazy mare."

"You love me really." She untied him and helped him to his feet. "Anyway, let's get the hell out of here and back to dear old Blighty. I'll meet you outside. Don't be long."

Before he had a chance to reply, she slung one of the Walthers over her shoulder, shoved Ramos' still smoking cigar in her mouth, and casually sashayed out of the room.

Job done.

Time for a celebratory drink.

Final Kill: Chapter One

The moon hung low over the rooftops of Pimlico, silhouetting the long-dead chimneys of the large town houses in this part of London. Despite the recent rainfall, a sinister mist lingered in the air, giving the wide, empty streets an almost Victorian feel – as if Holmes and Watson might suddenly appear under one of the many lamp posts that studded the pavements. To further add to this anachronistic atmosphere, a 1963 S-Type Jaguar in racing green was parked on the corner of St George's Square. Sitting inside, a man and woman watched the first-floor apartment of the building opposite, waiting for their night's work to begin.

The woman (codename: Acid Vanilla) rested her forehead against the window and sighed. It was a long, drawn-out kind of sigh. The kind of sigh that would normally elicit query from a companion – perhaps asking after the sigher's wellbeing – but not today. Not in this setting. Next to her, the man (codename: Banjo Shawshank) teased at his impressive moustache in the rear-view mirror.

"All I'm saying is, these days it's hard to know what women want." He twisted the ends of the moustache as he spoke, more than aware of the cliché. "To be honest, I don't think they know themselves. That's the problem."

Acid Vanilla didn't reply. Banjo had been talking incessantly for the last hour and she was getting antsy. The job should have been completed by now. Boxed off. She should be at home. She watched out the window as a woman in a Burberry overcoat waited for her dog to defecate at the foot of a tall tree. The woman looked to be a real piece of work. Nose in the air. Snooty. The dog just as much. On the tree, a sign read, *Bag It & Bin It.* A tenner said that wouldn't happen.

"Take this graphic designer chick I was seeing a few weeks back," Banjo continued. "One minute she's all over me like Weinstein on a starlet. Pull my hair. Spank me. Then the next morning she gets needy because I won't go for a walk up to Primrose Hill. I got out of there sharpish, I can tell you. Talk about mixed messages. You see what I mean? Hey, Acid. You listening to me?"

Acid shifted her focus to two droplets of rainwater on the other side of the glass and watched as they zig-zagged to the bottom of the pane where one engulfed the other to form a larger droplet. Then they disappeared into the foam abyss between the window and the doorframe.

"Yeah, mixed messages," she murmured. "Awful. You should write a blog post about it."

"Oh. My. God. Have you heard yourself? No one writes blogs these days. Jesus."

Over by the tree, the dog finished its business and the woman led it away, leaving a steaming pile of turds in their wake. Acid smirked to herself. She was good at reading other people. Always had been. It was just herself she had problems with.

She scanned the street. "Where the bloody hell is he? You sure this is the correct address?"

Banjo leaned over her and eyeballed the building. "Yep, Raaz confirmed it. Says he gets home between half eight and ten. So anytime now."

A familiar prickle of annoyance tickled Acid's nerve. Technology's encroachment on the industry always bothered her whenever she considered it. She pined for the good old days when fieldwork was visceral and exciting. It was more dangerous too, but she liked that. You had to think on your feet, keep your wits about you. Scrapes happened, sure, but how you got out of them sharpened you, prepared you for the next job. These days it was all too safe, too regimented. Off-site tech-wizards like Raaz Terabyte analysed every eventuality, saw problems before they happened. Acid wasn't a Luddite; she understood the importance of technology. But this wasn't the life she'd signed up for.

She clicked open the polished walnut glove box and pulled out a photo. The guy looking back at her wasn't a looker. In fact, he might have had the most average-looking face Acid had ever seen. His hair was average-length, mousy, parted to one side. Under that were a pair of average eyes, an average nose, lips, ears. John Brown. Even his name was average.

Still, John Brown's actions recently were anything but average. He had a list of crimes a page long: fraud, embezzlement, blackmail, mistreatment of illegal workers. But the main reason for Acid and Banjo being here tonight was that he'd royally screwed over his business partner and was now systematically destroying his reputation too. Not to mention stealing a client list worth well over eight figures.

Understandably, none of this had gone down too well with the business partner – a no-nonsense Scot called Brian Rand - and he wanted revenge. In fact, he wanted it in the most bloody and painful way possible. So he'd done his research, asked around in his secret gentlemen's clubs, spoke to people with knowledge of the sort of services he was after – nefarious businessmen, Russian oligarchs. One name cropped up time and time again. The best in the business for what Rand required.

Annihilation Pest Control.

Which was how Acid Vanilla and Banjo Shawshank came to be outside John Brown's apartment building on this cold September evening.

Acid glanced at Banjo. "Are you ready to move? Soon as we get eyes on him?"

"Relax, babe. I have done this before."

"Well focus, please. And quit the cute talk, okay?"

Acid shoved the photo back in the glove box and removed her trusty Glock 19 along with a suppressor and push dagger. Banjo watched her with a stupid grin on his face.

She arched a perfectly groomed eyebrow. "What now?"

"I can't believe you're still using that hunk of metal."

"It's not let me down yet."

She screwed the suppressor onto the end of the gun as Banjo pulled out his own pistol, a Colt M1911, and held it in the light coming from the streetlamp.

"Now this – this is a real man's weapon." He peered down the length of the barrel.

"A real man?" Acid said. "Hmm. Wonder where we can find one, this time of night."

It took him a second to register. "Get lost. You know you want me."

"Sure I do."

Banjo was starting up again, bemoaning the lack of decent masculine role models in modern literature, when Acid shushed him down.

"I think that's him. There, with the briefcase."

A man had emerged from the small grassy area on the opposite side of the street. They watched as he scurried down the side of a black Mercedes SUV. Then he scurried up the short flight of steps that led to the building and frantically pushed his key into the lock. A security light came on, highlighting his dumpy potato face.

"That's him." Acid zipped her leather jacket. "Give it five, then we'll move. You ready?"

"I'm always ready." Banjo winked at her. "Ready for you anytime."

Acid fingered the trigger of the Glock, imagining how good it would feel to put a bullet through her colleague's cheek. Caesar wouldn't be happy, but it'd be worth it. She looked at her watch. Maybe later.

"Come on, lover boy." She slapped Banjo on his skinny-jeaned thigh. "Time to go to work."

Grab your copy...
vinci-books.com/final-kill